To Steve,
You are going
to have a ball!
Eric Coop 2018

STAR ENFORCERS CREW BACKERS

CAPTAIN
Stefan Anderson / Anthony Reres / Dennis Condon

LIEUTENANT
Denise Jones *(Natural Body Care Professional)*
Brian Gregory

BRIDGE OFFICER
James Ficker / Michael Blatherwick *(Jackowick Toys)*
Derek Shackleton / Daniel Stalter *(Stealing Fire Comics)*
Philip Hughes / Stephen Greco

SPACE DOCK MASTER
Ryan Brady (www.CamdensComics.org)

SPACE DOCK SUPERVISOR
Robert Salley (Creator of Salvagers) / Philip Hughes

A moment to honor the three creators that have shared their passion for the worlds that they have written and illustrated throughout their careers. These three men have sacrificed their time and effort to show others the fountain of diversity that should be shown in the realm of entertainment.

These talented people of the entertainment industry were the driving forces to our own vision for a diverse cast of characters and to create meaningful and thought provoking stories.

Even though these three creators are no longer with us today we still celebrate their visions for an inclusive and prosperous future for all human kind.

Jack Kirby
Dwayne McDuffie
Gene Roddenberry

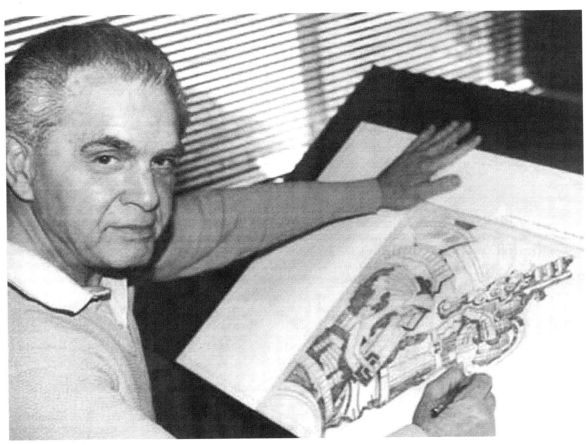

August 28, 1917, New York City, NY - February 6, 1994, Thousand Oaks, CA

Jack Kirby, original name Jacob Kurtzberg (born August 28, 1917, <u>New York</u>, New York, U.S.—died February 6, 1994, <u>Thousand Oaks</u>, <u>California</u>) American <u>comic book</u> artist who helped create hundreds of original characters, including <u>Captain America</u>, the <u>Incredible Hulk</u>, and the <u>Fantastic Four</u>.

Kirby left high school at age 16 and worked in <u>Max Fleischer</u>'s <u>animation</u> studio on <u>Betty Boop</u> and <u>Popeye</u> cartoons before teaming up with fellow artist <u>Joe Simon</u> in 1941. Working for Timely (later <u>Marvel</u>) Comics, the pair created <u>Captain America</u>, a star-spangled super-soldier who quickly became the publisher's most popular character. Kirby and Simon collaborated on a number of titles over the following years, exploring the crime, <u>horror</u>, and humour genres, and they created the first romance comic in 1947. Kirby and Simon's professional relationship was strained by the challenges of working in an increasingly competitive and uncertain market, and by 1956 the team had drifted apart. Kirby responded by turning to <u>newspaper comic strips</u>, and his *Sky Masters of the Space Force* was a moderate success.

By the late 1950s Kirby had found steady work with National (later <u>DC</u>) and, increasingly, with Marvel (then known as Atlas Comics). He started on western and <u>monster</u> titles at

Marvel, and Kirby's creatures—<u>behemoths</u> with names like Goom, Sporr, and Fin Fang Foom—boosted sales for the struggling publisher. In 1961 Marvel editor Stan Lee outlined the story of an ill-fated trip into space and its super-heroic consequences. Using the "Marvel method," which stressed collaboration between writer and artist, Lee and Kirby turned that premise into *The Fantastic Four*. Kirby's artistic skills gave the book a visual punch, and, with his experience with romance comics and Lee's knack for dialogue, they captured the soap-opera feel of life in a superpowered family. Whereas previous superheroes tended toward inhuman perfection, Kirby and Lee found success with everyman characters whose failures and flaws resonated with readers. Marvel's next new title, *The Incredible Hulk* debuted in 1962 as Kirby and Lee's monstrous take on Robert Louis Stevenson's Jekyll and Hyde story. The "Marvel Universe" was soon filled with Kirby creations, such as the X-Men, Silver Surfer, the planet-devouring Galactus, and a revived Captain America. In 1970 Kirby left Marvel over creative differences with Lee and joined rival DC. The following year he launched a trio of comics—*New Gods, Mister Miracle*, and *The Forever People*—which he envisioned as finite series of interlocked stories that would eventually be collected in a single volume. Though these books were canceled long before the conclusion of the planned epic saga, Kirby's "Fourth World" characters, most notably the planetary despot Darkseid, became integral parts of the DC mythos. Kirby returned to Marvel in 1975, but he left again three years later after stints on *Captain America, Devil Dinosaur*, and *The Eternals* (a book that bore more than a passing resemblance to *New Gods*). He worked as a freelance animator during the 1980s and retired in 1987. Throughout his half-century career, Kirby stretched the boundaries of comic storytelling, and his expansive body of work ultimately earned him the nickname "the King of Comics." Although his influence within the industry was unquestioned, the legal rights to the characters that he had helped to create remained a matter of debate. In 2009, several weeks after the Disney Company announced that it would acquire Marvel for $4 billion, Kirby's heirs issued dozens of copyright termination notices to Marvel, Disney, and an assortment of Hollywood studios. Marvel countersued, and courts twice found in favour of Marvel, ruling that Kirby's work had been "for hire," thus granting him no claim to the relevant copyrights. In September 2014, just days before the U.S. Supreme Court was scheduled to discuss the case in conference, the litigants reached an out-of-court settlement for an undisclosed sum.

Reference by: Encyclopedia Britannica, written by Michael Ray

February 20, 1962, Detroit, MI - *February 21, 2011*, Burbank, CA

Dwayne Glenn McDuffie, was born and raised in Detroit, Michigan. The middle son of Leroy McDuffie and Edna (Hawkins) McDuffie (now Gardner), Dwayne attended the prestigious Roeper School for gifted children before going on to earn undergraduate degrees in both English & Physics as well as a graduate degree in Physics, all at the University of Michigan. (Go, Blue!) He later also studied filmmaking at New York University's Tisch School of the Arts.

Dwayne first entered the comic book industry as an Editor at Marvel Comics, thanks to his NYU friend Greg Wright with whom he recreated the DEATHLOK character into the one in use today. With artist Ernie Colón, Dwayne also co-created the comedic Marvel team book, DAMAGE CONTROL.

Frustrated by the lack of diversity of both characters and creators in comics, Dwayne—together with Derek Dingle, Denys Cowan, and Michael Davis--co-founded MILESTONE COMICS (later MILESTONE MEDIA), the first African-American owned comic book company in history, with a mission to provide a wide array of characters, content, and creators that more accurately represent the racial, ethnic, religious, and gender diversity of real life. (Also? They were just outstandingly good books. Seriously. If you haven't read them, seek them out. Now. You won't believe what you've been missing!)

STATIC, ICON, HARDWARE, XOMBI—to name just a few. Throughout his career in the comic book industry, Dwayne created or co-created these and more than a dozen other series, in addition to writing stories for too many other titles to list but here are some highlights: JUSTICE LEAGUE OF AMERICA, FANTASTIC FOUR, SPIDER-MAN, BATMAN: LEGENDS OF THE DARK KNIGHT, CAPTAIN MARVEL, AVENGERS SPOTLIGHT, HELLRAISER, ULTRAMAN, even THE TICK, and BACK TO THE FUTURE. Dwayne also co-created THE ROAD TO HELL with fellow writer and Milestone editor, Matt Wayne, the inaugural Director of the "Dwayne McDuffie Award for Diversity in Comics," established posthumously by Dwayne's widow, Charlotte (Fullerton) McDuffie, along with the "Dwayne McDuffie Award for Kids' Comics."

Dwayne transitioned into the animation industry as a Story Editor and Writer on the Emmy-winning Kids WB series, STATIC SHOCK, which he co-created and for which he won the 2003 HUMANITAS PRIZE.

Dwayne was also a Producer, Story Editor, and Writer on Cartoon Network's JUSTICE LEAGUE and JUSTICE LEAGUE UNLIMITED animated series, for which he received a 2004 WRITERS GUILD nomination.

With artist Glen Murakami, Dwayne redeveloped Man of Action's BEN 10 animated series into BEN 10: ALIEN FORCE then BEN 10: ULTIMATE ALIEN—98 episodes of what became and continues to be an on-going, blockbuster, 230-episodes-and-counting franchise for Cartoon Network.

Dwayne also wrote the animated features JUSTICE LEAGUE: CRISIS ON TWO EARTHS, ALL-STAR SUPERMAN, and JUSTICE LEAGUE: DOOM, as well as episodes of WHAT'S NEW, SCOOBY-DOO? and TEEN TITANS, all for Warner Brothers.

For his indelible work in animation, Dwayne was posthumously presented with the WRITERS GUILD OF AMERICA's 2011 ANIMATION WRITING AWARD, the first African-American in history to be so honored.

The winner of 3 EISNER AWARDS for his work in comic books, 11 PARENTS' CHOICE AWARDS, 6 "BEST EDITOR" awards, the 2009 INKPOT AWARD presented by Comic-Con International, and a GOLDEN APPLE AWARD from his alma mater for his "use of popular art to promote and enhance human dignity," Dwayne McDuffie's life's work exemplified both diversity and excellence. He led by example while presciently stating, "From invisible to inevitable." The man may be gone, but his mission lives on.

"I learned to read from comics. I learned to dream."

-Dwayne McDuffie

"Thank you for sharing his life with us Charlotte." -Eric Cooper-

August 19, 1921, El Paso, TX - *October 24, 1991*, Santa Monica, CA

Gene Roddenberry, byname of Eugene Wesley Roddenberry (born Aug. 19, 1921, El Paso, Texas, U.S.—died Oct. 24, 1991, Santa Monica, Calif.) American writer and television and film producer, creator and executive producer of the popular science-fiction television series *Star Trek* (1966–69), which spawned other television series and a string of motion pictures. Roddenberry briefly attended Los Angeles City College, flew B-17 bombers during World War II, and was an airline pilot (1945–49) and a sergeant on the Los Angeles police force (1949–53). He then became a freelance television writer and contributed scripts through 1962 to several network programs, including *Dragnet*, *Highway Patrol*, *Dr. Kildare*, and *Have Gun—Will Travel*. In 1964 he began trying to sell the idea of *Star Trek* to producers, but not until Sept. 8, 1966, did the first episode debut on the National Broadcasting Company (NBC) network. The series was repeatedly threatened with cancellation, but the program's ardent followers, known as "Trekkies," formed fan clubs and initiated letter-writing campaigns to keep the series alive until Sept. 2, 1969.

Star Trek chronicled the 23rd-century adventures of a cast of characters headed by Capt. James Kirk, Mr. Spock, and other officers of the starship *Enterprise*. The 79 aired episodes of the series presented an optimistic view of life in the future as it traced the crew's mission "to explore strange new worlds; to seek out new life and new civilizations; to boldly go where no man has gone before."

Star Trek enjoyed astonishing success in syndication and eventually spawned an animation series (1973–75), a series of theatrical films, and three spin-off television series. Roddenberry was a producer on the first film based on the original series, *Star Trek—The Motion Picture*, which was released in 1979. It was followed by nine more *Star Trek* motion pictures, with Roddenberry serving as executive consultant on the first three. Beginning in 1987, he was also executive producer of the sequel television series *Star Trek: The Next Generation*. He also wrote *Star Trek—The Motion Picture: A Novel* (1979)

Reference by: Encyclopedia Britannica

Eric M. Cooper: Main Author & Creator
The beginning of Eric's career in writing started through a love for science fiction at a young age. He drew spaceship battles on paper and let his mind drift into outer space as he attended grade school. As Eric reached his early 20's he went through some mental depression, but at the same time he found an escape from his reality through writing novels which became his self therapy. Today Eric M. Cooper has produced his own series of 'Caption Novels' called Knight Seeker; a sci-fi charged superhero, writer of his own comic books, and an editor of exclusive press comic books from other creators. Now he's on even a wider path of writing which will include Star Enforcers, and the newest superhero called Merge. Eric's main motivation for writing is to give his readers a true escape with meaning and purpose, and at the same time he will be teaching people about themselves and their own potential in this universe. www.KnightSeeker.com
Photo by Eric Moran aka 'The Smoke'

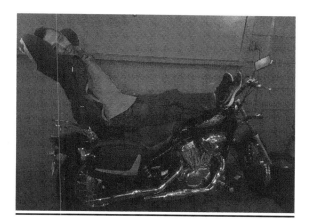

Star Enforcers Co-Writer: My name is Miles Simon, and I like to write nerdy things. I'm a lover of comics, fantasy, science- fiction, and roleplaying games. When I'm not busy writing some awesome shit, I work customer service day jobs, and spend my time playing roleplaying games or video games. I love writing for a lot of reasons. One of them is that I get to give someone a great story, and let their imagination run wild. I love to see the smile on someone's face as they immerse themselves into a wonderful world, and I love that I can give someone that smile. I hope at some point, you read this book and had a good time. And if you did, you're welcome.

Star Enforcers: Main Editor

Thomas Chervenak grew up in rural Minnesota, but now lives and works within the Minneapolis/St. Paul metropolitan area. He has spent much of his free time performing as a musician, both vocally and instrumentally. Past performances include everything from rowdy tavern songs at Renaissance Festivals to Beethoven's Ninth Symphony with the St. Paul Chamber Orchestra to acting as an interim Music Director at his church. Tom enjoys reading a wide variety of books, Science Fiction and Historical Fiction being the preferred types. His favorite authors are Anne McCaffrey (Science Fiction), Jeffrey Archer and John Jakes. Tom's interest in costuming is evident from his membership with the 501st Legion as well as his time performing with the Minnesota Renaissance Festival. Tom is also married and a father of two.

<u>Art Director of Star Enforcers</u>

At the age of 41 the artist known as Phoe-nix Nebula has begun to amass an impressive resume in the field of art. His productions range from children's books, coloring books, illustrations for both novels and comics, murals, logos, and now using his background in martial arts and as a music producer poet/lyricist to produce a vibe unlike any other. In 2017 he looks to debut his first self written/drawn graphic novel Chronicles of the Melanknights which will be preceded by Fancy, a build up to the graphic novel itself. He also uses his gifts in the arts of healing through visual channels creating a line of work centered around helping people find their path in this life as well as healing the wounds suffered along the way. Look for 2017 to be the breakout year for this rare and exclusive talent. Stepping into the light of center stage has never been his goal but it seems destiny has other plans. instagram- phoenix.nebula.9 facebook- Phoe-nix Nebula /
biz page- Unique Individuals Ink

Donovan Petersen is a concept design/storyboard/sequential artist who resides in Las Vegas Nevada. He is a 2006 graduate in Media Arts and Animation from the Las Vegas Art Institute. He enjoys learning and expanding his skills and has worked on movies, childrens storybooks, comic books, promotional materials, and many other varied art projects. He'll gladly talk your ear off about comic books or movies, whenever you want. He'll take as many friends as he can get, so go to his Facebook page where you can view a wide array of his past projects and he can be contacted directly at donovanpetersen@gmail.com

Blair Smith is the colors artist for the cover, and works with other independent comic book creators. For more into https://www.facebook.com/ArtofBlairSmith

Credited works:
The Living Corpse
Knight Seeker
Dynamite Comics
Hound Dog Comics
Shaolin Death Squad Comic

Paris Alleyne, Graduated from Max the Mutt College of Animation, Art & Design. He is a Freelance comic book illustrator from Toronto. He is also a penciler and a digital colourist. He has worked with IDW, Red 5 Studios, Red Stylo Media and a series of independent publishers as well as on my own personal stories. To add he is the main artist to the 'Haven' Comic Book.

First concept cover illustration for Star Enforcers

I loved comic books when I started reading Thor, The Black Panther, Superman, and Batman. I always felt that if I ever got the chance I could draw for Bob Kane, or maybe even Stan Lee, but I was only at the young age of 6. My mom noticed my passion so she got me a book on painting muscles, and my Aunt was an art teacher so I had some guidance in becoming an artist. Underground Comixxx new book lineup is outrageous because we are working with people like the Black Panther Party, T. Marton, Jake the Snake Robert's, Michael Jia White, Eric Cooper, Wayne Sutphin, Phoe-nix Nebula, Jesse Marks, and a few others. We have sold well over 2,000 comic books and well on our way to 3,000 sold. My artwork is inspired by my parents, the Black Panther Party, Jack Kirby, The Sims Brothers, Brother-Man, Dwayne McDuffie of Milestone comics, along with Denys Cowan. TV also had an impact on my artwork as well when I watched Bruce Lee, and Kung-Fu movies! As I was growing up I've seen people stand for something such as Alex Haley, and Malcolm X. These two men made me want to give back to my community so I started my own comic book company which was my childhood dream. I have characters that have substance such as Soul, he is a good brother. He's essence existed before the birth of Christ and he was awoken in a child's body in the 1960's. He was raised by BBP Huey Newton, and Bobby Seal. Soul and his brother helped to stop the first crack house from existing, but unfortunately this change in history caused a ripple effect in time and the sectors of space because aliens have been watching earth for thousands of years. The aliens were forbidden to invade Earth but after the ripple in space and time Earth became a target and The Protectors of Sector 5 teams have to stop them and fight for the 10 Point Program which was inducted by the Panthers. Jabaar L. Brown started a company that is diverse and gives back to the inner city's children. He teaches art at The Boy's and Girl's Club. He doesn't just teach them art but he also teaches the youth to write which helps their own temple of life their body and their minds. He encourages them to have goals because dreams are empty if you don't take action. Underground Comixxx is about the people for the people, the comic book fans, and to have diversity in every thing that we do. Underground Comixxx C.E.O. Jabaar L. Brown

My name is Jonathan Piccini, I was born in Italy in Assisi in 1990. Since I was a child I've had a passion for drawing, I do not know how many sheets of designs I've drewn in kindergarten and elementary school. I mainly drew anything that came to my creative mind, and the rest of my class mates remained stunned. During adolescence I began to cultivate a passion for reading various types of comics like Spiderman, Batman, Nathan Never or Tex. During class I would start to draw these characters, so much that most of the time I would be reprimanded by my teachers. During high school I had the opportunity to know a comic artist by the name of Claudio Villa. After seeing his work and asking so many questions I knew what I was going to become a "designer". When I entered the school of comics I was over the moon, I did not know what was waiting for me. I had so many thoughts in my head and I could not wait to start. I was fortunate to know other aspiring artists like myself in the world of graphic illustration. They were all different and with their own unique personalities. I'm happy to have known formidable cartoonists such as: Daniele Bonomo, Emiliano Mammucari, David Messina, Rodolfo Torti, Paul Grella, Fabio Mantovani, Sara Pichelli and Enrique Breccia; it is only thanks to them that I'm starting to draw more 'properly. In these years I have learned many things and read many comics. Sure I had my moments of difficulty but my tenacity and commitment has helped me to overcome my obstacles. For now I enjoy doing commission work on designs and to participate in projects for young artists. If there are greater opportunities in the future I would like to pursue them. I want to become an official designer for a publishing house and create new projects for events. Special thanks to Eric and Phoenix for giving me the opportunity to participate in this project, I hope to work with you guys again in the future ......

Kevin Grevioux, is an honorary likeness to the character Tactical Officer Onyx. Kevin is a screenwriter, producer, actor and a graphic novel creator who has 20 years experience in the film industry. After graduating Howard University with a degree in microbiology, Grevioux cameto Hollywood where he acted in several films including, *Alien Nation, The Mask, Congo, Batman Forever,* Tim Burton's *Planet of the Apes, The Hulk* and *Men In Black II.* Kevin also co-created the successful Underworld franchise, which was his first produced writing credit. He was also a co- producer on the filmseriesand played the character RAZE. Grevioux has just completed production on his latest filmfrom a screenplay he wrote *I, Frankenstein* produced by Lakeshore Entertainment.It was based on his original graphic novel. In addition, Grevioux is a prolific writer in the comic book/graphic novel world. He has workedfor both Marvel andDC Comics having written such characters as *Spider- Man, Blade, Iron Man,Batman, Superman, the Phantom* and the critically acclaimed *Adam: Legend of the Blue Marvel* for Marvel which he created.

He has established an independent creator-owed comic book/graphic novel company called Darkstorm Studios. Under this imprint Kevin hascreated *ZMD: Zombies of Mass Destruction, I, Frankenstein, Monstroids, Shurika, Skull & Guns, The Gray Men, Alius Rex and Battlesphere.* As well as Astounding Comics, which producesall-ages titles such as *Valkyries, Njuma, Cryptokids, Guardian Heroes, The Atoms Family,The Toy Box, Mighty Girls, The Vindicators* and *The Hammer Kid.*

Grevioux animation credits include The Atoms Family, an unproduced pilot for Starz and episodes of both Ben 10: Ultimate Alien and Avengers: Earth's Mightiest Heroes.

Evan Chan is an honorary likeness to the character Elumeni Golic. Evan is a first generation Asian American. He was born in Cleveland, Ohio. The son of two immigrant parents from China & Vietnam. At the age of 2 he moved to Delaware where he would spend the majority of his life growing up. He faced much adversity through teasing for his overweight appearance and racial ethnicity. The tough balance of growing up in America would later shape his core beliefs. He had become open minded to all types of people due to what he had to go through. Fast forward to adulthood he attended a University in Philadelphia with a degree in business and he has a passion for finance. His hobbies include staying in shape at the gym, loves to cook unique dishes, playing the piano, loves reading the news about the stock market, really enjoys going to comic conventions and participating as a cosplayer, and he embraces the nerd culture. Evan's future goals is being a wealth advisor, or equity researcher, working on Wall Street, and to establish his own restaurant towards the end of his career on Wall Street.

Author's Personal Notes: This project was one of the longest that I have ever done. I was fortunate to have a cool co-writer by the name of Miles Simon that helped me along this unchartered territory for Seeker Entertainment. My main art director Phoe-Nix Nebula has been a great illustrator to work with and the way he handled this small staff of artists has made my production of this novel even easier. Even though this novel was suppose to be released in 2014 life and other responsibilities came up, but like in Hollywood not all goes as planned; especially when it comes to timing of releases. I am confident though that Star Enforcers was well worth the wait. "Engage Slip Stream Drive!" *Illustration by Paris Alleyne*

SETTING:

The setting takes place in the Andromeda Galaxy on multiple planets that are occupied with different ethnics of humans, and a large variety of skin colors, even some spotted. The humans also have their different varieties of sexual orientations. There's also an array of aliens that are humanoid in this galaxy.

THE PEOPLE AND POWER FIGURES:

The colonies are controlled by the Flow Council that keeps the peace. To enforce law and order they use galactic police officers called Constables. When situations call for more drastic measures the Elumeni are called in to enforce the law.

The main threats to the law of the galaxy are ship pirates, gangs, and warrior societies that thirst for power and dominance over the galaxy. Some of these law breaking factions have Acers that serve them.

To control complete chaos in the galaxy the Flow Council has the ultimate weapon at their disposal. A spaceship the size of an aircraft carrier which was developed by ancient beings that are extinct was kept in an underground cavern. A planetary exploration team discovered it and accessed the ship's computer system which has a robotic pilot. The pilot informed the humans that the ship is called the Solar Sword; a weapon that destroys stars. The Flow Council has only used this destructive craft once to eradicate an uncontrollable deadly disease that was spreading among the population of the Darwin Solar System. Once the Solar Sword fired its beam it caused the sun to explode and destroy the entire solar system. The ship itself was not harmed due to the fact its hull is composed of a highly resistant metal, which is not found in this galaxy.

THE ELUMENI:

The Elumeni are the most effective killers. They have an honor code same as a samurai, and have the powers of Elementals. Elementals can control the four elements; earth, fire, wind, and water. They can only master one of these elements, but have a small control of the others. Their iris color reflects the element that they are a master of; example Water- Aqua eyes, Earth – Honey Brown eyes, Fire - Red eyes, Wind- white eyes (Just the center pupil will be visible) When using their full power their eyes will glow. The Elumeni are born with their powers and are put into training at a young age to serve the Flow Council. They are trained on the planet Technar. There are small numbers of them scattered around this galaxy. To come upon any of them is very rare. Any weapon in their hands they use with killer proficiency; from a simple knife, to a gun. They are trained to injure and kill their opponent in the most effective target areas.

The elementals when born are by law to be placed into the Elumeni training facility on a moon called Talon: A moon that orbits the planet Primus. Talon was uninhabitable until a core of engineers designed and built a bio dome the size of a small city with a large underground facility for the Elumeni Order. While on Talon the elementals are trained to live as part of the Elumeni Order, educated in history, the sciences, and to pilot starships. The moon orbits Technar, a planet two times bigger than Earth and has the same atmosphere. While on the planet the elementals are trained to use their powers, to hunt, and to kill. The inhabitance of Technar are powerful and dangerous wild animals which provide an impressive challenge for the elementals in training.

The planet and the moon are protected by a dampening field to scramble any sensors that try to probe the area. In addition to this security measure cloaked orbital weapons platforms are placed in the area. Any spacecrafts that come within range of the planet must enter a security code to avoid being fired upon by the automated weapons platforms. Only the Elumeni and Constables have access to the pass codes to safely pass through the defense perimeter.

The elemental lifestyle is difficult. They only have contact with their birth parents four times a year. Their parents are taken to Talon to watch their children train so that they might be inducted into the Elumeni Order. Unfortunately some of the elementals die in the training and the trials to become Elumeni.

Most elementals become a part of the Elumeni Order by the age of twenty five. Others that choose to not participate in the trials are forced to live their lives on Talon and Technar. The reason this action is invoked is due to the fact that if a corrupt organization were to get hold of an elemental they would pose a serious threat to other beings. The Acers which are the unlawful Elumeni are troublesome enough to the peace in the galaxy.

CYBERNETICS:

The home and training planet for the Elumeni called Technar was once used to wage a war on the machines of the past, called Eliminators. The war waged was between Elumeni and Eliminators. The Eliminators are able to take the form of humanoid skin types. Eliminators were an attempt to wipe out all life forms.

The war was waged because cybernetics were not their own people and had formed a sense of consciousness. Once the war had ended, the Flow Council of that time had formed a peaceful end with the Eliminators.

Today, the members of a modern day cybernetic society have earned a place on the seat of the Flow Council. After all, they fought for their rights. They represent all cybernetics.

CURRENCY AND LIFESTYLE:

Every planet society has its own paper currency, but interstellar currency is only accepted as Gem-Pressed-Latinum. G.P.L. is composed from rare gems, and is molecularly compressed into a rectangular shape no bigger than a credit card, and just a little thicker. Then a layer of platinum surrounds the edges of the rectangular pressed gems. There are 5 GPL types from lowest to highest: Topaz GPL= 1 credit, Safire GPL= 5 credits, Emerald GPL= 10 credits, Ruby GPL= 20 credits and Diamond GPL= 100 credits.

To function in the society you need to earn currency to eat, live, and survive. Working consists of government Flow Council jobs, agriculture, self employment, prostitution, and other methods of illegal activity such as unauthorized gambling, and selling illegal drugs.

TECHNOLOGY:

Tech info: Power source for ships come from charged liquids which are spun around in a centrifuge that power the space vessels.

Technology limits: There are no matter transporters for anyone. There are also no matter replicators. Hologram tech exists but they can't be formed into solid matter.

Weaponry: Guns that shoot bullets, sonic rifles, Guns that shoot lasers. Star vessels have missiles and torpedoes along with laser cannons and invisible shields barriers. Cloaking devices are only aboard specially designed ships.

PLANETS:

Forest worlds, full of vegetation and the natives of these planets live a simple life. Most of them are farmers, and do not express that much of an interest in technology. Most of their structural cities are very small. Most Elumenis that are the masters of earth are born on these types of planets.

Volcano worlds are quake active at times but the value of these planets are the metals that are mined. The natives of these worlds are excellent with engineering, and mass production. The cities are small but most of the buildings are extremely tall. Most Elumenis that are the masters of fire are born on these types of worlds.

Water worlds contain very few land masses, and most of the natives live in ocean cities. The natives of these worlds express a vast appreciation for the sciences. Most Elumenis that are the masters of water are born on these types of worlds.

Floating landmass worlds are highly unique. Not all the land masses float but a majority of them do. It is caused by the unusual gravity properties of these planets. The natives of these worlds are more in touch with enlightening the spirit. Their major cities are among the clouds. Most Elumenis that are the masters of air are born on these types of worlds.

Other worlds such as ice giants and desert worlds are made into penal colonies where prisons are forced to mine for jewels and ores. There are also resort/reservation planets that only have animal life; of course the true sportsman can't pass up hunting at these planets.

FLOW COUNCIL BACKSTORY:

The Flow Council is composed of ambassadors from all civilized worlds in this galaxy. The Flow Counsel is a large forum to discuss matters that impact other worlds and the stability of the galaxy. It is also a place of judgment and a means to carry out the law.

The planet Primus was discovered by a small group of unaffiliated explorers. Primus has a toxic gaseous environment, and ¼ larger that Jupiter. The planet was completely uninhabited and had no remains of life forms, yet there seemed to be some kind of civilization that lived there. There were ruins of buildings that still stood on the planet, and ancient machinery that was inoperable. What may have happened to whatever civilization that had existed there is a mystery. However, the planet could not be mined, and had nothing of worth; the only thing of any value was the Solar Sword, a weapon of extreme power. Once the Flow Council was informed of the Solar Sword's existence, the entire planet was taken over by them and none who are not of high ranked Constables, Elumeni, Flow Council ambassadors or otherwise approved by the Flow Council are allowed anywhere near the planet. Those who are not allowed near or on the planet are destroyed on sight.

JABAAR L. BROWN

Star Enforcers: Prologue

I had to live. I did what was required for me to stay alive.

I am Vas'Kis. I was born into a world where my race was drafted as the slaves of mercenaries. Their powerful air ships ripped through our skies and explosions and intense artillery fired onto our people. The advanced technology highly outmatched our weaponry.

They enslaved us. They killed us. They used our planet for its resources: food, land, water, everything. I learned their language because I was born into a prison camp, run by them, on one of their ships. Their head-to-toe body armor showed no expression; we just feared them. Their bodies looked like ours. Five fingers, two arms, two legs, a head. We had no idea if they had our red skin or our black hair. In the end, it didn't matter. They were our oppressors. Who cared what they looked like?

We weren't allowed to speak our own language. When we did, the oppressors thought we were planning something, plotting something, so we were beaten, often until we were unconscious.

One day, new men came to watch over us. They were going to grab the children, myself and others, to sell into slavery. My parents held my shoulders tight as a man in lavish clothing examined us. His face was exposed and it was the first time we'd seen a person who wasn't of our race. His own guards watched his surroundings, making sure my fellow people, and especially our oppressors, didn't turn on him.

The man decided he wanted me. In outrage, my father pushed back the men trying to take me. And he said "Khash Fin Sai Saz Rah!" I didn't know what that meant. The oppressors raised their guns and ordered my father be gunned down. Bullets ripped through his body. Black blood splattered to the top of my head and bits sprinkled into my left eye. I was too shocked to close them.

Mother screamed. She, too, was gunned down. In immediate response, one of the men grabbed me. I saw a small black box with buttons at his side. I remembered seeing one of these before. I had seen a man set the same device before. He used it to wipe out a room of my people to make room for more healthy ones to sell into slavery. I still remembered the combination of the buttons he used to cause an explosion. I pressed the buttons I could see, and slid beneath his legs.

The oppressors were stunned, the man was terrified, and my people went back into their cage. I ran to a hallway and turned left, shielding myself from the blast. I am certain I killed some of my people that day. I needed to survive. That moment is my only regret. I killed my own people to save myself.

I ran. I remembered the layout of some of the ship. The areas where they kept rifles. Areas where there were more of my people. I grabbed a rifle I could barely carry. I strapped a belt of grenades to my waist. I remembered which ones were explosive and which ones stunned. I think I heard them call it a flash-bang.

I started typing combinations to lock down the room I'd already left when I heard men coming down a hallway that led to mine. I threw a grenade in preparation for their arrival and I heard screams as it exploded. I remember smiling and laughing a little bit. Then I was confused. These were new actions and feelings. I was nearly an adult with 8 years in my life, and I hadn't known laughter.

I finally saw one of my oppressors. I knew those eyes. The man had purple skin, horns, and black hair. There was shock in his eyes as he saw a young boy holding a rifle and firing at him. Bullets ripped through his body and he fell to the ground. He tried to scream.

I ran to his fallen body and he looked into my eyes. He was gurgling on his own blood. That unusual feeling came back and I laughed again. I looked to see a control panel that needed a finger print and an eye to open. I knew that it was the way to freedom for my people. I saw the man again, gurgling on his own blood. I had found my path.

I took a knife strapped to his boot and started cutting into his fingers. His eyes opened wide in pain, but he was unable to scream. The only time he could make any noise with his mouth was when he coughed blood. Even then, he couldn't scream. I took the knife to his eye ball and reached the blade into his retina. I was surprised at how durable his flesh was. Halfway through cutting into his eye, he died from blood loss. I was disappointed.

I had what I needed. I put his fingers and his eye to the scanner. The man inside had expected one of his own to enter. He found one of his slaves holding a rifle. The cage was locked and he was raping one of my people. She was screaming and crying and struggling. The man backed away from her, his eyes filled with fear. I put bullets into his knees.

I grabbed keys located on the nearby table and walked over to my people's cage. I handed the crying woman her clothing. She dressed. Tears were still running down her face. I smiled at her.

"Don't cry," I told her, handing her the rifle. "Make him cry."

She took the rifle from my hand, and put bullet after bullet through the man's chest. She returned the rifle and grabbed a pipe near her, and started beating the man to death. Red blood splattered onto the pipe and I could see the anger on her face. She glanced at me and I nodded my approval.

I led my people back to the rifle room and soon twenty of us were equipped with rifles, grenades, and other weaponry. I killed many of the oppressors, none of them expecting the slaves to be carrying weapons. We ran from the ship and we were outside. This was our own land. I looked around at the barrenness, the cement, and the dead bodies of my people decaying in our streets. I smelled the air and I knew that we had to run. We had to go underground.

Two years later I was 10, an adult. I read and researched everything I could about the existing universe. There was something to hope for, something the oppressors feared: the Constables. The Constables were Flow Council's soldiers. Their army and their police force. Their officers and their assassins. Their vanguards for justice. They were our hope. I needed to get to them. I needed to get their help.

There were nearly 200 of us. And each of us wanted to fight. We lived underground, eating food stolen from our oppressors. We had fires to keep us warm, and weapons to keep us safe. The dust always got in our throats, our noses, our lungs. We'd often cough and gag on the dirt surrounding us. We stewed in our own fecal matter, had no luxuries, and nothing but each other.

Those of us who fought and killed people wore the stolen armor of our oppressors. It looked dark black. Often times it was stained with the blood of our fellow Amrasians, or by the blood of our enemies. Either way, it was a strange comfort knowing blood had been spilt. Almost as if knowing that chaos had ensued. It was our trophy. It is hard to explain.

Those who couldn't fight, the sick and the old, wore rags of clothing. Sometimes, some of my people found old clothing belonging to our once strong government. But often, if we could find articles of clothing, pieces of parchment, or something of the older civilization we'd use to have, we'd pin it to the cave. It was a reminder that once we were strong, and we would be again. Rarely, considering our unbarring hatred, you would see someone wearing the casual clothing of our oppressors.

We had an elder. An old woman. Kaisin was her name. Her face wrinkled, a burn mark was on her left eye, rendering it useless. Her dead flesh held together like the tight stitching of a piece of clothing forcibly sewn together.

Kaisin told me we had a religion. A way of life showing forgiveness to those who hated us. And to those who hurt us. I kept her alive and around because she taught me words of the old language, of our language, a language ripped from us. I was fighting to get it back. But with every useful word of our old tongue, came a useless word of forgiveness and peace. Nothing was more irritating to hear. But I put up with it. For the good of knowledge.

Eventually, though, she came around to my way of thinking. After the third dozen of dead bodies we dragged into our cave and do our best to bury. The stink of the dead hung in our savage home. It wore on her sanity, and on her sense of compassion.

Kaisin told me that in normal times, there was a time for compassion. There was a God who would teach us, and to choose a disciple. Weeks passed, however, and soon she said she didn't believe this was a time for compassion. It was a time for war, a time for defending our own. I asked if there was a god for this person. She said there was one, in the form of a woman. Naming herself Sinzo, and choosing to kill evil ones, and to defend the innocent. This Goddess became a heroine of mine, an idol. I begged for stories of Sinzo. Hearing how she slaughtered the barbarians who would come after her people, our people. I imagined, and felt childlike in my hunger for slaughtering the guilty, and protecting the innocent.

We raided ships and stole food, weapons, and one day, an Artificial Intelligence. It was a gray metallic box that spoke to us. A voice, who started telling us things about the universe. Its voice was synthetic, made to sound positive and gentle. It sounded like a female. It spoke in the tongue of our oppressors, the tongue that had been raped into our mouths, into our brains. It taught a girl, Ki'Sha, slightly younger than me, about ships. It taught how ships flew, how they traveled from system to system, the fuel that was used to operate them.

Ki'Sha said she could take us to the ones who would save us. To these saviors, these protectors of the galaxy, the Flow Council. Men and women and even a cybernetic being that represented their own respective people. We learned that there were dozens of other alien races out there. Possibly even more.

I and a band of nearly 20 of my people would sneak onto a ship owned by our oppressors, kill them all, steal the ship, and then Ki'Sha would pilot us to our saviors. They would learn of the injustices done upon us. And they would take action against our oppressors. The Flow Council governs all of the galaxy, and they must save us.

Hitting the ship was easy. We knew a group of our people hadn't yet been taken as slaves. Their tents were surrounded by our former buildings that were now rubble. Their location was obvious. I suppose they simply hoped they weren't important enough to be taken.

My soldiers waited for the Oppressors underground until a ship came to take them all, to enter to their small camp, rape the women, take the children, and kill the men. Our explosive devices were waiting for them. I watched from a balcony as body parts, innards and blood sprayed about the front of my peoples' camp. I smiled.

When the majority of the Oppressors were dealt with, we took the stragglers of the ship by gunfire. Our people stormed the ship, used one of the half alive Oppressors to get onto their ship, then gunned him down.

I personally escorted Ki'Sha. Our one hope for salvation was not going to be killed. Not by these men who dared to set their feet upon and cause atrocity to the people of Amras, my planet. We made our way through hallways and into the cockpit. We killed the pilot offering surrender. Ki'Sha sat in his seat and wiped the red blood off the dashboard.

"I can get us there," she told me.

"Do it, then," I replied. Ki'Sha pressed buttons and spoke to an Artificial Intelligence. Soon, the ship started to float into the air, and we could hear humming and roaring from the engines, as the ship prepared to rip through our planet's atmosphere.

Twenty minutes later we arrived to Flow Council space. A voice demanded to know who we were through the intercom. It told us to state our business or be arrested. We explained that we were of Amras and that we needed to talk to the Flow Council concerning our planet.

They demanded we open our hull and let them board. My people were skeptical, and looked to me for direction. I shrugged.

"Their weapons and numbers are superior. What would we do against them if they wanted to kill us?" I asked. "In any event, we are here to negotiate and beg for assistance to our people, not cause fights."

Their people boarded us. A large group of soldiers in suits that ran head to toe. They spoke of not infecting themselves with our sickness, but also being careful not to infect us. I wanted to say something back in response, but I was too in awe of something. Something on their chests. Something we'd all wanted to see. Something we'd heard about for so long. We saw it, finally. The voice told us about it, this insignia, an infinity symbol. The symbol had stars running down its middle. We saw the insignias on their chests. We knew what it was. The sign of the Flow Council. The sign of the men and women, and synthetics, who would protect us, and help us take back our land.

The men and women that boarded our ship, the soldiers, had small devices, scanners, in their hands. A blue light from a small beacon it would go up and down our bodies. They had vials to inject into us, filled with clear liquids. The soldiers had their guns raised at us, still not trusting us. Why would they? We were covered in red blood, with weapons on our floors.

"Hold still," a woman ordered, while scanning me. She looked at her device, this rectangle piece of metal in her hand, with a screen. She looked at the device that scanned my health.

"He would die in a matter of hours if we didn't give it to him, sir," the woman said to one of her fellow soldiers, one that his gun pointed at me, staring at me through his glass helmet in mistrust. "If we're going to bring them to Integra, they need the antibodies."

Her commanding officer nodded.

They sprayed us with things. They injected us with things. They told us that it was because we didn't have the immune system to handle the Flow Council's homeworld. I showed them trust. They seemed so shocked, so astonishingly surprised to see us. I suppose they'd only heard about us through news reports or stories. The red skinned people of Amras.

We followed their ships. Some of their soldiers stayed behind to watch us, to make sure we wouldn't turn on their allies.

"Did you know about us before? About our people? And our plight?" I asked one of them.

He said nothing. He simply kept his rifle aimed at my face.

"It seems you did. You didn't seem too surprised about my arrival. Why haven't the Flow Council helped us? Why haven't you aided us in our time of need?" I asked. The man I was looking at gave no answer.

A woman in one of their uniforms looked at me and seemed to have pity for my ignorance of the universe and the pain of my life. So she told me, "The Flow Council just command us what to do and where to go, and they abide by their own jurisdictions and laws."

"We're innocent people," Ki'Sha stated, as she was still flying the ship. "Why didn't you help us? Why do you have a law allowing us to die, to be tortured and raped and killed?"

"We're not allowed to interfere with races or planets that we have no claim to," she answered. "Or, rather, the Flow Council isn't. The Flow Council commands us to do things, and the Constables just obey."

"Constables?" one of my people asked.

"Soldiers." I answered to him. "Men and women who act in a variety of ways to serve the Flow Council. Be it politics, gunfire, space-based warfare or assassination."

"The Constables aren't assassins," a soldier said to me.

"Sure you are," I replied. "You simply fight for a cause you find to be just, not just money."

"We should stop talking to them," the woman said. "They're primitives."

"No," I stated. "We're simply embracing a savage side of our nature, in order to survive. And if you meant that our technology is less advanced, then I apologize that our ancestors adapted to our planet and became intelligent at a time slightly before yours did."

The pale skinned woman scoffed at me, and the rest of the soldiers didn't look at me as if they were disgusted. I know they weren't, they were simply insulted and their pride was wounded, because I, a primitive, had said something smart to them. And they had no response. A hid my smile.

After several minutes, we arrived at Integra. Integra was a moon, orbiting a single planet. It was the home base of the Flow Council and the training facility for the Constables. Looking down at this moon, terraformed to sustain life and hold a large, glorious city, was something you can't describe without words.

Buildings, gleaming lights, and ships flying through the air. People walking everywhere, happy, careless. It was a sight I had never seen. I'd heard about our cities being better, but not like this. We still had stone and had just invented gunpowder and useful ways to use it. These people had cars that floated through their city and shining lights to guide their paths. They had people to take care of them, and a government that wouldn't abandon them or fall in their time of need.

Stepping outside the ship, I breathed deeply. The air felt better than my world. I smelled clean air around me. I hadn't known the scent of an atmosphere that didn't combine blood, guts, and fecal matter with the exhaust from the ships roaring through our skies. The artificial sunlight hit my skin, and I could feel its warmth. It was moment of pure serenity, of freedom.

And then the Constables made it end. They told me to walk with them. One of them shoved me forward, forcing me to stumble in the direction he wanted. I was on a bridge made of pure smooth metal. Multiple flying cars zoomed through the air below me. I reached out over the edge with my hand and felt a strange force push me back. Something I couldn't see or hear or touch just forced me where it wanted me to be. I yelped in surprise. The Constables laughed.

"Integra has magnetic fields to prevent people from falling off," one of the soldiers said.

"Incredible," I replied.

"That must require a lot of power," Ki'Sha stated. "I'm surprised you put that much power and energy into stopping people from killing themselves." A soldier laughed at her.

"When you have the money and power to do it, you can actually care about your people," the soldier stated, smiling while she did it.

"False security," I smirked, in a happy, positive voice. The soldiers looked at me, confused. "The little things matter, to keep everyone thinking the Flow Council can protect them from everything. Fascinating."

We kept walking on the bridge. I looked up to see the headquarters of the Flow Council and the Constables. It was a pyramid made of glass windows. Statues circled the entirety of them, each of a different race. All of them looked humanoid with differernt colored skin, sometimes horns, one even looked somewhat amphibian. There was always a male, and a female, standing side by side, holding each other's hand. Except one statue. It looked a robot, and it stood alone. That confused me.

As we walked the halls of this great pyramid palace, people looked at us in shock. Blood covered foreigners, all of which were surrounded by Constables. My smiling at them occasionally did nothing to calm their unsettled eyes.

"Where are you taking us?" I wondered to the soldiers.

"To be questioned by our commander," was the answer.

"We need to speak to the Flow Council." I stated.

"Ha! The Flow Council doesn't have time to--" A loud sound beeped throughout the building. A synthetic voice started speaking over the intercom. I think it was supposed to sound male. **"Constables escorting the Amrasians, bring them to the Flow Council's chambers immediately,"** the voice stated. I chuckled.

"We should get you cleaned up," A female soldier said to us.

"No," I replied. "I want them to see us like this. I want them to see what our lives are like. I want them to see what it took for us to get here and how seriously they need to take our words. And the voice said immediately, so let's go immediately."

The Constables nodded and complied by shoving us in the right direction.

I could see the doors of the Flow Council in the distance. As we arrived, the two great golden automatic metal slabs slowly opened. The insignias of many different races and armies were imprinted onto the doors. These were the races I'd heard about from the voice.

As the doors opened, these men and women of different races were standing in a very large stadium. I and my allies were in the arena looking up at them. To finally see all of these people who were to help us brought complete shock and amazement. It brought hope to my mind that I could not express in words.

"Flow Council," I stated, "We are in need of your help."

"Desperately," added Ki'Sha. I put my hand out, to stop her from talking. I needed to say the words, and I needed to say them quickly.

"Our planet has been overtaken by oppressors with technology more advanced than ours, weapons more superior, and people more ruthless. Our race is being sold as slaves, and slaughtered as animals." I raised my two arms and hands with five fingers. "As you can see, we're very much like you. We're capable of speaking, of walking, of intelligent life. We're an intelligent people, and we're being slaughtered. Please. I beg of you. Assist us. Assist our race. Assist our planet."

"You make a compelling argument," a female Flow Council member replied to me.

"Compelling, but not reason enough to interfere with a planet to which we hold no jurisdiction," a male member added.

"We can't take action on something we don't own," another member stated.

"Don't own?!" Ki'Sha yelled. "Our people are being decimated by the thousands! We're being sold in chains! People are being raped and tortured and executed! You're supposed to stand for good and justness, but instead, you sit here and you--!"

"Ki'Sha!" I shouted, stopping her from yelling. I looked back to the Flow Council. I pointed to the blood all over me.

"You see what we are. You see what we did to get here. What must we do for you to help us?"

"There is one thing," a cybernetic voice stated. I looked up to see a robot standing amongst the Flow Council. This shocked me. "My people were once not a part of this Council, a time that was shorter than most of you would choose to remember." The synthetic life form then looked to his fellow members. "We swore allegiance to you. And you accepted us. By the same logic, it could be done for them."

"That was at a time of war, D.A.X.!" an ambassador shouted. "We made that deal to save lives!"

"And now I'm asking you to make the same deal to save lives again," the robot replied. The room was in silence.

"They'd need an Ambassador," a woman stated.

"Vas'Kis will do it!" one of my people shouted in pride.

"And Vas'Kis is?" a woman among the Flow Council wondered. I stepped forward.

"Me," I stated.

"He looks rather young," a man said.

"The Flow Council has no age restrictions," someone else replied.

"I'm over 200 years old," the cybernetic stated. "To me, the majority of you seem young. Age makes no difference in capability of leading your people. This boy has fought his way here, simply to speak to us. He knows the plight of his people, and what it will take to help them. He has shown leadership."

"He makes a good argument," a woman replied to the cyborg.

"I will be vanguard of my people," I said. "I will represent them and fight for them and work in every capacity you deem necessary to insure their safety, acceptance, and respect in your society. I will do whatever is necessary."

"Wouldn't a representative from your own government be more suited?" an ambassador wondered.

"Our people are overrun by advanced oppressors, whatever government we had is now destroyed," Ki'Sha replied.

"Hmm, very well." an ambassador replied.

"You will be their ambassador?" The cybernetic asked me. "You will take an oath?"

"I will do everything to protect my people," I stated.

"What is your last name?" an ambassador asked me.

"Last name?" I wondered in confusion.

"A name for your bloodline," a purple skinned man stated. "It is everything."

I looked to the floor and pondered for several seconds.

"Sinzo," I stated. "I am Vas'Kis Sinzo."

"Then say these words, Vas'Kis Sinzo." An ambassador told me.

Each ambassador typed something into their console and a holographic image appeared in the middle of the room. I looked at it and knew the words. I sank to my knees, closed my eyes, and began.

"I, Vas'Kis Sinzo, shall defend my people. Valiantly. Loyally. But I know I must defend others. I shall. I am one with the Flow Council. I am one with the galaxy that the Flow Council has sworn to defend and protect. I shall use the Constables when necessary, I will respect the wishes of other races, and I will defend them as if they were my own. The people that the Flow Council defends are my people, and mine are theirs. The Flow Council are my brothers and sisters, and I am their brother. I am loyal only to the defending of my new people, and I will follow the rules the Flow Council has set before me, as I will enforce the rules that have been created, and that I shall create and adjust. I am Ambassador to the Flow Council, and I will forever serve the people, not simply myself."

I opened my eyes.

"Rise, Vas'Kis Sinzo," The cybernetic stated.

"I thank you, android. You words may have saved my people." I said to him.

"I am D.A.X.," the android said, "and I only followed the oath you just took."

I nodded. "My first order of business is to enact a plan to free Amras. My planet. My people. Your planet. Your people."

And I did. I fought. And I am still fighting. I will not stop until injustice is gone.

-Vas'Kis Sinzo
Ambassador to the Amras

Integra

My people started to acclimatize to the Flow Council's world. Integra was the artificial base for the Flow Council's operations. A large amount of the Amras were as astonished at the world as I. I smiled at their bloody and dirty faces. Some of them didn't know how to keep existing, some were overjoyed at being freed, and others saw us changing from one army of oppressors to another. Those who rebelled against the Flow Council confused and saddened me.

Ambassador D.A.X came to talk to me as I stood on a balcony, looking at my people as shuttles dropped them several buildings away, where Constable scientists could ensure their health in this new artificial climate. Looking at D.A.X close up disturbed most of my people. Red eyes looking at you, strands of metal connecting to his jaw to make fake muscles, metal teeth and skull, he had a simple face, and he didn't show emotion.

"Enjoying the sights, Ambassador Sinzo?" The cybernetic asked me. I nodded.

"Yes, actually," I responded. "This is a new start for my people. They'll be safe. And we'll no longer have to deal with the oppressors." D.A.X nodded. It was rapid and sudden, and didn't seem like a real nod that a person would do, but I understood his intent to nod, to show understanding, to act like a person. I looked down in silence, thinking to myself. "Why didn't you save us?" I asked.

"You were outside our jurisdiction." D.A.X. responded. I didn't understand still.

"We were innocent people. Dying. Being sold into slavery, being raped, being tortured, being murdered. Why didn't you save us?" D.A.X remained silent for several seconds, still staring into my eyes.

"82 years ago, there was an uprising of men and women seeking to leave Flow Council space. Politicians, former Constable soldiers, former spies, and citizens left because they no longer wanted to live under a rule of a government system that claimed authority over the entire galaxy. A galaxy we still aren't able to travel all the way through. A galaxy we still don't even remotely understand." I was still confused.

"What are you saying, D.A.X?" I asked.

"The Flow Council still stated that they had dominion over those who attempted breaking from what we deemed as our rule. In leaving, those who left us persuaded additional men and women that they were not free, and that they needed someone to protect them from us. Because we demanded rule and order, and they demanded freedom. These men and women, they wanted to go to a 'Mystic Sea of Opportunity.' To space, unexplored worlds, and to the vast corners of the galaxy that the Flow Council, with all their power, had no real dominion over. They soon named themselves the Mystic Seas, and turned more to their cause. War began. Thousands died, all because of our ego. I was alive, I remember everything with clear precision. Deaths upon deaths occurred. And soon, we had no way to end this war. We committed genocide upon their colonized worlds, and many of their people came back to us in fear. Those remaining, who did not beg to be returned into the Flow Council's worlds ran. And they are still running. Calling themselves the Mystic Seas still, but now, they are but a small mercenary squad. A sad reflection of what they once wore. All that truly remains of them is their hatred for us."

"This is why you didn't protect us?!" I shouted, slightly in outrage.

"Yes." D.A.X. answered, bluntly. "You see, after the incident with the Mystic Seas, we created laws and rules, stating that we did not own everything, and we could not simply do whatever we wanted. We allowed lives of the innocent to die because we did not want to contradict our own rules. We did not want to start war once more with the vast amount of mercenaries about this galaxy. We did not want to create a situation like the one that happened 82 years ago. We did not want to create the Mystic Seas once more." My eyes widened. I was incapable of crying. Incapable of expressing pain. But I knew it. I knew pain.

"You allowed us to die." I said. "How many?" D.A.X. couldn't show emotion with his face, but altered the tone of his voice slightly, from a monotone robotic sound, to something somewhat more personable and sympathetic.

"How many what, Ambassador Sinzo?" D.A.X. asked me.

"How many worlds are controlled by mercenaries? How many of them are free from our wrath? How many innocent lives do we allow to receive a slow death because we aren't willing to do what is necessary, and cause war, despite the consequences?" I said to D.A.X, outraged, and saddened.

"Dozens," D.A.X. said to me. "Dozens."

The Solar Sword

A meeting was called of the Ambassadors. There were several that I was not asked to attend, and I wasn't told why. I didn't mind the exclusion. So long as my people were not being harmed, the other Ambassadors could discuss their business in private. I never understand why they excluded me so many times until today.

Someone new was in our midst. The newest Ambassador to the people of Acquis, and their multiple planets. A young man named Santos Hernandez. Slightly tanned cocoa skin, a short kept haircut, cleanly shaven face, and sporting the Flow Council robe that everyone wore. The dark blue colors, the Constable insignia on the shoulders, and a symbol representing his world on the front. Their symbol was simple, a drawing of a drop of water.

I'd read about the people of Acquis. One of the first races to create the Flow Council, along with the Daporans and the Minostas. As the Minostas still have yet to show their face to Flow Council meetings, curiosity swells the mind about them.

We got along with boring delegations, talking about the amount of money to be used to fund certain projects, allocation of Constable forces, discussing laws to adjust, more strongly enforce or remove altogether, those boring things.

We also did a customary welcoming of Santos, and allowed him to settle into the way of being a boring, boring Ambassador. Finally, after the monotonous talk, we got to something far more interesting. The discussion of the Flow Council's ultimate super weapon. The destructive power on the lips of everyone in the galaxy, the Solar Sword.

The planet Primus which Interga orbited was discovered by a small group of unaffiliated explorers. Primus has a toxic gaseous environment and ¼ larger than Jupiter. The planet was completely uninhabited and had no remains of life forms, yet there seemed to be some kind of civilization that lived there. There were ruins of buildings that still stood on the planet, and ancient machinery that was inoperable. What may have happened to whatever civilization that had existed there is a mystery. However, the planet could not be mined, and had nothing of worth; the only thing of any value was the Solar Sword, a weapon of extreme power. Once the Flow Council was informed of the Solar Sword's existence, the entire planet was taken over by them and none who are not high ranked Constables, Elumeni, Flow Council ambassadors or otherwise approved by the Flow Council are allowed anywhere near the planet. Those who are not allowed near or on the planet are destroyed on sight.

The starship is the size of a large aircraft carrier. The A.I. on the ship is a robotic pilot; it informed the explorers that the ship awaited commands to be activated. The reason for the ship's name is because the vessel has the ability to destroy a star and cause the planets in the targeted solar system to be eradicated by the devastating shockwave. The ship was used only once, to destroy an uncontrollable and deadly disease spreading in the Darwin System. The Solar Sword has since been used as a looming threat towards whole planets. It is never stated that the Flow Council would use it again, but the few populated planets that are not aligned with the Flow Council do fear the possibility of the Solar Sword being activated. However, the only planets not aligned with the Flow Council are mostly planets that have inhabitants that have not discovered space travel yet or planets ruled by mercenary gangs.

PHOE-NIX NEBULA

Star Enforcers: Chapter 1

"It doesn't matter what planet you're on or who you're working for or how it's being done, guarding for illegal drug shipments is always a shitty job," Morenko thought to himself.

"Not what I expected when I signed up for the Mystic Seas. I expected more adventure, excitement, gunfire, risk, and danger." Morenko would later regret the thought.

Though he liked the black armor, the painted white crescent moon on his chest and the assault rifle with the scope attached… he didn't like guard duty for illegal drug shipments. It bored him to no end.

Morenko's purple skin, shaved head, short bull horns at the top of his head, and blue eyes meant he came from a bloodline that was respected in the galaxy; he came from the species known as the Torrie. A race commonly seen as the most military prominent. They also possessed the largest population in the galaxy.

Inside the warehouse, the Mystic Seas guards wore the exact same armor as him and similar guns and scopes. The guards were a well organized army, making certain that every inch of their base was secure. The guards weren't all the same race. A lot of them looked pretty different. Some had paper white skin and blue hair, a few had red skin and black hair, there were even a few whose skin instantaneously adapted when in certain light. Mainly their numbers derived from Torrie, like Morenko.

Their numbers were in the double digits. On top of this army of mercenaries, there were even more guards outside to make sure that no one got in. The green cargo boxes contained their smuggled drugs. Morenko was clueless as to what the narcotics were, but didn't bother to care.

Suddenly, the red skinned, black haired general named Az'Ramo started yelling, "Hey! What the hell was that?!"

Guards started looking at him in confusion. There was a slight delay as Morenko's headset translated what Az'Ramo said. Morenko, being someone who spoke the main Flow Council language, had to adjust to this newfound change quickly. The thing that still jolted Morenko was he heard one thing coming from his headset but Az'Ramo's lips looked as though they spoke something completely different.

"What was what, sir?" someone asked. Az'Ramo was forced to wait for a split second as his own translator repeated the inquiry.

"The signal to the guards outside just went out for a second!" Az'Ramo screamed as he looked down at the device wrapped around his wrist. These Affixes were used by the Mystic Seas mercenaries and most travelers of the universe and were capable of establishing a wireless connection to almost anything. They assisted in retrieving information, downloading files, converting signals, and other useful functions. Depending on the user and the programming, the Affix could assist in nearly anything. Most used it for simple communication, wireless connection and analyzing device.

"They're back up now, sir," a guard noted. "It might just be a glitch in the signal, you know, like the last time?"

Az'Ramo charged the guard, grabbed his throat, and intensely pulled him close. "Are you questioning me, you worthless piece of shit?!"

Az'Ramo was notorious for being ruthless, so the guards got in line quickly. The guard who Az'Ramo attacked suddenly got ready for action.

"N-no, sir," the guard stuttered. "We'll check it out, sir."

The guard activated his Affix and spoke into it. "Men. Come in. Can you confirm status?" The guard listened to his Affix as static went through. There was no voice on the other side.

"I think their signals are glitching," the guard suggested cautiously towards the irritated general. Az'Ramo shot the guard a look of ferocity. "But, uh, we should have some men go outside just to make sure."

"Good idea. You and several others check it out." Az'Ramo waited angrily and impatiently for the guard to answer him.

"Yes, sir," the guard agreed with a nod.

Morenko watched as the guard, who looked as if he was about ready to wet himself, raised his gun and readied for a fire fight as he took several others with him. The others raised their guns, ready to blow something's head off. As the armed henchmen walked to the large double doors that led outside, the head guard lifted his hand to open the door.

The door exploded before he could touch it. The sound roared in the room and several guards by the door were flung to the other side of the warehouse, like rag dolls being thrown off a skyscraper. The explosion took the guards by surprise.

The smoke cleared to reveal a bulky, seven foot man. The dark skinned man wore a cold, emotionless expression as he walked casually into the room. His chest was covered by dark gray armor, but his arms were completely uncovered. He wore tan cargo pants and black combat boots. The man had some weight in his step, as he walked in slowly, but with such power and stride that he must have commanded quite a bit of muscle.

The man carried a black shotgun with a blue grip. The shotgun had six barrels at its end. The grip connected to the chamber which held six individual shotgun shells. The gun was known as the Artington, a powerful shotgun known for strong recoil and heavy weight. It wasn't popular due to the sheer weight behind it, but was feared for its unrivaled stopping power.

The man readied his Artington, blowing apart several guards who stood before him without hesitation. His face remained emotionless as their blood splashed towards him. There was no anger in his expression. No happiness. No sense of regret. His demeanor was calm, collected, and uncaring for the lives that he was taking.

The guards in the warehouse took cover, readying their weapons. All took cover but Az'Ramo, who started shooting at the man and screaming in fury.

"Hey! Light his ass up! We're the Mystic Seas! We don't run! We don't cower! We fight!" The guards in the warehouse listened to his words, feeling the need to kill the intruder who stood before them. They shot at him, but bullets and laser beams had no effect. Following each impact upon his skin, a shimmering rainbow light appeared before quickly vanishing after a lazer made contact with him. When a bellet impacted his skin it only dented it. The Mystic Seas did not falter and kept attacking.

Not until Az'Ramo's head was torn apart by an unseen sniper did the guards lose confidence. A cocoa skinned man with short straight black hair walked through the door whilst carrying a single silver pistol. The armored vest strapped to his chest had very thin bits of impact absorbing blue metal. His grey long sleeve shirt, black pants, and black combat boots were worn and scuffed. He wasn't the sniper, but this man walked with confidence, indicating he was the leader

The man calmly directed, "All right, wipe them out. Just make sure to leave a few alive for questioning."

Following his orders, the doorway became crowded. A blue-skinned man appeared. Skin tight black material covered everything but his arms and feet. Fins came from the back of his head and gills from the sides of his neck. This amphibian/mammal combination had a wiry frame and quick in his movements.

His gun, known as a Gravits, was mostly used by law enforcement. It was designed to simply propel enemies backwards, non lethal. Still, the guards hit by his repulsor felt their bones break. Other guards were knocked unconscious as they were slammed against walls, cargo boxes and other guards. The blue man moved quickly and did not fear the guards shooting at him. Although he appeared untrained in weaponry, he seemed stronger and faster than most. Maybe all of his species were like that. Morenko wasn't sure.

Morenko kept watch on the door and knew when the sniper walked through. She was feared by just about every Mystic Seas operative as she gunned down Mystic Seas mercenaries repeatedly.

A smile grew on Bryna Stoli's face as she looked at what was left of the commander Az'Ramo. Her long dark red hair rested on her shoulders as she looked at her custom gun. The gun seemed to encase her bullets in a blue glowing core of energy meant to rip through armor. She used a headset and electronic visor so that she could identify and hack opertation systems with simple voice commands while under fire. She appeared to be the most likely candidate that sabotaged the signals. Bryna's custom made blue armor has gold streaks that trailed ran from her shoulders to her boots.

Finally, a woman with brown skin and long straight dark hair walked through the door. She wore black armor with gold lining down the arms and legs and used an assault rifle with precision, almost beauty. None of the Mystic Seas knew her name, but recognized her weapon as of Constable origin. Her desire to find direct kills and her psychological motive to kill without emotion was unmistakable. There was no anger. No aggression. Only a need to kill quickly and eliminate her targets. She was killing like all she wanted were numbers. *Was that who they were? The Constables?* Morenko wondered briefly.

The thought didn't matter. What did matter was this small team was ripping his Mystic Seas squad apart. He started his shift with over fifty others, and just five people had reduced it to twenty. Morenko couldn't believe it.

The five continued walking casually, all of them firing in precision. The blue skinned man started to run towards the cargo box that was Morenko's cover. Morenko noticed an acid gun lying by one of his dead comrades.

He knew the acid could melt solid steel. In desperation, Morenko grabbed the acid gun and shot at the blue skinned man. The green acid cloud surrounded the blue man and Morenko assumed he was dead.

Morenko watched in shock as the blue man raced through the smoke, the green cloud dissipating at his movement. The man ran quickly towards Morenko, jumped and turned his body in mid-air, elbowing Morenko in the throat. Morenko couldn't catch his breath and was growing unconscious from pain. Before he could even grab his neck in agony, the blue man used a hand to grab one of Morenko's legs and flung him nearly eight feet into the air. The repulsor gun sent Morenko flying over twenty feet and slammed him into a wall. Morenko felt a rib break and his head slam into the metal. He started to see everything go black. His head was aching. He felt dizzy and unable to get up. His eyes shut as he lost consciousness.

Morenko awoke. He was surrounded by dead Mystic Seas mercenaries. The few guards left alive were confined with metal restraints around their wrists and ankles. Morenko knew they had lost. He looked up to see Bryna Stoli pointing a gun to his face.

The cocoa skinned leader of this team started talking in a serious tone. "The shipments. Where were they going?"

Morenko looked at Bryna Stoli's gun in fear. He knew that the Mystic Seas would make certain of his death if he told them anything. He did not know the intentions of this squad and he wondered if he would get out of this alive. The leader of the unknown soldiers spoke again.

"Look at your options, you don't have much room for negotiation. Either tell me where the drug shipment is going or--"

Morenko spoke in defiance. "You and this Stoli bitch don't scare me. We are the Mystic Seas. We don't succumb to you!"

The leader spoke again. "You do realize that we just killed about fifty of you, right? You were lucky enough to stay alive. Don't take that for granted. You can either tell me what I want to know, or well…"

Bryna Stoli interrupted in a heavy Russian-sounding accent. "I can see that you know who I am. If you know who I am, you know I will blow your head off if you don't answer him."

Morenko knew she wasn't bluffing. There were other mercenaries in the room and Bryna had been known to kill whenever necessary, and often times when it wasn't.

Morenko needed to make a decision and he needed to make it now. "This shipment was going to Martin VI, where we have a base that holds drugs and other cargo to be later sold to the highest bidder. This shipment had already been bought, and we were preparing to hold it on our base until the buyer decided to pick it up or we sent it out. I don't know who we were going to send it to or why they wanted this drug, but--"

Bryna interrupted him, "You don't know who wants this drug or what it is?"

"No. But you-you don't have to kill me. I can work for you. I'm good with guns and--"

"We just knocked your ass to the wall in under two minutes, you don't seem that good to me," Bryna noted sadistically. "It seems you don't have anything to offer us, little man."

Morenko started to worry. Bryna smiled.

"No." Ordered her leader. Morenko was both surprised and relieved.

"Why not?" asked Bryna.

"Have Onyx take him and the rest aboard the ship. I'll explain why later."

"Alright, makes no difference to me," replied Bryna. The Captain walked away. Bryna signaled for the big, tank built man and the woman who fought flawlessly to come to her.

"What do you require, Bryna Stoli?" As the man spoke in a robotic monotone, Morenko immediately knew this wasn't a man. He was an Eliminator robot. A machine created to kill. At least he knew why bullets were bouncing off him. If they had fired armor piercing rounds, they maybe could have stopped it. But with the caliber they were using, they didn't stand a chance. Morenko started to feel even more unsettled to be near a killing machine.

Bryna answered, "Onyx, take the little men aboard the ship. Have the crew put them in confinements and hold them in containment cells. We'll do interrogations later."

"Orders understood and will oblige." Onyx picked up Morenko by his shoulder and forced him to walk. The other Mystic Seas mercenaries followed.

Bryna spoke to the other woman. "You did pretty good back there, Anukis. I think you took out more than I did."

René Anukis spoke back, "Thanks, Stoli." They exchanged a smile of comradery. "Where's the Captain going?"

"I'm not sure. I think he's going to talk to Tika." replied Bryna.

"She's probably looking at drug samples."

"Probably. I just hope she doesn't get caught up in her own head and distracted," René said.

"You know that she will, she always does. Smart girl, but her dropping in and out of a conversation can be a bit annoying," replied Bryna. René smiled in agreement with her squad mate.

René and Bryna both watched as their captain walked to a 15 year old girl. The girl's hair was long and black, reaching to her lower back. Her skin was a light brown. Oddly though, her eyes were purple, which was not a common trait of her species.

The Captain asked "Find anything?"

"The drug they were sending out is similar to Red Rage. It might even be Red Rage, I don't know," Tika replied.

"Red Rage?" Asked the Captain.

"Yeah, it's a destabilizing drug that when administered into most higher evolved organics, mostly through injection, increases the levels of natural testosterone within their-"

The Captain smiled and interrupted her politely with a hand on her shoulder. "Tika, you're getting stuck in facts and science again. Just tell me what it does." Tika laughed in response then nodded slightly.

"It's a drug that makes people get violent and angry. Sometimes they get sexually aggressive too. Thus gaining the affectionate name, 'Red Rage.' It's highly addictive and usually requires a lot of manufacturing. Making Red Rage isn't cheap. Most mercenary groups use small doses on their soldiers. I'm not sure if this is Red Rage though. I can't tell because I haven't seen the effects when administered. And I haven't studied the sample yet. I wonder why it's being mass produced, it's kind of more effort to make Red Rage than it's worth."

"Does it really matter?" asked the Captain.

"I guess not, Captain, I'd like to take some samples of it aboard the ship for research. It's fascinating. And who knows, I might stumble across something."

The Captain smiled. "That's why you're the medical officer, Ms. Shamari. We'll put in a request to let you take some samples."

Tika Shamari smiled and nodded. The Captain put his hand on her shoulder, smiled in return, and walked away. As the Captain walked away, he saw Javal and Aiden Dakar talking. Javal's blue face and trusting attitude was a comfort to every one of the crew.

Aiden Dakar was blonde and had a five o'clock shadow. Aiden's blonde hair was cut short. The strands of Aiden's hair were several inches in length, and the ends of his hair tended to tip up at the slightest. He was in his late 20's, but the stress he was under made him look as if he could have been in his 40's. Though he always hid it with a smile and a joke, Aiden carried a terrible burden.

The Captain waved at both Aiden and Javal. They returned the wave.

"Lookin' pretty as always, Captain. When are we gonna see you in a skirt?" Though Captain Hernandez normally wouldn't laugh at those kinds of jokes, Aiden always made him think lightly. And he couldn't help but chuckle at his immature humor.

"When I get my hair done and shave my legs." Replied Captain Hernandez. Aiden's smile grew wider and the Captain walked away in mild amusement.

"I'll admit, you and the Captain's little back and forth is always entertaining," noted Javal. "Nice work on the bomb. Why did you come up with something that incinerates a door before making the initial explosion?"

Aiden stopped smiling and had a look of complete focus on what he was thinking about. "I got the idea from the X-46 Acid gun, a modified version of the gun you just got shot with. Just put the acid into the bomb and let it defuse the door, then right when the integrity was weakened, boom. Bomb goes off. Similar to the X-46, except it just explodes with more acid. I made it because I was worried that the initial explosion wouldn't blow away the door. And if it was too loud, then it would draw too much attraction and we might have been slaughtered when we first entered the doors. I needed something quiet to weaken the door before the explosion. So, a strong acid to wear it down first seemed like the most logical choice."

"Smart idea."

"I thought so. Simplistic, yet effective." The two stared out into the distance, both entranced with science. "Speaking of acid guns…" Javal looked back at Aiden, his thought broken. "I didn't know that you could take a point blank acid gun shot. An acid that can melt through solid steel, none the less."

Javal shrugged. "Benefits of being a Daporan. Invulnerable to fire, ice, acid, toxic atmospheres… lotta stuff. It's funny; I bet my ancestors would have never even thought of being invulnerable to things that we experience as a part of life every day."

"Wish I was you. But then again, I wouldn't have this beautiful face; though the fins on your head are artistically stylish." Aiden said with a joking voice as he pointed to his face. The two laughed in enjoyment. They turned to see Bryna and René approaching.

"We should get back to the ship." René Anukis ordered.

"Yes, Officer Anukis," replied Javal.

"You ladies ever think that you take yourselves too seriously? I feel like I'd pull a muscle if I kept the serious face you two muster," Aiden sarcastically wondered.

René was not amused by his comment. The blonde explosives expert had seemed to strike this chord before, but he just couldn't help himself.

"You ever think that you don't take yourself seriously enough?" René asked with a stone cold expression. Aiden stopped smiling.

"Because I do," she continued. "It hasn't happened yet, thank God. But if your immaturity gets in the way of the crew's success on a mission, there will be ramifications, Dakar."

"Yes, ma'am. It will not affect this mission or any mission in the future. I apologize if my attitude has indicated otherwise," Aiden stated in obedience. Bryna saw Aiden weaken and didn't like it.

"Hey," Bryna called to René, catching her attention. "Let the little man say his stupid jokes if he wants to."

"Are you questioning an order?" René inquired sternly.

"Knock it off," Bryna rebuked. "You do not threaten me. Don't jump down my throat for defending a friend. Besides, you're not in charge of whether or not I stay here, so back off."

René walked closer to Bryna, meeting her eye level, as she crossed her arms, trying to give a serious demeanor. Bryna tilted her head slightly, and raised her eyebrow, indicating that she was not impressed.

"She has a point, Officer Anukis," noted Javal. René shot Javal a look of intensity but Javal's calm expression did not falter. "You don't need to take everything so seriously. Let Aiden act the way he wants. He does his job well and he's here for that and only that. His behavior isn't interfering with it." René uncrossed her arms and nodded, knowing that Javal was right. "Besides, we've been on the ship for two months, and we're probably going to be on it for even longer. Let loose a little with his humor."

"Alright," agreed René. "I won't question your priorities on this squad again, Dakar, at least not when it comes to your sense of humor."

"Thank you, ma'am," responded Aiden appreciatively.

"So, we should probably go aboard the ship, right?" Javal speculated to the whole group. The group of four agreed and walked towards the destroyed double doors of the warehouse.

As they exited the warehouse, they looked up to see the midnight stars and felt the cold night air on their faces. The dirt ground was easy to walk through, though the dusty feeling all around them was slightly annoying. Captain Hernandez, Tika Shamari, and Onyx, along with the Mystic Seas prisoners waited outside patiently.

"Good, we're all ready," announced Captain Hernandez. The Captain pulled his Affix towards his mouth and spoke into it. "Bridge, this is Captain Hernandez. De-cloak the Enforcer. We're coming aboard with Mystic Seas prisoners. Prepare containment cells for all of them immediately. Also, set up a signal connection with Director Tollus, we need to brief him in on the mission."

"Yes, Captain Hernandez," agreed a militant sounding man through the Affix.

The area before them suddenly turned into a ship. The spacecraft was twenty five yards in width of its main hull with a length of one hundred and twenty yards. The Slipstream propulsion wings were monted on the front area of the ship which spanded fifteen yards on each end of the hull. The ship's black and blue colors were a little hard to see at night, but none the less, it was a beautiful four deck destroyer class vessel which resembled the look of a lobster or crayfish.

The ship's ramp started to descend and was welcoming the squad to come aboard. Onyx forced the Mystic Seas bounty hunters to enter first. René and Bryna had their guns aimed at them, just as some reassurance. The team walked into the main hull of the Enforcer after the bounty hunters entered Deck Four.

A side ramp lowered on the bottom deck of the ship, and the mercenaries were met by the crew of the Enforcer, all of them dressed the same. One had pitch black skin, another two were pale, one with blonde hair, and the other with light brown. The last one had dark hair, brown skin, and almond-shaped eyes. They all wore blue uniforms and their guns were pointed at the prisoners.

"Take them to the holding cells. They're having trouble standing up right now, so I doubt they'll be a problem," commanded Capt. Hernandez.

"Yes, Captain," answered one of the guards. The Mystic Seas mercenaries were escorted with guns at their backs.

Hernandez turned to his main officers. "Let's go to the briefing room, I believe Director Tollus will want to hear from all of us this time."

René Anukis nodded in agreement. "You heard him," she told the others, "Let's go."

They all followed Hernandez down on a hallway on Deck 2 to a large single door. Captain Hernandez typed in a series of numbers on the control panel to its side and a high pitched beep occurred in response

"Captain Miguel Hernandez of the Enforcer. Recognized. Welcome, Captain," stated the computer device in an automated woman's voice. The doors opened for the squad, and they walked into the briefing room.

A large circular metal table filled the center of the room with computer terminals around the room's perimeter. The group sat in the chairs around the table and faced the hologram in the middle of the table.

The hologram was of a man the mostlyeveryone in the room respected. Director Tollus was in charge of all of them. His skin was purple, his eyes red, and his black hair black was styled in a Mohawk, and he had short bullhorns at the top of his head.

"Crew of the Enforcer," he said. "What do you have to report?"

"As instructed, we investigated a drug shipping operation run by the Mystic Seas and shut it down," Capt. Hernandez responded. "We took several of the mercenaries as prisoners and have them confined within our ship."

"What drug were they trafficking?" asked Director Tollus.

"Well," started Tika. "I think it was Red Rage, a drug used by a lot of mercenary groups. It ups aggressive tendencies. I can't be sure if it's Red Rage or not because I've never studied it."

"Why were they mass producing it? Don't you generally lose more than you gain with Red Rage?" asked Director Tollus.

"I don't know, sir. I'm requesting to have a sample of it for study."

"I don't care, have fun with it. Deliver whatever you discover to the Flow Council," answered Director Tollus.

"Yes, sir. Thank you, sir," responded Tika.

"Where was the drug going to?" wondered Director Tollus.

"A Mystic Seas operative said it was going to Martin VI," answered Bryna Stoli.

"Do we know why?" asked Director Tollus.

"On Martin VI, there's a Mystic Seas holding base. Once their products are sold, they either hold the products or send them to the buyer. He didn't know what was in the cargo boxes, or anything about who bought them," answered Bryna.

"Maybe he was kept out of the loop on purpose. Less liability," Ren`e Anukis theorized.

"Probably," answered Bryna. "Tollus, the mercenaries should be put in separate holding cells that are not near other prisoners. The Mystic Seas isn't just a mercenary band, it's a force that holds to a powerful belief system. Therefore, they have a far reach and could influence prisoners to kill them while inside."

"Fine, on one condition. I want you to keep one of them. Separate him from the others," Tollus directed.

"Keep one of them, why?" Hernandez wondered.

"They might hold future insight on any of the Mystic Seas that you might run into. They're far different than they used to be, less powerful, but still, they are a force that the Flow Council doesn't want to get out of hand. Keep one of them."

"How about the little Torrie that was about to piss on himself?" Bryna wondered with a chuckle.

"Fine, whatever works," Tollus uncaringly agreed. The hologram of the purple skinned man turned to the Captain. "Hernandez? What do you want to do with the prisoners aboard the ship at this time?"

"I think that we'll interrogate them for a little while; then hand them over to the Flow Council."

"All right. Following standard protocol, I will disavow any knowledge or alignment of you if they decide to speak of you. Once I have gone offline, I will delete any history or recordings of this transmission, and I must order you to do the same."

"Of course," Capt. Hernandez acknowledged.

"Yes, anyway--" blurted Director Tollus, trying to change the subject, "I have another mission for all of you. Don't become husks of lazy uselessness in the absence of something to do. Hernandez, report to my office tomorrow. I'll fill you in on the details about it."

"Understood, Director Tollus," affirmed Captain Hernandez. The hologram immediately disappeared as Tollus was finished with the conversation. Hernandez looked to his crew. "Good work out there today, all of you. Tika, keep me informed on the drug samples and what you find."

"Will do, Captain," answered Tika with a sense of duty and respect.

"Now, all of you, I suggest you get some sleep and relax once we get underway to Integra. Knowing Director Tollus, we've got a big day ahead of us tomorrow."

PENCILS: DONOVAN PETERSEN / INKS: JABAAR L. BROWN

Morenko sat in a dimly lit room with nothing on its blank white walls. He shifted in the uncomfortable metal chair but his cuffed wrists limited his mobility. All he could look at was a woman standing before him. Her dark skin and hair matched her Constable black armor that looked like it had been molded to her body.

René Anukis had a command tone in her voice as she looked at Morenko. "Let's get a thing straight. You are a prisoner if you don't accept this offer. You go to prison. You pay for your crimes. There is no retribution for your past actions."

Boredom echoed in Morenko's mind. He hadn't had water in since he'd been revived from consciousness several hours ago. He needed them to believe he was an actual viable threat and not appear weak.

"And what is this offer, exactly?" Morenko wondered, his head still ringing from the pain.

"You join this ship and become a part of its crew," René responded. She crossed her arms in contempt for Morenko. Standing over him, her attempt at intimidation was working.

"And what does a member of this crew do, exactly?"

"Whatever we tell you to do." René uncrossed her arms, and got closer to Morenko's face. "We tell you to stand guard duty with a loaded rifle, you do it. We tell you to scrub the ship, you do it. We tell you to go down onto a hostile planet, with hundreds of people firing at you, preparing to torture and murder you, you do it."

A bead of sweat went down Morenko's forehead as he asked, "And for how long?"

"Five years," René said. "You serve this ship for five years. If you survive, you go free. You get some money, you get a little transport ship, and you get a clean slate. Officially, you will not be a convict in the outside world. To the Flow Council, you will have committed no crimes. And you're free to do whatever you want, wherever you want. Even if that includes going back to the Mystic Seas or whatever other half-assed terrorism or mercenary group will take you, just to get killed or incarcerated by a group of Constables all over again."

"And if I say no? Then, what? I go to prison?" Morenko asked, rhetorically. "Prison sounds like paradise in comparison to being your personal slave for five years. Being confined to my own small room, where I'm safe from gunfire ripping my flesh apart sounds pretty great right now."

René backed away from Morenko. "Let's look at the facts. You associated yourself with, and worked for, the Mystic Seas, a known terrorist and mercenary organization and renowned enemies of the Flow Council. That will gain you no leniency with the sentencer."

Morenko looked away from René, attempting to break eye contact from the woman trying not to add fear to his pain. René only stepped closer to Morenko, to make him know her presence, and her power in the room.

"That, you were smuggling, what we can assume, is a very rare, very illegal drug throughout the galaxy. That crime in it of itself gains you time in prison. And, your final offense that I know about, is shooting at seven Constables attempting to take you in. You fired at seven officers of the law, seven peacekeeping soldiers. You attempted to kill. That gives you life."

"At least in prison, I'll be alive." Morenko stated, looking René in the eyes, and attempting to convey strength.

"You know, as well as I do, that the Mystic Seas kill their traitors," René smirked and a slight chuckle echoed through her mouth.

"But I didn't betray them."

René sarcastically shrugged. "Sure, you say you didn't, now. But what if they heard that I said that you told me where to find them? What if they hear that Morenko, a no-name Torrie wanted to make some money by selling out who he was working for to the Flow Council? And sure, it didn't work. Those Constable assholes locked you in prison, and they didn't pay you. But you still sold out your brothers in arms out to the assholes who locked all of them up."

Morenko's expression turned from feigned strength to sincere fear as she continued. "And then, one day, you're stabbed. Ruthlessly. And then your corpse, unworthy of burying, is shot into the cold depths of space. And that's all that is left of Morenko, of the Torrie, traitor to the Mystic Seas."

Morenko was afraid and didn't know what to say or do.

"Why? Why so much effort to get me on this ship?" Morenko muttered, his body shaking in nervousness.

René backed away from Morenko, and walked behind him, forcing Morenko to turn his head, attempting to see her as she paced back and forth behind him.

"Not my decision. Someone important wants you alive." Morenko was surprised.

"Why?"

"I don't know and I don't care," René stated. "All I want to know is, are you going to make the smart choice?"

"As if I had another one." Morenko replied.

René laughed.

Dawn's light cast slight shadows on the Flow Council Moon, Integra. The artificial sunlight, used to compensate for the lack of the sun's rays, had been dimmed to give the population a sense of time. Pills and injections were required to provide much needed supplements that would have occurred naturally from a sun.

Many citizens felt the air smelt, tasted, and felt almost too clean. The artificial atmosphere attempted to make all races inhabiting the planet feel as though it was the same air as their homeworld. This wasn't necessarily achieved, but many adjusted the best they could. Integra was filled with skyscrapers and not a single building was in disrepair. Like all Flow Council controlled and funded worlds, everything was meant to be perceived as perfect.

At the center of the large city was a pyramid fifty-five stories tall covered with black mirrored windows. Strobe lights one the edges of the skyscraper warned flying vehicles if they flew too close to the structure. At the very top of the building was the red scanning light that identified this as Constable headquarters of operations.

Director Tollus was in his office on the fiftieth floor. Across his desk was Captain Hernandez. Tollus had given Hernandez his new assignment and the captain was not pleased. .

"I don't want an Elumeni on my ship and I don't want to send my squad into a mission that is so damn suicidal," Hernandez spouted in protest, looking the director in his blue eyes.

Even though he held the rank of director, as a member of the warrior-like race known as the Torrie, Tollus still worked out in the training rooms every day. The shadows on his purple skin defined his muscles. With his short black Mohawk, and short bull like horns, he looked like an ancient Roman gladiator. His race had dominated a number of planets before the Flow Council was established over a century ago. The Torrie relinquished power back to the original inhabitants in their sector of space. They had adapted to interact with varying species in harmony instead of intimidation.

Director Tollus was a stern man and he rarely tolerated any disagreement. He suppressed his aggressive nature and turned to Hernandez to get him under control. Director Tollus wondered if the Captain had been insane or simply assuredly confident that a Torrie would no longer act aggressively put him in his place.

"Be careful of your tone, Captain Hernandez, and keep in mind that the Enforcer is a Constable Fleet Vessel, not your own personal ship. We provide the instructions to you and your crew, not you. I don't request, I order. You don't deny, you follow. You and your crew are in no position to ever argue."

The captain lowered his volume, knowing that Tollus was right, but he would not give him the pleasure of agreeing with him.

"You tell me that when you get rid of me, or when I die on one of your damned mission impossible," Hernandez sighed and crossed his arms around his chest and continued. "So who's the Elumeni that I have to babysit on this fool-hardy assignment?"

The director huffed and thought to himself, *"His rebellious nature will always irritate me. What is far more irritating is that he is the most capable."* He spoke professionally and walked over to his window to watch the sun rise over the mountains of the other buildings on the horizon.

"The Elumeni that you are taking with you on this assignment is an earth elemental. His name is Golic. From what I'm told, he is a well-mannered warrior, and one of the best skilled combatants."

"He may well be, but anytime an Elumeni is involved in anything, my crew is in danger, and Lieutenant Anukis has an unprecedented hatred towards all Elumeni."

A sly grin came upon Tollus' purple face as he turned around from the large window. "Stop talking and listen. Deal with it, Captain, and get the Ambassador's son back before the information about this operation goes public. Golic will be waiting by your shuttle."

"Yeah, I hear you. Your voice travels you know?"

Tollus remained silent and simply slowly raised his arm, and pointed for the Captain to walk out of his office. As he left the office, Hernandez shook his head very slightly to show his irritation and disapproval.

As the captain reached his private shuttle sitting on the top of the Constable Headquarters, he saw three Elumeni standing by his craft. One of them approached the captain as the other two departed without fanfare. Hernandez realized that this Elumeni must be Golic.

Golic approached, his bronze chest and shoulder armor signifying him as an Earth Elemental. He had beige skin with slightly slanted brown eyes. Even though he stood five feet nine inches, his face was full and a decent muscular build. While the top of his was covered with short black hair, he had a pony tail that reached the middle of his fourth lower vertebrae.

Golic did a subtle bow to Hernandez as a sign of respect, "Constable Hernandez, I am Elumeni Golic. I'm here to accompany your crew on your next mission."

Hernandez noticed that Golic called him *"Constable"* and not *"Captain."* Hernandez wondered if this was a sign that Golic did not acknowledge his Captain status, but he wasn't sure.

Hernandez did a bow of his own in return, "Yes, I am aware of your presence on my ship. I still don't understand why this was necessary, but I will do what I can to make sure this mission succeeds." Hernandez never liked speaking so formally.

When the initial contact was completed, Hernandez and Golic boarded the shuttle. Hernandez got into the pilot seat and Golic sat behind him as he closed his eyes and meditated. The captain ignited the booster and the shuttle craft left the atmosphere of Integra.

While Golic was meditating, Hernandez had time to be lost in his own thoughts, since piloting a shuttle was second nature to him and it required very little attention. *"I can't believe that I'm still in this damn outfit of an operation. Go here, go there; do what we tell you without question, and we'll make sure that you and your crew will be in the clear of any illegal charges.*

"Being an undercover constable is hard work when you begin to question your superiors and their decisions. But when you are under mandatory service to the Flow Council for five years, you do what you are told or face a prison sentence with heavy labor. Not to mention that your ass becomes some big brute's property. My rear already feels pretty worn out.

"My mandatory service to the Flow Council started three years ago when I was sentenced to serve eight years in the Space Constable Academy. Being born and raised on Aquis IV with three brothers and two sisters was quite boring. I happen to be the youngest of the bunch. Our mother loves us very much and she's

truly a nurturing woman. As for my father, he's the ambassador of our world, and sits on the Flow Council. He always had high expectations of his children.

"My siblings and I are very intelligent, but the others excelled in math and science. They're textbook savvy, but those were not my strong points; I'm more of the creative one, and a risk taker. I couldn't see myself being a renowned professor at a university or stuck in a laboratory all day, sitting on my ass at a desk; it was just not my calling.

"I want my life to be filled with action and adventure, so in my teenage years, I hung around the wrong type of crowds. I was part of a few street gangs, did some illegal gambling, and hot-wired a few luxury flying cars from time to time to sell at chop shops. I liked having my own jewel pressed latinum and not having to ask for it from my parents.

"I was caught a few times by the authorities for a string of misdemeanors and public disturbances, but being the ambassador's son, I only had to perform public service and thankfully I was not subjected to a criminal record.

"When I turned twenty, I left the family home and moved in with a girlfriend I was dating that my parents disapproved of. Mia Diaz was not a model citizen and she had a small criminal record. She had ties to a space pirate group and got me involved in raiding vacation cruise liners. We wore masks during our raids to protect our identities and gloves so that we did not leave any finger prints behind.

"We had a string of successful raids that stretched from my star systems without any major incidents, but that changed three years ago when we raided a space liner named the Utopia. The cruise liner was carrying a ship load of vacationers, but it also was secretly carrying a team of twelve undercover space constables. When our team of twenty pirates started to shake down the passengers for their valuables, we were taken by surprise by the constables.

"A gunfight ensued and I did what I could to protect Mia

and myself without killing any of the constables, by using a repulsor rifle instead of a deadly weapon. But Mia, she brandished a pair of silver hand caliber pistols. Both pistols were engraved; one read Chaos, and the other Mayhem. She fired several times and killed one of the constables and wounded another. Mia had no problem killing anyone that got in her way, but her life soon came to an end when one of the constables shot her two times in the chest. She went down immediately and coughed up a great deal of blood. She told me to leave the pirate life behind and live with a purpose. She knew that I was meant for better things. With her last breath, she looked at me then smiled and then her life was gone.

"I stood to my feet to look at the constable that shot her and I rushed the bastard. It was the squad captain Mintog. He was a big brute with the ramming horns at the top of his head. He did not intimidate me and I stood my ground as we fought. I was bloody from our first exchange of gunfire and laid on the floor. Mintog called me a punk ass and I was so enraged that I got back up onto my feet and unexpectedly delivered the hardest kick that I could to his left knee. When he lurched forward, I kneed him in the chin. Mintog fell to his side, but only briefly. He shrugged off the blow and stood up. With a short sprint he rushed his butting horns into my chest area that sent me flying, back first, into a support beam, which knocked me out.

"Mintog came over to unmask me and took me into custody when he found out who I was. It's a good thing too, he might have killed me that day if I was any other person. Like I said, being an ambassador's kid does have its advantages. My other pirate comrades were not so lucky as only two others survived that dismal day.

"I was made to stand trial in front of the Flow Council, and Mintog was present to give his account of the events aboard the Utopia. My father was also present as my attorney. He was not the happiest father in the galaxy that day but he loved me and defended me well against the prosecutor at the trial. My father told them that I was of good worth and that I needed direction. He furthermore asked for Flow Council to be lenient in their sentencing.

"When the verdict was reached, the Flow Council gave me two options for my sentencing. The first option wasn't all that palatable; serve an eight year sentence performing heavy labor at a mining penal colony. The second option, which I still have some regrets about, was joining the Space Constable Academy for my eight year sentence, and having Mintog as my commandant. That decision became a living hell for me, and Mintog made sure of it during my first year in the academy. He instructed the other trainers under his supervision to push me to quit the program. There were times when I wanted to quit, but showing that bastard that I can take anything he threw at me kept me going.

"Within two years I graduated at the top of my class and gained the respect of Mintog for being able to take whatever he threw at me. I was assigned to different missions and moved up the ranks quickly to first officer, in order to serve out the last six years of my mandatory sentence. I thought that with six years left to serve, it would not be so involved and I could finally leave all this behind me."

"Then only six months into my space assignment onboard the USS Grande Torino, I was approached by Director Tollus. He told me I was to take command of the newly designed stealth destroyer class ship, the U.S.S. Enforcer. Tollus told me that I came highly recommended by Commandant Mintog. The crew and the missions that I would be assigned to would be a true use of my talents since we would be working as undercover constables."

"The Enforcer officers are a bit rough around the edges and I did not expect that I would be working with constables that have issues in their past. I feel like a guidance counselor at times to a boat-load of children, but at the same time, I can somewhat relate to them. This new mission is highly dangerous and I have no idea how things will go, but this will be a true test for the people under my command."

In the darkness and coldness of space, the only thing visible were the stars and the lone small space shuttle as it slowed from its normal speed. The planet moon of Integra was to the rear of Hernandez's space craft. Hernandez was still leery of the Elumeni behind him, but Golic still seemed to be meditating at the moment.

The captain rolled his fingers over the control panel of the shuttle to activate the communications system. "Onyx it's me. I'm slowing on approach to the ship."

An electronic voice responded over the shuttles speakers "Understood Captain, I'll meet you in the hanger bay. Bay doors opening and awaiting your approach."

Small runway lights started to appear in the darkness of space until they stretched forty feet in length. Hernandez guided his shuttle toward the lights as the rest of the ship remained cloaked. Any average person that looked at this site would find it very odd to observe two parallel lines of lights and nothing else, but Hernandez and the crew were used to it by now. Only three ships had this capability, but the Enforcer was the only ship in operation. Hernandez know where one was located and the other was at a secret location.

Once through the magnetic field that separated the hanger bay from the vacuum of space, the captain's ship hovered over its holding area. The shuttle touched down gently onto the deck as locking claps grasped the craft to keep it in place. There were three other crafts in the bay: two drop down ships and one other shuttle.

The Enforcer was also equipped with a number of life pods if the ship were to experience a devastating disaster. Two members of the non-militant crew were busy working on control panels in the bay as they ran safety and diagnostic checks.

The rear of the shuttle opened and Hernandez, along with Golic, walked down the ramp. Onyx was there to meet them.

The automaton noticed the conflict on his commanding officer's face. "Captain Hernandez, based off of your facial expression, you appear to be struggling with the assignment that we have been given by the director."

"No kidding. This is Elumeni Golic, please escort him to the briefing room. I'll be there in a moment; I need to go to the bridge first."

The captain made his way to the level-lift to travel three decks up to the command bridge.

As the door slid open, Hernandez noticed Ren`e sitting in the captain's chair while she assumed the role of acting captain. "Being the first officer does have its advantages," she said to herself from time to time.

René looked into Hernandez's direction and spoke, "Hello Captain. Does our hard ass director have another doozy of an assignment for us?"

Hernandez rolled his eyes upward and smirked, "You can say that again. This time it's a Priority Two Mission."

"A Priority Two assignment, what the hell did Tollus get us involved in?" she was determined to know.

"That's why I came to talk to you before I call everyone to the briefing room. There is an Elumeni coming with us on this mission."

"What?! There's no way in hell I'm working with an Elumeni. You know how I feel about them," Ren`e protested and placed her hands onto her hips.

The captain could tell she was disgusted, but now was the time to act as her superior officer. "Yes I know, but you will just have to deal with it, Lieutenant. Now go to the briefing room and keep a cool head."

"Yes, sir," she replied, rolling her eyes as she walked off the bridge. Two other non-militant crew members on the bridge witnessed the conversation and looked in the captain's direction.

Hernandez just shook his head as the two went back to the work of maintaining a steady orbit around Integra.

"I'm going to need a vacation after this," Hernandez said, comically. He sat in his command chair and tapped a com switch on the arm rest. "All Constables, report to the briefing room."

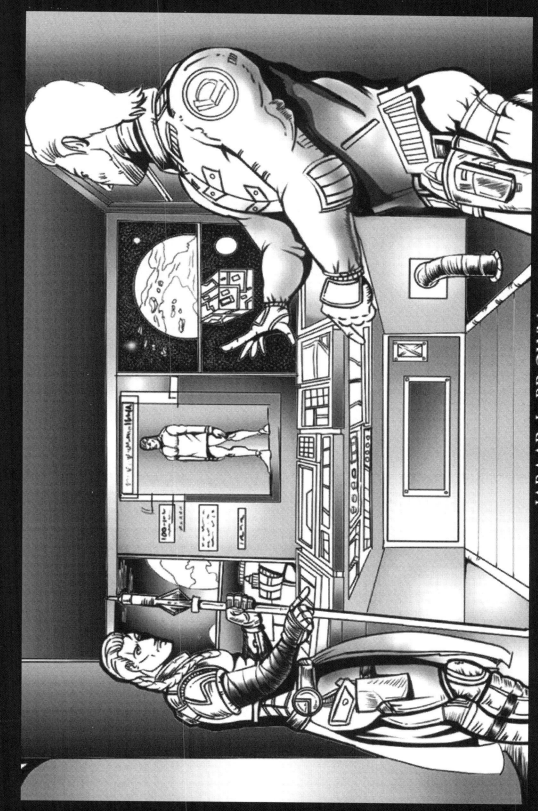

JABAAR L. BROWN

Star Enforcers: Chapter 3

The captain made his way to the briefing room after departing the bridge. The meeting room was located on deck two, one level below the command center. Hernandez took his time walking to the secluded room. He respectfully nodded his head as a few of the non-militant crew greeted. He had an uneasy feeling about how his crew would handle their new task.

"Some of us may not return from this mission in one piece," he thought in the back of his mind.

Hernandez reached the conference room door, which was locked to prevent non-authorized personnel from obtaining access. As he stepped up to the door, he heard the command, **"Identify please."**

Hernandez placed his open right palm onto a black panel plate next to the door.

"Identification verified. Welcome, Captain Miguel Hernandez."

As the locked door slid open, the captain walked into the conference room with a sober expression on his face. Hernandez looked around to observe that his team was present and seated in the semi-circular room. Several team members were looking pointedly at Elumeni Golic.

The briefing room had fourteen comfortable chairs, each containing a computer terminal on the arm rest. Three similar chairs were at the rectangular table in the center of the semi-circle. As Hernandez reached the center chair, René Anukis continued to give him a look of displeasure from her adjacent chair. Javal, the ship's chief engineer, was on the other side.

The captain directed his attention to the constables and spoke authoritatively. "I called this briefing to inform you of our new task. Director Tollus has assigned us to a Level Two Priority Mission and has insisted that Elumeni Golic join us. We will be traveling to the gaming moon Roule` and infiltrating the Treasure Planet Casino. Our primary objective is to retrieve Ambassador

Larott's son, Jaffar. The casino owner, Voltory Bolore, has placed him under house arrest. Jaffar's been charged with raping, and murdering, one of the female patrons at the casino."

The large view screen behind the officer's table showed a front profile image of Jaffar followed by a split screen image of Voltory Bolore.

"So let me guess. Our job is to save face for the Ambassador before the situation becomes a media frenzy?" Aiden asked.

"That is correct, Aiden," the captain answered.

"Was there an amount given for his bail?" Bryna wondered, trying to figure out the intentions of the casino owner for holding the ambassador's son captive. She was quickly accessing all the general information she had about Voltory on her chair's computer terminal. She barely broke away from the computer screen to glance toward Captain Hernandez. Her fingers were steadily typing to try and find any bounties placed on the casino owner.

Elumni Golic spoke for the first time. "Yes, there was, but Ambassador Larott refuses to pay it. He believes that his son is innocent and he wants his name cleared. The mission also requests that we investigate the crime scene."

The frown on René's face was evident she was not in the mood to hear Golic speak. "So the ambassador wants us to do the dirty work for him, and you're along for the ride, to make sure that we get Jaffar home safely? Or do the Elumeni have other intentions?"

Golic looked in Rene`s direction with the rest of the crew. He crossed his arms and answered the stubborn woman. "Yes, I am along on this mission to make sure that the ambassador's son is returned safely. However, there is an additional reason for my presence. The Acer working as head of security at Treasure Planet Casino. This creates the potential for additional difficulty."

Most of the constables let out groans of discomfort at the news. The captain took offence he had not previously been privy to this information. "An Acer? Why wasn't I told about this? Do you understand the kind of risk we are taking here, Golic, when we are facing an Elumeni gone to the wrong side of the law?"

"Director Tollus wishes you to be on a need to know basis, Captain. This Acer is the main reason why I am accompanying your crew. The Flow Council wants the Acer to be taken in, dead or alive. Her name is Solara, and she is a fire elemental. She is my primary objective; the ambassador's son is yours," Golic replied, once again defending his position.

Golic used his computer to display an image of Solara on the main view screen. She was humanoid, like most of the elementals and had tan skin. The irises of her eyes were red, indicating that she was a master of fire.

"Talk about putting us into the pit of fire," Aiden Dakar chimed in.

Tika thought carefully before speaking, "I would suggest that we avoid the squabble with the elementals and just focus on getting Jaffar back to his home world."

"I concur with Medical Constable Tika; our mission priority is to retrieve Jaffar," supported Onyx. "Anything beyond that will further jeopardize the safety of the crew."

"You won't hear me complaining about that, Captain. We get the ambassador's son and get the hell out of there, with or without Golic," René agreed with the other constables and gave the Elumeni a smirk.

"You have quite the tongue, Lieutenant." Golic shot back. The captain smiled for just a moment and then tried to ease the tension between the Lieutenant and the elemental.

"Golic, it's all a part of her charm, and I do share her rational thinking. We'll try to make sure you come back with us, or Director Tollus will have my hide. Report back to your stations, we will depart for Roule` in twenty minutes."

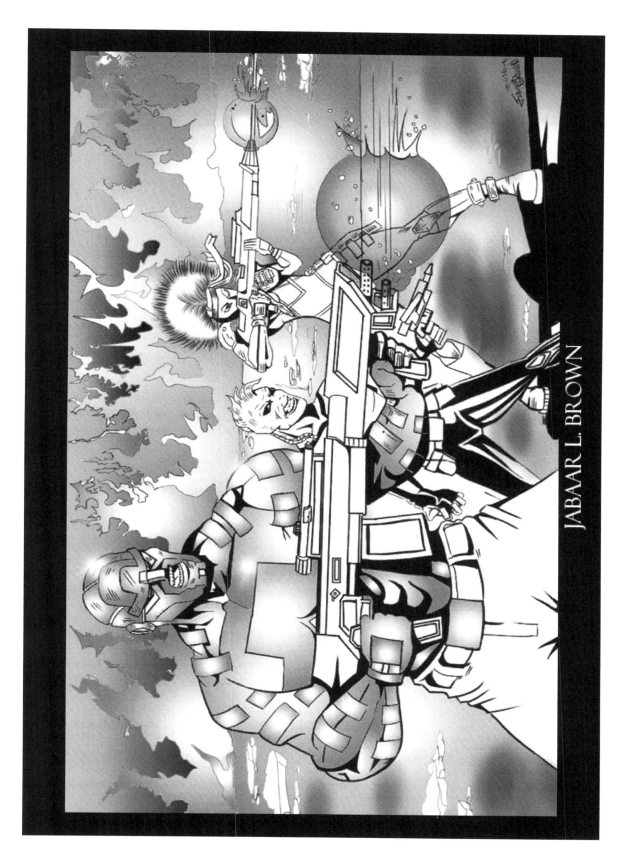

JABAAR L. BROWN

Star Enforcers: Chapter 4

"I need some Red Rage right now. My blood's too calm. I need something to make this day good," thought Kenkias. Kenkias Loro was red-skinned with black hair and full black eyes. His pissed off expression was below his high and tight. Less than two decades ago, Ambassador Vas'Kis Sinzo inducted the Amrasian as the newest addition to the Constable Task Force.

Kenkias strode down the hallway and yanked the door to his apartment in anger and frustration. It had been a long day and he had never truly been happy with his life. He slammed the door behind him in ferocity and looked about his living room. Black leather couch, metal coffee table in front of it, alcoholic beverages on the table in their bottles, and a few guns mounted on his wall.

Kenkias' black and red armor was starting to annoy him. It was heavy and it rarely had to be used. Unfortunately for him, it was mandatory for the job. The Treasure Planet Casino on the gaming moon of Roule` demanded high standards for their security.

The agitated guard abruptly sat down on his couch, ripped the armor covering his right arm from bicep to wrist and threw it to the floor. Kenkias' red arm was now exposed. He pulled out a needle containing the glowing red liquid known as Red Rage from a compartment in his armor. Kenkias flexed his arm and started to inject the Red Rage into his vein.

Kenkias once again started loving the feeling in his arm as the Red Rage flowed into a vein. He started to sweat and breathe heavily and a smile grew on his face. Kenkias finally felt relaxed. He let his head rest on his couch and closed his eyes.

Suddenly, he heard a slight footstep from the other side of the coffee table. Somehow, someone had gotten into the room without him noticing. Maybe they had been hiding in his apartment and were waiting for him. Kenkias opened his eyes.

"You'd better get out of here right now," he demanded in a cocky tone at the three people in front of him wearing armor.

Onyx raised his shotgun and pointed it directly at Kenkias's face. Bryna was on one side aiming her own shotgun and Captain Hernandez casually stood on Onyx's other side.

Captain Hernandez smiled and asked, "Now why would I do that?"

Kenkias started getting angry again.

"Do you know who I am?" he shouted ferociously.

"Kenkias Loro--" Bryna started, "A native of the planet Amras. A world within the Flow Council's jurisdiction, outfitted with limited and primitive technology. The planet's resources were ravaged, the people were enslaved, and slowly decimated by the mercenary gangs who had banded together to use your world and its people for their own uses. The planet begged for the Flow Council's assistance and after the matter was made highly public, the Flow Council finally intervened. Now, the Amras people have a seat on the Flow Council. A few Amrasians still resent both the mercenary groups that enslaved them and the Flow Council along with the Constables for not saving them."

Onyx continued in his cold, monotone, and robotic voice. "A small percentage of Amrasians formed a sect of rebellion and are labeled terrorists by Flow Council law. Flow Council records state that Kenkias Loro was a Constable for a short time but was removed of all duties for taking bribes from criminals he had previously arrested."

Bryna continued. "Now you work for a casino outside Flow Council jurisdiction. You aren't bad at your job necessarily, but you have no true talents. You got into this line of work like most people do, being an ex-Constable. You're not a very unique person in any way. Simply put, you're not worth watching, and no one would notice if you infiltrated the casino."

Bryna talked about Kenkias' entire life story like it wasn't even worth mentioning. This made the already agitated Kenkias even angrier. And with Red Rage in his system, his body was starting to want to kill something.

"If you did infiltrate the casino, that would highly convenience me," stated Captain Hernandez with a smile.

"I won't do a damn thing for you," responded Kenkias, still in his rage.

"Oh, I don't need you," began Captain Hernandez, "I just need someone who can look like you."

The Captain turned to Onyx and nodded.

Onyx locked his focus on Kenkias and his eyes started to glow a static blue. His outer shell and what appeared to be skin started to flicker. Red blotches started to appear on his dark brown skin and black metal spikes began poking out of his bald head. As each second passed, he started to look more like Kenkias. Soon his head looked like it was covered with black hair, his physique had changed, and his eyes turned black. Kenkias felt like he was staring in a mirror.

Kenkias was shocked when he realized what was going to happen. These people didn't need him, they just came to his apartment to take him so that there wouldn't be two of him going around in the casino. The Red Rage coursing through his veins took over and Kenkias wanted murder. The blood in his body started to pulse and he leapt off his couch. With a roar, he started to charge Captain Hernandez, trying to get his hands around his throat.

Before Kenkias was fully upright, Bryna pulled the trigger on her shotgun, ripping Loro's head apart.

Captain Hernandez turned to Bryna in shock.

"What the hell was that?" Hernandez barked.

Bryna looked up at him and shrugged her shoulders.

"What was what?" she inquired in confusion.

"I didn't tell you to fire your weapon!"

"So?"

"The mission wasn't to kill him! We were just supposed to take him and make sure that he didn't alert the casino of--"

Bryna cut him off. "I didn't hear of taking him. I heard of taking a target away from the location. How does killing an insect impede the mission?"

Captain Hernandez started to get angry. "If Onyx can't get the information he needs on how to act as Kenkias, that's on you! You'll have endangered the mission and--!"

"He's already reviewed the security tapes of him I retrieved when I hacked the casino. He saw him up close and heard enough voice samples of him. An Eliminator doesn't require any more than that," stated Bryna in defiance and confidence.

"Technological expert Bryna Stoli is correct, Captain. I do not require anymore of Kenkias Loro than I have received. He is useless to the mission and it will not be endangered by Bryna Stoli's actions," affirmed Onyx.

Captain Hernandez didn't care. "God dammit, Stoli. Don't fire your weapon unless I tell you to!"

Captain Hernandez and Bryna stared at each other. Bryna realized she needed to agree with the Captain in order to fulfill what she really wanted.

"Yes, sir," she muttered in a fake respect. The captain detected a sense of anger in Bryna's voice but was too angry to care. He turned away from her and pulled his Affix towards his mouth.

"René," started Captain Hernandez, "Loro is a no go. But Onyx has what he needs."

"What?" asked René Anukis. Her voice sounded slightly distorted through the Affix. "He's a no go? What happened?"

Captain Hernandez frowned slightly in seriousness, "Bryna happened."

René couldn't help herself. "Hahaha. Sorry, haha, that isn't funny. Are you coming back aboard the ship?"

"Affirmative. Get the rest of the constables and Elumeni Golic prepped to hit the casino."

"Understood."

The casino was filled with tables for gambling, card games, dice games, and slot machines. The casino was fast paced, crowded with aliens of all sorts who were enjoying themselves. While some patrons gambled, others were getting drunk, having a good time with the prostitutes of both genders, or just wasting the night away.

The guards stood in their red and black armor, ready to stop whatever and whoever threatened the casino's activities at a moment's notice. They watched what they thought was Kenkias Loro walk up to them. His same old pissed off face was there.

"Hey, Loro," greeted one of the guards, "where you been?"

"None of your damn business, that's where," answered Onyx.

The guard shrugged, "Whatever, man."

They continued to watch the entire casino to see what was going on. They immediately noticed when a couple of engineers approached them. One was blue skinned and the other had blonde hair, a five o'clock shadow, and a smirk on his face.

"Can I help you boys?" inquired one of the guards.

"Yeah," replied Aiden. "We're here to do an inspection of the reactor for any chance of overload or leak possibilities."

The guards looked back and forth at each other. One of them put his Affix up to his face. "Hey, communication tower, are there any engineers scheduled to check out the reactor core?"

"One sec," replied another guard through the Affix. A slight pause occurred. "Yeah, it's here. They're scheduled to check the reactor and take note of any possible overload or leak possibilities. Have someone escort them down there."

"Understood," answered the guard. He turned toward Kenkias. "Hey, Kenkias, you just got here, you want to escort 'em down?"

Kenkias shrugged. "Sure."

Kenkias motioned for Javal and Aiden to come with him. "Follow me, boys." Javal and Aiden walked with the disguised Onyx down to the elevator.

The hotel room in the casino had more people than it would normally contain. Tika was examining the room while Captain Hernandez stood attentively. René had her rifle out and was ready to fire upon any intruder or anyone who would threaten their safety. Bryna had paid attention to her wrist device, making sure that her tech was working.

"There's clean up and bleach everywhere, covering up any possible evidence that could be gained. This scene has been way too sanitized to get a proper idea on what happened," noted Tika.

"Is that going to be a problem?" asked Captain Hernandez.

"Yes. I can't get a proper clue of what was going on in this room," replied Tika.

"So, it's going to be difficult to find evidence to clear Jaffar's name?" wondered Captain Hernandez.

"Yes," answered Tika. "I don't even get why the casino owner got involved with this. It would have been more effective if he had called in a squad of constables. It doesn't seem like he's the kind of man who would care about something like this."

"Maybe he was keeping him for the money?" inquired René.

"No," stated Captain Hernandez. "I've been involved in this kind of crap. I know the kind of man that Voltory Bolore is. I know that kind of casino owner. He makes enough money with sales from his casino and whatever underground and illegal activity he probably does. Judging from Kenkias Loro and his addiction to Red Rage, Bolore probably has a lot to do with this. He doesn't need bail money. This is about something else."

"Maybe it's personal?" wondered Tika.

"Not a bad theory," noted Captain Hernandez. "Bryna?"

"Yeah?" she said, looking up from her Affix.

"Could you check Flow Council records to see if we can find out a connection between Voltory Bolore and the ambassador?" asked Captain Hernandez politely.

"Sure.", responded Bryna. She started tapping on her Affix, looking for information that the captain requested.

"Thank you, Captain," noted Tika in appreciation.

"Of course, Tika. I do what I can to help my crew," replied Captain Hernandez.

"Damn it," blurted Bryna abruptly.

Hernandez turned to her in slight surprise.

"What's the problem?" asked Capt. Hernandez.

"The Flow Council put up firewalls for the information you needed," responded Bryna.

"Can you hack past the security lock outs?"

"Yeah, but it might be traced back to the Enforcer and we could get into big shit for that. I could do it, but there's a risk involved. It's your choice, Hernandez," stated Bryna.

"Don't. We can't have the Flow Council knowing that we're hacking into their database. This crew gets enough scrutiny as it is," answered Captain Hernandez thoughtfully.

"Alright," replied Bryna.

Captain Hernandez turned to Tika. "Sorry, Tika. I can't take that risk."

"It's okay, Captain," assured Tika. "I just wish I knew what was going on with this, you know?"

"Me too, I . . ." agreed Captain Hernandez.

Suddenly, a beeping sound came from Bryna's Affix, causing silence to come over the entire group.

"Oh, shit."

The group looked to Bryna in her statement. She was slightly concerned.

"What's the problem, Stoli," inquired René curiously.

"A merc group I had to deal with some time ago uses a particular signal for communications." Bryna looked down in thought and then continued.

"They really hate me. I took out about twenty of their squad when they went after me for a hit job. They've been after me ever since as a matter of pride. I set up an alarm for whenever their signal got within 50 yards of me... it just went off," Bryna explained in a serious tone.

Captain Hernandez pulled out his pistols and calmly replied, "Well, that's worth some concern, I guess."

The engineering room was huge. About half of it was taken up by the huge blue reactor. The blue glow from the reactor illuminated the room through the bulletproof and radiation sealing glass. The entire room was made of gravel, most likely to help shield whatever possible radiation would escape as a result of an overload.

Aiden started working on his bomb and placed it on the reactor itself.

"You are certain this will work, Aiden?" asked Javal.

"Yep," confirmed Aiden." The schematics work out perfectly. The bomb'll go off and every radiation detector in this place will think the reactor is on the verge to overload."

Aiden focused on the bomb without a break in concentration. The black bomb with glowing blue buttons made beeping noises as Aiden set the right time sequence.

Javal had something on his mind, despite Aiden's reassurance.

"If the bomb is just to send a wide spread signal, why do we need to evacuate the room?" worried Javal.

"The bomb could screw with our electronic equipment," answered Aiden. "And honestly, I'm not too sure how Onyx would test to that. He might be deactivated and our cover would be blown. Plus, I'm not in the mood to haul a big ass Eliminator robot out of here."

"Are you certain your equations are correct, Explosives Expert Aiden Dakar?" asked the disguised Onyx in his robotic voice.

"Gettin' a little scared, Onyx?" joked Aiden with a smile. "Don't worry; this room will shield us from any possible electronic power surges. We'll be safe once we're right outside of the engineering room. It's the being up close and personal that I'm worried about."

"Understood," replied Onyx. Though Onyx was a machine, Aiden was surprised to see human qualities in him, as did Javal. But, neither of them had had much experience with Eliminator robots, especially one as sophisticated as Onyx.

But this was no longer a time to think. An unexpected guard walked into the room and saw the bomb. He noticed Kenkias Loro was doing nothing about it and quickly pointed his rifle at Aiden and Javal.

"Don't move!" he shouted, nervously, as he started to reach for his Affix.

Quickly, Onyx grabbed his arm and broke it like a twig. The guard dropped the rifle and was about to scream in agony when Onyx covered his mouth. Reaching around, Onyx placed his other on the back of the guard's head and gave a twist. Aiden and Javal winced when they heard the neck snap. Onyx released the guard and the gravel scattered as he fell. Javal went to the dead guard in shock.

"Onyx! You--you killed him...," said Javal in disbelief. The event transpired so quickly. Onyx acted without a second's hesitation.

"Yes," responded Onyx, without even acknowledging Javal's shock. Javal had forgotten how cold and deadly Onyx could be when necessary. Javal shook off his feeling of disbelief and started to think logically.

"Did he get the signal sent out to the other guards?" asked Javal.

"Unable to tell based off of current signals, Engineer Javal. Insufficient data," responded Onyx. Javal put his Affix to his mouth and spoke into it.

"Bridge, this is Javal. Do you read me?"

PENCILS JON. PICCINI / INKS JABAAR BROWN

After a moment, the voice of Ensign James Felipe aboard the Enforcer could be heard. "Affirmative. What is required, Engineer Javal?"

"Ensign Felipe, a casino guard may have sent out a signal, we need to have it traced and blocked to any further links. Can you do that from the Enforcer?" asked Javal.

"Yes," affirmed the ensign, "Hold momentarily."

Javal put down his arm and looked to Aiden. "Aiden, is the bomb armed and ready?"

"Yup. I'll set it for 20 seconds. That's about how much time we'll have to hightail it out of here. Just give the word and I'll set it to blow." explained Aiden.

"Understood, wait for further instructions." commented Javal.

"Wouldn't it be simpler and more effective to have created an explosive weapon which could have been activated by remote?" wondered Onyx in his robotic voice.

"Oh, huh. I'm an expert in explosives and I didn't think of a simplistic explosive option. That sounds a lot like what an explosives expert that the Flow Council hand picked would do." remarked Aiden sarcastically.

"Stop mocking Onyx, Aiden." said Javal in a light mood.

"Haha, sorry, Javal. Couldn't resist." Aiden smiled while still working on the bomb.

Aiden looked to Onyx and started talking. "Yeah, actually, I thought of that, Onyx. But in a place this massive, I was afraid that the signal for the bomb could be detected, identified, and hacked. Then they'd know of our presence and the distraction part of the plan would fail. As well as, you know, my internal organs from the wave of guards coming in."

A beep came suddenly from Javal's Affix, meaning that the crew had called back. Javal put the Affix to his mouth and started to speak.

"Ensign, please tell me something good." pleaded Javal.

"We shut down the signal from the guard, and it didn't get out to the entire casino," James answered.

Javal and Aiden felt relief from the news. However, Ensign Felipe continued, "Unfortunately, a signal was sent out to a single person. We're haven't been able to trace it."

"Probably the casino owner," theorized Aiden.

"Data states that is unlikely," commented Onyx. "Data suggests Treasure Planet owner Voltory Bolore does not usually involve himself in intruder affairs. It was most likely Voltory Bolore's head of the guards; the Acer known as Solara."

Javal and Aiden started to worry slightly.

"Well, shit." remarked Aiden. "Think we should just make a break for Jaffar after I set the bomb as planned?"

"I'm not sure that we have much of a choice," replied Javal in a startled voice. He put the Affix close to his mouth again. "James, can you cut off the signal to whoever he sent the intruder alarm to?"

"Already done, sir." the ensign replied.

"Thank, you," said Javal. "I'll call if we need additional assistance."

"Yes, sir. Over and out," replied the ensign bridge commander as they logged off.

"Hopefully Golic will show up to protect us if that crazy killer of a bitch shows up," noted Aiden. "And hey, maybe she doesn't know where we are."

"Even if she doesn't, the guards will eventually notice that this guy is missing," worried Javal.

"Then I guess it's time to set the bomb," noted Aiden.

Aiden pressed a few buttons on the bomb until it lit up and read 'Armed'. Aiden pressed the button for it to detonate.

"Detonation in twenty seconds," announced a female robotic voice. Aiden looked back at Javal and Onyx with an urgent expression.

"Run like hell," ordered Aiden without pause. Onyx and Javal followed his advice and rushed to the door leading out to the engineering section of the casino as Aiden followed. The three of them got out of the door that lead to a long hallway and quickly shut the door.

Aiden's Affix started to beep.

"There she goes," said Aiden. The lights in the hallway started to flicker on and off. "Huh, suspected that might happen. Don't worry, that'll just add to the belief that the reactor is about to overload." assured Aiden.

Four guards in red and black armor approached Aiden, Javal, and the disguised Onyx with their guns up. Onyx saw that their cover was blown and decided to revert back to his normal form.

"Hey!" screamed one of the security personnel. "Put your goddamn hands up!"

"And the alternative if we don't?" asked Aiden in a mocking voice.

"I'll blow your brains out! I mean it!" barked the guard in response.

"Ah, well that's a tad bit more of a compelling threat than I've heard in the past few days," joked Aiden, attempting to stall them. A loud voice boomed over the intercom system that distracted the guards' concentration.

"Attention casino customers and personnel! The casino's reactor is on the verge to overload. Evacuate to your vehicles immediately! This is not a drill or a hoax. Evacuate immediately!" ordered the demanding voice.

Aiden's had been prepared for this announcement. Taking advantage as the guards' concentration that was broken; he rolled a bomb toward them. A guard felt it bump his boot and looked down.

"Oh sh--!"

Before the guard could finish his scream in shock, the bomb went off. Killing all of them. Aiden had just enough time to take behind Javal and Onyx, who were immune to the firebomb.

Aiden got off the ground. "So?" he began, "Let's go find Jaffar, shall we?"

"This is the way to the prison area, let's go." Javal nodded and pointed them forwards.

"Tika, take cover. Take out your repulsor gun. Use any chemicals, acids or whatever you want to use that you've cooked up. René and Bryna, get your weapons ready," ordered Captain Hernandez.

"Sir, I've fought these cowards before. I'll take them down," stated Bryna.

"I'm the Captain, Bryna. You take orders from me. Not the other way around. None of us fight alone," replied Captain Hernandez.

"Whatever," remarked Bryna defiantly. "Just don't get in my way."

Captain Hernandez was annoyed at Bryna's attitude, but he knew that at this point, giving orders to Bryna was futile. This was no time to get angry and bark orders. Imminent danger was coming, he and the others needed to get ready.

Captain Hernandez, Bryna, and René readied their weapons before leaving the room slowly and cautiously. The trio looked down the hall and saw the mercs striding with pride and anger in their tan and black colored armor.

"Kill the Stoli bitch!" ordered the leader in rage. "The other two don't matter!"

Before his men could take a shot at them, Bryna threw out a flashbang grenade, blinding them.

"Take out the henchmen! The leader's ass is mine," screamed Bryna in a bloodthirsty and vengeful tone.

Despite their ever growing annoyance at Bryna's defiance, Captain Hernandez and René followed her orders and took out each and every henchmen without missing a beat. The blood from their bodies splattering and stained the fancy white carpeting in the hall.

Bryna ran quickly and furiously at the leader. She hit him in the face with the bunt of her rifle. His face clenched in pain as he spit blood from his mouth. Bryna kneed him in his groin, causing more pain and forcing him off balance. She grabbed his arm and dropped her rifle. Kicking out the leader's leg, Stoli forced him to crash to the floor, face first. Bryna then stomped at his arm and felt it snap. She knocked him out by elbowing the back of his skull.

René watched in marvel as she saw Bryna's unnecessary, yet still highly effective close combat skills.

"Well done, Stoli," noted René.

Captain Hernandez wasn't amused or impressed. He was angry. "I said follow my orders, Bryna! As you can't, I suggest you go wait on the Enforcer!"

Bryna was not affected by his demands even slightly.

"It was I who was responsible for taking out the entire squad, sir. Not you. Perhaps you should listen to me more, no?" she stated proudly defiant.

René walked closer in to back Captain Hernandez up, as a lieutenant should.

"You need to follow orders, Stoli. And you also need to learn when to shut the hell up," stated René using her authoritative voice.

"You're one to talk," replied Bryna.

"What's that supposed to mean?"

"You know what I mean. Getting angry at Golic, a true warrior who is not only deadly but completely essential to this mission. And the man was nothing but polite. You need to learn to be silent better than I, Anukis," explained Bryna.

"Hey!"

The three turned to see Tika approaching them. She was putting away her repulsor gun as she walked up close to them. "Does it really have to be that the 15 year old girl who is the only one acting like an adult? It is not a wise choice to argue, especially at a time like this. The both of you need to realize something. And that is you need to either let each other in on what is bothering you, or let it go. Then find a way around it or use it to your advantage. If you don't, this team will not prosper."

"I'm the Captain, Tika." stated Hernandez seriously. "I'll resolve these issues, not you."

Tika raised her eyebrow in suspicion. "Resolving an issue when you're a part of it doesn't work, Captain. You know I'm right."

Captain Hernandez and René looked at Bryna as she stared right back at them. The three decided to put their anger aside for the sake of the mission. Captain Hernandez looked down at the merc leader.

"What do we do with this guy?" asked René as she looked down at the Merc, examining his armor, guns, and pondering his entire existence.

"We should probably take him aboard the ship and interrogate him on why he's here," proposed Hernandez.

"Doesn't sound like a bad idea to me," replied René.

Hernandez looked to Bryna.

"Bryna? He's probably already afraid of you. Maybe you and I should handle his interrogation."

"Sure," Bryna nodded in agreement.

Captain Hernandez felt a slight feeling of relief that Bryna followed his order without question. Captain Hernandez put his Affix to his mouth.

"Bridge, this is Captain Hernandez. We were unable to recover any evidence to clear Jaffar. However, we do have a mercenary here for pick up. Prepare an interrogation cell."

"Yes, Captain," responded a crew member.

Any further conversation was impossible as the casino alarms sounded. "Attention casino customers and personnel, the casino's reactor is on the verge to overload. Evacuate to your vehicles immediately! This is not a drill or a hoax. Evacuate immediately!"

"Looks like Aiden set off the bomb," Captain Hernandez said calmly. "Hopefully they'll be able to get Jaffar out safely."

The Captain picked up the unconscious mercenary leader and slung him over his shoulder.

"Regardless of the others, we have to get out of here. We can't risk Bolore catching us. I guess the rest is up to them. Move out to the nearest elevator."

"Aren't you glad I made sure this hotel section was closed off, Captain?" asked René sarcastically.

Captain Hernandez shook his head with a smile and followed the other three down the hall in a hurry while carrying their captive.

Jaffar was unable to break free from the restraints keeping him in his chair. The ragged clothes given to him by Voltory Bolore barely covered his paper white skin with black dots. He was scared as he looked around at the metal-covered room filled with metal cargo boxes.

The armed casino guards never took their eyes off Solara. Her red lips set in her tan skin and black hair matched her red eyes. The eyes had no mercy or remorse; just bloodthirsty rage and destruction. Solara walked with power and ferocity even in the most meaningless tasks, and the guards quickly followed her orders. She wore a skin tight black top that left her belly open so she could have easy access to her knives strapped to her sides. Solara's black pants were also skin tight and her black boots were pounding the metal floor as she impatiently wanted to kill something.

All of the guards stared at her and knew what it meant when they saw her, a being who was more powerful than they could ever hope to be. Solara was an elemental and could control the elements and destroy people as if they were insects. And Solara was an Acer, one who wouldn't even give a damn of killing these men in an instant if they failed in their duties.

A guard nervously asked, "S--Solara?" He almost wet himself as she looked in his direction. "Um, not to question you, but how do you know the reactor isn't on the verge of overloading?"

Solara smiled as she saw the guard's scared expression. "Guard 37 was sent to the reactor room to check on Guard 68 and never reported back. I believe Guard 68 is a traitor and is responsible for a fake signal. Maybe there was a bomb used to confuse the sensors."

"So, why haven't we alerted the rest of the guards, or Mr. Bolore?"

Solara smiled once more. "I'm guessing that whoever it is wants the little polka dotted Jaffar. And whoever they are has some prowess. They're good, probably professionals sent here for the Ambassador's son. They're probably worthy fighters. I want them for myself."

As the guard nodded nervously in fear, the door exploded into the room followed by Onyx, Javal and Aiden. Onyx quickly shot the two guards and turned to find Solara. To his surprise, Solara moved before Onyx could even point his gun at her and took cover behind a cargo box a few yards behind Jaffar. Onyx and Aiden ran quickly to free Jaffar, seeing as how he was the first priority.

Unexpectedly, Solara surrounded herself with fire and quickly shot it at Aiden and Onyx. Before it could reach them, Javal instinctively threw himself in the way knowing he would not be affected.

Javal held his ground as he took fire and shouted, "Onyx, you're the most capable of protecting Jaffar! Get him out of here! That's what's important! I can handle the Acer!"

Onyx used his cybernetic strength to break Jaffar's metal wrist and ankle restraints. As he ripped the restraints apart, Jaffar looked in amazement at Onyx, thinking that no human could break those restraints with their bare hands until he realized Onyx was an Eliminator. Aiden and Onyx freed Jaffar and started to run out of the detainment area.

"We got him Javal, let's go!" shouted Aiden as he looked back at the engineer surrounded by fire.

Javal turned back to face Solara while she still wielded the flames around him. He aimed his repulsor and fired. Solara flew several yards and hit the wall.

She quickly stood up and rushed Javal. As she was running, she pulled out her knife and drew it down Javal's arm, forcing him to drop his repulsor pistol and scream in agony.

Solara quickly turned and stabbed Javal through the slightly burnt and black skin tight material covering his chest.

Javal tried to utter another scream but couldn't. All he could feel was Solara's cold blade stuck inside him. All he could hear was her sick and quiet laughter in his ear. All he could see was Solara pulled her knife out of his chest and reaching toward his throat.

Her knife was pushed aside by a large rock. Golic jumped down from the air duct followed by at least seven more floating rocks, each the size of a human head. He tossed several more in Solara's direction.

Solara dropped her knife and started to run toward another door. Gathered two fire balls in her hand, she threw them toward Golic to distract him. As Golic used his floating rocks as a shield, Solara opened the door and ran out of the detention area.

Aiden and Onyx came to Javal's aid as he fell to the floor from the knife wound. Jaffar did not know what to do so he remained by the second exit door.

"I will kill the Acer. Move your teammate to safety," ordered Golic to Onyx and Aiden.

Onyx picked up Javal and his repulsor rifle as the engineer tried to cover his wounds and stop the bleeding.

Golic followed Solara through the door into a long hallway. Solara, fire surfacing around her, stood waiting for Golic. Golic waited.

"An Elumeni?" noted Solara. "My, my, I haven't killed an Elumeni since I was 12, when I decided that getting to kill whoever I wanted was more fun than being one of them."

Solara smiled as she was getting more and more excited for a fight with Golic.

Golic did not smile.

"You will pay for your sadistic crimes with your life, Acer," Golic declared courageously. The door closed behind him as he met his challenge head on.

PHOE-NIX NEBULA

Star Enforcers: Chapter 5

In a dimly lit large executive office suite, smoke filled the air with a sweet smoky smell. The expensive Korona suit hugged an athletically built human who gave orders from behind an impressive crystal carved desk. He pulled the cigar from under his mouth and placed it into the ashtray.

"Is the shield dome up yet? And what is the status on the reactor?" Voltory asked in a sober dry tone to the uniformed person sitting across the table.

"Yes it is Mr. Bolore," the high ranking security officer replied. "The shield is fully engaged and all communications outside of the dome have been terminated. Someone recently hacked into our computer matrix to terminate communications to our security officers, but I am trying to reestablish the security lockout links. I'm reading that the reactor is in normal stasis. The only conclusion I can come to about the reactor showing a meltdown would be that an electro magnetic pulse device was used that gave a false reading to the reactor core."

Satisfied by the security officer's response, Voltory ventured another question. "Very well, now where is my head of security?"

"Unknown sir, the last sign of her was in the holding cell area," the security officer informed him.

"Oh, really. Get me some eyes down there, I want to know what's going on," Voltory ordered, rolling his well-trimmed finger nails on the crystal carved desk in a controlled rhythm as the officer quickly started punching buttons.

"I found her sir. She is . . . fully engaged with another combatant. Who could provide such a challenge?" the security officer asked in disbelief.

"Display it on my viewer, lieutenant," Bolore instructed, wondering the same thing.

Once the order was given, the large one hundred inch plasma screen viewer displayed a floor littered with seven dead security guards. The image shifted to blood trickling from a nose. Zooming out, Solara appeared holding a sword. She looked tough as nails with her sword in her hand but the audio indicated she was breathing considerably heavy. As the image continued to zoom out, her opponent could finally be seen. Golic stood toe to toe with her and he was carrying a pointed battle staff.

"Oh this is interesting, indeed," Voltory said and rubbed his clean shaven chin.

"Should I send backup to her location?" the lieutenant asked.

"No. I actually want to see how she does against him. If my head of security can't handle one lone Elumeni, then I may have to consider a better replacement. Anyhow, give me a visual on Jaffar's cell. I to make sure that he has stayed put."

"Yes sir… Umm, sir, I don't…," the lieutenant uttered as the visual showed an empty cell.

Voltory huffed, reached for the sweet smelling cigar and smashed the lit end into the base of ashtray, extinguishing it. "This has all seemed to be a distraction to get Jaffar out of my prison area."

The casino owner stood up and crossed the carpeted floor to a weapon's cabinet. He entered an access code on the control pad and the hydraulics engaged, forcing the secure case to open with a hiss.

Eyeing the lovely assortment of weapons, he finally reached for one of his favorites. It was a jade green colored rifle which had a laser scope that would make his task easier.

"When I find Jaffar, I'm going to charge his father double for the inconvenience. Lieutenant, stay here and keep me posted."

"Understood, Mr. Bolore," his second in command responded.

"You and you come with me. We have some hunting to do," the casino owner ordered as he pointed to the two guardsmen standing by his doorway. In unison, they turned and followed as he exited the executive office and headed toward the level lifters.

Not too far from the detention area, Onyx, Javal, and Aiden were making their way to the lobby of the casino. They were herding Jaffar, who was not too worse for wear. Javal's injuries from Solara's blade made him weak and Onyx was required to carry him over his shoulder. Onyx, being a cybernetic being, was still in the lead, even with Javal's weight. The casino guards were sparse, an advantage the jail-breaking team had not expected.

Aiden was keeping careful watch for any hostiles they might encounter. His custom-made gun was designed to fire rounds that would explode on impact and he kept it at the ready as they moved through the hall. When the group finally stopped running to rest in a dim corner of the hall, Aiden shamelessly panted, "Jaffar, how the hell did you get into this mess?"

Jaffar was catching his breath and answered, "I don't know. I was just gambling and doing quite well when this woman came over to the Parises Dice Table and offered me a drink. We had a few of them as time went on. I had no idea why I was beginning to get aroused and I tried to hide it at the gambling table. Apparently she was aware of it and she asked to go up to my room for a good time. Once we got there, I could not contain myself and I became an animal. I deserve to be locked up. I'm not even sure what truly happened. All I know is that when I woke up from my drunken stumper, there was blood all over my hands, and the casino officers were standing over me with their guns pointed in my direction. The woman's body was in a twisted wreck on the floor near the bed."

"Does your male species normally react that way around females?" Onyx asked as he carefully set Javal on the floor very to avoid injuring him further.

"No, we don't at all." Jaffar added as he shook his head.

Before Jaffar could continue, three security guards moved through a door and started making their way into the hallway. Their guns were drawn as they looked for the infiltrators.

"Three incoming targets," Onyx whispered as he scanned the hall after he heard a pressure sliding door open down the corridor. Onyx and Aiden pressed their backs against the wall in an effort to blend into the dimness of the hallway. Fortunately, the emergency strobe lights were not flashing. They aimed their weapons at two of the nearest guards, and fired one round each. The two guards were fatally wounded, one in the neck, the other in the chest.

"Oh shit!" the last guard said as he trotted backward and fired his weapon, almost hitting Aiden in the head. The frightened guard had almost returned to the sliding door when Onyx locked onto him and shot him in the leg. Once immobilized, a second shot to the head to ended his life.

A repulsor round fired from the other direction took Aiden and Onyx by surprise. They quickly turned around to see a guardsman make a sickening thud as he fell backwards and landed head first.

"He came out of that entrance," Javal pointed with is repulsor, "and was about to shoot you. I don't think he saw me in the corner."

"Good to see that you heal somewhat quickly, I was beginning to worry a little about you," Aiden said as he watched Javal gingerly struggle to stand. He was still bleeding, but his wound was beginning to heal.

"Not all that quickly. It still hurts like hell, but I am mobile," Javal responded as he gritted his teeth.

He looked in Jaffar's direction. The ambassador's son had noticed him holding the glowing purple blood back with his left hand. Droplets the entire length of the hallway glowed like a trail leading to the intruders. "Not to worry Jaffar, it's just a flesh wound. All I need is some time to heal and some coffee."

"Oh boy you and your coffee Javal," Adien commented knowing how much that their engineer loved coffee.

"Maybe so, but your blood sure as hell left a trail for the guards to follow us by. Here, take this," Jaffar said and tore a part of his prison cloth to help Javal contain his bleeding and offered it to him. "Who are you guys?"

Javal accepted and tied the cloth material over his wound. "We are undercover constables sent here by your father, to clear your name and to get you home safely. So are we ready to get out of here before the whole security force comes down on us?"

"I would recommend a steady pace to exiting these premises," Onyx advised.

"I would not debate you on that call. I wonder how the captain is doing?" Aiden said and let loose with a round of explosive fire bombs as a fresh group of casino guards once again came through the door.

The Enforcer's crew of thirty five tended the ship while waiting for a transmission from the constables. All communication was cut off, unfortunately, when the casino's defense shields were engaged. The crew had been trying to establish communication with Bryna, but even her advanced Affix would not respond to their hails. The crewman sitting in the captain's chair decided it was time to assume command of the ship. Initiating a yellow alert, the crewman brought the ship out of orbit.

The constable ship remained cloaked as it passed through Roul`e's atmosphere. Luckily, the exterior plating on the ship could easily handle the intense heat as the ship flew through the ionosphere. The night's cloud cover was sparse and clouds separated as the ship passed through them and hovered in position. They were a few kilometers away from the Treasure Planet Casino.

"Javal, what's your status?" Capt. Hernandez asked as he carried the mercenary captain over his shoulder.

"We have Jaffar, Captain, but we are running into some resistance. We should be on the lobby level in a few minutes. I was wounded by the Acer, but I'll be okay. Golic has engaged Solara," Javal responded. The firing of his weapon was heard in the background of the communication.

"Good, we'll rendezvous in the lobby in about five minutes," Hernandez concluded as he and his team reached the level lifters. "René, get a level lifter," the captain ordered. "I don't want to take the stairs thirty-two levels down.

Bryna was scanning for any resistance and she and the captain heard a group of security officers running up the emergency stairwell.

René and Tika reached the level lifters. She pushed the down button. "Damn it, there are security lockouts on all of them!"

"Bryna, get over here, I need you to get these level lifters working immediately," Hernandez ordered as he placed the knocked out merc captain on the floor. He took out his pistols and kept a watch over the passageway as he heard the emergency doors open down the hall.

"I'm on it." Bryna said as she passed the helplessly unconscious merc captain. *"I should just kick the shit out of him now while I have the chance. Yannis, you're so lucky that Hernandez wants you alive, or I would have ended your life when I first had the chance."* she thought in the back of her mind.

A disturbing howl came from the far corner of the hallway. What appeared to be a canine snout appeared down the hallway accompanied by three more. Large great white shark-like teeth were displayed as drool leaked from the mouths of these beasts. Sharp Wolverine-type claws reached from the paws of four tiger sized animals.

"Oh, damn! We have kill-hounds coming towards us," René shouted as she fired her weapon into the skull of one of the beasts. It fell against a neighboring kill-hound as brain matter and blood splattered against the wall. The three remaining kill-hounds went into a rage after losing a member of their pack. Using their claws, the beasts climbed up the walls and rushed towards the constables.

"Send these bitches to hell," Hernandez cried to Tika and René. The roar of three people firing their weapons was continuous. The kill-hounds were extremely hard to hit as they dodged and bounced from wall to ceiling. The first volley of bullets did not hit their mark and they came closer. During the second round of firing, Hernandez scored a hit on one of the beasts and sent it falling from the ceiling to the floor.

The remaining pair of kill-hounds were only fifty meters away, and the constables became nervously uncomfortable, knowing the fact that they could be ripped to shreds and eaten alive.

"Bryna, come on! We are about to become canine food if you don't get that level lifter working." Hernandez said urgently.

"I just got access to the controls. It will be here in a couple of seconds; just hold them back. It's hard to try to hack any systems in the hotel after the security locks on the main computer of the hotel were put into place," Bryna responded in a frustrated tone as she was typing as fast as she could into her sophisticated Affix.

She took out her pistol and fired a shot that hit one of the kill-hounds in its wolf-like ear. The pain to its ear made the huge canine lose its balance and fall to the floor. It growled in agitation and took to a full sprint up the hallway. René, along with Tika, fired their weapons straight into its head, sending the beast falling forward and sliding to a stop from its momentum.

The last remaining kill-hound stopped in its tracks and thought about its own survival. After growling a displeasing tone, the beast ran the opposite way.

The chime of the level lifter could be heard and the doors slid open.

"My goodness that was close, I thought that we were on the menu tonight," Tika muttered, breaking the brief silence.

"We aren't out of the woods yet. Everyone get in now, and drag that merc inside," Hernandez ordered as a round of bullets and lasers came streaking down the hall.

The constables dove for cover on the level lifter and Yannis' body slumped on the floor of the carriage. As the doors closed, a bullet hit the mercenary in the left foot causing him to wake. He began to scream in agony.

PHOE-NIX NEBULA

Star Enforcers: Chapter 6

The Constable team looked down in shock to see that he was awake. Yannis held from the pain and the bullet hole with blood he saw in his left foot. He then looked up to see Bryna pulling out her shotgun. Yannis needed a way out. Before Bryna could pull her trigger, Yannis reached into his pocket.

"Hey! Back off!" shouted Yannis as he pulled out an explosive grenade and held his finger on the button. "You know what this is, right? I let go of this button, or if you kill me and my finger slips off this button, we all die. Right here. Right now. It explodes. That's it. So back the hell off. I'm getting out of here and you won't do a damn thing."

Bryna gritted her teeth and intensely glared at Yannis. She didn't twitch or move her gun away from his head.

"Stand down, Bryna," ordered Hernandez.

Bryna lowered her gun slowly. She hated not being in control of a situation, especially when an enemy of hers had power over her.

A smile grew on Yannis' face. "That's right, Stoli. Stand down, like a good little bitch," joked Yannis.

Bryna's eye started to twitch as she had an ever growing urge to slaughter Yannis with her own bare hands.

Onyx kicked open the door to the stairs. Aiden, Jaffar, and Javal followed. Though Javal was recovering quickly, he was still having trouble running. As they moved up a flight of stairs, Aiden saw that guards were following them from the flight below.

Aiden aimed down and pulled his pistol's trigger. The bullets hit one guard in the neck, two in their knees, and the last in his chest. Several other bullets hit the stairs and the wall behind the guards. The bullets exploded. Aiden wasn't the best shot, but with explosive bullets that wasn't important.

"They're right behind us," informed Aiden. "You think they all know where we are?"

"Data suggests that casino guard forces are entirely aware of our position," noted Onyx. "Prepare for combat on both fronts. Cover may not be an option."

"So what the hell are we supposed to do? Just shoot and hope we hit them before they hit us!" screamed an outraged Jaffar.

"Welcome to the world of high risk missions," stated Aiden. Jaffar saw more guards coming up the stairs as Aiden noticed reinforcements coming from above.

Bullets rained from the top and roared from the bottom. No one was getting hit, but Jaffar was getting worried and agitated as he ran. Aiden, Javal and Onyx kept their cool as they returned fire.

Onyx easily blew apart chunks of guards that were approaching him. Due to his calculated accuracy and strength, he was decimating the close combat forces. Jaffar looked as he saw blood and body parts fly around the stairway and was starting to get repulsed by the carnage. He tried as hard as he could to maintain himself.

Javal's repulsor gun kept guards from behind them at bay. Javal had even shot some of them down the stairs, causing them to hit walls and black out. Javal's speed had started to pick up as his wounds continued to heal.

Aiden dropped several bombs behind him in order to keep the guards approaching their rear further away. Those who noticed the bombs stopped in their tracks, making them easy targets. Those who didn't notice the bombs were blown apart when they walked near them. Either way, Aiden was taking care of the threat behind him, though he was starting to run out of both explosives and ammo very quickly.

After nine flights of running, shooting, and deafening explosives, they had finally reached the lobby.

They saw a battalion of casino guards who had their guns aimed at them. Before the guards could waste the Constables and Jaffar, Aiden threw his last explosive grenade at them, blowing apart most of them. Those who were injured or had escaped the explosion were killed by Onyx.

"Architect!" cried Jaffar in repulsion. "How can you people do this day after day?"

Aiden and Javal looked back at each other, then to Onyx.

"Someone has to rescue the Ambassador's son, Jaffar," answered Onyx.

"Honestly…, " started Aiden "—not all of us are here because we want to be."

Javal looked away from Aiden with a feeling of nervousness. The awkward silence remained for a couple seconds until Javal noticed something else.

"Hey, where's Captain Hernandez? He said that he'd be with everyone else with some mercenary captain. Where are they?"

Aiden, Javal, and Onyx looked at each other, each trying to see if the other had some idea as to where the rest of their team was.

"Well, they can handle themselves, can't they?" asked Jaffar.

"I hope so," responded Aiden.

"Another thought occurs," stated Onyx. "Elumeni Golic has not returned from his confrontation with Acer Solara."

Golic hadn't tasted his own blood since his training on Talon. He tried to hold his own against Solara, but she was relentless. Her sword kept coming towards his body, again and again. Golic was losing energy and didn't know how much longer he could keep up the fight.

Solara's blade met with Golic's spear repeatedly as Golic tried to keep her at a distance. Solara's sadistic laugh came constantly as she saw Golic's lowering energy and resolve. She knew exactly what he was thinking. That his efforts may be hopeless, and his strength may be failing him. Despite all of the teachings, that being on the side of righteousness gave him strength; he was weak compared to Solara's never ending madness.

Golic swung again at Solara's head to try to get her to back off. Though she was thirsty for Golic's blood, she could wait. Like a vulture trying to get its food, she could wait.

Golic took several quick steps back. He closed his eyes and began to focus. He opened them and Solara saw that they were glowing. Golic had no expression of pain or emotion, only of complete focus. He was going to use his elemental powers to kill Solara.

Golic raised his arm at her and suddenly huge piles of concrete came crashing through the windows. Solara smiled as she saw Golic's desperation to want to kill her. She easily avoided the boulder-sized concrete chunks by simply flipping backward away from them.

Solara and Golic started to lose their footing as the boulders crashed through the floor, causing it to collapse. The hallway's floor started to crumble and crash in on the one below it.

Golic's eyes stopped glowing as his body started to slip down into the next floor. Solara was falling as well. The two elementals lost their weapons as they painfully dropped to the floor below.

Golic tried to rise quickly, but he saw that Solara was already up and running at him. Her own eyes were glowing bright red and fire was surrounding her. Golic didn't have enough strength to summon his own elemental power, so he grabbed his spear and threw it at Solara. Solara dodged and it missed, hitting the remains of the upper floor behind her.

Solara then shot an extreme amount of fire at Golic. Golic managed to evade most of it but still felt the effects of flames singing his skin. Golic felt the pain as he rolled away in an attempt to get to safety. Solara delighted in the smell of burnt flesh.

Golic backed against the window, trying to get away from Solara, but Solara merely laughed. Once again, she surrounded herself with the remaining bit of her summoned flames and created an explosion of fire.

In panic, Golic summoned head-sized bits of concrete to his aid to block the fire, but it wasn't enough. The shockwave pushed Golic through the window. He hung from at the sub-basement window and looked at the floor of the canyon forty stories below. He was losing his grip and a fatal fall would occur if he hit the ground.

In desperation, he forced his eyes to glow as he summoned gravel from the ground. He needed to land on the floating rocks and get to safety, but he didn't have the strength to summon it quickly enough to prevent injury. As he lost his grip, he fell thirty feet. Golic felt his legs break as he hit the large chunks of gravel.

His eyes did not stop glowing despite the pain. He let himself float slowly down to the ground. As the concrete reached the canyon floor, Golic lost concentration and the ability to remain conscious.

Solara looked down to see the unconscious Golic and merely laughed. She knew he would no longer be able to stay awake. She thought she'd send some guards to round him up, so she could have something to torture later.

The lobby level lifter door opened and Yannis limped out with his hand on the live grenade.

"Now!" he yelled, stretching his arm behind him. "Goodbye Stoli! I hope you rot in hell!" Before he could pitch the grenade into the elevator, he felt a cold robotic crushing his hand. He looked up to see Onyx, staring at the grenade intensively. "No! Stop!" he cried.

Bryna watched every second of it. Even though she was not the one to kill Yannis, she was satisfied in watching him break down.

"That's right. Cry," she said. "Like a good bitch."

Yannis looked to Bryna in absolute fear, not wanting to die, pleading for her to help him with his eyes. She simply smiled.

The bomb went off. Yannis was killed instantly as the shrapnel ripping through his body like it was ground beef. Onyx's right hand was ripped apart, and the shotgun strapped to his right leg was damaged. Robotic may he be, but his body was not invincible and an exploding short range grenade could cause a lot of damage. Without emotion, Onyx looked at Captain Hernandez and awaited his next orders.

Captain Hernandez, René, Tika, and Bryna ran out of the level lifter. Hernandez and Tika were concerned with Onyx's hand while René and Bryna scanned the room to see if any other guards were approaching.

"Onyx, are you alright?" asked Hernandez in worry.

"I am operational, Captain," replied Onyx. "Repairs will be needed. Right hand is unable to complete tasks and Constable issued shotgun is damaged beyond repair for this mission. Must switch to the laser pistol for left hand." Captain Hernandez knew that Onyx would not be needing any consolation as would someone else, and that he would survive.

"Hey!" Jaffar stated in Captain Hernandez's direction. "Are you the Captain of all these people? Are you going to get me out of here?" Captain Hernandez nodded.

"I'm Captain Hernandez of the U.S.S. Enforcer. My crew is here to rescue you from the captivity of Voltory Bolore," explained Capt. Hernandez.

"Thank you for confirming that last piece of information I needed," Voltory Bolore stated as he walked into the casino lobby. With a wave, fifty guards appeared, surrounding the entire team of constables. Bolore held his special custom-made jade-green assault rifle toward Captain Hernandez, the blue laser scope placing its dot directly over the captain's heart. He smiled, knowing he had captured those who were the cause of his recent anguish.

The crew turned and looked at the fifty guards. They all knew that there were too many to fight. If they shot one, the other forty nine would kill them. Still, they kept their weapons ready. Voltory Bolore cleared his throat and prepared to speak.

"Now, what shall I do with you Constables?"

JONATHAN PICCINI

"Well it appears that you have yourself in a very difficult spot, Mr. Bolore," Capt. Hernandez spoke to the casino owner in a confident manner. He had his silver pistol pointed at the distinguished gentleman.

"Hahaha, surely you're joking, captain. Look at your situation. You're out-numbered and out-gunned."

Even though Voltory might lose some of his security force and risk being shot from the courageous captain, he still felt as though he had the upper hand. Still, the confident smile on the captain's face perplexed him.

"Are you ready to have this place leveled, burying you and all of us inside?" Capt. Hernandez pressed.

"You are playing a very weak hand of cards, captain. Just give us back Jaffar and leave before I have all of you shot, starting with you," Voltory declared.

"A weak hand, you say? Right now I have the wild card in my deck. That wild card is a fully armed cruiser at the front porch of your casino, and in…" the captain looked down at his Affix to see the time, "ninety seconds my ship will open fire if we don't communicate with them."

"Yeah, right. We've been constantly scanning for military ships in our sector and current scans indicate that there are none to be found," Solara spoke as she emerged from one of the lobby entry doors.

Many eyes looked at her. She walked determinedly toward her employer. She still held her sword and it was laced with blood.

"I'm not bluffing. By the way where is Elemuni Golic?" the captain asked hoping that the warrior had not lost his head to this torturous woman.

"Oh that's his name. He took a bad step. I'll fix him up later. Now hand Jaffar over to us or I'll surely burn all of you nice and slow till you beg me to kill you quickly by ramming my sword down your throats," the Acer said as a flame gathered in her left hand.

"Watch your tongue bitch!" René uttered and aimed her weapon directly at Solara.

"Voltory Bolore, are you willing to risk the lives of everyone over this person?" Hernandez reaffirmed.

"Yes, I am. He's not just a person he's a rapist and a killer and I will do with him as I please. He killed one of my prostitutes so that makes me judge and jury here. You constables have no jurisdiction in my place of business, and you pose no threat to us," the casino owner surmised.

"He's right, captain, I did kill her. I must have blacked out from the drink I was having. I don't remember anything that happened that night," Jaffar admitted.

"I will not allow you to interrogate him or hold him without a proper investigation into the crime," Captain Hernandez said, hoping Voltory would reconsider his decision.

"You now have twenty seconds to stand down your forces," Onyx interjected using his internal circuitry to sync with galactic time.

Realizing that Onyx was an Eliminator and they don't bluff, Voltory decided to check. He tapped a gold circular device the size of a dollar coin surrounded by diamonds while his other hand remained on the trigger of his weapon still aimed at Hernandez.

"Lieutenant at Arms, scan the area within a ten mile radius of any vessel activity."

"Yes sir, scanning… I'm not detecting anything out of the ordin… wait a moment. I don't believe this," the lieutenant gasped in shock.

"What are you talking about?" Valtory demanded. He did not like surprises.

"Sir, a ship within a mile of our location has appeared out of nowhere. It's raising shields! Red Alert! Red Alert!" The floor came alive with flashing red strobe lights.

The Enforcer de-cloaked outside of the casino and preparations began for a missile attack. Two panels opened and revealed missiles tubes swiveling into position as four air-to-surface missiles were launched toward the casino. The missiles exploded upon reaching the defensive shield dome of the Treasure Planet Casino. Customers inside the casino shouted in terror as they thought an earth tremor had struck. The shaking was so great that slot machines fell onto the floor spilling casino coin credits. Outside, explosions lit the night sky as the yellow shield dome protecting the casino shimmered.

The security personnel were baffled. A cruiser had never attacked the casino before, and casino's defenses and personnel were only trained to encounter small class vessels threatening, but rarely ever attacking, the gambling establishment.

Aiden took advantage of their confusion. He reached into his vest for his last remaining bomb. Rolling the canister toward Voltory and his forces, it exploded a few seconds after touching the floor. The huge rush of purple smoke engulfed part of the lobby and blinded mostly everyone.

The security guards began firing in different directions trying to hit or wound the constables. Shouts of pain and surprise could be heard through the thick purple fog. The team of constables immediately fell to the floor and Tika grabbed Jaffar and forced him down to the carpet as well. She told him to stay still and not to move.

The constables had practiced this scenario and were prepared. They reached into their side pockets and grabbed therir infrared glasses. Onyx, being an Eliminator, had already intiated the heat sensing vision of his optical receptors. The constables took aim with their firearms.

"Just wound them; especially you Stoli," The captain commanded.

Stoli huffed in irritation not liking to be told what to do so often, but she made sure that she was the first person to fire as she looked for the strongest heat signature in the lobby.

Solara's grunt of pain showcased Bryna's excellent marksmanship as the Acer's left knee was shattered. Losing her concentration, the flame in her left palm disappeared as she dropped to the floor in pain and let go of her sword. Solara had never been shot before. She clutched her wounded knee as blood oozed between her fingers and dripped to the floor.

Javal used his repulser rifle to send a dozen guards crashing against the walls and onto the floor while Tika shot five guards with special mini tranquillizer dart rounds. Without ammunition, Aiden enjoyed watching heat signatures fly through the air or drop to the ground. René aimed her shot gun at shoulders and legs, and seven more guards succumbed to severe pain from their flesh wounds. Bryna was very selective kept shattering knee caps, sending the casino security forces to the floor. Even though Onyx had only one good hand, his was extremely accurate firing with his laser pistol. He scored hits on the shoulders and thighs of more hostile security forces. As for the captain, he fired four rounds with his silver pistols at two carefully chosen targets.

The casino was returning fire at the Enforcer. Two rocket launcher mounts rose from the base of the forty story tower and fired ten surface to air missiles. The ship's plasma laser arrays that were mounted on the front SlipStream Engine Wings were activated to target and destroy the oncoming warheads. Nine of the missiles were destroyed as searing hot beams of light struck the warheads causing them to erupt in an orange and red plume of exploding light. The last missile made it through the laser defense systems and collided with the Enforcer's shield grid. The impact explosion slightly shook the ship but it was not damaged.

The bridge crew returned fire and four more rounds of high yield missiles shot towards the casino. Rotating cannons from the casino's roof attempted to destroy the incoming missiles. The high caliber bullets hit two of the missiles exploding them in mid-air, but the other pair made it through the defenses and once again struck the shield dome causing it to buckle. The casino shook once again and a few of the crystal decorative chandeliers fell onto the lobby floor with a loud crashing sound.

"Solara I don't care what kind of pain you're in, get rid of this got-damn smoke, right now!" Voltory cursed at the top of his lungs.

Solara pushed her pain aside and focused on her limited power of wind. She directed her right hand, covered in her own blood, to form a whirlwind of air, as the other hand continued to cradle her knee injury. Within moments the purple smoke had gathered near her and she pushed the well contained purple tornado to the other side of the lobby. When the smoke was finally clear, only eight of the guardsmen remained standing. Voltory appeared from behind a marble pillar where he had hidden for cover and noticed that his two personal bodyguards were wounded in the ankles, as they tried to endure the pain. Capt. Hernandez was still pointing his pistols at them.

"Mr. Bolore, the shield dome can't handle another missile barrage and its integrity is down to twenty three percent," the Lieutenant at Arms alerted the casino owner over the P.A. loud speaker.

"So Mr. Bolore, are you willing for us to talk things through, or do you want to see your casino crumble all around you with us inside?" Hernandez warned the owner as the constables returned to their feet unharmed, Tika pulling Jaffar to a standing position. The ambassador's son was a little shaken as he saw a number of guards moaning and gritting their teeth from the wounds they had received from the determined constables.

"I would suggest doing as the captain says," a voice boomed through the lobby. "He is not the kind of person to be taken lightly, and I could level this place in seconds with my powers of earth."

A large slab of rock hovering four feet off of the floor emerged through the purple haze of smoke from the other side of the large lobby area. To everyone's surprise, Elemuni Golic was sitting upright on top of the slate.   His broken legs were extended out to lessen his pain while his upper body was was supported by a slab of rock. Solara disgustedly looked up at Golic since her leg had been injured as well. Bryna smiled slightly seeing the look on the Acer's face, as though it was poetic justice. Golic focused his attention on Voltory and his brown eyes were glowing.

Voltory loved his casino and did not wish for it to be destroyed. The Treasure Planet Casino was a life time of hard work, and to lose it within minutes would be foolish. He huffed and spoke into his communication device and lowered his jade green weapon. "Lieutenant, deactivate the security grid, and stand down all weapons."

"Sir?" the lieutenant questioned.

"That wasn't a request Lieutenant."

"Yes… Yes sir," the lieutenant responded and did as he was told. The rocket launchers and rotating cannons retracted back into their normal positions. The yellow defense field deactivated leaving the casino vulnerable to the Enforcer's weaponry.

The crew aboard the ship was ready to launch a new round of missiles, but could tell that the hostiles inside the casino were surrendering.

"Guards put down your weapons," Voltary told his eight remaining fully functional guards. They were hesitant at first since the constables were targeting them. "Do as you're told!" The owner barked, and they immediately lowered their firearms.

"We have established communication with our ship, and the crew awaits your command captain," René informed Hernandez much to her relief.

"Mr. Voltory Bolore, my crew and I are here to investigate the crimes against Jaffar Krytis. Do you consent to our investigation?" Hernandez stated.

The casino owner shrugged his shoulders, "Do I have a choice?"

"I will take that as a yes," Hernandez responded. "René tell the crew to stand down. We'll take things from here."

JONATHAN PICCINI

Captain Hernandez looked at his crew who were patiently awaiting his orders. He knew he'd have to get evidence for a reasonable defense for Jaffar, first and foremost.

"Onyx."

"Yes, Captain," replied Onyx.

"I'd like you and Bryna to go the security room and I want you to tap into the video surveillance. Bryna will be there for additional technical support, to block out any possible viruses and get past any firewalls. Can the two of you do that?"

"Affirmative," stated Onyx positively. Bryna simply looked at Captain Hernandez, shrugged, and followed Onyx to the stairwell.

As Onyx opened the door, Bryna's eyes widened.

"Shit, Dakar. Did you have to blow up everything?" she exclaimed in surprise. Aiden let out a chuckle as Bryna went up the stairs.

Captain Hernandez turned to Golic and evaluated his painful and injured state. He then pointed to Tika.

"Tika, get Golic immediate medical attention."

"Yes, Captain," responded Tika. Tika walked over to Golic, pulled out her medical kit and began working on Golic's injuries. Golic kept his gaze on Solara. She stared straight back at him.

"What you staring at ground feeder? Do you want to continue this outside?" the fire elemental said to Golic.

"No, I do not wish to continue this. I consider this a stalemate. I was under orders to bring you back dead or alive, not the Constables. I will return for you another time. Maybe not today, nor tomorrow, but sometime soon," Golic replied to her taunting.

"I look forward to the day, and I expect that you will not have the help of the Constables to pull you out of the fire next time. It'll just be me and you," Solara obliged and used her wind power to hover above the floor to exit the lobby to attend to her wounded knee.

"Captain?" asked Javal.

"What is it?"

"This casino has an impressive shielding matrix. The Enforcer might benefit if I got some data on it. It's possible I could find something to improve the shields on our ship."

"Fine," confirmed Hernandez. "Have Bryna hack the database for shielding schematics in a few minutes."

"Thank you, Captain," responded Javal.

René never let down her gun from the guards and looked at them all suspiciously. Captain Hernandez walked over to her and started whispering in her ear.

"Look, these guards seem to be scared of you. We'll need to interrogate them soon. Right now, the most important one to question is Bolore. Take them all aboard the Enforcer and I'll meet you there to interrogate Bolore in a few minutes."

Captain Hernandez backed away from René and she gave a simple nod without breaking focus.

"Alright, hands behind your heads," ordered René. "And I swear, try anything and I'll pull the trigger."

The eight guards still standing moved out slowly in a line as René pointed her assault rifle at them. The wounded guards would remain behind until they received attention from the casino's medical staff.

Onyx and Bryna soon reached the security center and entered to find all the guards standing with their hands behind their heads. Bryna pulled out several devices and placed them on the guards.

"These are explosives. They're triggered remotely. I can see you from this room. Try anything, and I press a button and you all explode, understand?"

The guards nodded to Bryna and walked out of the room.

Bryna started working with her portable computer. The firewalls were being disabled and the system was soon open for Onyx to get into it without any complications.

"Go ahead, the firewalls are down," informed Bryna. Onyx closed his eyes and waited for a few seconds. He opened them and they turned a glowing red.

"Uplink established, retrieving data," Onyx stated in his cold and robotic voice. "Estimated completion time is five minutes, forty eight seconds."

"Whatever," Bryna blurted as she continued working on her portable computer.

"So, what makes the shields of this casino so interesting?" Aiden asked Javal.

"Most shields act as a barrier for a single type of shielding, either physical, like from the Enforcer' weapons, or electronic, such as signals. On the Enforcer, we have two separate operating systems, as do most ships. If we can find whatever it was that allowed this casino's shields to scramble both hacking and communication, while protecting it, then we could use about half of the power of our shields. Half of the power would enable us to keep the shields up for about twice as long as we normally do. Or make them twice as strong, depending. I'll have to screw around with the shield settings later."

"Fascinating," remarked Aiden.

Captain Hernandez walked over to Tika as she was working on Golic with a tool. She was scanning Golic's body with a green light and looking at the tool's readout.

"How's Javal doing?" asked Captain Hernandez.

"His legs are broken, but with injected robotic stabilization probes, he should be on his feet in a matter of days. He'd be able to do physical work to the intensity he did today in a matter of a couple of weeks," Tika answered. Looking at the displayed results she continued. "It seems he also suffered burns from the Acer's attacks. He should be in massive amounts of pain."

Golic looked at Tika, with an expression that seemed to say *"I'm right here."* Tika looked away in slight discomfort.

"How are you feeling, Golic?" wondered Hernandez.

"The side of right deserted me today," announced Golic dejectedly. "I must find what allowed the Acer to defeat me in battle. Perhaps the side of right was a lie. Perhaps everything was a lie. Perhaps I need to find the placement of anger… for right now that is all I can feel."

Tika and Captain Hernandez looked back at each other in worry.

"Are you doing okay?" asked Tika.

"My body shall recover, as you said. But I must discover what shall be of my mind and spirit." replied Golic.

Both Captain Hernandez and Tika paused for a moment in awkward silence, and tried to collect themselves in order to say something to Golic.

"You lost a fight. It happens," assured Captain Hernandez. "Live and learn from your mistakes."

"Your sincere words echo with hollow meaning in my mind," replied Golic. "Training shall be required, yes. But it is in the mind where I was weak. Solara did not hold back, she did not get tired, only her rage and blood thirst was needed. Perhaps I need to find a similar emotional drive to accomplish the goals that are required of the Flow Council."

"Do you want a sedative?" asked Tika. "Something to ease the pain?"

Golic shook his head.

"Pain is what shall remind me of my failure," stated Golic. "I refuse to forget it."

The uncomfortable feeling of being around Golic changed for Captain Hernandez when his wrist device started to beep. He looked at it and saw that René was establishing a communication uplink.

"Captain, we have Bolore as well as his guards in holding cells. I'm awaiting your presence so we can interrogate Bolore." explained René.

"On my way now," affirmed Hernandez. "Tika, when Onyx comes down, have him carry Golic to the Enforcer and put him in the medical bay. Even though he only has one arm, he can still carry him. Then we'll all take a look at feeds from the surveillance cameras."

"Understood, Captain," answered Tika. Captain Hernandez started to walk to the Enforcer.

Bryna waited patiently for Onyx to finish the data upload. She received a call on her wrist communicator from Javal and patched it through.

"What do you want, blue man?" Bryna asked in boredom.

"Ah, blue man. That's original," noted Javal sarcastically. "I'd like it if you could hack the database for info on this casino's shields, if at all possible."

"Sure." Affirmed Bryna. "Onyx has established a link to Treasure Planet's server systems, I can use that link to find the data you want. I'll send it to you when the download is complete. Is that it?"

"Yes, thank you."

Bryna closed the established link and started working on her wrist communicator. She typed in the words "shields" and let her wrist device get to work. She waited for a few minutes before the download completed and she sent it to Javal immediately.

Finally, Onyx started to move. "Upload completed. We are to deliver this information to Captain Hernandez and the rest of the crew for obser--"

"Just one thing though." interrupted Bryna. "What if we just watched it right now, just you and me? I'm curious if Jaffar did it or not."

"He did commit the crime. However, he did not do it intentionally."

"What do you mean?"

"I can not inform technical expert Bryna Stoli until direct orders given by Captain Miguel Hernandez, at which time, I will--"

"Stop talking, I can see the end to this discussion already. Let's just rendezvous with Hernandez and the rest of them."

Onyx nodded slightly in agreement as he and Bryna left the room to go back downstairs.

Bolore was bound hand and foot to his metal chair. Other than the chair, everything else in the eight by six foot room was white. He knew this was an attempt to scare and break him so that he'd give up secrets. He looked up to see René Anukis standing over him, looking angry and intimidating. He smirked as Captain Hernandez walked in and looked from René to Voltory Bolore.

René Anukis moved behind Bolore as Captain Hernandez stood in front of their prisoner. Bolore smirked as he recognized their attempt to scare him by surrounding him. He'd done it to others himself.

"I'm sorry, Captain, but do you really think this is going to scare me?" inquired Bolore sarcastically.

"We're asking the questions, Bolore. Not you," came the voice from behind him.

"Right," Bolore sarcastically agreed as his smile grew wider. "I know what you are, all of you. You're Constables. You're the soldiers and scientists that work for the Flow Council. And the Flow Council has rules, I know them well. You don't even have any jurisdiction to be here. Under Flow Council Law, I have law and jurisdiction to this moon to which I have legally purchased…"

"Those rules won't provide any protection here," informed Captain Hernandez in a calm and collected tone.

"What?" Bolore squinted his eyes in slight confusion.

"Take a look at us, Bolore," ordered Hernandez. "Do we look like we're in Constable issued armor and uniforms to you?"

Bolore raised an eyebrow as he started to wonder what Hernandez was getting at.

"Do we look like we follow their rules or are restricted by their regulations?" Hernandez continued.

"You—you can't do this. You can't hold me and I don't have to answer without my…" Bolore's eyes widened as he realized that the situation may be much more serious than he thought.

René interrupted. "I don't think you were listening. We can do this. Because we don't operate under Flow Council Law. There are no rules. No regulations. Just you in restraints and us with guns."

"This—this is a pathetic attempt." Bolore blurted in nervousness. "You can't do this to me. I know you can't."

"Bolore, do you remember who was on my crew?" asked Hernandez coldly. "Do you know who Bryna Stoli is?"

"By reputation."

"Then you should know that she would never be with Constables or the Flow Council willingly. The Constables and the Flow Council would have put her in prison, right? I mean, she's murdered dozens, maybe even hundreds across the galaxy. So why isn't she in prison?"

Bolore's mouth started to tremble as Hernandez continued. "I'll tell you why. Because she's on something else. Something where we work outside of Constable and Flow Council jurisdictions. I even have an Eliminator as part of my crew. One that isn't connected to the Hive Mind. This crew doesn't have to follow any rules. We make our own. And my rule right now is to get you talking by any means necessary. Now, what do you have to tell me?"

Captain Hernandez pulled out his pistol and put it to Bolore's head. Bolore's eyes opened with intensity, his teeth gritted, his nostrils flared with desperation to save himself.

"I was given a great deal of money, resources, and research development for my casino in order to drug random employees of

Treasure Planet with Red Rage. I started with my lower paid staff, you know the ones who couldn't affect that much if they had bad reactions. Well, they wouldn't affect anything important."

René rolled her eyes at Hernandez as she became frustrated with Bolore's statement.

"I figured that was all this group, or organization or whatever wanted. Tests. On whoever. But then they demanded that I did it to people who were in the casino too. They called it social tests. To see if it could stay in their system and not have any side effects. But the kid, the ambassador's kid, he killed one of my agents. A woman who was supposed to monitor his blood level but instead, he, he had a spike in his adrenaline. He killed her."

"And you thought that you could get a ransom?" Hernandez inquired.

"I thought 'Why not?', right?" Bolore responded.

"Where is your employer now? This one with so much money?" René wondered.

"I don't know. He stopped contact as soon as the Ambassador's boy was in our custody," Bolore answered.

"You mean when you kidnapped him," René stated aggressively.

Bolore smiled and laughed in fear.

"Yes, I'm a bad, bad man. I've done bad things. Put me away. Can you pull this gun away from my head now?" Bolore asked as looked toward Hernandez.

Hernandez looked up at René. René looked at her pulse scanner to know if Bolore was lying. René gave Hernandez a nod to let him know that Bolore was, in fact, telling the truth.

Captain Hernandez got up and signaled for René to follow him. The two of them left the interrogation room and waited for the door to automatically shut before they started talking.

"That was easy," stated René. "Your file didn't mention anything of having any training in interrogation methods, Captain. Where did you learn how to do that?" Hernandez shrugged.

"When you go through rough patches, you learn how to get the answers you need," responded the Captain.

René nodded with a smile as the Captain's wrist device started beeping. Hernandez pulled his wrist device close to his mouth.

"Go ahead," he answered.

"Sir, this is Bryna. Onyx has recovered the data, and he's carrying Golic on his shoulders back to the ship. The rest of the crew is coming aboard with us. Golic will be put into the medical bay. Everyone else is ready to view the surveillance tape. Tika in particular is pretty curious about it."

"Understood, we'll meet you in the debriefing room soon. Captain Hernandez, out."

The Captain turned off his wrist device and looked at René's expression of disgust.

"Everything okay, Anukis?" Hernandez asked cautiously.

"Everything will be okay when that freak gets off our ship."

Hernandez frowned with displeasure.

"What is your problem with him, exactly?"

"It's not just him, it's all Elementals. Freaks who have the power to kill with a single thought. The rest of us require weapons or armaments to do that kind of damage, but they can just toss us aside like we're insects. I don't see how you can be okay with them."

"They're flesh and blood, not freaks or monsters like you make them out to be. And I think that Golic is a good man, even if he seems a bit… under the weather at the moment."

"I'll just be happy when he's off the ship, Captain."

Hernandez looked away from René and nodded.

"Do you know what you're going to do about Bryna yet?" René continued.

"No. She has been disobeying orders, acting recklessly, but to be honest… she helped each and every mission. I don't know what to do about it."

"Just because she did actions that happened to benefit the

mission this time, doesn't mean that her actions won't blow it all to hell next time. She doesn't always know best and there won't always be something she can just fight, hack, or use brute force against. Her arrogance and recklessness is liable to get someone killed. We need to attend to that."

Hernandez nodded in agreement as he looked René Anukis in the eye.

"And you need to attend to your problem to Elementals. Your hatred and mistrust of them is liable to get someone killed. You know it, I know it. Work on it."

René lowered her eyebrows and closed her eyes at Hernandez in irritation. Capt. Hernandez's focus did not falter as René started to show signs of aggressiveness. The two Constable's wrist devices interrupted their glares at each other. They both pulled their devices closed to their mouths.

"This is Captain Hernandez, go ahead."

"Captain, it's Tika. We're ready in the debriefing room."

Hernandez smiled, happy that something was going right, even if it was something as simple as his crew going to the debriefing room.

"Alright, how's Golic doing?" inquired Hernandez.

"He is stable but he's refusing pain killers and any type of medication that would assist with his discomfort. I'll be able to get him on his feet and he'll be okay physically, but I won't lie, I'm concerned with his current mental state. That Acer seems to have done a number on him."

"Understood," replied Hernandez. "René and I will be in the debriefing room momentarily."

"Affirmative."

René and Hernandez decided to put their differences aside and turned to walk toward the debriefing room.

The remaining crew sat around the debriefing room's table, waiting for Captain Hernandez and René Anukis.

Bryna sat impatiently as she wanted to know if Jaffar was guilty.

Javal was looking through the hacked shield schematics on his wrist device. He was entranced with the blueprints and layouts of the casino's shielding. Being an engineer, Javal couldn't help but love thinking about every single component of the blueprints.

Aiden sat in his chair with his eyes wide open. His body was relaxed as his hands were behind his head, but his mind couldn't help but go to dark places.

Onyx sat in his chair patiently, awaiting orders.

Tika was checking Javal's vital signs on her wrist device.

Jaffar sat nervously, as his entire body started twitching as he knew what he'd see on the screen that will most likely shock the entire room. He killed a woman and the stress of viewing this video made him start to sweat.

Finally, Hernandez and René walked into the room. Bryna turned to see them.

"Good, you're here," Bryna exclaimed. "Let's watch the surveillance tape."

"Onyx," announced Captain Hernandez as he nodded. "Play all relevant tapes pertaining to Jaffar's accused crime in chronological order."

"Yes, Captain," replied Onyx. "Though it should be noted for the record that Jaffar has admitted to the crimes monitored on the surveillance cameras."

Onyx then closed his eyes for a few seconds. As he opened them, they started glowing red. Suddenly, the large plasma screen near the debriefing room table, a light showing the surveillance camera's footage came up.

The first footage showed a prostitute at a gambling table, talking up Jaffar as Onyx announced the tape.

"Time of day: 11:13 P.M. Location: Gambling tables. Surveillance camera 6 recording. Beginning tape."

Onyx kept his cold expression and his glowing red eyes as the rest of the crew watched the surveillance start to play.

125

Jaffar smiled as he talked to the prostitute. They both talked politely as she started to rub his shoulders. Jaffar calmly and politely tried to get her to back away. It seemed that the prostitute walked away from Jaffar, in an attempt to later get him comfortable.

"Surveillance Camera 4 recording," announced Onyx. The angle shifted as the prostitute walked over to the bar. She ordered a drink and waited for the bartender to give it to her. The bartender seemed to be in on the operation, seeing as he responded simply with nods and served the prostitute a drink without asking for a tab or money for the drink. The prostitute gave him a nod, and signaled him to walk away.

The prostitute looked behind her to see if anyone was looking and pulled a vial containing glowing red liquid.

"Red Rage," stated Tika. "Onyx, pause the tape."

Onyx looked to the Captain for approval. Hernandez gave him a slight nod to make sure it was alright.

Tika looked to Jaffar. "Jaffar? You said that you were aggressive during the prostitute incident?"

Jaffar looked down at the ground in discomfort as he thought back on his bad memory.

"Yes," he affirmed.

"Uncontrollably aggressive?" Tika continued.

"Yes," Jaffar confessed, and Hernandez was intrigued.

"What are you getting at, Tika?" wondered Hernandez.

"Do you remember what I told you about Red Rage on our last mission, Captain?" asked Tika.

"Vaguely. Some kind of drug that affects aggression, right? And is usually used to…" Hernandez paused. "Bolore just said that the prostitute tried to seduce Jaffar. Could Red Rage be used for that?"

Tika nodded. "Technically, yes. It can drive some to be more sexually active. It changes from species to species, however. Some races like, well, Javal's would not feel the same effects."

"Could you tell me why my race wouldn't feel the same effects?" Javal asked, curious that he and his race were mentioned.

"Your race doesn't have sex drives the way most races do," began Tika. "They also don't have the same aggressive behavior caused by hormones. It's probably due to your partial amphibian nature."

Javal nodded as Tika continued. "But most forms of higher evolved species throughout the galaxy have developed in fairly similar ways. It's why most from other planets can breed without complication. But, I doubt that this girl used just Red Rage, it's probable that she mixed it with something else to boost Jaffar's sex drive."

"Like what?" inquired Hernandez. Tika shrugged.

"I don't know, there's a lot of them. Which one she used probably doesn't matter. But it had to be one that wouldn't mix with either the Red Rage or the drink and accidentally kill Jaffar."

Tika stood for a moment while thinking.

"Onyx, continue playing the tape," ordered Hernandez politely.

"Yes, Captain Hernandez," obeyed Onyx.

The tape continued as the prostitute started pouring the red rage into a drink. She was careful to put a certain amount. Just as she was about to check and see if someone was watching, a customer bumped into her. The jostle caused her arm to shake, adding a slight bit more Red Rage into the drink.

"Aha," exclaimed Tika. "An overdose of Red Rage. Probably what made Jaffar be so aggressive. Curious to see if the Red Rage while mixed in the drink forced a longer period of delay to aggression than usual. I should look into Red Rage more. Maybe…"

"Tika, you're getting into your head again," Hernandez interrupted.

Tika smiled and nodded in acknowledgement.

The crew continued to watch the tape as the prostitute offered the drink to Jaffar. Jaffar smiled and took a drink of the alcoholic beverage spiked with Red Rage. He set it down and continued to gamble. Tika pointed out when his pupils started to dilate slightly and he started sweating and smiling. Jaffar then picked up the drink and started drinking more of it in an addicted manner.

Hernandez remembered as the guard named Kenkias whose role Onyx assumed had the same effects.

"Hmm, immediate addiction," noted Tika. "Interesting."

The crew watched as Jaffar saw every moment in slight horror and disgust. Hernandez knew what had transpired next and felt no more need to keep watching.

"Onyx?" asked Hernandez, trying to get the Eliminator's attention.

"Yes, Captain?" responded Onyx, his eyes going back to normal.

"Does Jaffar's story corroborate with the remaining security cameras?"

Onyx nodded.

"Then I feel no more need to watch anymore of this, turn it off."

Onyx once again turned his eyes red cutting out the large visual screen before he reverted them back to normal.

"I think it was a good mission, all things considered," noted Javal.

"Oh definitely," agreed Bryna in sadistic happiness as she remembered Yannis being killed.

Hernandez thought to himself for a moment.

"Shield data has been recovered from the casino, Jaffar was rescued, Bolore was taken into custody… even if the Flow Council won't find sufficient evidence to hold him. As for the Acer and the armed casino forces they were defeated," said Hernandez in agreement to Javal's verdict. "Yes, it was a good mission. Good work out there… most of you, anyway."

Hernandez looked at Bryna who rolled her eyes. Then Hernandez looked at René who stared right back at him. They both looked away.

"Everyone return to your posts," ordered René.

"Agreed." Hernandez nodded. "Jaffar, we'll deliver you to your home world Lylax. I'm sure your father will be relieved to see you again. You won't be charged with anything, that's for sure. And our reports will vouch for you."

Hernandez's reassurance seemed to have little effect on Jaffar. He simply nodded and looked to the ground in slight shame.

"Now, everyone return to your posts. Tika, I want you to check on Golic every fifteen minutes."

"Yes, Captain," accepted Tika.

"I'll set a course and fly us to Lylax momentarily. Javal, I'd like you to handle the repairs to Onyx's damaged limb."

Hernandez waited as the crew left. When Jaffar finally stood from his chair and walked past the captain, Hernandez put his hand on Jaffar's shoulder.

"It's not your fault, kid. Don't blame yourself," he said. "You saw that you were drugged."

Jaffar nodded, but Hernandez saw that his words were empty to the Ambassador's son. Jaffar left the room like the rest and the captain was left with his thoughts.

"What a truly shitty day to be the Captain of the Enforcer. On top of everyone else's problems that I've already had to deal with, now I've got René and Bryna. Bryna has to learn to trust me somehow and René has to learn to let go of her anger. I wish I had access to their history to know why they're so damn pissed off all the time. Ah, well. Another problem for another day."

The Captain walked out of the debriefing room, hoping that his next mission wouldn't require so much babysitting.

JONATHAN PICCINI

Star Enforcers: Chapter 9

After returning Jaffar to his home world, Lylax, the crew of the Enforcer reported to space dock. The trip to their destination took thirteen hours using faster-than-light Slip Stream technology. The crew needed time to rest and prepare for their next assignment. Everyone hoped the Enforcer would be docked for several days so they could go to their living quarters on the space station to truly stretch out and take in some much needed rest, relaxation, and privacy. The constables had been on the vessel for over a month, and they also needed some time to themselves.

After the thirteen hour journey the Stealth Destroyer class starship reached the space dock. Chalice had been constructed inside an asteroid that orbited the giant planet Primus. The construction took three years to complete, and once operational it was used by both the space authorities and civilians. Mixing the military population with the civilians provided a unique balance. The civilians felt safe on the station because of the military presence and the constables they felt normalcy in their lives when surrounded by non-militant people. The civilian population on the station provided the constables with services and entertainment that made them feel as though they were back on their own home worlds.

The Enforcer approached in cloaked fashion and was finally cleared for docking. The secret location within the asteroid was hidden by a hologram of the rock face covering the doors. The only potential breech was while the doors were open. As the large metal doors parted, the vessel used its thrusters to ease into port. Once the Enforcer passed through the asteroid hologram the cloaking shields morphed the illusion around the outlines of the ship momentarily. The doors closed behind the Enforcer and the cloaking device was disengaged.

René piloted the ship as it passed by the U.S.S. Warlock, the other Stealth Destroyer class ship. The construction to the Warlock would near completion within two months. Some of the

Enforcer's crew observed the construction crews welding and installing circuitry throughout the sister ship.

"I wonder who will be the captain of the Warlock?" René asked as she was lining up the Enforcer with the docking clamps.

"I'm not sure; I have a few names to suggest, but it's too early to tell. Whoever it is, though, I hope the crew has an easier time working together than we have," Captain Hernandez replied with a hint of sarcasm.

"Hmm, yeah we'll see. This crew has not had a casualty yet. Not bad for six months I have to say," René rebounded with a sly smile.

"Dually noted, Lieutenant. I'll pass that bit of optimism to the newly assigned captain of that ship," Hernandez replied as he tapped the communication channel on the armrest of his command chair. "Enforcer crew, prepare for docking."

"Chalice port command, this is the U.S.S. Enforcer, we are in proper alignment to dock. Ready to engage docking clamps," René announced.

The Enforcer was holding position between the arms of a u-shaped structure a few meters larger in width than the vessel. Four docking clamps extended to secure the ship. As the clamps engaged, the Enforcer shook slightly while transferring the weight of the superstructure.

"Docking is complete. Connection tubes engaged to the air locks of the ship. All personnel are secure to disembark," René informed the crew through the ship wide communicator.

"I can't wait to take a nice long shower and relax in my tub back at my apartment," René said while deactivating her pilot station and standing up from her command chair. She looked over to the captain after the large main view screen confirmed deactivation.

"That sounds like a good idea. As for myself I'm going to go over to the promenade and hit the Black Jack Pub. They have a seasonal ale from Melva IV that I heard goes down really smooth with a melted cheese and meat sandwich. After that I'm heading to bed."

"Sounds like a plan," René agreed with a smile.

René's smile was short-lived and diminished instantly as she saw the person who emerged onto the bridge in a metal wheel chair. Tika was following her patient who refused to have her wheel him around the ship. The wheel chair was not motorized and Golic used his arms to power his transportation.

Golic faced Captain Hernandez and bowed his head in respect. "Captain, before I depart I would like to thank you and your crew for your hospitality."

He glanced momentarily over to the lieutenant. He knew it would annoy René and Golic felt it would give him the last word. As they say in life, kill your adversary with kindness. The lieutenant in returned grunted and left the bridge to go pack her things before she could earn a reprimand.

"Is she always like that?" Golic asked.

"She has her moments. The lieutenant is a good person but she has issues with Elementals. But anyhow I thank you Golic for your help on this assignment. I hope your injuries heal swiftly," Hernandez bowed in return.

"Thank you captain. And thank you Doctor Tika, for your care," Golic bowed his head to Tika and she returned the gesture.

Departing the bridge, Golic saw by the same three Elumeni that saw him off before the mission with the Enforcer crew waiting to welcome him. Golic did not say a word to the three, but rolled his wheel chair past them with disappointment and anger on his face. He felt like a failure since he had been defeated by Solara. That burden would encourage him to train harder so the next time they met he would defeat her and remove her head. But first he had to become mobile, and the micro medical droids would do their work in repairing his legs quickly before deactivating and extracting themselves out of his body.

"How do you think he will recover after this?" Hernandez asked the medical officer after Golic left the bridge.

Tika had mixed emotions in her response. "Golic is a tough character, and he still refuses to take any pain medication. He will make a full recovery physically since the nano medical bots are doing their job in his body. Emotionally, I am afraid he will need counseling. I just hope he doesn't embrace the anger he is feeling."

"I understand where you are coming from. Hopefully he can bury the hatchet, but I feel as though this will not be the last time we'll see him. Well Tika, you can disembark and I will inform the crew of our next assignment after I see Director Tollus tomorrow."

She smiled as she left to pack her belongings from her ship quarters.

The captain was the last crew member to leave the Enforcer after inspecting the ship before the maintenance crew came aboard to restock the ship with new supplies and equipment. He saw all of the constables and the thirty five members of his non militant crew to thank them for a job well done. Hernandez was relieved to see Onyx's arm had been repaired while walking through Javal's workshop. With the proper metals in storage to effectively construct a new arm for the Eliminator, Javal's expertise with mechanics and robotic technology gave him talents to use the tools he had to bring the cybernetics being back to full efficiency. Onyx had never been damaged on a mission before but all was right with the Enforcer as Captain Hernandez left his ship. He stuck to his plan and proceeded to the Black Jack pub to have his much awaited seasonal ale before returning to his living quarters on the space station.

Artificial sunlight dispersed the dark and created a feeling of morning the residents of the Chalice Space Station. The station was on the dark side of the asteroid and shared a similar thrity-six hour orbit around Primus as the Flow Council Moon Integra.

The increasing light caused Miguel Hernandez to wake as the light filled his room. He yawned and stretched out his arms. He removed the blanket from his body, sat up in his bed and crossed his legs. He placed his hands together and closed his eyes to pray to the creator of the universe. Miguel did not follow an established religion, but he thanked the creator each day for another day of life. His mother and father were religious but never forced their children to worship, even though their faith kept the family united. Miguel remembered the words his father spoke, "A family that prays together, stays together."

During Miguel's teenage years he strayed away from his spiritual life and embraced the philosophy of unlawful individuals. He had learned many things from these people, both good and bad. But when he was captured and sentenced to serve in the Constable Academy he had time to think about his life and his situation. By coincidence, he stumbled upon his training director Mintog praying in the dojo area late at night. The trainees had never seen Mintog pray, and he chose to keep his personal life from others. The training director heard someone approaching and realized it was his student Miguel by the way he walked. Mintog invited the young cadet over to pray with him. At first Miguel hesitated, but he decided it was time to get his life in order. Each day following that chance encounter, Miguel always tried to pray if time allowed. Today was like any other as he continued his daily devotional.

He looked out of his window and watched the citizens of the station in their daily activities. Residents were taking the train tubes to their place of work while others jogged as part of their exercise routine. A few of them slept in as Miguel wanted to do. A great benefit of being in a controlled habitat environment was one world never having to worry about rain. The watering systems took care of all the various vegetation. If Miguel wanted rain, all had had to do was step into his bathroom and take a shower using the rainfall mode and play a thunder soundtrack over the speaker system.

Once his shower was complete Miguel started to brush his teeth. Hearing a chime in the living room, he knew Director Tollus was trying to establish visual communication.

"Oh man, what does he want so early in the morning? It better be important," Hernandez said as he placed his hands on his hips.

Miguel wrapped a towel around himself and quickly walked into his living room.   The visual call alert chimed once again.

"Computer, patch call through; security code 3474."

The forty-five inch plasma screen came alive and displayed the Space Constable insignia. The horizontal infinity sign with a star in the open area of the symbol, and a row of four stars running verticaly down the center of the icon faded as the computer acknowledged, **"Security code approved."**

The view screen was replaced with the image of Director Tollus with his purple face, short horns, and blue eyes sitting at his office desk in full uniform. He raised his bushy black eyebrows in surprise.

"Oh a little informal aren't we?" came the director's voice from the speakers surrounding the gathering area of Miguel's apartment.

"I was just getting out of the shower," Miguel chuckled as he gestured toward his blue towel. "So what can I do for you this fine morning?"

"The Flow Council has called a meeting for this morning. They have specifically requested Lieutenant Anukis and you to appear before them at 0-nine-thirty. You have two hours.

"We have never appeared before The Council before in regards to a mission. Is it really that important?"

"I'm told that it is of the utmost importance," Tollus replied sternly.

Miguel exhaled. "Alright, René and I will be there on time."

On the planet moon Integra, the Flow Council gathered at the usual time for meetings and debates at the Great Hall of Aura. The Great Hall was a fifty story building that had the appearance of a gigantic torch. What made the vertical cylinder truly unique from was the skin of bronze metal plating fashioned to look like flames. The entrance of the Great Hall surrounded by mirror coated shatter resistant windows which gave this gathering place a magnificent appearance.

Lt. Anukis and Capt. Hernandez entered through the tall doors and were ushered through the security scanners by fully armored guards. As the pair looked down the eight foot long narrow passageway they could see additional security guards that carrying highly lethal weapons. They felt intimidated just looking at them.

As René walked down the hallway, the sensors embedded in the walls showed her skeletal structure and the outline of her skin, which was normal procedure. But what alerted the security personnel was the glock pistol in a holster that she was carrying behind her back which was covered by the red and black leather jacket that she was wearing. The captain had his pair of trusty pistols strapped to side holsters hidden under his black unbuckled denim jacket.

Four armored guards, ready to take action at a moment's notice, stood at the end of the scanning equipment with their weapons pointed upwards at the ceiling. Upon reaching the guards, the constables reached into their pockets to retrieve their badges. Before they could pass between the guards, a pair of individuals dressed in formal two piece suits stepped forward from behind the enforcers; their sashes went over the left shoulder and wrapped around their midsection.

"You two can wave your badges all you like, but no weapons are allowed in the Great Hall. Protocol requires you to check in your weapons," the Elumeni wearing the white sash stated as he extended his hands to relieve the constables of their weapons.

"Oh, really," René huffed and placed her hands on her hips. She stared at the wind elemental's eyes, seeing only a black pinpoint of a pupil surrounded by a white iris.

"Yeah, really. Don't think for a moment that those badges will get you any special privileges here. So give up the weapons or there will be constable soufflé on the lunch menu today," the Elumeni said as his eyes glowed red, matching his sash. The flame appearing in his right hand lent weight to his words.

"Hey ease down, we were invited here by The Council and Director Tollus. It's too damn early in the day to get into an altercation. Lieutenant, relinquish your weapon, and do it now," Hernandez ordered as he slowly handed over his pair of silver pistols, Chaos and Mayhem, to the wind elemental. The captain knew these Elumenis were just doing their jobs. The fire elemental, however, was being a wise ass, and looking for any reason to start a fight. René unhappily grabbed the firearm from her back holster and gave it to the nearest armored guard and not the Elumeni; she did not want to give them any personal satisfaction.

"Very good Captain Hernandez, The Council awaits your arrival," the wind master grinned.

When he met René's eyes his grin turned into a smirk. The lieutenant's reaction was a huge smile knowing that she pissed the wind elemental off.

"Fine, fine, just remember one thing. I want my pistols back; if anything happens to them, if they even have one scratch in any way shape or form, your ass is mine. And afterwards whatever is left over I will leave for her," Hernandez retorted and walked towards the council hall as René followed.

"He really thinks he's some kind of bad ass, doesn't he?" the fire elemental commented as he strolled over to his fellow Elumeni after extinguishing the flame in his hand.

"Honestly, Captain Miguel Hernandez is not a person to be messed with. Not only was he trained by Commandant Mintog, he was one of his best students. No one else has come close to his skills. Since I have to do background checks on all visitors that are invited here, I can confirm that he is as tough as he says he is. And every member of his crew holds an elite status," the wind master concluded.

"He just looks like a typical constable to me. And his lieutenant, I would like to kick her ass," The fire master commented.

"Leave them be, if you challenge the captain or anyone on his crew, you do so at your own risk," the wind master recommended as he walked away and carefully secured the constables' weapons making sure that he treated them gently.

The two constables arrived at a closed two-story door controlled by the building's central computer.

"Miguel, what in the Architect's name are we doing here? Normally when anyone has to appear before The Council it is by visual communication, not in person," René asked, trying to understand the reason behind this odd request.

"I don't even know myself. Director Tollus just ordered that you and I had to be here at O' nine- thirty hours for an important session," he answered.

"It sure better be important or I'm going to give Tollus a piece of my mind," René lightly ranted.

"Yeah, you and me both." Hernandez agreed and stood still at the main door.

"Please wait for retina scan before entering," the central computer spoke and shot a harmless red beam into their eyes. **"Security access approved. Welcome to the Great Hall of Aura Captain Hernandez and Lieutenant Anukis."**

As the huge bronze door automatically opened, Director Tollus was there to greet them. He had a serious look on his purple face that indicated that the matter truly did deserve the constables' attention.

"Thank you both for showing up on time. The Council has been deliberating before the two of you arrived," Tollus told them briefly.

"About what; and why does it concern us?" the captain asked his superior.

"The Council will inform you," Tollus assured them.

"I hope someone does, they are totally ruining my day off," René mumbled.

Tollus did not bother to look as her. She was Miguel's problem, not his. Dealing with Miguel was hard enough for him as it was, since the captain was very unconventional in his methods. Still, Tollus appreciated that Hernandez successfully completed his missions.

"This way, please. The Council shall address the two of you. And be on your best behavior," Tollus pleaded.

"Oh please; there's nothing to worry about. I have more class than most of these bureaucrats put together," René spouted after sucking her teeth. Miguel just raised his eyebrows at the comment, and the director shrugged his shoulders and shook his head.

The trio proceeded down a dark tunnel that was illuminated with an abundance of white light at the end of the walkway. Chatter echoed through the hall by the people on the other side. There didn't appear to be any arguing, just a soft form of talk amongst the group.

Director Tollus emerged first from the entrance tunnel with the constables right behind him. Upon seeing their invited guests the chattering stopped almost immediately from the array of ambassadors and their entourage from different reaches of the galaxy.

The Great Hall was a circular forum two hundred feet in diameter. The ten-story high ceiling disappeared into the darkness, but the floor of black and white marble was clearly visible. The illumination of the Great Hall came from lights at the base of thirty-one large pillars. The thirty pillars surrounding the room were fifteen feet tall and topped by a circular platform with four chairs. The pillar in the center of the Great Hall towered over the other pillars. It's single chair chair belonged to the Monitor. The Monitor's pewter colored gavel blended into his long grey robes. Raising his hand, he banged the gavel onto a black metal slab and called the hall to order.

The Monitor stood up began to stroke his white Fu-Man-Chu mustache. The Monitor's large yellow eyes stood out from his green reptilian skin. He began to speak.

"The Great Hall of Aura calls Captain Miguel Hernandez and Lieutenant René Anukis of the Constable ship U.S.S. Enforcer to be asked about the possible threat of the drug epidemic Red Rage and its effects on our galactic society. Director Tollus of Constable Headquarters is also recognized and present for this discussion session."

Miguel cleared his throat before speaking. "Honorable ambassadors, especially my father Ambassador Santos Hernandez, we stand here before you today ready to share whatever information we have about the drug Red Rage. Please know that Constable Tika Shamari, our medical doctor, has very little knowledge of where it comes from, or how it affects individual beings. Even now, she continues to evaluate all she can to learn as much as possible about this drug."

Even though he addressed the entire Flow Council, he looked at his father on one of the thirty platforms. The remaining chairs held his assistant and two personal guards. His father nodded in approval of the level of respect his son showed to The Council.

"Captain Hernandez, the Flow Council wants to know if you have any leads as to where the drugs may be coming from?" The Monitor asked.

"No, I'm afraid not. We have stopped a few big shipments of the drug into our protective sectors of space during the last couple of weeks, but none of the captured prisoners know who is supplying the drug," Hernandez honestly said.

"How about that crooked casino owner Voltory Bolore? Does he have some kind of connection to all of this?" Ambassador Larrott spoke as his son Jaffar sat beside his father.

"There isn't much more we can get out of Voltory. The only worth-while person we could have questioned was the prostitute but she's dead, unfortunately. This is through no fault of Jaffar.

He was an unwilling pawn in this scheme," René informed the group.

"Serves that whore right for what she did to my son," Ambassador Larrott shouted and slammed his fist on the armrest of his chair.

"Father, please. She's dead now we don't need to add any further disgrace to the incident," Jaffar said trying to calm his father's rage.

The lights at the base of a pillar turned red. The Monitor turned toward the pillar and bowed to the ambassador. "Ambassador. You have signaled that you have something important for our discussion. I invite you to share with the rest of The Council."

The ambassador, D.A.X., was a thinly built Eliminator that preferred his natural mechanical form rather than cover his endoskeleton with bio skin. The other Eliminators seated near D.A.X. appeared to be bodyguards, as their muscular endoskeleton closely resembled Onyx.

"I speak for the Matrix Collective. We have looked over the data from the constables' last two assignments. It appears as though the individuals that should be questioned are the mercenaries. These outlaws have been present in both instances. Observations would suggest sending the crew of the U.S.S. Enforcer to interrogate the mercenaries on their home world of Scar. That is where we will possibly know the true location of where the drug Red Rage is being produced, and it may possibly be produced on the planet itself in secrecy."

The lights of a second pillar changed to red. A female ambassador, resembling a lioness, bowed to D.A.X and The Mointor. "Ambassador D.A.X.'s theory sounds very wise. The mercenaries I believe may hold the key to eradicating the drug epidemic. They may even be producing the drug themselves. Mercenaries and terrorists never talk, so I would doubt that they will reveal who is behind it. My sector has been constantly in turmoil once Scar, which was originally a penal colony, became the home planet and breeding ground for mercenaries and terrorists. To save my sector, I would not even mind using the Solar Sword to wipe out the entire solar system and obliterating most of them once and for all."

As the volume increased in the arena, Ambassador Hernandez pushed his red attention button to speak to The Council. He stood, but waited patiently to be recognized. There was very little order as the talking grew in volume with no clear order.

The Monitor banged the pewter gable, "Ambassador Hernandez has the floor."

The chattering ceased as everyone looked to Ambassador Santos Hernandez. Miguel was curious to hear what his father had to say.

"I would not recommend using the Solar Sword in such an abusive and reckless act. That weapon is a resource that should only be used as a last resort. Also, sending the crew of the Enforcer would place them in a volatile situation that would be highly dangerous," Santos expressed his concerns as a wise council member and as a father.

Miguel was gratified to see that his father was truly concerned about his safety as well as the people under his command. The other ambassadors were not interested in the safety of one ship when others could take its place. His ship the Enforcer was considered a testing project for problem constables who needed to be dragged through the burning coals of duty before being seen as a valued worth to society.

"If I may speak?" the head constable spoke aloud amongst the chattering.

The Monitor pushed a button on his control panel that returned the three pillar lights to white. A second button surrounded Tollus with red light from beneath the marble floor. .

"Director Tollus you may speak," The Monitor acknowledged.

"Thank you Monitor; I must agree with Ambassador Hernandez. To send the crew of the Enforcer to planet Scar would be suicide. There must be another way."

The red light faded from around Tollus and returned to Ambassador D.A.X.'s pillar. "Director Tollus, your emotions along with those of Ambassador Santos, should not be part of this discussion. The Enforcer crew has been equipped with the most advanced technology our worlds have to offer. It is most logical for the crew of the Enforcer to effectively infiltrate and extract whatever information is needed to stop the production of the drug. According to its charter, the Enforcer and crew members are the property of the Flow Council and at our disposal."

The hard honest truth was finally revealed. It hurt Captain Hernandez to have his suspicions confirmed. The crew of the Enforcer was a rag tag of fugitives and offenders who were at the Flow Council's whim. René hated the fact that that damn electronic ambassador was right as she slightly bit her bottom lip in frustration. This crew was under contract to serve five years on the Enforcer to make amends for their past unlawful crimes.

The gavel fell once again onto the metal plate three times, and The Monitor spoke, "All ambassadors we have heard the situations and the possible solutions. The Great Hall must come to a vote on either to dispatch the Solar Sword to obliterate the Scar solar system or send the U.S.S. Enforcer on this mission to interrogate and pursue leads in the location of these drugs. All in favor of using the Solar Sword switch your pillars to red. Those in favor of the U.S.S. Enforcer mission keep your pillar lights remaining white."

Pressing a large button on his console, The Monitor plunged the arena into darkness.

Morenko was in a large club on Integra. Mostly meant for young men and women who wanted to cut loose, they had the opportunity to be stupid, angry, and dance and forget about their problems. Flashing lights and pulsing music littered the room.

The club was mostly filled with the staff of the U.S.S. Enforcer. Each of them doing different things to cut loose. Their captain who they were forced to show respect to was nowhere to be found, so they felt a need to scream, shout, move their bodies, and put burning alcohol down their throats.

Morenko sat at a small metal table by himself and stared at two of his fellow "Constables" dancing with each other. A Torrie woman, with her hair in a Mohawk, was having her neck bitten by a human with his hair in dreadlocks. They were both feeling each other's bodies, and the human's neck was being scratched. Blood was dripping on the woman's fingertips, and the human just grunted in response, uncaring about the pain, almost enjoying it.

"Animalistic, aren't they?" a female voice said to Morenko. Morenko looked behind him and saw a red skinned woman with long, black hair. Her hair was tied into a ponytail, to showcase her entire face. The woman looked somewhat middle aged, but had a look about her, that seemed to suggest she was an energetic, very capable person.

"You want me to buy you a drink?" Morenko wondered. The woman laughed.

"No, I'd never want you to buy me a drink." She stated. Morenko looked to her black dress, and noticed a Constable insignia on the left side of her chest.

"Who are you, Constable?" Morenko asked.

"'Who are you, sir?' is what you meant to say," the woman replied to him. Morenko's eyebrow rose. "I'm your superior. You're a Constable now. So you answer to me."

Morenko knew a basic chain of command; he knew how to follow orders when someone above him spoke. So Morenko nodded, and let the woman speak.

"Yes, sir." Morenko said to her.

"You weren't born on the Torrie homeworld, were you?" she asked, watching as Morenko shook his head. "You see, the Torrie follow Gods. They cut their hair in different ways in order to signify the God they follow." Pointing to Morenko's fellow

Torrie on the dance floor she continued, "That woman over there? She follows Gonz, the Goddess of War."

The Constable in the black dress looked back at Morenko. Morenko stared at the woman's face, noticing a faint scar running down her forehead, then looked at her eyes.

"I don't follow their Gods," Morenko said. The woman laughed again.

"Obviously not. Your head is shaved. If you were on their world, they would leave you alone completely, but only if you followed your God, and did nothing. Affected no one. And were not part of their world," the woman described. "I think that God is called Fink."

Morenko shrugged, not caring about what she was saying.

"Why did you sit here, sir?" he asked, sipping his gin on the rocks.

"Because you aren't part of the Enforcer, not really," the woman stated. "And you don't hold allegiance to anyone. You don't care about the Mystic Seas, the Torrie, the Flow Council, or this new crew you're forced to serve with. Really, you'd like money. You'd like to be free. And I can give you your freedom."

"Can you now?" Morenko wondered. "How is that, exactly?"

"You're a grunt, working the bottom of the ship. You guard it, wait for something to happen, and never fire your gun. Because that's all that Hernandez trusts you to do. Which is smart, to not trust you."

"He gave me a gun. I can do a lot with a gun. He must trust me somewhat." Morenko replied.

"He doesn't care about what you could do. Miguel Hernandez, Bryna Stoli, René Anukis, that free-willed android, they'd destroy you. The android alone wouldn't even need a weapon. And Hernandez doesn't fear death, because he doesn't appreciate life."

The woman allowed her words to sink into Morenko's brain. "So no, he doesn't trust you, he just gave you a gun, and he knows that if you did something stupid, they could kill you easily. But we don't want you to use the gun on them, we want you to do something much, much better."

"And what is that, exactly?" Morenko asked.

"We don't care about the lower staff," the woman said. "Try your best not to kill the seven top personnel. Especially Miguel Hernandez and Aiden Dakar. If they're killed, that could be a large problem."

"Why would I commit what is essentially suicide for you?" Morenko wondered. "All alone, fighting against seven unstoppable killers? I've watched them. They fight without weakness."

"Money. Freedom. They're glorious things."

Morenko's head tilted, still listening to this woman's words.

"How long do you think you'll survive after your five year sentence? What will you do? Be a mercenary again? Get almost killed by Constables again?"

Morenko looked down, remembering his past failures.

"No, you need our help."

"I'm listening," Morenko replied, with a desparate tone in his voice.

"We have something planned. You probably won't have to fight against the seven of them, but even the best of plans can fall apart," the woman said, grabbing Morenko's drink on the table and slowly drinking all of it.

"What am I supposed to do, exactly, and when?" Morenko wondered.

The woman finished his gin and gently set it down. "Keep your Affix tuned into the public communications, when you hear the phrase come in from a distress beacon or some other call from outside the Enforcer saying 'We need assistance. Our crew is scattered, our people are dissipated, and they're inside, and we can't get away,' destroy the slipstream drive, preventing the Enforcer from escaping, and then take the nearest shuttle you can out of there."

The woman took out a lighter and a cigar. She put the cigar in her mouth, and calmly lit it, sucking in air in order to keep the cigar burning.

"Give me your wrist," she ordered.

"Why?" Morenko asked, confused.

"Because the other traitors will need to recognize you," The woman stated.

Morenko understood, and gave her his wrist. The woman took the cigar out of her mouth, and put the burning end onto Morenko's skin, singeing it. Morenko gritted his teeth and exhaled in pain as the heat seared his skin. When the cigar was finally extinguished by Morenko's skin, the woman blew on his wrist, wisping the bits of cigar away, and then set the cigar next to Morenko's glass of water.

"Why are you doing this?" Morenko wondered.

"Because the Enforcer is getting too close," the woman answered.

Morenko was confused, but then realized, he was getting money, he was going to be free, he didn't care what would happen aside from that.

"Keep the cigar. It's good, if you can get past the fact that I burnt your skin with it," she said as she stood and left.

PHOE-NIX NEBULA

Star Enforcers: Chapter 10

Ambassador D.A.X turned his light white immediately while at the same time the Ambassador that represented the sector closest to Scar turned her light red. The illumination gradually returned to the room as most pillars white had white lights again. A few pillars were turning red. Miguel's father stood while his pillar remained unlit.

The Monitor looked at him directly.

"Ambassador Hernandez, you are not making a decision. Do you wish to recluse yourself?" inquired the Ambassador.

Santos put his hand on his chin and thought to himself. He then looked to every other Ambassador who mostly had kept their lights white. Santos closed his eyes in slight pain, as he knew that his son would have to dive in head first to Scar, one of the most dangerous places in their galaxy. He then looked to the Monitor in discomfort.

"I might as well, but it doesn't matter much, does it? It seems as The Council has made its decision." stated Ambassador Hernandez.

"Indeed," Ambassador D.A.X. agreed. D.A.X. had not realized it by his comment, but Santos felt somewhat angered by the statement. It was almost as if D.A.X. was being sarcastic or somehow insulting him. Santos took a deep breath and let the feeling go, knowing that D.A.X. would not comprehend the emotion that he had accidentally caused.

"With Ambassador Santos Hernandez's recusal, the majority of the Flow Council favors sending the crew of the U.S.S. Enforcer to the mercenary ruled planet of Scar to extract information regarding the Red Rage drug," announced the Monitor.

Santos showed his discomfort and displeasure in the action of the Flow Council on his face, and met the eyes of his son. Miguel looked at his father and gave him a look as if to say "I'll be fine, Dad, don't worry."

"If I may, Monitor," pleaded Miguel.

The Monitor looked down at the Captain.

"Proceed, Captain Hernandez," affirmed the Monitor.

"Thank you, Monitor," stated the Captain. "Our team is strong and we can get the information that is needed. Obviously, from the vote just cast, most of you agree. I understand that a few of you may be skeptical, but we are capable. And if we are wrong, then you may take secondary action. But please, for those who chose for the Solar Sword's use, do not lose faith in my crew's capabilities, or in the capabilities of the Constables themselves. The Solar Sword is a weapon of massive destruction, I do not believe…"

The Monitor interrupted, "If the Captain doesn't have anything regarding the mission to add, I must order that he does not involve himself in weapons politics in the Flow Council meeting room to which he has been given no power."

Miguel understood that he was being rubbed aside and stepped back.

"The U.S.S. Enforcer crew will leave for Scar immediately, and will give any information directly to the Flow Council database. Director Tollus, Captain Hernandez, Lieutenant Anukis, you are all excused."

Tollus gave a slight head nod in respect to the Flow Council. "Thank you, Monitor." Tollus said.

The trio left, all of them with one thing on their mind, the planet Scar. Once outside the Flow Council chambers, Tollus decided he needed to discuss the mission that was ahead.

"This planet is a notorious breeding ground for mercenary factions, bounty hunter groups, and underground terrorist agencies. I hope your crew is ready for it."

Hernandez nodded, "Of course they are. We have Bryna Stoli, I'm certain she knows a thing or two about Scar's facilities and operations.

"We can do this," Ren'e assured her superior.

Tollus smiled in newly found confidence.

"Then the best of luck to you all. Keep me updated," Director Tollus saluted to his two Constables as they returned the salute. Tollus left to go seek out his quarters.

"Let's get out of here, the planet full of ruthless murderers and assassins awaits," stated Hernandez.

René nodded and the two Constables left the way they came in. René stared down the Elementals that watched her every move.

"Your weapons, as promised," stated the wind Elumeni, as he handed Hernandez his silver pistols.

The fire Elumeni handed René her firearm.

"Don't die too quickly now, I'd like an opportunity to test you out myself," antagonized the elemental.

René grunted in frustration, but before she could take action, she felt Hernandez's hand on her shoulder. She turned to see him shaking his head in disapproval. René knew that the captain was right and continued walking. Hernandez and René exited the building, both with the topic of the Elumeni on their mind.

"Listen, back there… not all Elumeni are like that," assured Hernandez.

René raised an eyebrow in skepticism.

"Most of them are more like, well, warrior monks. But Elumeni are rare. Especially after the Eliminator-Elumeni War about sixty years ago, the Flow Council wants to make sure elementals are on their side. Even the arrogant ones."

"They're all arrogant," stated René. "I don't think you get it, Hernandez, because you've been in the thought process of not wanting control over your safety, but I do."

"What's that supposed to mean?"

"I read your file, I know all about you. The only reason you're even a Constable, let alone on the Enforcer, is because your daddy bailed you out of trouble and this was the best alternative."

"My father has nothing to do with my…"

"Please, without the big ambassador, you'd be in prison right now."

Hernandez's nose started to snarl in instinctive anger. "And why are you on this crew, huh?" Hernandez started. "For whatever reason, the Flow Council or Tollus or whoever the hell it is doesn't want me to know your, or damn near anyone's, history. Why did you join the Constables? What makes you so high and mighty?"

"I joined the Constables because I see a point in protecting human lives and those who are endangered by power wielding scum who think they're above the law, like the Elementals."

Hernandez shook his head.

"The Elementals are not our enemy," he pleaded. "I don't know what problems you've had, but you need to get over them. I've had a rough life too, but you don't see me trying to kill every casino owner or back alley thug I see. I've moved on, why can't you?"

René stood and stared at Hernandez in anger and silence. Hernandez realized that his attempt at getting to René was pointless, and that whatever she was going through, was on her, not him.

As the two Constables made their way through the halls, ready to get back to the Enforcer, they saw that someone was waiting for them. A man with red skin, black hair, sporting the Constable insignia tattooed on his neck proudly. He was wearing the uniform of a Flow Council Ambassador.

Captain Hernandez and René knew who he was immediately. Quite possibly one of, if not the most famous, Ambassador in existence, Vas'Kis Sinzo. Vas'Kis looked on Hernandez and René with a glance of disapproval, and yet respect.

"Sir," René stated, as she put her fist to her chest, and tipped her head downwards ever so slightly, while keeping firm eye contact with the legend that stood before her.

"Miguel Hernandez and René Anukis," Vas'Kis Sinzo stated. "I heard what you had to say in there. I was impressed with your drive and admiration in there today."

Miguel nodded. "Thank you, Ambassador." Hernandez responded.

"I simply wish it was put in the right place," Ambassador Sinzo continued.

"I was arguing for the lives of the innocent. I don't see how that could be the wrong place," Hernandez replied.

Sinzo's eyebrows raised slightly in response to the young captain's belief.

"Innocent lives," Vas'Kis stated, reiterating the Captain's words.

"Innocent lives," he repeated. "Innocent lives."

Now with bitterness and discontent in his voice. The Captain and René both easily recognized this, and while both remaining respectful, each of them started to feel uneasy as they gazed upon the grizzled war veteran.

"Is there a problem, Ambassador?" Captain Hernandez wondered, in an almost pointless effort to break his discomfort.

"Yes, Captain. Yes, there is a problem," Sinzo said. "I know you weren't born in a world of chaos and destruction and pain, so you do not understand my anger in why you say the word innocent."

The Ambassador looked to René. "You might understand how I feel, Lieutenant," Sinzo stated. "You know who I am, I assume."

René nodded, "With respect, who doesn't, sir?"

"Clearly, not enough people sitting in that chamber," Vas'Kis retorted, gesturing with his eyes to where the Flow Council's meeting was held.

"I'm afraid I don't understand, sir," Captain Hernandez muttered.

The Ambassador looked dead into the Captain's eyes.

"Then let me enlighten you," Vas'Kis told the Captain, with vague aggressiveness in his voice.

Vas'Kis looked away from the Captain, as if his mind were simply somewhere else, in another memory, another life.

"History books are written about me. Lectures are spoken about me; my plight, my pain, my rebellion. They call me hero,"

Vas'Kis shook his head. "But I'm not. Too many died. Too many suffered. Too many people were born into a life, into a world in which all they knew was voided, disrupted, corrupted lives."

Vas'Kis shook his head. "My planet's wildlife, its plants, its people, its entire livelihood was disrupted and destroyed. It was diseased."

"But it was still a life," Hernandez argued.

"No. That is not life. That is worse than death, boy," Vas'Kis rebuked. "Do not confuse life with meaning, the two aren't synonyms."

Hernandez and René looked to each other in confusion at Vas'Kis' statements towards them, each attempting to communicate subtle signs of displeasure in the situation.

"Everything was taken from us--" Vas'Kis continued. "--and it will never be regained. My people are a shell of what we may have been. We live off the boot of a government that would have easily abandoned us, had I not made such a drastic plea for assistance. And, even now, I have to wonder 'Did I do the right thing? Is this really a life worth living?'"

Vas'Kiz looked into the eyes of Captain Hernandez once more.

"And I can honestly say, without any doubt in my heart, that the pain my people had endured would have been welcomed with the swift end, along with sending our captors, our rapists, our persecutors and the people who had destroyed our land along with us. Only then, could we have known peace."

Vas'Kis shook his head, "Not this life."

Vas'Kis had weakness in his voice, it was difficult for him to actually speak and get through the pain of his memories to say the next words.

"Not this empty shell of purpose that I'd given to my people."

Vas'Kis moved closer to Hernandez, his body stature slightly aggressive.

"So the next time you claim to do something in the name of innocent lives, I suggest you think about the reality of the horror of those lives, not the fantasy of something greater that you'd like them to achieve."

As Vas'Kis walked away, Hernandez shrugged, as he was unaware of how to feel about the Ambassador's words.

At twelve hundred hours Hernandez and René walked to the Enforcer's docking bay and saw the rest of the crew. The captain ordered that the main officers meet in the debriefing room at fourteen hundred hours, after making sure that the Enforcer itself was fully operational. That job was handled by Javal with the assistance of some non-militant crew, Onyx for weapons, and Bryna for the database and hacking systems.

René walked to her room, pushed the unlocking combination on the computer panel screen next to her door and allowed it to open. As she walked through, it automatically shut.

The lieutenant's room was well furbished. A made bed, a small database computer, a televised screen for entertainment, and a mini bar with bottles of alcoholic beverages.

René walked to the bar and poured herself some Scotch. The taste of the drink started to invoke memories.

"Every time I think back to what makes me who I am, I need a drink. Some say it's soft poison, some say that it's the sign of an alcoholic, some say it's just depression, but I don't give a damn.

No one understands my struggle, my pain, my loneliness, and all of the things that have been taken away from me.

I was a small child, living on Royale III with my parents. Royale III was just another casino world. A planet that was privately owned and found before the Flow Council could technically declare it to be in Constable space. So whoever ran the world basically owned whoever lived there.

My parents who loved me. My parents who got involved with the wrong crowd. My parents who were addicted to narcotics. Before I could even remember, I was taken from my parents and put into foster care. Not that I can blame the authorities for taking me away.

But really, that's not why I was taken away by the crooked casino thugs that passed for authority on the twisted casino world. My parents were murdered. The order was given by a casino owner, one whose name doesn't even matter anymore. He's been dead for a long time. The murderer who he hired was an Acer, an Elemental that the casino owner used for muscle.

I looked at the autopsy report repeatedly. My parents' burned skin, crushed bones, and mangled necks and arms. The Acer tortured them. For fun. For sport. Like my parents were playthings, animals.

All because the two people who were to support me in life...who were to give me love and lessons and support and compassion... they owed money. As if, somehow, their lives equaled a few thousand JPL (jewel pressed latinum).

All Elementals are the same. Self righteous freaks who use the unnatural powers they've been given to destroy those they see as weaker than them. No matter their fake attitude of tranquility or if they're just bloodthirsty, they're all the same. No regard for anything but their own power and dominance over us or over themselves.

No one is above the law. No one is above murdering innocents. No one is allowed to revel in their indecent lives based on the suffering of a little girls' parents. So I joined the Constables. To stop anyone who thought they were above the law. Anyone.

These people I see don't regard any form of law or order. Particularly Stoli. A former mercenary. Well, she still is a mercenary. Just working for different people now. These people probably see the Constable's laws and regulations as some demanding and forcing restrictions, when really, it's designed to help people who can't help themselves.

I would call what I'm doing disgusting if it didn't have to be done. It would be disgusting if there weren't people who exploit technicalities of the law to harm innocent people. It would be disgusting if I didn't have to do it. It would be disgusting if there was any other way I could do what was necessary. It would be disgusting if I didn't love it so damn much.

In the academy, I excelled in weapons training and tactical approaches. Hand to hand combat was taught to me, but I didn't use the training as much as I used pure rage. Rage is what kept me going and what will always keep me going. Nothing can kill it, even if they kill me.

A few years passed after training, and I was under the command of Commandant Amadus. A man who'd been a decorated soldier for the Constables for decades. He was an icon to those who believed in the ideals that the Constables represented. He was a leader who could command with simple facial expressions. And when he spoke even the fewest words, you couldn't help but be drawn in and listen. He had olive green skin, an athletic physic, and light grey eyes. Even in his older age, you could see that he had the spark of a soldier.

One night, he invited me to his quarters. He'd done that with some of the crew. I had assumed that he was trying to use some speech on them to motivate them, or to get to know the crew better. But there was something I didn't notice that I should have. He had invited only women to his quarters.

When I walked in, he offered me a drink, and me being who I am, I accepted.

Amadus looked at me after I drank it. He looked at me with a smile, and it wasn't one that I liked. One that felt like he was trying to peer into your mind, your soul. I started to feel woozy and like I couldn't stay awake.

He started talking about how much of a beautiful woman I was as he got closer and tried to kiss me. I resisted and pushed him away. He started to get angry and tried to wrestle me to the ground.

Then, it happened. I got angry. Very angry. Rage took over. The drug slipped drink didn't matter anymore. I just felt anger.

I snapped Amadus' arm like it was a twig. He screamed in pain as I beat him in the face until his purple blood started to seep into his carpet. Before I killed him, I stopped myself and left his room. I let him gurgle on his own blood, barely alive.

When I opened the room, the guards saw that I had beaten Commandant Amadus to a pulp and placed me under arrest.

A few days later, I was in a Constable holding cell. That's when I met Director Tollus.

He sat down and laid down my file in front of me.

"Before I go into any of this, I do not approve of beating a Constable hero. One who saved colonies and cities in multiple battles on multiple occasions." Tollus' words had no effect on me. I didn't give a damn. "But... I do not approve of rapists. Not even in the slightest. And from some of the female officers whom I've spoken to, they've been assaulted. If I would have known that this was going on right then and there, I may have done the same thing. Now, I have good news and bad news, Corporal Anukis."

"What's the bad news?" I asked sarcastically.

"The bad news is that the Flow Council tends to let Constable heroes get away with damn near everything. So he won't be locked up, just set away from female officers."

"That's disgusting." I remarked.

"I agree. It's crooked, it's wrong, it's sickening, but it's their decision, and I need to work with the Flow Council more than fight with them on a decision they won't change. And also, you will be charged with assaulting a superior officer. And the sentence for that is—"

"Seven years, I know."

"Yes. But I have a compromise."

"And what would that be?"

"I'm putting together a force, an experiment, a team of those who are on the wrong side of the law, and are trying to seek redemption."

"I shouldn't have to seek redemption for what I did."

"I agree. And if I were in charge of everything, I'd give you a medal for what you did. Hell, I may have joined in, myself. But, this is a good thing. You are interested in high risk missions that will help innocents, correct?"

"Correct."

"Then this is directly up your alley. You will be set up with a crew, and a ship that has state of the art equipment from the entirety of the Flow Council's planets combined. Are you interested, Lieutenant Anukis?" I was surprised at Tollus' remark.

"Lieutenant? I'm a corporal. I've never been a..."

"If you join this team I'm putting together, you'll be a lieutenant. Your high tactical ratings and comprehension levels speak for themselves. You deserve to be a lieutenant, nothing less. This doesn't seem like it now, but this is the opportunity of a lifetime. Do you accept?"

"Who will I be working with, exactly?"

"You'll be taking orders from me, the Flow Council, and maybe certain Constables."

"I know that, but which Constables will I be assigned to on this ship?"

"So far I only have one, a Captain. But he's damn good. I'll build the team more as I find more who fit the description of extremely talented, but having trouble with the law."

I couldn't help it, this sounded amazing. It sounded like something I needed to be part of, not just wanted to be a part of.

"I'm in."

Tollus smiled, and that was the beginning of it all. I can't believe I'm almost out of scotch, dammit."

René set down her glass. As she was preparing to refill her glass, the intercom beeped, indicating that the repairs were complete and that she needed to report in to set the course to planet Scar.

René walked away from her personal bar and got into her armor plated uniform. Once equipped, she left her room, and her memories along with it, for now.

PHOE-NIX NEBULA

Star Enforcers: Chapter 11

"Captain's Log, Star Time: Alpha Xenos eighteen hundred ten hours. I rarely do vocal log entries because it feels kind of odd talking to myself. This may be my last entry if my ship and its crew meet an undesirable end on this next assignment, so I might as well say something. Anyhow, the ship's crew is underway to planet Scar under stealth cloak mode. Scar is a volcanic world which was at one point a penal colony where prisoners mined ores and metals. But the status of the population has changed dramatically over the years and the planet is now a home for mercenaries, terrorists, and bounty hunters.

"I myself have only been around space pirates which helps me to be diverse in dealing with the inhabitants on the planet, but for the most part these people are brutal. I just hope that we can find a lead on where the Red Rage drugs are produced to end the epidemic. Well, in fact, it was not considered an epidemic till one of the Flow Council's children was affected by the drug. Before that Red Rage was looked at as a nuisance; go figure.

"Since the planet is foreign territory to most of the crew, I've requested Bryna Stoli to report to my quarters so that I can obtain any personal insight that she may have on the environment that we are entering before I call the constables to meet in the briefing room tomorrow morning."

Just before Hernandez was about to say his next sentence for the log a door chime is activated.

"End Captain's log and save," he commanded and the computer beeped with an acknowledgement.

The captain was seated on the edge of his bed, still dressed in his normal attire as the night shift approached. He stood up from his bed and tried to think about the questions he wanted to ask Bryna. The door chime rang again, but this time it chimed five times noting the inpatience of the person on the other side of the sliding door.

"Enter," the commanding officer said as he turned to face the sliding door.

Bryna Stoli walked into the captain's quarters with a hurried stride. "You requested to see me?" she asked in a frustrated manner.

"Yes I did." Hernandez said and walked over to one of the three observation port windows in his room. He peered out and watched the stars streak by as the Enforcer was traveling at faster than light using its Slip Stream drive.

"Well it would be nice if you spit it out so that I can get on with the rest of my day," Bryna insisted, having no patience for the captain.

"I'm just a little worried about the crew and how they will handle the assignment on Scar," Hernandez admitted as he turned to face her and he placed his hands on his hips.

"I understand some of your concerns," She returned with a smile. She felt gratified that Hernandez had to consult with her in light of the current situation.

"I doubt that. You probably don't have any concerns about being on Scar. You were practically raised around their people," he countered.

"On the contrary Hernandez, I'm a wanted mercenary, and also I still intend to find the Rycuda so that I can give them the brand of justice that they so rightly deserve," Bryna informed him as she tapped the sophisticated sidearm in the left leg weapon holster.

The captain looked into her eyes with a serious manner. "I don't need you to go running off on some damn personal vendetta."

"Oh really, and what makes you think that you can control me once we land on Scar," Bryna verbally shot back at him.

"Don't try to play this game with me, Stoli or I swear you will lose. In other words, don't test me," Hernandez scowled.

"I'm not playing any games here, but I will tell you this, the people of Scar only respect bad asses. You can't be soft, we have to be affirmative and very direct," she told him.

"That's good to know. So what do you expect to find once we get there?"

"The environment is somewhat hostile at times; it's a criminal's paradise. No one on the planet is innocent of anything, so don't be afraid to put a bullet into anyone's head. Rest assured they would love to put a bullet into one of our heads. We will all have to wear cloaks to blend into the population.

"Why is that?" the captain asked.

"The planet surface is covered in ashes that come from the active volcanoes on the planet. It's almost like falling snow. The cloaks help with keeping the ashes out of our faces, and also to conceal our faces. The towns are controlled by whoever has the most muscle in the area," she told him as she propped her back on the side wall to relax from standing.

Hernandez would offer her to sit down but he knows that she rarely can't stand being around him.

"So who should we be looking for that may have the answers that we are seeking, and where do we find such a person or group of people?" Hernandez inquired.

"We will have to land in a province called Voodoon. There we can try to find a man named Brillen. He is the head of a terrorist organization known as the Spearheads."

"Ah yes I've head of that group. All the members have small spear tip tattoos on their foreheads," Hernandez said, tapping just under his hairline. "The Spearheads mainly have caused havoc on certain planets by destroying political structures and government buildings."

"Yes that is correct," she confirmed.

"Will Brillen be a tough man to find and deal with?"

"Yes to both, but if we offer him something that he can't pass up he will seek us out. He is only as tough as what you can provide for him."

"I understand. That will be all, Stoli, you can report back to your station. Thank you for your time," Hernandez sincerely told her.

"I'm just doing what I have to do," Stoli said without fanfare and walked out of the captain's quarters.

At o'six hundred hours, the constables assembled in the private briefing room. The officers were very attentive and they looked well rested. But some concerns still filled their minds. Hernandez was in the room fifteen minutes early and was the first person to be seated. He greeted all the constables as they came in, and Stoli was the last person to come into the room.

"Stoli, thank you for being on time," The captain told her.

"Yeah and with a minute to spare. I had to download some extra information before this briefing. I believe it will be essential for this assignment," Bryna stated as she took her seat along the semi circle of chairs.

"Very well then; Constables as you know we are on approach to the planet Scar and are due to arrive in two hours. Our assignment is to make contact with a man named Brillen Cardac. He is the terrorist group leader of the Spearheads. We will be able to locate him in the Voodoon province. Stoli can you tell us more about this individual?" Hernandez extended the floor to the former mercenary.

Bryna connected a wire from her sophisticated pistol into a plug in port that was on the side of the computer panel on the armrest of the chair she was seated in. The image of the terrorist leader could be seen on the large view screen. Brillen was a grey-skinned human with a very rough pitted face that was scarred. He had a scar on his left cheek and a second scar ran down his right brow that extended to the upper part of his cheek bone. On his forehead he bore the red tattoo of a spear tip. His eyes were dark blue, and he possessed a very intimidating look.

"Brillen Cadac, is a notorious terrorist, and has the reputation of carrying out some of the worst acts of terrorism in the

Tango Quadrant. He has an information network of people and spies that covers a vast deal of territory. He has a loyal band of followers and personally trains his top people. His followers will protect him at all costs especially since some bounty hunters dare to try to cash in on his head. What we have to do is draw him out. He will be almost impossible to find because he stays off the grid."

"How do you suppose we do that? He seems to not want to make any appearances for just anyone?" René asked.

"We will have to hold something of value to get his attention," Stoli told the constables.

"Something of value you say, and what do we have that is valuable on this ship to trade? There isn't enough jewel press latinum on board to get an audience with Brillen," Javal added.

"We do have something of value that will lure him out of hiding," Bryna offered.

"Oh and what is that Stoli?" Hernandez inquired anxiously awaiting her suggestion.

"It's not what Hernandez, it's who," Bryna affirmed.

"Stoli, what the hell are you talking about?" Hernandez asked. It frustrated the captain whenever Stoli held back information.

"The who is me," Bryna said to them. The constables looked surprised by the suggestion.

"Why would he risk revealing himself in public when almost every bounty hunter is after him?" Aiden asked Bryna.

"Because I was the one who scarred the right side of his face, and it's a scar that fuels his need for revenge against me."

"Stoli, do you make enemies everywhere you go?" Hernandez injected.

"Only to those who are targets and the people that piss me off," Stoli shot back.

"I will remember that." The captain grinned.

"If I may say something."

The constables looked into Onyx's direction as some swiveled their chairs to face the cyborg.

"This is highly unadvisable. This plan would put the crew at risk, and possibly losing Bryan Stoli's life."

"Risk is part of our job description, Onyx. There are no guaranties that any of us will return from this assignment at all, but to sacrifice ourselves for the good of the many on that planet even though most of them are harden criminals is what is needed here," Captain Hernandez reminded the officers so that the wrath of the Solar Sword can be averted.

"There are innocent children on Scar. They don't deserve such a sentencing. The children should have the right to grow up and choice their own path in life," Tika informed them of the importance of this assignment.

"I hate to say it but she's right," René agreed with Tika's rationale.

"So how do we deliver Constable Stoli into Brillen's hands without her being savagely beaten or killed by the hands of everyone else on the planet?" Javel asked.

"Bryna, tell me what's the bounty on your head?" René asked.

PHOE-NIX NEBULA

Bryna smiled at Rene's question.

"I'm worth half of what it took to build this ship. And the number keeps climbing," Bryna answered. A few Constables raised their eyebrows in slight surprise.

"Okay, we offer you as a bargaining chip," began Aiden. "But how do we do it? What are the specifics? How do we get you in and out without getting you killed?"

"I know quite a bit about Brillen, Dakar, and quite a bit about Scar. We'll hold a simple meeting where I'll be captive. Onyx and Tika will serve as the mercenaries who will be holding me captive."

"Why them?" asked René. "Wouldn't the Captain and I be more suited for something like this?"

Bryna shook her head.

"Obvious military training, without the mercenary scars to deter suspicions? I don't think so. The two of you would be spotted as the Constables within seconds. Onyx is a natural infiltrator. He won't be discovered."

"And why me?" asked Tika. "Won't I be a little easy to spot as non mercenary?"

"On any other planet, yes. But the case isn't the same on Scar," stated Bryna. "Sometimes mercenary bands kidnap child geniuses, like yourself, and have them do their tech work. Usually as slaves, other times as trainees against their will. You'll blend in with no questions asked. Just let Onyx do the talking, and you'll be fine. And besides, we'll need you to come along so that we know the properties of Red Rage. The meeting will probably be in their base of operations where Brillen will feel the most secure."

"Technicians expert, Bryna Stoli, the numbers of the Spearheads mercenaries would overwhelm us in a direct firefight. I judge this plan of operations unsound." stated Onyx.

"Ah, there's more to it. René and Aiden will infiltrate their basement level. Their basement holds all of their valuables and resources. Dakar will plant explosives and René will provide cover," explained Bryna.

"We don't stand much of a chance." blurted René.

"The basement level doesn't have any guards within it, just guards outside of it. Ever since I tried gunning for him, Brillen's become a coward. He uses most of his security staff to protect him, and leaves everything else easily available," Bryna elaborated.

"And how does planting explosives on some valuables and resources help them from not killing you?" asked the Captain.

"Without his needed resources, Brillen's entire terrorist operation would crumble. He wouldn't dare kill us when we have that kind of upper hand."

"How are we going to get in there?" inquired Aiden.

"There's a building that's normally used for the Spearheads' attempted escape if they ever needed it. It used to contain small ships so that they could get off planet in case a mercenary group or the Constables would raid their base. Now it's just empty. The tunnel system is offline, but still available for use. They won't be able to detect you in there. You should be able to get in, plant the explosives, and get out without being seen."

"Okay, maybe Javal and I should go with René and Aiden, to give some backup. It doesn't sound like we'll be doing anything else anyway," said Captain Hernandez.

"No," objected Bryna. "You two have a different job. And, out of all of us, the one that the two of you are most capable of doing."

"And that is…?" wondered Javal.

"The two of you need to pilot the Enforcer and rain fire on the base itself to weaken the outer defenses. Then, once everyone is secure and out of there, get us from the roof, or another escape alternative if something goes wrong."

"Okay," agreed the Captain. "What will we do to get in the base?"

Bryna smiled.

The Enforcer was on approach to the system that was formally known as the Cronar system, renamed the Penal Solar System when planet Scar was turned into a penal colony. Of the five planets orbiting the sun, Scar is the only planet that has life. Orbiting the planet are two moons; both are lifeless and about the quarter size of Scar.

The cloaked constable ship slowed down to Sub Stream speed as René did her best maneuvering possible to avoid hitting other ships and debris surrounding the planet. There was a mixture of small and large spacecraft sharing the orbit around the planet. Battle damage from engagements was visible on a number of vessels, and others were in obvious need of repairs as sections of their hulls had been breached. Those in the worst shape had been abandoned and space scavenger drones could be seen cannibalizing the ships for parts to sell at discounted rates.

Javal watched some of the scavenger drones from the view screen in engineering and hoped that those beasts would never try to attempt a desecration of the Enforcer.

The Stealth Destroyer Starship reached the ionosphere of Scar and inserted itself into the volcanic smoke and clouds that covered the planet. Only some of the land masses were visible from space. Rivers of lava flowed along the surface of the planet merging like networks of veins. The lava falls looked magnificent but were extremely dangerous to most life forms.

Only twenty five percent of the planet surface contained water, but it had a blackened look and was not suitable to drink. The acid content was poisonous to non-indigenous life forms.

As the Enforcer entered the upper atmosphere, the bridge crew observed a small flock of winged beasts called hornwings, similar to dragons. The group of six were as large as horses with horns and dark grey short fur, the large talons on their feet had immense crushing power to snatch their prey. The constable ship passed within one hundred feet of the hornwings during its descent. The creatures were spooked by the roar of the engines and they broke formation, but quickly reformed their flying pattern and carried on since they were not able to visually see the cloaked vessel.

Back on the bridge of the Enforcer, Onyx spoke in a monotone voice, "Captain the ship's scanners have detected a suitable landing site."

Miguel's attention shifted from the main view screen and he swiveled in his command chair to look at his tactical officer.

"Location?"

"It's a cavern two point eight miles from Brillen Cardac's compound," the Eliminator answered.

The captain's eyebrows rose.

"Excellent, feed the coordinates to the lieutenant's control panel and engage whisper mode. René, take us in."

"Yes sir," she replied and took meticulous effort to steer the ship towards its landing destination. She flew over the small town called Voodoon. The inhabitants had no clue that a cloaked constable ship was above their head. They tried to not look up anytime during the day that volcanic ash fell from the sky, and this day was no exception.

The spacious cavern was at the side of a small mountain. René landed the ship with ease and powered down the engines. The purple shrubs provided some cover to the entrance of the cavern. Through the view screens they watched as large insects the size of small dogs flew through the air and pointed out the sharp mandibles that could tear through regular flesh with deadly results from just one bite.

Lt. Anukis got up from her flight panel and looked over to Onyx, "Hey, big, tall, and handsome. It's time for us to make you beautiful."

An hour later, the interior of the ship appeared from the eight foot opening at the rear of the ship. As a gangplank met the dusty cavern floor, two individuals descended into the cavern. Tika disembarked first, wearing a dark grey cloak and hood that extended down eighty percent of her legs. Her face had a dark impression as she used an eyebrow pencil to arch her brows that gave her a scolding look. She wore black lipstick, and her nails were painted the same color. The light body armor she wore was black with silver trim. The medical officer felt strange being dressed in such a manner, but she kept reminding herself that it was only temporary.

The individual walking next to her was Onyx. The tactical officer was wearing a black cloak that dragged on the ground as he walked. Under the mysterious cloak, Onyx had morphed his body into a woman's style body armor that was navy blue with red trim. René had selected the image of this female so that his appearance would complement their assignment. She chose the image of an Asian woman in her young thirties named Kora Nagotu. She was currently a prisoner in constable custody, faced with life in prison for being a professional assassin. She had a reputation of being very treacherous and Onyx adjusted his body language and movement to accommodate his current role. The Eliminator kept close to Tika as they walked into the town of Voodoon.

When the duo reached the outer edge of the town, it looked like a setting in an old western movie. The structures in town were only two to three stories tall, and the buildings where made from concrete instead of wood. The roads in and out of town were covered with ash and a taxi driver was busy dusting off his vehicle to make it presentable to any would be passengers.

Tika noticed a mother walking with two children that appeared no older than ten years old. Both children carried pistols while the mother carried a shotgun. Tika knew her assignment would help protect the children of the planet who didn't have a choice in life. For most kids their age, once you were able to hold a gun, you better be able to use it.

Voodoon's main attraction wasn't the shops of merchandise or places to eat a meal, it was a place of business called Wicked Titties. Tika shuttered at the idea of going into such an establishment, but she was told by Bryna that it was the most likely place to meet a member of the Spearhead Terrorist organization.

Onyx looked down at the shorter constable.

"Medical Constable Tika Shamari, make sure that you stay close to me. This location has a high probability of violence," the Eliminator said as he noticed the amount of patrons entering the gentleman's club brandishing an assortment of guns and bladed weaponry.

"I see your point," Tika replied, her eyes widening when a large brute of a man walked into the place carrying a Gatling gun.

The scent of sweet tobacco wafted through the air as the pair walked through the double doors. Hookahs were sporadically spread around the establishment and the smokers enjoyed their relaxing drugs. Customers were also seated at tables and around a bar area circling a large stage. Most people were watching the female dancer with turquoise and long white hair. Her sensual body had an unusual feature, a third breast that was in the middle of her chest area.

The dancer schmoozed the fifty-two men in the audience. The eight female patrons were enjoying the atmosphere. A few were interested in watching the dancer, but most were there for business.

The dancer's music was being played by two male musicians; one playing a guitar, and the other was beating a bronze metal vertical instrument that kept the rhythm and tone.

Tika and the disguised Onyx removed their hoods, and ash fell to the floor. A small roving machine moved over to where the new ashes fell and quickly vacuumed the particles up into its containment canister. Onyx felt privileged that his function and purpose was not as menial as the robot that cleaned up the club.

A few of the patrons took notice of the new arrivals and a few of the customers gasped when they saw the appearance of Kora Nugotu, with two long range pistols holstered at both legs. The whispers grew louder and more intense. Tika looked like a serious bad ass even though she was still a teenage girl. People took her seriously just because of the person that she was accompanying. Tika pulled a dagger from her holder and cleaned her black finger nails with the tip of the blade while her pistol remained within the left holster.

Onyx began scanning the club in hopes to find a member of the Spearheads. Within seven seconds, he targeted the four men sitting at a table in the corner

"Follow me," Onyx said and stepped towards the gentlemen of interest.

Tika walked alongside the Eliminator, her heart starting to race as the duo approached the group of men. Long range rifles and hard liquor drinks littered the table. They talked amongst themselves as they oogled the exotic dancer shaking her sensual behind.

Before the undercover constables could reach the corner table, Onyx was stopped by the large man still carrying his Gatling gun. The man had tan skin and a shaved head. His face was rough and unshaved. His jaw moved around as he worked the wad of chewing tobacco in his mouth. The large man began to speak as he spit a discharge of chewing tobacco by Onyx's boots.

"You have got a lot of nerve showing up here on Scar, Kora; especially after assassinating my brother," the man said and stared the disguised Eliminator down.

Onyx thought quickly as how to address the man without blowing his cover.

"And who the hell are you?"

"I am Bounty Hunter Gul Nar, the brother of Tuk Nar!" the man shouted aloud to get everyone's attention. The patrons' attention was now focused on the two; even the dancer stopped moving to take notice. The men at the corner table stood so they could get a better view.

Onyx had access to most known criminals in their galaxy. His advanced memory matrix accessed the name of Tuk Nar in the matter of one and a half seconds.

"Ah, Tuk Nar, the wanted felon and professional jewelry thief. When he successfully stole the Martos Royal Family Jewels, the family paid me to kill him and recover the jewels before he could sell them on the Black Market. Don't blame me for doing what I was paid for," Onyx countered with a female sassiness that Tika didn't expect from the sophisticated automaton.

"Well spoken. I hope you enjoyed it, as this will be your last time speaking. Now that I have you here, I plan to avenge the death of my brother and place your head at his tombstone," the big brute said, and placed his hand on the barrel of the Gatling gun that hung on a hook to the side of his leg.

"Hey, both of you quit it. There will be no fire fights here. Take that shit outside right now," the owner of the Wicked Titties protested. "I don't need any of my patron's shot and or damage to my club."

The man had a big mouth for being only five foot tall and having a weasel like face.

"You better get out of the way or you'll be next, little man. Don't worry, if I damage something, she'll pay for it with her dead body as collateral."

"Alright, go kill yourselves, just don't break anything," the owner said and went behind the bar to watch the ensuing challenge.

Tika backed up as did the other patrons. Gul was not concerned with Tika, she was small and insignificant to him. Her weapon was not a worry to him. He was totally focused on the figure that resembled Kora. Gul Nar took ten steps back to give himself some room before the intended duel. Onyx just stood there and had not moved one inch. Tika had no idea what the Eliminator was planning.

"I'd put my hand on my weapon if I were you, assassin," Gul warned, looking at the pair of untouched long range pistols at her side. The barrels of the Gatling gun started to spin waiting to fire out several rounds in the matter of a millisecond.

"Alright, damn you then. On the count of three, draw your weapon. One... Two...,"

"Three!"

Onyx's feminine voice completed the count as the Eliminator quickly drew the pair of dark blue pistols from both leg holsters and fired one round from each. Onyx used precise accuracy to defeat his adversary. One round hit the large bounty hunter in the left knee, and the other went straight for Gul's trigger finger. The velocity of the metal slug's impact detached the trigger finger from his hand. Gul Nar fell to the floor in pain as he could not stand on his one leg. He could not believe how quickly he was shot by the assassin before he could raise the barrel of his weapon. The Eliminator re-holstered the pair of pistols, then walked over to his fallen opponent and stripped him of his weapon and threw it to the other side of the floor.

"You bitch; why didn't you kill me?" the defeated man asked outraged by the turn of the event.

"I only kill professionals," the disguised cyborg said and kicked Gul Nar in the face, knocking him out.

The owner of the establishment ordered some of workers to toss Gul Nar out into the street.

Tika breathed, a sign of relief that the short altercation was put to rest. It was now time to make contact with the Spearheads. Onyx had most certainly gotten their attention as everyone went back to whatever they were doing.

When the undercover constables were within a few feet of the four men, one of them spoke. The edge in his voice echoed the feelings showing on the other three men's faces.

"Very interesting addition to today's entertainment, Ms. Nugotu. Your display of marksmanship is impressive."

The Eliminator put his hands on his hips and pursed his lips, "Gul Nar was an object in my way and I have very little tolerance for foolishness."

"Luckily, she took action, or I would have had to put him down myself," Tika said with a smile, twirling the dagger in her right hand.

One of the men laughed, "Oh, little one, you have a lot of spunk, I see."

Tika immediately threw the dagger in the man's direction and the blade drove into the wooden table next to his drink. The man appeared to be outraged. Onyx was about to un-holster his pair of pistols to protect her, but Tika had already drawn her pistol and had the barrel aimed at the man in the corner. Onyx simply raised Kora's eyebrow as Tika displayed her skills with weapons.

"I don't take well to being treated like a child or being disrespected. I may be young, but I sure as hell know how to take care of my business," Tika spoke out in a collective and serious tone.

The man immediately backed down in fear of having his face blown off and the other three men remained motionless as they remembered seeing the disguised Onyx's marksmanship. All four men sat back down.

The man who first spoke to the undercover constables said to the duo, "Okay, damn it! Okay. So what brings you two to our table?"

Both Tika and Onyx looked at each other. Kora Nugotu's voice was clear. "We're here to offer a valuable commodity to your sovereign leader."

Brillen sat in his huge meeting room. He fingered the scar on the left side of his face. He gritted his teeth in anger as he thought of the knife slicing his dark orange skin from his cheek into his jet black hair. Remembering the attacker, he shivered in fear.

Brillen's throne-like chair had provided comfort and power over the men in the room for over three years now. His armed terrorists, wearing black and red armor that filled the room, were his guards.

Each guard was equipped with high caliber assault rifles, a set of grenades, and combat knives. A black spear tattooed on each forehead proved undying devotion to Brillen's cause.

Brillen's messenger, Arako, approached him. Arako's skin was grey and his blue hair was half burnt off. Arako wore lighter armor than the rest, and carried a wrapped object in his hand, roughly 10 inches in length and 2 inches in width. Arako bowed to Brillen, and began to open his mouth.

"Sir," Arako began, "a couple freelance mercenaries approached a few of our troops today. They say that they have captured Bryna Stoli."

Brillen's eyebrow rose in intrigue.

"So, Bryna's spate of murdering across the galaxy has finally led to her capture," Brillen said. "Delightful. But how am I supposed to know that they're telling the truth?"

"They sent this, sir."

Arako handed the object delicately to Brillen. As Brillen unwrapped it, he uncovered Bryna Stoli's famous combat knife. Her initials of "B.S." were carved into the handle. The trail of blue and gold leading from the handle to the tip of the blade represented the former mercenary band which, while in existence, Bryna had been a part of.

"Is Stoli alive?" Brillen smiled in happiness.

"Yes, they have her in restraints on their ship, and they are waiting for your response," his messenger informed him.

Brillen was overjoyed. He fingered his scar once again.

"Send them to me. I'll gladly pay them in exchange for the bitch who carved my face."

PHOE-NIX NEBULA

Star Enforcers: Chapter 13

The outside of the Spearheads' compound was a four story building with few windows. The shut-down former ship base had a single door locked from the inside. The gray paint was falling off, giving the appearance that it had been abandoned for months. Upon close scrutiny, however, a faded Spearhead insignia was visible above the door.

René and Aiden both approached the building in cloaks. Both of them had light body armor beneath black hooded trench coats and concealed weapons. The body armor was black and grey, no Constable insignia of any kind. Their appearance gave them the look of normal inhabitants, perhaps a married couple. René looked at her Affix as it did a quick scan of the building.

"There doesn't seem to be anything powering the building, so I doubt we'll run into any trouble," stated Aiden.

"Any life signs in the building?" wondered René.

"The building cloaks life signs, but I doubt anyone would be in there when it's shut down."

"Alright, let's do this," commanded René. Aiden nodded in agreement.

The blonde explosives expert walked to the door and removed a small, coin sized bomb from his belt compartment and placed it on the key lock. Aiden then took a few steps back to safety and spoke into his Affix.

"V-X-1: Detonate."

At Aiden's words, the small explosive combusted, forcing the lock to pop off allowing the Constables access to the inside of the building. René walked forward and slowly opened the door. René and Aiden walked through and closed the door behind them.

Within the warehouse, dust covered the floors and walls. The room, large enough to hold space ships and engineering decks, was empty. Doors leading to different rooms and sectors of the warehouse remained closed. As René and Aiden lowered their hoods, ash fell to the floor. Aiden and René both tapped their

Affixes to light up their body armor, illuminating a ten foot radius within the darkened room.

"I hate Scar," noted René. "It's like thousands of smokers are blowing in your face every two seconds. My lungs feel like they're on fire. I feel sorry for the children forced to live in an environment with sadistic mercenaries and ruthless ambitionists. If I had the power to take all of the murderers and sick bastards out on Scar, I would, but, as the Flow Council likes to remind me time and again, I'm restricted by them to do what they say, not what's right."

"I understand your pain," replied Aiden. "It's a hopeless cycle of death and misery for any innocent involved. Yet the Flow Council does nothing because they don't want to risk the man power, and anyone who wants to make this place better themselves is snuffed out in a matter of minutes."

René shook her head in disgust. "Let's get this over with. The sooner we get done with this hellhole, the better."

"Agreed."

Aiden looked down at his Affix to see the floor plans for the building mapped out.

"There," Aiden pointed to a door on the far left side of the room. "That seems to be the way to the elevator. Well, what was the elevator. We're going to have to climb our way down."

"Fantastic," remarked René sarcastically, as she pulled out her assault rifle.

"Really? Do you always have to carry that thing around?"

"Better safe than sorry."

"True."

The two Constables continued walking as René held her assault rifle in caution, while Aiden looked through his explosive plans on his Affix in curiosity. Suddenly, René heard something near the other end of the warehouse, where the darkness made it unable for her to see what it was. Instinctively, she fired. The deafening bullets pulsing out of the rifle startled Aiden as he covered his ears in shock.

"What the hell?!" shouted Aiden.

"I heard something. I know there's something over there," responded René intensively.

"There's nothing in here! It's just you and me and maybe, maybe, a rat or two. But congratulations, you might have killed a rodent. Now could you stop being so damn paranoid and put that rifle away? I'd like to walk out of here with all of my appendages."

Fifteen feet behind Aiden, a hissing sound started to echo throughout the warehouse. Aiden's face went from sarcastic shock to confused concern.

Aiden turned quickly and saw several seven foot long Acidpods. The creatures' bodies had multiple segments, each with two legs. The creatures' antennae dangled over their green eyes as they slowly crawled towards their targets. The corrosive acide dripping from their mouths started to melt the solid metal beneath them.

The Acidpods were another native of Scar and had evolved to handle the harsh volcanic environments. They were known to burrow into non volcanic land and create tunnels, similar to that of ants, just on a much larger scale. Acidpods are also regarded as extremely hostile and territorial.

"Well…," stammered Aiden, "I guess you did hear something."

Tika and Onyx, still disguised as Kora Nagotu, guided Bryna into the Spearhead base. Bryna' restraints and ragged clothing gave the appearance to the Spearhead forces that she was truly a prisoner.

The main entrance to the Spearheads' headquarters was a metal base with equipped mercenaries, all guarding the elevator in a precise fashion. The large communication screen over the elevator covered the entire wall.

The guards walked to the disguised Onyx.

"Hand us the prisoner and leave," demanded the guard.

"What?" blurted Tika. "No, we had a deal. Give us the right amount of J.P.L, and you'll get Stoli."

"Hand over Stoli, now. Or else we'll . . ."

The guard was cut off by an incoming signal from Brillen.

"Guard, stop trying to piss off the people bringing us the bitch that carved my face," ordered Brillen. "Stand down and go back to your post."

"Yes, sir," obeyed the guard, as he walked back to the front of the elevator and stood calmly.

Brillen's attention shifted from the guard to Bryna.

"My my, Bryna Stoli. Right here in my base. This is too damn good."

Brillen felt his scarred part of his face and turned his head.

"Remember this, Stoli?" he said as he displayed his scar.

Bryna smiled. "I still haven't gotten your bloodstains out of the rag I used to choke your men to death. I kept it as a trophy, to remind me of what a broken man sounds like, crying and scared."

Brillen's face turned to anger and intensity.

"Bitch, I'll keep your head as a trophy to remind everyone what happens when someone crosses me!" shouted Brillen.

Bryna snickered at Brillen's response.

"Yeah, keep laughing, Stoli. Keep laughing until I cut your fingers off with my steak knife." Brillen then looked at the two that had brought Bryna in. "You two, thank you for bringing Stoli to my humble home."

"We didn't do it for free," stated Kora. "The deal was we'd get something for this."

Brillen smiled, "Of course, of course. Just come up the elevator with Stoli and I'll give you more J.P.L. than you could imagine."

Brillen's statement was, of course, a lie. What Brillen was really planning was to kill the two of them in his throne room, where he felt the most secure and had the largest guard force. The Constables knew the lie, and were hoping he would try to trick them. Tika nodded in false reassurance.

"Alright, that sounds reasonable," agreed Tika. "We'll be up there in a bit."

Brillen nodded in the sadistic pleasure that he thought was to come.

"Good, good," muttered Brillen. "Come on up, we'll negotiate what I'm sure will be a very large sum for you both."

Tika gave a fake smile and signaled for the disguised Onyx to push Bryna to the elevator. Bryna walked slowly to the elevator as the guards stepped aside for her. As the elevator doors opened, and Bryna stepped inside, a smile grew to her face. An answer she'd spent years searching for was finally about to be attained.

Javal had remained on the Enforcer's engineering deck. There were a few others there checking maintenance, power, and weapon systems, but Javal was reviewing the Enforcer's blue prints, a sight that brought back old thoughts and memories.

"The Enforcer's blue prints. Where it began. Where everything began. I haven't gotten use to being on this ship, with these people. These people who aren't from the same world as mine. These people that can't survive the things I deem normality. These people who can't even pronounce my family's surname. These people who, despite their fragile forms, put themselves in violence and aggression. Something I don't understand.

"Looking at most of them, there's the same expression on their faces. That they're lost. That they're looking for a goal, or trying to find a purpose, but can't find someone to hold onto. They can't find someone who understands them. They don't have a true family. I suppose I'm just being a bit biased. Where I was raised, family meant everything.

I was born on the water planet of Dapora. Though my people originally evolved from, well, fish type animals based underwater, we had risen from our oceans and lived on land. The land is a harsh environment in comparison to other planets. Volcanic eruptions, emitting toxic gasses. And when winter came, the conditions outside were near freezing. So now, we're invulnerable to most conditions, except the vacuum of space.

"My people mostly believe in coexistence and solving things through non-violence. We don't see the point in fighting each other when we can create new ways to live peacefully.

"My family is a long line of diplomats between us Daporans and the other races in the galaxy. Something I do believe in, yes. But I feel as though I'm a foreigner to any belief system that the other races have. Any words I present are usually argued by one question: "What do I get out of it?" I can't do that. I can't sit in a room with selfishness and hatred, it's too depressing.

"So instead, I became an engineer. The science of technology and physics fascinates me. And it's all the same language to everyone. Physics is an undeniable truth, and there is no hatred between me and these tools I create, just science.

"But that's not how I got on the Enforcer. That's not why I was forced to sign on to this for five years. I'm here because of my one and only younger brother, Kaisa.

"He's nearly half my age. The other races can't tell the difference between a forty five year old Daporan, and a twenty two year old one. He looks almost exactly like me to them. Kaisa is brilliant, an expert hacker who could disable just about any system. His mind is very systematic, like mine. He did not like the life of peace on Dapora like I had, however. He was always a dreamer, wondering what mysteries there were beyond the stars. He was fascinated by the idea that there were other races that waged forms of war on each other and did not always choose a path of peace. So, Kaisa left. He went to the slum planet of Garka.

"Garka had multiple races and was notorious for death counts among its inhabitants. It was city-like and originally intended to be a colony for the Torrie, but a battle during the Elumeni/Eliminator war forced the power grid system to be offline.

"The Torrie were evacuated, and so the Mystic Seas mercenary band bought the system, rebuilt it, and rented it out for cheap prices. Once there were enough inhabitants, they were forced to remain and assist the mercenaries. Otherwise, they'd be forced to leave the planet, something that most didn't have the money to do.

"It is, for all legal intents and purposes, a legitimate planet, and the Flow Council can't do anything about it.

"Kaisa left our home planet without telling my parents, and entrusted me with where he was in case he was in danger. After a few months, Kaisa contacted me and asked me to come to Garka. I departed, wondering what was going on, and found that Kaisa was in trouble.

"He said that the Mystic Seas were forcing him to hack and steal a blueprint for a new ship to be built, called the U.S.S. Enforcer. I stayed and tried to negotiate with the Mystic Seas, but they wouldn't listen.

"Soon, the Constables arrived. The Mystic Seas operatives and the Constables waged a gunfight outside while I protected Kaisa from the few Mystic Seas inside his apartment. I was forced to kill them with a pistol that was in Kaisa's room. I hated killing them, and I always will. The sad part is, I know I'd do it again.

"The Constables defeated the Mystic Seas outside and stormed into Kaisa's apartment. I dropped the pistol and put my hands up. They demanded to know who hacked the Flow Council security for the blueprints.

"Kaisa was extremely important to me, everyone in my family is. He's my little brother, and he made a mistake. He has so many years left, so much to learn. I can handle myself in a fight, I know that. I couldn't let him take the blame and go to prison; he had a life ahead of him.

"I stepped forward and said 'I did. I put a virus into the system and hacked the security for the blueprints. I'll insure that they're returned if you provide transport for my brother and I off this planet.' The Constables nodded and took us away. Kaisa still lives with the guilt that I took the blame and not him, but I'd rather he survive with a bad feeling and learn a lesson, than have to endure the years of a prison sentence.

"I spent one week in Constable prison, until someone knocked on my cell door and walked in. It was Director Tollus, purple skin, Mohawk, bull horns and all. He had a file in his hands and had several armed Constables behind him. Tollus ordered the Constables to wait outside while he talked to me.

"So, Javal... I can't actually pronounce your last name,"
he began. "Hacking the Flow Council database and retrieving classified blueprints of the U.S.S. Enforcer. Pretty serious crime."

I turned my eyes away from him.

"I just want to serve my time, sir," I said.

"Uh huh." Tollus opened the file. "So, hacking? That's odd, isn't it? Your brother was listed as an expert computer analyst on your home world. And you're an engineer, with no hacking tech skills listed. I'm surprised you suddenly acquired the expertise. Your brother must be a fast teacher?"

I knew where he was going. I knew he knew the truth.

"What do you want? Mister..."

"Tollus. Director Tollus. It's not so much what I want, as what you're willing to give. The way I see it, you have a choice, Javal. Either deny that your brother did it, force me to go into an investigation and put him in prison, with you along with him, by the way. Lying to the Flow Council is almost as serious as hacking into their systems."

"Or?"

"Or you could put that engineer expertise to good work on the blueprints of the ship that your brother stole. He will be safe, and you will be working on the Enforcer for five years, minimum."

My eyes widened in slight shock.

"This—this isn't right. You shouldn't be allowed to do this."

"Oh, I know, it's terrible. But I suppose that's the repercussions to your brother's actions, huh?"

"I started to feel something I'd never felt before for this man, anger. But I knew I had to do it. For Kaisa. For my baby brother.

"I'll do this. But if I do, my brother is to be unharmed."

Tollus stood up and put the file in the metal trash can in my room.

"One thing about the Torrie, my race, my people, we have a code of honor. Your brother shall not be harmed, I give you my word."

Tollus then took out a lighter and set fire to the file.

"And this whole story, this whole investigation on your brother is over."

I stood up and bowed before Tollus. Despite whatever danger that might come to me, I was grateful that my brother was to be unharmed.

"Thank you, Director Tollus. I will not take this for granted, and I will serve your Enforcer ship honorably."

Tollus smiled and nodded.

"Good. We're leaving. We'll put you into light weapons and spec ops training for a few months, then put you aboard the Enforcer. Your Captain's name is Miguel Hernandez, and your lieutenant is René Anukis. We'll be building up more of a squad later, but it'll take some time to find the right experts. I'm sure you'll fit right in with them."

"Yes, sir."

"Family and protecting my brother forced me to join the Flow Council and it forced me to join this ship. The crew of the Enforcer disturb me. I feel lost and confused aboard with them. So many of them angry.

"René still has a hatred for all Elumeni, a prejudice that I wish I could rid her of. Bryna brings a mindset of hatred and destruction with her, for reasons I do not know. They're all so angry and confused. It seems they have no compassion. I wish I could help them. I wish I could be their family. But it seems they don't want to let me in. I don't feel angry anymore; just sorry for these shipmates who I wish would call me friend."

Suddenly, Javal's Affix buzzed. He listened in, it was Aiden and René.

"Agh! God damn it!" shouted René in anger.

The Captain's voice was heard through the Affix.

"What is it, lieutenant? What's going on?" asked the Captain in confusion and slight worry.

"We have acidpods down here! I'm trying to shake them off, but the crawling bastards are still on us!"

"René, run," stated Aiden in a calm and serious voice.

Suddenly, a huge boom was heard through the intercom.

"What is going on?!" Javal demanded to know in distress.

All that came through was static.

"Javal, get up here, now," ordered Hernandez "We're going in with the Enforcer. If we can get the Spearheads to think that we'll blow them all up, Bryna might have time to escape and get whatever she needs to know. Then we can rescue René and Aiden."

"Understood, Captain. I'm coming to the bridge!"

PHOE-NIX NUBULA

Star Enforcers: Chapter 14

Inside the Spearhead mercenary compound, Brillen, group leader and proprietor of the fortress licked his lips at the expected arrival of the pesky adversary he was so eager to kill.

"But then again, why kill her. That's too quick and easy of a way out for her. Perhaps I need to think of a more suitable punishment. I may start off with having someone measure my scar and give Bryna a lashing to her back for each and every millimeter measured. To hear her scream would be such music to my ears. After that I will have the bitch bound and gagged with her ass up in the air ready to be raped repeatedly as I watch. But I will do the honor in being the first to tap that ass. I never liked sloppy seconds. Then once all my men are done spilling their seed into her I will slit her throat and have Stoli gag on her own blood. That is when I will render her punishment paid in full."

Brillen heard the chime of the elevator make it to the top floor. He straightened himself in his plush velvet chair. The distinguished man was wearing a black robe with gold threaded impressions of symbols woven into the silk black fabric. He had the appearance of royalty even though he was on a planet that contained no true government or laws. It all came down to how well an individual can fight for their life and one's possessions.

The elevator door opened and the first person to step out was Tika. Her expression indicated a person that meant business. Behind her Brillen could see Bryna Stoli. His heart skipped a couple beats in excitement. He could have drooled on the spot, but he kept himself contained. Kora Nugotu's form followed Stoli out of the elevator.

Without being obvious, the undercover constables noticed four extra men in the room armed with large machine guns and sabers. The law enforcement trio knew that they had to be Brillen's finest men who were entrusted to protect him till the bitter end.

The four protectors eyed the expected guests and in unison disengaged the safety locks on their weapons.

Brillen stood with his arms wide open.

"Greetings friends, minus one. Welcome to my humble abode."

It was truly an understatement since the place was very spacious. Marble flooring, a large crystal chandelier, a full service bar with a wine cabinet, a collection of fine paintings and statues to decorated his lavish room. The only thing that was missing was a throne, but the chairs in the room were plush and dressed well enough to make anyone feel comfortable.

"Hmm… thanks for the heart felt greeting, but you are still full of shit, Brillen," Bryna spoke first.

Kora pushed Bryna which made her fall to her knees. Stoli could not stop her momentum since her hands were cuffed behind her back.

"Shut up before I tape your mouth shut," Onyx disguised as Kora warned her. Bryna was surprised how well Onyx played such a role as he pointed the pistol to Bryna's temple. The four protectors aimed their automatic weapons at Onyx. Tika revealed her daggers as she grabbed two of them after removing her cloak.

Brillen put his hands up, "Stop all of you. This was supposed to be just an exchange; Bryna Stoli for a wealthy sum of Jewel Press Latinum. So can we get on with business without all the drama?"

Tika spoke, "You know what, he's right. Let's talk business and get back to our lives."

Everyone eased up on their weapons.

"Well it's time to make the deal and get the hell out of here. Where is our J.P.L.?" Kora asked Brillen in a blunt tone.

"Sure, let me show you what I have for you and your charming young partner. By the way what is your name?" he asked, turning toward Tika. "I should know who is worthy enough to tag along with Kora Nugotu."

Brillen wanted to add her name to his list of kills. He had no problem killing other assassins or bounty hunters that had supposedly crossed him on deal negotiations.

"My name is Shalah Vallair, and I don't take well to being called a 'tag along'," Tika stated sternly.

"Well noted, my mistake," Brillen replied and clapped his hands.

Two of his personal guards went to a large window that was twenty feet wide at the side to the room. Visible through the window was the volcanic landscape which extended past the town of Vodoo. The familiar and all too common ash fell to the ground. Under the view of the landscape was a black chest two feet high and two feet long. The two guardsmen picked up the chest and walked it over to deposit it in front of the bounty hunters.

"Here is your payment and a bonus as gratuity for your exquisite work," Brillen said as one of his men unlocked the latch on the chest to reveal its contents. "Two hundred thousand J.P.L. inside, you may count it if you wish."

"Just more of your blood money," Bryna said in a hateful tone.

"Shut it, Bryna. You should be thankful that I can buy you so that I can do what I will with you. All the other people, and one other person that wants your head on a platter would have you killed in a heartbeat. I think I will let you live just a little bit longer, though you'll probably prefer the other option."

Brillen replied and spat in her direction, his spittle landing an inch from her knee. Bryna's eyes looked as though a fire burnt behind them. She tried to stand up as quickly as possible and hope to take a bite out of him with her bare teeth.

"How dare you bring him into this! I'm going to kill your ass!"

Onyx, disguised as Kora, held her down with one hand to calm her. Onyx knew that this bickering would get them nowhere and time was running short.

Underground, René and Aiden were running down a tunnel followed by three acidpods. The huge insects were spitting corrosive acid in the constables' direction, but luckily, the corrosive bio concoction could only stream out five feet. The acid was only meant for making it easier for the large creatures to tunnel underground and partially as a defensive mechanism. The centipede like insects were not predators, but were extremely territorial.

René and Aiden slowed down as they ran through a large cavern that was very humid. The constables could see a number of the huge insects, but what mainly caught their attention was one of the creatures that was nearly two times the size of the others; the queen of the acidpods. A dozen acidpods gathered around the queen to protect her from the would be intruders, hissed and snapped their huge mandibles to scare off the uninvited guests. On the ceiling of the cavern was a large webbing to keep roughly fifty larva eggs in place of her unborn young.

"Oh crap! Let's get the hell out of here!" Aiden shouted as the three acidpods were still in pursuit. Aiden glanced back and saw a shooting of the acid immediately corrode a large rock that he had almost stumbled on. René did not want to fire her weapon just yet to ward off the creatures. She was concerned that she would alert some of Brillen's guards to their location.

Aiden was starting to become winded by all the running around and took action by reaching into his side pocket and taking out a concussion grenade. He threw it behind him after he set it to a three second delay. The three acidpods had no idea what the device was and paid no attention to it. The head acidpod was closest to it and one quarter of its body was blown apart and that portion of the tunnel started to cave in. The other two acidpods stopped their pursuit when the cave came crashing in.

Aiden stop running and took a few breaths. René slowed down and looked back at Aiden's handy work and shock her head.

"Damn it, Dakar that was not the smartest move to make. You could have given away our position; which could lose us the element of surprise," she frustratingly told him.

"Hey, I was getting tired of running; besides we have at least another quarter of a mile to go before we are under Brillen's compound," Aiden said defending his action.

"Alright, but I'll tell you this, if you gave away our position I'm going to make sure I grab one of the acidpod larva and put it in your bed back on the ship. It'll give a new meaning to bed bug," René said and walked off in a skulk.

Aiden rolled his eyes and he was thankful that she was starting to develop a sense of humor.

After another five minutes of walking, the lights on their weapons shining reflected off a rectangular carving in the tunnel area that was nine feet in height. There were also four acidpod carcasses laying a few feet before the rectangular tunnel. René bent down and visually examined one of the huge dead insects and noticed the wounds inflicted on the exoskeleton.

"What killed them?" Aiden asked.

René stood up to address him, "The rounds used were from a high caliber rifle."

"That means we had better be careful." Aiden responded and readied his grenade launcher. René checked her rifle to make sure the safety feature was disengaged. As the two Constables peered around the corner, they could see lighting illuminating the new tunnel. They turned off the lights on their armor and weapons and headed toward the light.

Suddenly, an unusual stepping noise caught their attention. They quickly retreated to the Acidpod shells.

"What the hell is that?" René whispered as they heard servos and gears coming towards them.

Aiden shrugged his shoulders, "I don't know, but whatever it is, it sounds big. We should hide."

The two constables made themselves scarce by keeping low to the ground and hiding in two large crevasses across from the the lighted tunnel. They watched the entrance and were surprised to see a chrome and titanium steel-plated robot as it came into view.

The red sensory eyes along with the chrome head of the killer machine gave it a menacing look. The robot had numerous burn marks and scarring on its metal exterior from being in the heat of battle. The eight foot tall mech assault robot stopped at the edge of the rectangular entrance as though it was a boundary. It looked around for any movement or a target for its high caliber rifle mounted on the left shoulder. The Assaulter was only used on the battle field but somehow Brillen had been able to purchase this one.

Once satisfied that there was no threat to its owner's property, the robot turned around and walked slowly back into the interior of the corridor from which it came. The Assaulter turned the corner and headed to another area to complete its patrol. Both constables came out from the wall crevasses and breathed a sigh of relief that the robot did not detect their presence as they saw it leave.

"Dammit, this is going to be a problem. I've never seen one of those Assaulters up close before," René admitted quietly, just in case the robot had enhanced hearing.

"Let's try to find the elevator before that thing finds us," Aiden suggested.

"I know what you mean but I was expecting to take on real guards, not something like that. I might as well have a pellet gun," René admitted raising her gun. "I don't think this would penetrate the Assaulter's armor."

"Well then maybe you should leave the big boy to me," Aiden winked at her as he turned in the opposite direction.

They found the elevator at the end of the tunnel under the center of the Spearhead Compound long with a large walk-in vault. The area looked peaceful and it was perfect for an easy escape if the fortress was attacked or access to his valued possessions. Two security cameras were stationed by the large vault that was six feet tall. Aiden was surprised that it was not more sophisticated than a combination safe with a dial. But then, when you have an Assaulter as the protector of a safe, what more else would a criminal need? Aiden was already thinking of how to get into the vault.

Rene pointed to the two surveillance cameras as they slowly panned around the safe room area. Before they could be spotted, the lieutenant took out her silencer attachment from the boot section of her armor. Aiden knew what she was going to do next. Lt. Anukis attached the silencer to the barrel of her weapon and fired off two shots that disabled the cameras. The reduction of noise did not alert the Assaulter, but they knew that sooner, and definitely not later, anyone watching the monitors would alert the robot.

Aiden quickly walked over and looked at the safe as Rene took off the silencer and stood waiting for the Assaulter, turning her weapon in the direction where it most likely will be needed.

"I can hear the damn thing approaching, how much longer do you need, Dakar?" Rene asked eagerly as she tried to relax her trigger finger from the intensity of the moment.

"All I need is about twenty seconds." Aiden said as he reached into his backpack and pulled out the X-46 Acid Gun. He fired two shots and the large steel safe door started to dissolve away on contact. A melted hole of two feet in diameter displayed the contents inside the vault. Aiden shined a light into the safe and his eyes widened in surprise. He immediately rushed over to Rene as he could see the large steel figure approach them from down the corridor. The Assaulter was not made for running but it kept at a regular walking pace. Rene had a clear shot at the metal guardian as it detected them.

"Lieutenant we have an issue," he told her.

"No shit. Come on, come and get some of this!" Rene yelled as she aimed her long range rifle and chose the most possible vulnerable spot of the mechanized warrior. She fired and as the bullet left her weapon, it collided with the left glowing eye port of the sentry robot. If the Assaulter felt pain it did not show any indication of it as it shot the shoulder cannon at the constables. The shot was misaimed and impacted the wall.

Back in Brillen's meeting room,

"The payment is adequate but why are you exceeding the bounty that was set at one hundred fifty thousand J.P.L.?"

Brillen smirked, "You question my generosity, Kora? I'm giving you two and an extra fifty thousand J.P.L. because I appreciate your services and I have more than enough to replace that with."

"Are you speaking of your underground vault?" Tika inquired.

"How did you know about that?" Brillen questioned.

Upon hearing a boom underneath them, Tika smiled. "We have a team of operatives securing your assets as we speak."

"Oh really now?" Brillen said as the guardsmen guns turned on both Onyx and Tika as the alarm siren alerted everyone in the compound.

"Hey relax, relax, we're all friends here remember. Besides we needed some security just in case you tried to kill us before we got our payment," Tika told them trying to calm the tension.

"You two and your team must be ready to die. No one can access my vault," the Spearhead leader confidently informed them.

"Oh, don't think so highly of your security measures. If you doubt our capabilities why don't you contact your guards down in the vault area?" Onyx disguised as Kora said.

"I don't believe that it's necessary. So tell me, what did you ladies plan to gain by coming here? Taking more than your fair share or something more sinister than that? If it's more sinister I'm dying to hear it. Besides I believe I have the upper hand anyhow," Brillen surmised as his men had their weapons trained on them waiting for the first sign of aggressive movement.

"You're not concerned about losing the contents in the vault?" Tika asked perplexed by Brillen attitude.

"Not one damn bit. There's nothing in it anyhow." Brillen smiled, "As I said before, why are you here?" The four protectors stood alongside Brillen as he pressed his advantage.

"Why did you move your possessions? It's unlike you, Brillen," Bryna confused by his actions.

"Ha, ha, ha… Bryna Stoli, things have changed and I have changed. I hide my valuables elsewhere; I only use this compound as a meeting place for negotiations and interrogations. I still want you dead though and by my hand. You two have thirty seconds to tell me why you're here or these charming gentlemen will begin firing into your heads."

"I'm tired of this act," Bryna said.

Upon giving the verbal to the smart cuffs, the metal bonds holding her hands behind her back opened and fell to the floor.

"We're here to find out what you know about the Red Rage drug. Because if we don't find out where it's coming from, Scar will be destroyed, especially since the Flow Council is connecting most of the dealers and sellers are residing on this planet," Bryna told him as she stood to face him.

"Bryan Stoli, I must admit that was a damn good acting job on your part. So the Flow Council is planning to use the Solar Sword. This can be a little complicated, but quite frankly, I don't give a damn. If that's all you came here to tell me as far as information goes, it doesn't give you and your band much leverage," the terrorist leader told them looking disappointed by their efforts.

"How about a Gatling gun targeted at your head right at this very moment," Onyx added, shedding his Kora Nagotu disguise and returning to the natural muscular physic of the Eliminator.

Onyx signaled for Captain Hernandez to decloak the Enforcer as he had established a com-link to the ship when they entered Brillen's meeting room. Captain Hernandez had the cloaked constable ship on standby awaiting any actions to be taken. The corner of Brillen's vision caught the decloaking constable vessel through his large window and he turned toward the Gatling gun on the top side hull of the ship aimed at him.

"I have to hand it to you, Stoli, this is a turn of events, but yet again, I have my ass covered," Brillen said with the utmost confidence.

Suddenly the crew of the Enforcer was on alert. The ship's detection grid had picked up a large object moving in on them.

"Captain, we have a contact bearing 3, 4 mark 5, 7," Javal said as the blip was moving towards their location.

"What do you make of her, Javal?" Hernandez asked as he was in the pilot's seat.

"Readings coming through now; the configurations confirm that it's a Hammerhead Class ship, and its defensive screens are up, and the ship is locking missiles onto us," Javal alerted the captain. The Hammerhead was a ship that was two hundred and fifty meters in length it was an elongated rectangular rounded edge ship. The ships were older but highly formatable and used during the Elumeni-Eleminator War.

Javal was familiar with the controls on the bridge and he was best suited for tactical when Onyx was not aboard the ship. The only worry to him was that this was the first time he has ever manned tactical in an actual battle.

"All hands red alert, raise shields!" the captain ordered.

JONATHAN PICCINI

Static burst from the ship's speakers as the U.S.S. Enforcer was covered in a blue electric field. The shields were raised just in time as the hostile Hammerhead ship fired two missiles at the constable vessel. The impact hit against the shields, causing a deafening boom.

Inside the ship, the crew went on red alert as they quickly engaged all of their stations.

"Shields down to 58%!" a crewman called out.

"Dammit! We can't take another hit like that!" screamed the Captain. "We have to get to the skies and out maneuver this damn thing!"

The Enforcer raised itself perpendicular to the ground quickly, soaring to nearly forty feet, then immediately shut off the rear propulsion system to become level. The Enforcer sent itself into lightning fast reverse as the weapons targeting system locked on to the Hammerhead.

"Preparing air to air missiles to fire!" exclaimed Javal.

"Understood!" responded Hernandez.

The Captain looked at the screen showing the hostile ship flying towards them.

"Waiting on firing order!" Javal desperately cried out.

"On my mark, dodge their fire, then send missiles and alter course to out maneuver them from behind. The missile fire will only slow them down, so we have to take this damn thing out from behind by disabling its engines."

"Acknowledged!"

Brillen watched from inside his palace as the Hammerhead chased the Enforcer into the skies and chuckled in glee.

"Now, men, kill those two, but leave Stoli alive. I want to save her for last."

Before Brillen's men could even fire their weapons, Bryna rolled to the left, finding cover behind the bar while Tika using her pistol quickly shot down the chandelier, sending it crashing to the middle of the room, confusing and slightly alarming Brillen and his men as glass shattered in their direction.

As the mercenaries were preparing to aim their weapons, Onyx used both hands to grab the remaining metal and unshattered glass of the chandelier. Planting his feet into the ground, he used his robotic strength to shove the chandelier into their direction.

The men scattered to avoid the chandelier's dangerous impact, searching for cover. Tika put a bullet from her pistol through the merc's neck approaching the bar. The guard fell and blood gushed from his throat as he died in agony, not even able to scream.

The other guards started firing from their rifles. Brillen bolted to the door behind him.

Bryna laughed sadistically, "Hahaha! Yes! Run little man! Run like the fucking coward that you are!"

Onyx and Tika ran to a statue at the right side of the room for cover. Tika slid behind it as Onyx merely jumped to find safety from the armor piercing gunfire.

Bryna crawled carefully and slowly to the dead guard on the other side of the bar counter. She saw that the bar had a wooden door that could easily be opened. Bryna kicked the door open, and dragged the dead guard's body for cover. Bryna removed the guard's helmet and took his radio headset, attaching it to her ear. Bryna then took the guard's rifle and checked the scope. Bryna smiled.

"I'm coming for you, Brillen," she whispered.

Back down in the underground cavern, the missile hit and impacted wall, sending Rene and Aiden flying. René slammed into a wall, Aiden rolled a few feet away from the Assaulter robot.

The destructive robot looked down and prepared to shoot Aiden with its missiles. Aiden quickly barrel-rolled in between the legs of the robot, and attached a small explosive to its leg. Aiden jumped to his feet.

"V-X-6, detonate!" Aiden yelled, activating the voice command.

The device exploded, disintegrating the Assaulter's leg. The off-balance mechanical gladiator fell to its left side.

Aiden rolled to his back, armed his grenade launcher, firing three grenades at the fallen Assaulter while cocking the gun each time in quick succession. A large cloud rose from the explosions, revealing the Assaulter with one arm, no legs, and most of its torso missing. The Assaulter was about to fire another missile. Aiden's eyes widened in fear, his grenade launcher needed more ammo and there was no time to reload.

Before the Assaulter could fire, Rene paraded the killing machine with gunfire, hitting its now vulnerable core components. The robot went into an electric shock as its core parts combusted. The Assaulter's undamaged eye finally stopped glowing, indicating that it finally deactivated.

"Thanks," Aiden blurted.

"Yeah," René sighed heavily with a nod. "Shit… that was a tough son of a bitch."

René and Aiden both smiled and laughed in relief. René's left hand held her ribs in pain.

"You alright?" inquired Aiden.

"Yeah, I'm okay. Let's just get the hell out of here."

"Alright," Aiden walked over to René and put her arm on his shoulders to confidently move forward to the vault.

An Enforcer crewman looked at his interface, seeing that the Hammerhead was preparing another attack. "Sir! Hostile ship is prepping to fire again! We need to move!"

"Not yet!" demanded Hernandez.

Capt. Hernandez waited for the ship to fire at just the right moment. The Hammerhead's missiles fired, roaring at the Enforcer.

"Javal, now!"

At the Captain's command, Javal cut the reverse engines and did quick-paced barrel rolls to the left, evading the missiles. The crew felt no change in direction, thanks to the Enforcer's gravitational systems that held them in place.

"Fire the missiles!" ordered Hernandez.

Javal entered the command code, making the ship fire four air to air missiles from underneath the ship.

The Hammerhead took the brunt of the hit, slowing in their pursuit. The Hammerhead's shielding held strong, but the ship still took some of the kinetic force.

"Hit was successful!" Javal exclaimed.

"Get on their ass and prepare to fire the Plasma Lasers, and the Gatling guns!"

"Affirmative, Captain!"

Javal forced the ship to race behind the Hammerhead and flipped the ship upside down, aiming itself at the Hammerhead's rear engines.

"Fire!"

The Plasma Lasers fired destructive supercharged rays, as the Gatling guns unleashed a blaze of high powered bullets which in combination tore apart the engines of the Hammerhead. The engines soon combusted and the Hammerhead ship exploded from the inside, sending giant pieces rushing through the skies.

The crew inside the Enforcer exclaimed in victory. Hernandez and Javal nodded and smiled to each other, triumphant in their success.

"Javal, land the ship on top of the Spearhead base," directed Hernandez.

"Yes, Captain," Javal agreed as he shifted the controls, changing the Enforcer's course to the Spearhead base.

Onyx ran past his cover, aimed his shotgun, and blew apart a guard that peeked his head out. His body hit the ground with blood and brain matter smacking to the ground. Two guards were left, both horrified. Bryna heard them through the radio headset.

"Dammit! They're going to kill us! Get ready, I'm tossing a grenade," informed one of the guards.

Bryna aimed her assault rifle, waiting for him to throw the grenade. The mercenary's hand raised above his cover, armed with a high powered explosive. As the grenade was to leave the merc's hand, Bryna released several shots into his arm, forcing him to drop the grenade.

"Architect, no!" the mercenary cried out.

The grenade exploded. The guards died instantly.

Bryna vaulted over the bar.

"Let me handle this," directed Bryna. "Brillen will wet himself at the sight of me with a gun."

At a loud explosion echoed outside the base, Bryna, Onyx, and Tika glanced at the window and watched a giant piece of the Hammerhead crash into a building near Brillen's base.

"Huh!" Bryna stated. "I guess Javal and the Captain took down the Hammerhead."

Bryna then heard Brillen talking through the headset.

"Automated turrets, activate. Heh, that Stoli bitch won't know what hit her." Brillen exclaimed joyfully.

Bryna smiled, "Dumbass."

She tapped her Affix to activate her custom hacking program. She waited for the door to unlock and for the turrets to deactivate. She smiled as her Affix's screen glowed green, indicating she was in the clear.

Bryna marched to the doors and kicked them open. The hallway had the same marble tiling as the room, as well as wall mounted turrets, some more paintings, and in front of a door that led to something else, the frightened Brillen.

Bryna aimed her gun up to Brillen, "Scared that your turrets can't protect you, little man?"

"I—I," Brillen stuttered.

"You—you… are shit out of luck."

Bryna fired several rounds into Brillen's knees. Brillen cried in agony as he fell over, holding his bloodied joints. Bryna walked to Brillen, delightfully watching him bleeding and screaming. Bryna put her knee on Brillen's back, forcing his body to the ground, as she aimed her rifle to the back of his head.

"What do you want?" pleaded Brillen desperately.

"Where is the Red Rage drug being manufactured?"

"How will I know you won't kill me?"

"Because if you end up lying, I'll have to come back and question you again," Bryna aimed her gun a few feet away from Brillen's head and let off a few rounds.

The sound of the bullets crashing against the marble floor frightened Brillen.

"And again," Bryna fired more, again terrifying Brillen.

"And again," Bryna fired more.

"And again."

"Alright!" Brillen screamed, wanting the nightmare to be over. "I don't know where it is! I swear to the Architect, I don't. This is bigger than mere mercenaries and my Spearhead organization."

"Alright. Now, on to my other question."

"Let me guess. Where's your--"

"Yes. Where is he? Where's Forlka Skine?"

"You're going to love this. Forlka Skine is involved in the Red Rage manufacturing. I think he's heading the mercenaries. The Rycuda started losing numbers, but Forlka as a general of sorts would be highly effective. So I suspect that's the plan or something to that extent."

"No, he's got to be lying," she thought. Bryna looked to her Affix. "Well, it doesn't seem like you're lying."

"What?"

"I had a device tracking your heartbeat and respiration. Even accounting for your intense pain and stress, it can tell if you're lying or not. Want to know what that means?"

Brillen remained silent.

"It means that's the only important information you've got to give me. So you're useless."

A bead of sweat dripped down his forehead.

Bryna chuckled, "It's time for you to die."

Bryna got off of Brillen's back and grinned as he tried to crawl away with just his arms at his disposal. Bryna shot two rounds into Brillen's shoulders. To end Brillen, Bryna ran to him, kicked his chest to roll him to his front, and then shot repeatedly to the lungs. Brillen was going to die in agony, coughing up massive amounts of blood and chocking on it until he had no blood left to choke on. Bryna walked away, laughing in satisfaction.

As Bryna left the doors to go to seek the rest of her team, she saw the horrified face of Tika Shamari.

"What?" Bryna wondered in sarcastic confusion.

"You just killed him! You killed Brillen! The Captain said to get the information!" Tika shouted in disarray.

"I did." Bryna stated coldly. "I just had some fun afterwards."

"You can't… you can't do things like that, Bryna. You just murdered him, which the Captain gave you no order to do! You're supposed to do what he says!"

"Right, and let the slippery little bastard get a free pass of life because the Flow Council and the Constables will want to cut him a deal? I think not. He's a psychopathic murdering terrorist, he deserved what he got."

"The argument can be made about you just as much as him," Tika pointed out.

Bryna remained silent and started to show an expression of anger.

"Just wait until the Captain hears about this!" Tika exclaimed.

René and Aiden walked into the vault. The two Constables gazed at the vault's inner chamber, filled with technology plans, stolen goods, and even deactivated robotic workers. The stolen goods ranged from crates filled with resources, rare metals and alloys and stolen Affixes littered about the ground.

The robots were built for simple uses, each one skinny and wiry in its frame. The cybernetic beings were all simple steel in their shiny gray color. They all had slight bits of dirt, dust, and scratches on them. The lights on the joints and eye sockets of the androids were all grey, as there was no power shining through their bodies.

"Damn," blurted René. "How much do you think all of this is worth, Dakar?"

"Dunno," answered Aiden. "A lot probably. I'm kind of curious about something."

René glanced at Aiden in slight suspicion.

"It doesn't have to do with the cybernetics, does it?"

"Uh… it might," Aiden joked.

Aiden walked over to one of the robots.

"What are you doing?" wondered René.

Aiden slowly started moving to one of the inactive cybernetics. The explosives expert started looking up and down the robot, searching for an on switch or an off switch, something to activate it.

"Dakar!" René repeated in frustration. "What. Are. You. Doing?"

"Trying to talk to it," Aiden responded calmly. A weak cast of green light shined from the robot's eyes and scanned Aiden's Affix briefly.

"Constable I.D. recognized. Welcome, Constable Officer," The robot stated in a monotone voice.

Every robot in the room lit up in activation.

In unison, the remaining cybernetics all stated, "Welcome, Constable Officer."

"Who are all of you?" inquired Aiden.

"We are the creation of the Constables. We are created to assist in the law enforcement of the Flow Council."

"And who created you?" asked Aiden.

"Dakar, why does that matter?" wondered René.

"Shhh," Aiden whispered.

"We were created by Declan Dakar."

Aiden turned away briefly and rolled his eyes in irritation.

"Of course you were," Aiden remarked.

"Who's Declan Dakar?" René asked.

"My father," Aiden bluntly explained. "How did you get here?"

"Terrorist Organization Spearhead captured us from Research Base Eva-9," the robots responded. "Terrorist Organization Spearhead leader Brillen attempted reprogramming us for use as an assisting force."

"And he was unsuccessful?" Aiden assumed in question.

"Unsuccessful upon us. However, successful upon reprogramming of Guard 7-8-20. Whose signal link has been unsuccessfully achieved. We assume Guard 7-8-20 was deactivated through military force by Constable agents."

"By us, you mean?" René inquired.

"Yes," the cybernetics stated.

"Dakar, why are they all talking at the same time?" René wondered.

"I think my father tried programming them so that they could all share a signal link and act and react according to what any cybernetic saw and/or was ordered of."

"What does that mean?"

"The robots would be able to act based off of what the other saw. So, if one robot sees something happen, all of the other ones know at the same time. They'd be the perfect guards to alert the Constables of any danger. One mind, multiple platforms."

"Huh?" René blurted. "Look at how they move though. How they operate. It's like they're just doing what they're ordered to do. Isn't that illegal? Aren't all cybernetics supposed to have free will?"

"Well, I think there's supposed to be a head control bot. One robot that commands all the others to do what is ordered of it.

All cybernetics are supposed to have free will, yes, but these appear to be simple platforms, not cybernetics of high brain functioning. So, it's, well, it's in the gray area."

"What was your father trying to achieve with this?"

"All cybernetics have a link mind, a collective signal that allows them to know what all of the other ones are thinking. I think my father built these androids either to understand how it might work better or maybe improve it. I don't know."

"Would he be convicted of something for this?"

"I don't think my father would be convicted of anything, but this would definitely be something that would make him be watched a little bit more. Well, not that our family isn't already watched."

"What do you mean?"

"You know the Flow Council base? The one on Integra?"

"Yeah?"

"My father built it. He built the base."

"Really?"

"Yeah. That's basically why I got a free pass for—well, for what I did," Aiden looked to the ground in discomfort of his own memories.

"Well, you didn't quite get a free pass," René stated. "You got ordered to be on the Enforcer ship."

"Yeah, but for what I did, I should be in prison for life," Aiden shook off his mental anguish "Doesn't make a difference."

Aiden looked to the robots, "Can you establish a signal link to a ship? Our communication system is out and we need to reach our crew."

"Orders understood and will oblige," The androids acknowledged.

Captain Hernandez sat in his chair and looked at a lower ranked engineer Constable.

"Power status?" inquired Hernandez.

"82 percent. Shields at 76 percent," explained the engineer Constable. "Approximate time for full Enforcer reboot estimated at 28 minutes, 7 seconds."

"Acknowledged," affirmed Capt. Hernandez.

Another Constable turned to Hernandez quickly.

"Sir," the Constable called out, getting the Captain's attention.

"Yes?"

"A weak signal is coming in, it is recognized as a Constable I.D. The signal signature appears to be cybernetic intelligence."

"That's odd," Hernandez stated. "And the name isn't recognized in the Constable database?"

"No, but we have the best identifying and hacking system there is, it's a Constable I.D."

"And it's coming from Scar?"

"Yes."

"It might be René and Aiden… I hope it's René and Aiden. Put it on the main communication system."

"Right away."

The Constable turned to his post and activated several interfaces. Suddenly a slightly static sounding voice of Aiden came through.

"Captain? Hey, Captain? Are you there? Let Bryna know that we're at the vault and that we're ready to blow it when they are," Aiden informed.

"Actually, I don't think that's going to be much of a problem," Hernandez replied. "Something tells me that Bryna did just fine. Do you need assistance getting back to the Enforcer?"

"Nah, there's an elevator in the vault, I think we can reach the roof if you can meet us there."

"Already here, Dakar. Is the lieutenant there too?"

"Yes captain, I am" René announced.

"Haha, very good," Hernandez chuckled. "We'll see the both of you soon."

PHOE-NIX NEBULA

Star Enforcers: Chapter 16

"Bryna did what?"

Captain Hernandez stood inside the meeting room along with Javal, Onyx, and the emotional Tika. Javal was checking the engines through his Affix but was still paying attention to the conversation. Onyx stood blankly alongside Tika behind two of the meeting room chairs. Tika herself had her arms crossed in frustration.

"She killed Brillen. And pretty damn brutally, might I add," shouted Tika.

"Well, that's kind of to be expected," Javal noted while still looking down at his Affix.

"Sure, she's, well, she's not the most normal person, not that any of us are, but I specifically told her to keep Brillen alive," Hernandez stated. "He's a terrorist. The Flow Council wants him to pay for his crimes as they see fit."

"Listen to me, Captain," Tika blatantly ordered.

Hernandez found it somewhat strange that Tika was giving an order, meaning that Bryna's offense was serious to her.

"Her anger is completely out of control. She just went berserk and killed Brillen because of their past. She disobeyed orders. She went nuts because it was fun. Because she wanted revenge. She might do this again. Who knows who will piss her off? What if one of us does? What's to stop her? If she isn't put under control, what's going to stop her from coming after us?"

Hernandez paused to collect his thoughts.

"I have to be honest, Tika. I don't know what can be done to control her, and I don't know if it's quite as extreme as you're making it out to be."

"Captain, we almost died because of Bryna's, excuse my language, bullshit. René and Aiden in particular were put into significant and unknown danger, and do you want to know why?"

A silence fell.

"Facial recognition of Captain Hernandez suggests he wishes to hear of your answer, Medical Officer Shamari," Onyx broke the silence.

"Uh… the question was rhetorical, big guy," informed Javal lightly.

Onyx stood blankly for a few seconds.

"My bad."

"My bad?" Javal exclaimed with a confused glance at Onyx.

"A phrase learned from Explosives expert Dakar. Is this an action that is disapproved?" asked Onyx, noting Javal's confused expression.

"No, I just--I didn't know you incorporated what other people said into your baseline personality."

"I seek to understand and evolve myself to better suit my role as a soldier to the crew of the Enforcer. Using phrases and mannerisms learned from comrades should, theoretically, create comfort to my presence."

"Uh, okay," Javal sat staring at Onyx, wondering the true potential of his programming.

"Boys," Tika interrupted, "Back to the matter at hand?"

Javal turned to Tika and nodded in an apologetic gesture.

"Why do you think Bryna's acting this way, Tika?" wondered Captain Hernandez.

"Because something from her past is bothering her," Tika answered

"And what makes you think that?"

"Captain, we've all been put on this ship for past crimes. That's the whole point of this squad, right? To utilize past criminals and make them work for the Constables in exchange for freedom in five years,"

Javal immediately looked up to Tika.

"It's not as simple as that," Javal countered.

"Yes it is, you're just overcomplicating things," rebuked Tika. "Captain. We need to talk to Bryna. We need her to tell us what the deal is and how we can help and how we can resolve it. If her past isn't resolved, she will self-destruct."

"To be fair, that can be said about just about any of us," Hernandez responded.

"The rest of us aren't letting our anger to endanger the lives of the crew, Captain."

The Captain exhaled slowly due to stress. *"Why was I picked for this?"* he thought.

"Captain, I've seen her rage. I know that kind of rage. That comes from a deep turmoil that sticks with her. She only acts this way towards those in her past, which with Bryna, is quite a few people. That rage that Bryna has is… it's damn near unstoppable. It makes her careless. It makes her reckless. It makes her a danger."

The Captain pondered Tika's words with care and calm thought. *"She might be right."*

Capt. Hernandez thought back to the multiple times that the team had gotten by the missions by the skin of their teeth, and how much it could have been avoided had the team functioned properly. The Captain wondered if these near death experiences and failures could be avoided if he knew everything he needed to about his crew. The Captain knew his decision before he spoke the words.

"Alright, I'll talk to Bryna."

"No, we'll talk to Bryna," Javal directed as he stood up quickly.

The room shifted to watch him talk.

"All of us have been far too distant from each other. Do you want to know how this team will succeed? Trust. If we all know, and I mean know, not just assume, that we can trust each other, then we'll be able to succeed. For every high-risk mission we've completed, it's been close to near death. That Elumeni Golic nearly died because he didn't trust or rely on us in that fight. And I, well I took a bit of a hit from that, too."

Javal rubbed his healed wound in slight discomfort in his memory.

"We need to learn to trust each other and we need to learn to be able to tell each other anything and everything. If we don't, we could die. Like we almost have on multiple occasions."

"It sounds more like you want us to be a family than a bunch of soldiers," Hernandez commented.

"Maybe that's what it takes to make this team work, Captain," Tika proposed.

"Alright," Hernandez closed his eyes to think of how to handle the situation. "Where's René and Aiden?"

"They're both in the medical bay. René had a brused rib from the encounter they had with that Assaulter robot so I treated her, she should be good now. I guess Aiden stayed behind to check on her."

"Okay. Send a message to René and Aiden. Tell them to escort Bryna to the meeting room and we'll all talk this out."

"Affirmative," acknowledged Tika.

"So, how're your ribs feeling?" asked Aiden.

"Like absolute shit, but, well, I can feel them healing. I can tell that whatever it was that Tika injected into me is working," answered René.

"Yeah, I can't believe how close that was."

"Me either. We haven't had our asses kicked like that since, well, since Javal got stabbed by that damn Acer."

"Yeah."

"I hate those freaks."

"Acers?"

"All of them. All of the damn Elementals."

Aiden frowned in shock and disapproval. "What? Why?"

"They're freaks with unnatural God like power. Did you know that even now they haven't been able to explain how they do what they do?"

"Well, just because they have power, that doesn't mean they all decide to do destructive things with it. In fact, the Elumeni are trained to be tranquil and decisive."

"It seems to me like a lot of them just use their power to bully people. And the Flow Council encourages it."

"Well, that's kind of what the Flow Council does with all of their power if you think about it."

"What do you mean?" René asked in confusion and wonder.

"Think about it. The Solar Sword, the Constables, The Elumeni, even us. Everything is a huge ploy to try to bully anyone who isn't aligned with the Flow Council to get onboard with them."

"Well, we're not legally aligned with the Flow Council. We're, well, we're what we are."

"Yeah, but doesn't this all feel like some kind of an experiment?"

"What do you mean?"

"I've been a top level scientist since I was 12 years old, I know a prototype when I see one. I feel like, well, I feel like the Flow Council wants to use us just to see if it'll work."

"I don't know, Dakar. I've respected the Flow Council and the Constables for a long time, they seem to do everything right."

"Oh yeah? If they really did everything right, I doubt that you'd even be here."

René's expression went blank as she thought about beating Commandment Amadus near to death, his blood dripping from her bare fists. She then thought about her arrest for defending herself from a rapist and how much being punished for it disgusted her.

"Okay, you got me there."

Suddenly, René's Affix beeped. René pressed its touch screen interface in order to check the message she received.

"What is it?" inquired Aiden.

"The Captain wants us to escort Bryna to the meeting room. And he, uh, he wants us to stay in the room when he talks to her."

"Escort her? Why would he want us to escort her?"

"He wouldn't say."

Aiden looked at René in confusion.

"It sounds weird to me too," René said, as she stood up slowly while holding her bruised rib. "Well, let's not keep the Captain waiting."

Bryna laid on the couch in her bedroom. The room had two sections, one where the couch sat in front of the center of the room, with a coffee table a couple of feet in front of it. Multiple computer interfaces were at the front of the room, each one running different programs and awaiting for Bryna's commands. Bryn looked at the brand new bottle of bourbon she had retrieved from the bar to her right. Of all the choices available, this was what she needed now. Opposite the bar was the door to her room. Behind the couch, two steps led to the upper section. On either side of Bryna's large bed were doors. One opened into the compartment that held her armor and weapons, and on the opposite side, a door to the bathroom.

Bryna thought back on her victorious murder of Brillen. *"Haha, that look in his eyes,"* she thought. *"I can't believe how easy he was. Little prick thought he could kill me. It's almost like he forgot that my name was Bryna Goddamn Stoli."*

Bryna then thought back to Brillen's words of *"Forlka Skine is there too."* Over and over and over again. *"Forlka Skine is there too."* She thought again. *"Forlka Skine."* Again. *"Forlka Skine."* Again. *"Forlka Skine."* A sound of a little girl screaming echoed in Bryna's mind spontaneously.

Bryna slammed her coffee table with her fist in sudden outrage, causing her bottle of bourbon to fall and shatter on the floor. Bryna watched the bourbon spill over the floor and didn't move to clean it up. She was consumed with rage over the name of Forlka Skine.

The door opened as the automated voice declared **"Affix I.D. identified. Welcome Lieutenant Anukis and Explosives Expert Dakar."**

René stumbled into Bryna's room slowly, but still managed to maintain authority and power.

"Get up," René demanded. "The Captain wants to speak with all of us."

Bryna sat up quickly to greet her squadmates.

"Why?" wondered Bryna.

"He didn't say," René answered.

"Fine. Let's go."

Captain Hernandez paced slowly awaiting Bryna. *"What am I going to say? How am I going to handle this? What will Bryna do?"* Captain Hernandez thought about this challenge in mild anxiety. Finally, the door opened and Bryna, René, and Aiden walked in.

"So, what's this about, Sir?" inquired Bryna. "Mission debriefing or something?"

"Sit down, Bryna," ordered Hernandez.

"Haha, I'm sorry, what?" Bryna mocked.

"I said sit down."

Bryna's face went blank, her eyebrows raised in suspicion. Bryna glanced to Tika and Javal, their eyes planted purely on Bryna, nothing else. Bryna slowly turned her head to face René and Aiden, both of them looking somewhat unaware. Finally, she looked at the Captain's hands. Bryna had seen the Captain enough to know that if there was ever to be a hostile situation, his hands were at his sides for quicker reach to his pistols. It seemed to be a reflex for Hernandez, not a conscious thought. Seeing his hands near his pistols, Bryna knew she might need to handle Hernandez.

"Alright," Bryna complied.

The ex-mercenary grabbed a seat pulled it out slowly, still keeping her eyes on Captain Hernandez.

"What's this all about?"

"It's come to my attention that your anger is becoming a danger to us and to our mission."

"Uh huh," Bryna replied calmly, her hand near her hip to reach for her side pistol.

"We'd like you to tell us what happened to make you start working for the Constables," Tika explained. "And we'd like you to tell us what made you who you are."

Bryna stared at Tika.

"That's none of your damn business, first of all. Second, if Tollus didn't tell you, I sure as hell don't have a reason to tell you."

René walked behind Bryna.

"Bryna—," René called, getting her attention.

Bryna turned her head up slightly, still keeping her eyes on Hernandez. An abrupt punch came to Bryna's right temple, causing her to slam into the meeting table violently.

"Answer when spoken to," ordered René.

Bryna grunted aggressively and kicked out René's left leg, pulled downwards and thrusting the back of her head against the metal table. Bryna's hands immediately went to her knife, which went to René's throat.

"You want to hit me again, Constable bitch?!" Bryna screamed.

René's eyes widened in shock.

"Do not hit me again. If you hit me again, I will slit your throat and you will die."

Onyx instinctively pulled out his pistol and aimed it at Bryna's head.

"Bryna Stoli, remove yourself from Lieutenant Anukis or I will fire," Onyx directed.

Bryna backed away slowly and put her knife back in its sheath at her left calf.

"Stand down, Onyx," Hernandez directed.

"Captain Hernandez, Constable protocol directs that--"

"Stand down, Onyx."

"Affirmative, Captain," Onyx put his pistol back in its case.

"Bryna," Hernandez began. "You are a danger to this crew due to your anger. You need to get past it. In order to get past it, you need to tell us what happened."

"And if I don't?" wondered Bryna.

"I'll tell Tollus to put you in prison. Because this, your one and only chance at freedom will not work. And whatever deal you made with Tollus will be off."

"Are you serious, asshole?"

"It's Captain, Stoli. And yes, I'm completely serious."

Bryna closed her eyes, thinking about what she wanted most desperately.

"Fine, Captain. But be forewarned, what you know can't be unknown."

"If you're trying to say that whatever happened to you is going to shock me, I'm pretty sure you'd be wrong."

"Oh, you have no idea, Sir. You have no Goddamn idea."

Bryna clenched her fist in the mental pain of remembering her past.

PHOE-NIX NEBULA

Star Enforcers: Chapter 17

"I live by one thought: weakness, fear and helplessness turns to strength, anger, and power when the wrong person tries to break you. My life was made from this thought. Its entire existence is this thought. And I will never forget it or the one who made me think it.

"The man responsible for my life and all of its savagery and brutality is Forlka Skine, my father. I was the offspring of this vicious and psychopathic mercenary and a kidnapped woman that was used to be his sex slave. I never even knew her name. All I knew about my mother was that she died in childbirth.

"As a child, I remember crying constantly. I was helpless as Forlka beat me mercilessly. He was a big, hulking, terrifying mercenary. He had red hair like mine, but it had started to fade grey. A scar ran from his forehead to the left side of his face. A gash that looked like it has been caused by a knife wound.

"Forlka Skine led a gang of mercs that operated with brute force. They called themselves the Rycuda. The entire gang of mercenaries wore black impact resistant armor. On the chest of the armor, there was a red painting of a wolf's head, which was the Rycuda's insignia. Though the Rycuda took jobs from whoever could pay for necessary funds, the goal was to take over territory and establish more of a reputation for their disgusting mercenary gang.

"I remember Skine and his mercenaries taking prisoners and torturing them. The mercenaries found the torture sessions humorous. Forlka never laughed. It didn't seem he got enjoyment from it. More like he thought it was necessary. I had never understood his motives for the tortures and I still don't. Forlka also allowed the men to take women of their choice and use them as sex slaves. Forlka no longer did it because the last time he had, I had been born nine months later. Of course, I didn't have a name at the time. I was always referred to as 'It.'

"I often brought around food and drink to the men as they laughed at the torture and beat their slaves. I wore rags, not proper clothing. I was treated like a pet, not a person. The men did

not dare lay a finger on me. Not a single one of them wanted to know what would or could happen if they did. This was despite the fact that Forlka beat me repeatedly, sometimes until I bled and went unconscious.

"The attacks weren't as punishment or from anger. Forlka just did it like clockwork. I knew that they would come, but that doesn't make it any easier for a little girl who just wants the pain to stop. I still cried, every single time. Anytime I spoke, I was beaten.

"When I turned 8, Forlka pissed off the wrong person leading a bounty hunter group. Someone who used technology and tracking as opposed to brute force like him. The man was named Al'ra Stoli and his group of bounty hunters were named the Martai. Al'ra and the Martai wanted my father dead as much as I did.

"Forlka had kidnapped Al'ra's family and used his wife and daughter for his men. They'd been beaten and abused so much that eventually they died from their injuries.

"I'll always remember what Al'ra looked like. His skin was vaguely pale yellow and his hair was blue. His hair was cut fairly short, so it kind of spiked up all around. There was also a single trailing tattoo that went back and forth like a snake; it ran from his forehead to his chin, running past his left eye. The armor that Al'ra's bounty hunters wore was of a dark blue armor with golden trails running down it.

"The fight started to rage at Forlka's campfire, on his home turf. Normally it would be an advantage for him, but there was no cover and no secret passageways. Neither side had an advantage over the other. Al'ra, his men, and women fought Forlka's mercenaries and the casualties on both sides were immense as gunfire was exchanged. If gunfire ran out, some used knives and their bare hands. Al'ra and Forlka were the best trained in hand-to-hand combat. They both slaughtered whoever got in their way. Al'ra was driven precision and revenge as opposed to Forlka's savagery and brutality.

"As the gunfight went on, I noticed something. My father was not paying as much attention to me. I could escape. Maybe go with these men who wanted to kill my father. I needed to escape. I needed to get away from Forlka Skine. I ran as fast as I could. I desperately wanted to go with this man who wanted to kill my father.

"Unfortunately, before I could reach him, a stray bullet got me in the knee. My little body went down. I was driven, however. I crawled to Al'ra.

"As Al'ra was blasting the mercenaries in rage, he felt a little hand tug on his pants. He looked down, ready to point his gun, and saw a sad, hopeful, wounded little girl, crying and bleeding.

"'Please…'" I said. 'Please get me out of here. Please let me go with you. I don't want to be hurt anymore. Please.' Al'ra looked up and saw that Forlka was escaping. He had a choice. Leave the little girl he saw to bleed out while he got his revenge or save her. I don't know why he did it. Maybe it was for his family, maybe he thought that he had to be a good person for them, and that if he wasn't, he wouldn't be the same father and husband that they loved. Either way, I saw this look in his eye that said 'I can't leave her.'

"'I won't hurt you, little one.' Al'ra said in his accent. His accent sounded, like, well, like how mine sounds. He picked me up and carried me to one of his men. He handed me off to a surprised soldier, whose name was Rik'Tal Shivasti. Rik'Tal was of the Amras race, the red skinned humanoids that Kenkias Loro was also a part of. Rik'Tal sported the same blue and gold armor that Al'ra and all his mercenaries wore.

"'Sir—I—I can't take the girl,' he muttered in shock.

"'Rik'tal, you must. She is but a scared little girl.' Al'ra pleaded. 'I can not leave her in this place. Tend to her, I am going to finish this.'

"'…Yes, sir.'

"Al'ra ran towards Forlka, intending to kill him. As Al'ra shot at the hulking figure of my father, shotgun in hand, Forlka turned to him.

"'You will die for the crimes against my family, monster!' Al'ra shouted in fury. 'They will be avenged! You will die today!' I was amazed as I watched this man try to kill my father. I desperately wanted him to kill my father. I wanted an end to the man who had beaten me to no end. A man who had made me scared to so much as breathe. I didn't understand much at that age, but I did understand revenge.

"Forlka shot Al'ra's knee out with his pistol. Al'ra fell to the ground. His shotgun fell a few feet away from him. Before he could reach it, he felt Forlka's boot crush his arm. Al'ra screamed in agony. Forlka picked Al'ra up by his throat, watching him try to reach for his gun. Forlka pulled out his knife and stabbed him in the chest. Al'ra screamed. Rik'Tal screamed. I screamed.

"Forlka pulled out the knife and smiled. Forlka knew that Al'ra was going to bleed out and it was going to be slow. Painful. Forlka also smiled because he knew the look on Al'ra's face. That his hopes were crushed. That he had failed his family and that he was going to die. Forlka dropped him and left him to wither away in despair.

"'No! No, no, no!'" I cried, still in pain. I struggled to get free from Rik'tal's arms.

"'No, little one! You can not-!' Before he could finish his sentence, I bit his arm deep and hard, drawing blood, thus forcing him to release me. Before he could get to me, I was quickly staggering to Al'ra's bleeding body. And before he could try to save me, he noticed that there were mercenaries closing in on him fast. He had to engage them and leave me behind.

"My arms and single strong leg moved as fast as they could to Al'ra's body. Al'ra tried to hold his chest as he was bleeding. He had this expression that somehow, in some way, he would not die. That he would get his revenge. But he was kidding himself. I arrived to his body.

"'No! You can't die! Don't die!' I shouted. My voice started to crack as more tears rolled down my face. Al'ra took my hand and smiled.

"'Little one... you can't be afraid.' His tried speaking again but his words were cut off by a bloody cough. 'Be Bryna,' he ordered in a withering voice.

"'What is Bryna?' I asked, now broken because of Al'ra's wound.

"'It means noble. Strong. You must be strong. You must be...'

"Blood started pouring from Al'ra's mouth. I held his head in my arms. I felt him stop breathing. I felt the one man in the entire existence of the galaxy who had ever shown me any shred of compassion and kindness die. And it was at the hands of the man who took everything away from me, my father. I looked up and saw that his ship was starting to take off. I felt anger. Not fear. Not depression. Anger. Revenge. I wanted my father dead.

"I looked down and saw Al'ra's shotgun. I picked it up and aimed it upwards as best I could. I tried to align it with the ship correctly to stop it and force my father outside. I pulled the trigger. The bullets merely bounced off the ship's plating. My shoulder dislocated from the recoil. I hit the ground in pain and I knew I had failed. The adrenaline had worn off finally and the blood loss and pain had gotten to me. I fainted.

"A few hours later, I woke up. I was laying on a bed in a spaceship. My leg was bandaged and my arm was in a sling. My shoulder and leg felt pretty numb, so I assumed that they injected me with something to speed up the healing process. I was wearing a clean gown. Clean clothing was something new to me. I looked up and saw Rik'tal looking down on me, smiling.

"'You bite quite hard, little one,' he said, trying to be reassuring with humor. Dakar kind of reminds me of Rik'Tal in a way. Rik'Tal was out of his armor and in a white shirt, cargo pants, and black combat boots. He had a bandage over his left forearm from my bite mark.

"'Did you kill him?' I asked, still angry about the memories of my abusive father.

"'No. Little one, why were you there? With them? Were they... using—were they—,' Rik'tal couldn't finish the sentence. The subject of what he was trying to say seemed to repulse him.

"'No,' I responded. 'He was my father.' Rik'tal's eyes widened in shock.

"'Your father?' he asked in disbelief.

"'Yes, My father,' I repeated.

"There was a long pause between the two of us as I let it sink in and Rik'tal tried to get over his shock.

"'You'll be feeling better soon, little one,' Rik'tal reassured, attempting to change the subject.

"He died, didn't he?" I asked.

"'... Yes. Al'ra died,'" Rik'Tal affirmed in a slightly depressed tone.

"'Al'ra was the man who tried to save me?' I inquired.

"'Yes. He was a good man.'

" I started to cry. 'He was the best man in the galaxy,' I stated in a broken voice.

"Rik'tal held my head and let my tears sink into his shirt.

"'What is your name, little one?' Rik'tal asked.

"I started hiccupping as more tears rolled down my face. Rik'tal told me years later that he would have thought it was cute if it wasn't so soul shattering.

"'I don't—,' I tried breathing as tears rolled down my chin. 'I don't have one. My father called me 'It' most of the time. I don't have a name.'

"Rik'tal frowned. He gave me a look that almost said 'I'm sorry.'

"'What am I to call you, little one?' wondered Rik'tal.

"I paused and closed my eyes in deep thought. Then I opened them and I knew what my name was going to be.

"'Bryna. I want to be Bryna,' I announced.

"Rik'tal's eyebrows raised slightly as he recognized this from Al'ra's words and knew where I got the name.

"'Okay, Bryna. Soon we'll drop you off at a Flow Council outpost. There you can be retrieved and you'll be put into a foster home.'

"'No. I'm staying here,' I demanded.

"'You cannot stay here... we... we are people who are bounty hunters. We can not—'

"'Teach me to be like him,' I ordered.

"'What?' asked Rik'tal in confusion.

"'I want to be like Al'ra. Teach me to be like him. I want to be like him. And I want to find my father. And I will kill him.'

"Rik'tal's eyes opened in disbelief. His jaw dropped.

"'I will not do that, Bryna. I can not do that,' Rik'tal finally told me. 'You are too young. You—'

"'No one is too young to make a life decision that they want for the rest of their life,' a tall woman with pale skin and a completely shaved head stomped into the room, cutting off Rik'tal.

"Her name was Valya. Her eyes had a strange blue sparkly glow to them. I later discovered that they had been augmented with cybernetics. Valya was an excellent tech specialist.

"'I started out when I was not that much older than her,' she continued.

"Rik'tal shook his head seriously and stood up to look Valya in the eye.

"'No. This is a child. We will not train a child.'

"'Look at her,' Valya directed as she pointed at me. 'Look at that anger. That fire in her eyes. That willingness to kill. This is a girl who may become one of the best bounty hunters in the galaxy. And if we train her right, she'll be just that.'

"'We are not training a child, Valya.'

"'You are not in the position to make decisions regarding her or anyone of this crew. I was second in command. Now that

Al'ra is dead, I make the decisions. You are training her. We are all training her,'

"Rik'tal looked down to the floor, away from Valya, as he attempted to find something to say, but was unable to. Eventually, his head raised and he looked at her eyes, passively giving into her demand.

"'Yes, ma'am,' Rik'tal answered before walking away.

"For 9 years, our little bounty hunter group roamed from solar system to solar system, each of us getting over our past by killing and capturing bounties on mercenaries and criminals. Eventually the system of mercenaries trusting other mercenaries didn't work as well as with no one left to kill. Valya didn't care enough about anyone but Rik'Tal or myself enough to keep the other bounty hunters in line. Rik'Tal himself didn't want to stay a part of the bounty hunter squad anylonger because he didn't feel we were dispensing justice anymore, just senseless J.PL.rewards. I didn't exactly agree with him, but I guess I understood.

"For the years up until my capture and enlistment on this ship, I took bounty jobs from whoever could pay enough. Sometimes it'd be a simple job, sometimes people would try to screw me over after I was done, and after a while, someone might have been trying to get revenge. I did simple business, I only caused pain when I had a score to settle. If I ever found any remnants of the Rycuda, I'd try to find them and find their leader, my father. Unfortunately, nothing ever turned up after I killed his little thugs.

"Anyway, about six months ago, I got pulled in to do this one job. I was supposed to meet up with these mob bosses on Lictora, a planet on the outer rim of the galaxy that the Flow Council had no domain over because it was too expensive to establish a connection there. So, it was mostly run by mercenary squads who fought on it for dominance. I was briefed that I would arrive there and help find and assassinate one of the rival leaders in order to gain power.

"When I arrived at the meeting room, it was completely closed off, just a metal room with a single door and some lights activated via affix. The facility was underground and I was met by three different Elumeni instead of guards. I knew each of them. They were all forces to be reckoned with.

"The leader was a Daporan female, the same race as Javal. She looked quite a bit like him, just in female form. Her name was Kalama, and she was a water elemental.

"To Kalama's left was a Torrie Elumeni. Unlike Tollus, he didn't keep to the honor system of the Torrie's military anymore and his hair was completely shaved. His right eye was cybernetic and there was a burn mark leading from his forehead down to his chin. From what I'd read, it was gained from a training exercise on Talon, the moon where Elumenis train and hone their skills before going into combat situations. The man's name was Aratar and he was an Earth elemental.

"The final Elumeni was a woman named Harmony. Her skin was a jade green and her hair black. She had slight, thin horns coming from the sides of her head that began at the top sides of her head, then trailed down to her chin and stopped at a pointed curve before going past her face. Harmony was a wind Elemental.

"The three Elumeni told me that they would be forced to kill me if I didn't come peacefully. My first instinct was to blow each of their brains out and get away before their Constable forces arrived. However, killing military is bad for business as it's just begging for every Constable and Elumeni in the galaxy to put a rifle up your ass and pull the trigger. I didn't want to be taken in though. So I had to be flashy.

"I closed my eyes, used my Affix to deactivate the lights in the room and threw down a flashbang grenade. I opened my eyes and made a break for the door. I hadn't counted on Aratar's cybernetic eye adjusting to light so quickly, which was unfortunate for me because he'd shot spiked rocks in my direction.

"Even without counting for that, I still had somewhat of an advantage. Hearing the rocks coming for me, I rolled to the ground, getting underneath the flying spiked gravel and I laid down on my back with my pistol out. I had to shoot him to prevent him from attacking. I fired. One bullet hit him in the bit of flesh that hung from the neck to the shoulder and another two got him in both of his knees. I knew that in a few days with the Constable's repair systems he'd walk just fine again.

"Aratar screamed in agony, so Kalama acted as quickly as she could, even with the lights being off and her eyes having been temporarily blinded. She stretched out her arms and suddenly I heard busting from the pipes in other rooms on the left and to the right of me. I knew what she was doing. She was about to summon all the water that she could into the room and aim it at my general direction.

"I shot at her hair, trying to startle her. From what I've heard and read about Elementals, using their abilities requires an intense amount of focus. So even with her training, she got a little distracted by a bullet whizzing by her. I used the opportunity to run towards her. I needed to disarm her without shooting her and giving away my position to Harmony.

"I immediately got up, ran at her, tackled her. As we rolled against the ground, I used the momentum from the running tackle to dislocate her left elbow by slamming down on her bicep while pulling her forearm out of its socket.

"Quickly, Harmony shot wind at Kalama and me, trying to separate us both. I hadn't counted on Harmony's willingness to affect her leader as well as myself with the wind. We both flew against the wall behind us. As I was forced against the wall by the powerful air blast, Harmony reactivated the lights and she could now see me clearly. As the wind stopped, and Kalama and I dropped to the ground, I grabbed Kalama by her throat and put a gun to her right temple.

"I said 'Back off Elumeni. I will kill your captain.'

"I had forgotten that all Elementals had some form of control over all four elementals. That little bit of information may have been useful to me at the time. Kalama used her still working arm to heat my pistol, forcing me to drop it in pain. Kalama quickly let her arm go limp, took her left forearm with her right hand, and reset her elbow.

"She turned to face me quickly and grabbed me by the throat. Even someone who's as peaceful in thought as an Elumeni will get pissed if you dislocate their bones. I'd never really felt the power that those blue skinned Daporans have until the moment that Kalama started choking me and lifted me off the ground with one arm.

"Harmony stared at Kalama in shock and slight fear.

"'That's enough, Kalama!' Harmony screamed, but Kalama didn't seem to be in the mood nor the duty to show me any mercy.

"I did know of a weak spot that the Daporans have, however, the gills on her neck. I did what I had to. I grabbed all four of her gills with both of my fingers on each hand, stuck my fingers inside them, and started digging into her flesh with my armored glove. Apparently, it's like someone stabbing your insides in a very sensitive area. Kalama muttered a muffled scream and loosened her grip. I used that opportunity to free myself of her hold, take my combat knife from its hilt with one hand, and cut her wrist. It was brutal and unpleasant to someone who I'd had no death wish against, but it had to be done. I flipped Kalama over to her back and quickly turned my aim to Harmony. I threw my knife in her direction and she moved to the side to avoid it.

"I quickly bent down, picked up my still somewhat warm pistol and aimed it at her knees. Harmony used her wind powers to soar to the air and tried landing on me. Or at least she tried scaring me off so that I'd have to move into another direction. I rolled forward and turned back to see Harmony about to turn to face me. I tried to fire a bullet at her, but she disarmed me by kicking the pistol from my hand.

"It was close combat now. The trick with hand to hand combat isn't to stop the other person until they drop, it's to let them attack you and redirect their hits, thereby allowing you easy *access to take them down. Harmony threw a punch at me to the right side of my face. I used my right elbow to deflect her forearm, thereby opening the weak spot by her ribs. I went low to deliver a punch, but Harmony saw it coming and elbowed me in the back of the head. I went lower to the ground from the momentum of the hit, but sprung up with a punch to her jaw. I felt a crack against my armored glove.*

"Harmony sprang back and tried to get some distance from me. I was afraid of her using her wind powers against me so I leapt at her, knee first. My knee hit her in the chest and the wind started to be knocked out of her. I quickly followed my attack by grabbing her by the horns on the sides of her head, brought her down to my knee and drove it into her nose.

"I flung Harmony to the ground as she moaned in agony and I saw green blood on my knee. I let down my guard for a second because I assumed she was down. Mistake. Harmony's eyes started glowing and suddenly an immensely powerful gust of wind lifted me off of the ground. I was propelled in the air, helpless. I tried reaching for the shotgun that was attached to the lower back of my armor, but it was of no use, I couldn't control my body. Harmony then brought me down in a hard thump against the ground.

"The pain was immense as I landed directly on the front of my head that took a beat against the ground. I looked up to see Harmony inject something into my neck. I later found out that it was a sedative that they were going to use on me in case I came peacefully. Harmony spared my life when she could have taken it. She could have easily taken my pistol from the ground, aimed it at the back of my head, and pulled the trigger. But she didn't. According to the Elumeni, you are supposed to kill a dangerous target. I still don't understand why she didn't do it.

"Anyway, I woke up about a day later, handcuffed in a cement room with one metal door and no windows. There were constable guards all over the room and Director Tollus was standing right in front of me.

"The first thing he said was 'Wow. Three Elumenis. Three of the best Elumenis in the galaxy to take you down. Aren't you just the mercenary psychopathic badass they said you were?'

"I laughed in joy at his comment. 'And who are you?' I wondered, still plotting an escape attempt.

"'My name is Director Tollus. I'm an operative of the Constables and the Flow Council. I have a direct interest in you.'

"'And what interest is that?'

"'You see, I'm putting together a, well, some people call it a squad. Some people call it an experiment. Some people are calling it the worst damn idea ever brought up, but with you? A hand to hand combat specialist, one of the highest ranking snipers galaxy wide, an expert hacker, tactical expert, and someone with firsthand knowledge of operating in, and defeating almost every mercenary operation there is? Well, I think it's going to be the most successful project the Constables and Flow Council have ever seen.'

"'If you know me, you know I work for the pay, not the morality. I don't think I'd fit in with your ideal Constable world.'

"'See, that's the best part. It's not a team of Constables. Well, technically a couple of them were Constables. But it's not a team of Constables. It's a team of convicts.'

"'Well, that's interesting.'

"'Isn't it though? But I know you, Ms. Stoli. I know that you're just stalling until you can find a way to do what you have to in order to get out of my facility. But, I know a little secret. Would you like to know what it is?'

"'Please,' I muttered sarcastically.

"'I know who your father is. And I know you want to kill him.'

"'You what?

"'Oh, and that's not even the best part. The best part is that if you work for us on this team, on this ship called the U.S.S. Enforcer, we will help you find your father. In fact, we will help you kill him. And I know how much you want to kill Daddy.'

"'You're willing to help me find and kill Forlka Skine?'

"'Oh, yes. And then, once we help you and you work for us for five years… you're free to go.'

"'Really?'

"'Yes, really. But something tells me you're going to love this job. Something tells me that you're going to want to stay forever. Because I know all about your bloodlust. Even fighting three Elumeni, some of the biggest Constable agents there are in this world, you were willing to kill them just to escape incarceration. So, I wonder what you could do if you applied those abilities to just a whole lot of scum and sadistic murderers who deserve that kind of attack? Because I think the galaxy needs quite a bit of cleaning. And you're the girl to clean it. Are you in?'

"'Director Tollus, it would be my honor to kill for you.'"

Bryna looked up to her squad mates as all of them stared back at her in disbelief and shock.

"Your… your father is a mercenary and you're trying to kill him? That's why you've agreed to work for the Flow Council?" Javal inquired.

"Yes. You're stuttering. Did I not make that clear?" Bryna wondered sarcastically and with a lack of emotion.

"Bryna. You can't seriously try to convince us that you're not in pain," Javal stated. "This… this isn't something that you can casually pass off."

"And it isn't. I just hope that all of you know that I will kill Forlka Skine. And none of you will stand in my way."

"None of us said we were going to," René declared.

"Bryna, this isn't healthy. Your mind is supposed to achieve a level of happiness and peace. You are promoting a thought process of unhappiness and pain," Tika explained.

"Hahaha. All of you trying to tell me that you know what true pain is. Hernandez, your father does nothing but bail you out of any trouble you get into. Your mother wasn't a forced sex slave. Your father never beat you until you bled. Your father never put true fear into your heart. You've never even had fear for your life, not true fear. Not the fear that a person is truly in control of you and could take your existence away from you in a mere moment. Do not try to tell me that you know what pain is. You cannot even begin to know what pain is."

"Bryna, you aren't killing your father," Captain Hernandez demanded. "If you do anything that goes out of line, I will throw your ass off this ship. No matter what Tollus says, no matter what the Flow Council thinks about your actions. I will toss your ass off this ship without a second thought and we'll see how long you last with no ship, no resources and no food on Scar or whatever other planet is near when you disobey my orders. You will obey my orders. Is that understood?"

"Killing Skine will benefit our mission. I'll be assassinating the general of the possible armada that is behind this manufacturing."

"Wait, what?" Aiden blurted.

"Brillen informed me that Skine is involved in the Red Rage facilitating and distribution. It's probably on a larger scale than we originally thought and there is probably another motive behind it."

"Why didn't you tell us this before?" René asked with blatant confusion and slight irritation.

"I would have, but the Captain decided that it was a good time to start interrogating me about my past," Bryna responded sarcastically. "I'm going back to my room. If you plan on throwing me off the ship, Hernandez, come in whenever you'd like."

Bryna walked out of the meeting room. Tika soon exited as well, but not before giving a look of worry to the Captain.

"Well, that turned out well," Aiden stated, trying to calm the situation. "Maybe we can celebrate this? The Captain decided to poke the bear and it didn't work out kindly for him today?'"

Looking to his squadmates, he saw that none of them were in the mood, and so he stopped grinning, and quickly left. Soon, everyone but Captain Hernandez and Lieutenant Anukis were left in the room.

"Captain, what is your problem with her assassinating her father, really?" René wondered. "She's killed lots of times before."

"This isn't healthy for her. Murdering her own father--"

"It sounds like her father has it coming," René interrupted.

"That's not the point, René. She's already so far distanced from normal, this won't help her mind."

"Captain, all of us are fairly distanced from normal. Is this about Bryna or is this about you?"

"What?"

"Captain, I know you don't like not having any control on this ship or in life. In fact, it's probably why you rebelled the way you did when you were young."

"What are you getting at, Anukis?"

"You need to accept that you can't control everything and that you can't always get people to do what you think is the right thing. There are some things you need to let go, like revenge. Completely justified revenge, I should add."

"Are you saying its okay for Bryna to murder her own father?"

"I'm saying that you need to stop worrying about what right and wrong is for her and what right and wrong is for all of us. All of us crossed that line a long time ago. I think you need to make the best of the chaos that's become our lives. There's no need to try to make it seem like it's any better than it actually is."

Captain Hernandez and René stared at each other in brief silence. Captain Hernandez, not knowing what to say, just looked away from his lieutenant and waved her off. René rolled her eyes and left the room. The Captain tapped his Affix, accessing the central Enforcer communication system.

"Crew, set a course to get us off Scar. I've had enough of this planet."

Bryna sat in her room, angered and dissatisfied with the previous conversation. She heard her door automatically open. She seemed to have forgotten to have the Enforcer's A.I. automatically lock it. She was surprised to see not Captain Hernandez come into her room, but René Anukis.

"Here to piss me off like the Captain? Or were you just in the mood to bash my face in again?" Bryna declared.

René kept her blank expression. The lieutenant looked up towards the ship camera and readied to order the ship.

"Enforcer A.I., deactivate recording protocol in this room, both visual and audio by order of Lieutenant Anukis," René demanded of the ship.

"Gonna try to kick my ass without the Captain seeing? You're the one with the injured leg, you should see Tika before I break you," Bryna advised.

"I'm not here to threaten you," informed René.

"Oh? And what are you here to do?" Bryna wondered.

"Have you heard anything about my childhood, Bryna?"

"Didn't know and didn't bother to care."

"My parents were murdered. By some piece of shit Acer. Some freak that had unnatural power and was ordered to do it by a nameless asshole who owned a casino because my parents owed him money. Because of the order by a vicious man and the act by an unbound freak, my parents died, and I was left alone. Because of one person, well, two people, my life is like this. I've accepted it. I'm not a well person. I wouldn't want to share my pain with anyone. I've never had a serious relationship, never loved anyone truly, never found a reason to really care about what is to happen to the world or to my life other than anger. I've accepted that. And you've accepted the way you are too."

"Just get to the point, Anukis."

"My point is, if I had the chance to kill the piece of shit that took my parents away from me, that made me what I am, I would do it in a heartbeat. And I will not take that opportunity away from you, nor will I let the captain or anyone else do it."

Bryna's eyes opened in complete shock. "Really now?"

"Really. You have my promise that no matter what happens, you can kill your father. And I will help you in any way I can. No one will stand in your way while I still draw breath. Because sometimes someone deserves death. The captain will never understand that. His life was too perfect. He was just a spoiled rich boy who never really suffered except through his own choices. We were born into complete and absolute chaos and we know how the world really works and how to make solutions for it. If you feel killing Skine is the solution to your problem, I'll make certain that you achieve it."

"Well, Anukis, you may be one of the few people in this world that I can now call a friend."

"Likewise. Let's get ready to kill your daddy."

JABAAR L. BROWN

243

Star Enforcers: Chapter 18

Captain Hernandez returned to the bridge from the briefing room. He was still contemplating what to do about Bryna's obsession of killing her father. To have a blood thirst such as hers would undoubtedly cause some complexities in the crew's future missions. Miguel decided to tolerate her attitude up to a certain point, but if she crossed the line, Bryna would be tossed off the ship. Hernandez had to acknowledge that his entire crew had issues, but some were definitely worse than others. He realized he had no control of their past difficulties; he just had to work within reason of his command.

When René saw the doors slide open and the captain enter the bridge, she primed the engines to depart the mercenary planet of Scar. Before Hernandez could reach his dark brown leather command chair, the regular crew members manning the communications controls turned to face him.

"Captain I'm receiving a visual transmission from Director Tollus."

"Place the communiqué on the main screen," Hernandez ordered, with a frown on his face.

He needed to inform the director that their mission to find the Red Rage facility was delayed. If the terrorist Brillen was still alive, he might have been able to report differently.

The image of Director Tollus came up on the large view monitor in front of the bridge. His purple skin, black Mohawk, and horns were clearly visible against the stunning mega city seen through his office window.

"Hello Captain Hernandez. I am ready for your status report on your mission to Scar?"

"Well, Director, things haven't gone as well as we anticipated," Hernandez began calmly, hiding his frustration.

"Explain, Captain."

"The mission was compromised when our investigation on Brillen lead to his death when he attempted to assault one of my officers."

"Before he was killed, did that officer have a chance to make that bastard squeal?" Tollus asked with a raised eyebrow eager to hear an answer.

"Nothing concrete. Just that a Forlka Skine is associated with those in charge of whoever is running this."

"He is what?!" Tollus replied in outrage.

"You… know the man, I assume," the Captain responded in slight surprise.

"Captain, he--he--" Tollus stuttered as he watched Bryna walked onto the bridge.

"He what, Tollus?" Bryna wondered.

Tollus couldn't think of what to say.

"He. What," Bryna stated aggressively, as if she knew what he was going to say.

"Forlka Skine has been incarcerated for… for over a year."

The entire crew was shocked.

"Were you ever going to tell me this, Tollus?!" shouted Bryna.

"It wasn't my decision to keep you in the dark, Stoli."

The crew was confused. Other than Bryna, only one other person pieced together the proper sequence of events.

"Oh," Tika blurted. "Bryna thought her father had been on the run for years. The Flow Council had him. And then--"

"Then they sent their men after me," Bryna interrupted.

"Right," Tika replied. "And they were supposed to kill you. Skine is out of prison."

"That's impossible," René declared. "Unless he broke out, which everyone would have heard about, only a Flow Council member could let him out."

"Why would they let Skine, a known mercenary out of prison?" Hernandez wondered.

"Because he was their first choice, not me," Bryna grunted.

"But something must have went wrong. He must have gotten free. But we couldn't know about him escaping, because the Flow Council were the ones to illegally let him out in the first place."

Tollus said nothing. His face was filled with discomfort as this information was being uncovered.

"So, what? You were going to have me killed and then Skine would join this crew? Was that it? But instead, you just decided that I was too valuable to keep alive once that Elumeni spared me. You sick piece of shit."

Director Tollus shrugged.

"I don't have to explain myself to you, Stoli," Tollus replied. "I was following orders. What information do you have?"

"If I may Director, we have a piece of evidence that a Constable is examining which may provide us with a lead," René said in defense of her crew.

"Oh really Lieutenant, and what pray tell are the findings?" Tollus asked looking over to the lieutenant along with the rest of the bridge crew.

René Anukis was now under the pressure of playing a wildcard that she hoped would pay off. She tapped her affix.

"Aiden, please link into the main communication channel. We are in need of your findings."

Within a few seconds, the screen split and Aiden appeared on the other half. His workshop was full of technical equipment, loose wires, circuit boards, and explosive materials. Dakar's lab was restricted due to its highly volatile elements. The room was fortified with thick alloy walls and its location allowed the workshop to be jettisoned from the ship if the explosive devices would ever pose a threat to the ship or the crew.

"I'm a little busy over here. What's up?" Aiden asked with his eyes steady, looking through the scope of an electron microscope that was on his work bench.

"If we could get your undivided attention, Constable, we would like to hear of what you've discovered on the planet that might give us a lead on where the Red Rage drug is being produced," Director Tollus asked in an even tempered tone.

Aiden turned away from the electron microscope when he heard the voice of Tollus speaking to him. He stood up from the chair in a bit of surprise.

"Oh, Director, my bad. Lieutenant Anukis and I discovered a batch of twenty cybernetic robots inside a locked vault in the voles of Brillen's stronghold. I extracted one of the CPU chips from one of the units. The robots were lightly covered in Red Rage residue from having been in contact with the substance. I have attached connectors to the chip to access its memory. I'm now decoding the chip to ascertain where the units were before Brillen's forces stole them from whatever freighter or ship they were on.

"How long will it take for you to decode the chip and grasp where the units had been?" Tollus asked with interest.

"I'd say it may take another thirty to forty minutes. Fortunately, I'm familiar with this design as it appears to be a copy of my father's designs."

Aiden turned and reached toward a control panel near his work bench. His image was replaced with that of a CPU's schematics.

Onyx's eyes glowed red as he quickly scanned the new display.

"I have an idea of this chip's design matrix. The chip's construction is somewhat of a lower grade from my own nano independent processors. Not as advanced, but adequate enough to establish hive mentality programming and function."

"Hive programming?" the captain asked, not aware that such computer programming existed.

They were used to advanced mechanical beings having independent Intelligence.

"Yes," confirmed Lt. Anukis. "That would seem consistent to what me and Aiden experienced when we came in contact with the robot units. They all seemed to activate at the same time and spoke in unison."

"Who or what was the controller?" Capt. Hernandez asked.

"There didn't appear to be a queen or individual controller," Aiden replied.

"It makes logical sense to believe that the automatons were used to manufacture or harvest the drug because they wouldn't be affected by the properties of the substance," Onyx theorized.

"Why would they respond to us and obey Constables, then?" René wondered.

"It is probable that the machines had an original mind created by Declan Dakar which was subsequently rewritten over time to suit the needs of whoever created the bodies of these machines. Once deactivated and then reactivated manually, they most likely lost their memory, their rewritten functionality, and reset to obey Constable ID and orders," Onyx thoroughly explained.

"I... guess that makes sense." René responded.

Suddenly, cybernetic Ambassador D.A.X. appeared on a new screen split.

"Director Tollus, the Flow Council and I have been monitoring your transmission to the constables and have come to an agreement. It is our decision that the 20 cybernetics be destroyed, along with any additional ones you find. These automatons violated the Neural Network Law since they are not part of what brings order and peace to our galaxy. Of course, the one among you is under the protection of the Flow Council and Director Tollus and is excluded from that Law."

Onyx looked at the Ambassador with glowing eyes for a few seconds. The bridge crew glanced over at their weapons officer, trying to ascertain if the statement truly bothered the independent mechanical sentient being. They knew he was so unique that he wasn't part of the Neural Network Law, nor would his programming allow it. Onyx was still a mystery to the researchers that found him and were continually examining his highly advanced circuitry.

"So, you want us to destroy the robots and find out who

manufactured them?" the captain asked, not too thrilled about taking on the tasks of two missions at the same time.

"That would be logical. If you find who created these illegal automatons, your crew will theoretically find the Red Rage facility. Director Tollus, we leave the rest in your capable hands," Ambassador D.A.X. concluded as the image faded from the screen.

"Captain you have your assignment. Good luck," Tollus said as he shrugged his broad shoulders and ended his transmission.

"I guess we have our work cut out for us," René said to break the silence.

The captain looked in her direction, seeing the back of her head.

"Indeed we do. So, lieutenant why didn't you tell me earlier about this piece of evidence you two obtained?"

René turned around in her swivel seat to look at the captain. Aiden remained quiet since Hernandez had asked his lieutenant the question. She had a small smirk on her face but the expression quickly disappeared when she addressed him.

"Well hmm, let me think about that one. Once I got back on the ship, I had to go to the infirmary for my injuries, which still hurt by the way. Then I got called to the briefing room to confront a crew member about her past, who at that time tried to slit my throat. After all the excitement, that one detail about the CPU chip that Dakar was analyzing must have slipped my mind," René stated, sarcasm reeking from her lips.

"Alright Lieutenant, I get your point. Now that you've caught your breath, I would like to say good work by the both of you and the rest of the crew," the captain acknowledged and René nodded with a grin, then swiveled back to the piloting controls.

"Captain, I'd suggest placing the ship on yellow alert. I detect five mercenary carriers coming out of slip stream and approaching our coordinates," Onyx informed Hernandez.

"Agreed. Onyx, take the ship to yellow alert. Those five ships must be some of Brillen's back up forces. How much time do we have till they get here?" the captain asked as bridge lighting took on a yellow hue, signifying the ship's alert status.

"Best estimate is four minutes."

Hernandez looked up to the view screen at Dakar's image.

"Explosives Expert Dakar, we have very little time to do any real damage to Brillen's fortress, and we don't have the time to send a team the underground area to destroy the cybernetic droids. Do you have any suggestions for a quick tactical solution?"

"Well Captain, being the beautiful and hilarious genius that I am, I'm sure I can come up with something," Aiden told him as he pulled a small data pad from his back pocket.

He thumbed through it for a couple seconds until he found what he was looking for.

"Captain, instruct the torpedo room to load torpedoes D-68 and D-69."

"Torpedo Room, unlock Dakar's special arsenal locker and load torpedoes D-68 and D-69," Hernandez ordered over the com system. "So what's special about these torpedoes, Dakar?"

"As you said Captain, we can't send a team to the underground area of the stronghold but these torpedoes will be all that we need. Each torpedo contains four small rotating drill tips designed to easily travel through rock and detonate at the desired depth," Dakar smiled, knowing that he provided the proper solution.

He ended the visual conversation and returned to decoding the CPU chip.

"Torpedoes loaded, Captain."

"Thank you, Torpedo Room. Lieutenant, take us up."

"Aye sir; engaging thrusters," she replied and the growl of the thrusters could be heard in the background, causing the Enforcer to lift off of the ground smoothly.

"Captain, we will be in killer range by the approaching force within less than two minutes." Onyx cautioned.

"Understood. How far up are we, Lieutenant?"

"We're fifteen hundred feet above the surface of the planet

Captain."

"That's good, maintain this altitude. Onyx, scan for the caverns under Brillen's fortress."

"I have located the caverns at three hundred feet below the surface. I am setting detonation controls for that depth," Onyx replied.

"Very good, Onyx. Fire when ready."

"Aye sir, firing now."

Two torpedoes darted out of the front of the ship from the weapons tubes beneath the bridge and sped on their way to the destination. The projectiles plowed through the roof of Brillen's compound and began to burrow through the hard cement. Upon reaching the desired depth, they exploded. Shortly after the detonations, Brillen's fortress could be seen collapsing into the ground.

"Everyone remember: don't piss off Dakar," Hernandez jokingly noted.

None of the crew seemed too amused with his statement.

"Captain, those five ships will be at killer range within twenty seconds," Onyx reminded him.

"Oh by all means, Onyx, engage the cloak."

"Cloak engaged," he replied, as a small high pitch hum could be heard.

"Excellent. Lieutenant, take us out under Sub Slip Stream speed, heading three four mark seven four.

"Aye, sir," she replied and took the Enforcer away from the path of the approaching ships and broke through Scar's atmosphere.

The incoming ships couldn't detect the constable ship as the crew hoped for. Hernandez stood up from his command chair.

"I'm going to Aiden's workshop to see what else he has found on the chip. René you have the bridge."

As Hernandez made his way down the Deck One pathway, the crew members that passed him glanced in his direction. Some of the crew members saluted him, most of them nodded in some form of respect, but several paid him no attention at all. What else could one expect from a ship load of prisoners, the captain thought.

Aiden's workshop was to the rear of the ship and there was a reinforced door that had the same restricted access like the briefing room.

"Computer, this is Captain Hernandez, open doors to Constable Dakar's workshop."

"Acknowledged, please verify by retinal scan," the ship's computer said and a green beam of light shot out from the control panel by the door.

Hernandez opened his eye and stuck it close to the beam.

"Retinal scan verified. Please enter Captain Hernandez."

The random types of procedures used to make sure who was who always interested Hernandez.

When the door slid open, Miguel noticed Aiden sitting in a chair near a large computer screen. There were a series of binary number and letter codes shown on the screen.

"Ah Captain, I'd figure you would stop be sooner or later," Aiden remarked, not looking or bothering to turn around.

"Yup, so were you able to unlock the transponder coordinates of where this droid was operating before it was abducted by Brillen?"

"I should have an answer any minute," Aiden informed him and turned away from the computer screen to look at his commanding officer. "So how did the drill torpedoes work out?"

"Your title is well deserved. This was the first time we ever used something from your personally designed arsenal, and I'm happy to inform you that Brillen's basement was not only destroyed, but his entire complex fell into the cavern."

"Wow! I'll have to take a look at the surveillance video when I get a chance," Aiden smiled.

"You know--" the Captain began to say. "All I really know about you is that your father built the base on Integra, and that you're a genius. And you didn't get your combat experience until after you were imprisoned, like me. You don't seem the violent type, in fact, you don't seem malicious or destructive to anyone at all."

Miguel shifted his body over to the work table and looked over to his explosives engineer.

"Tell me Aiden, what was your crime?" he inquired in a disarming fashion.

A beep interrupted from the computer screen.

"Maybe another time, Captain," Aiden responded, managing to avoid the subject.

Returning his attention to the computer screen, he added, "The computer has decoded the memory to give us a location of its primary operational tasks."

Hernandez looked at the screen as well and saw six distinct paths of travel and routes the group of robots operated.

"Most likely the group of robots was assigned to a freighter to smuggle the drug from place to place."

"All shipping lanes seem to originate from this set of coordinates," Aiden said and pointed to the set of numbers.

Miguel tapped his affix, "Lieutenant Anukis."

"Go ahead, Captain."

"I need you to pull up the star map and give me a location on these coordinates, sector five one nine one mark eight."

"I'm on it, Captain," René replied.

"Very good," Hernandez stated.

"Um, Captain?" René muttered. "The location, it's, uh, a Constable facility."

"I don't care. Get us there, keep the ship cloaked and scope out the facility. We'll make a plan of action from there."

PHOE-NIX NEBULA / EDITOR JABAAR L. BROWN

JABAAR L. BROWN

Star Enforcers: Chapter 19

The U.S.S. Enforcer was drifting slowly towards the station that the robots seemed to originate from. The station was mounted to a moon that orbited a gas giant. This system had only a few planets that weren't gas giants, and the few that were habitable didn't seem to have any life on them.

The station itself that the Enforcer had traveled all this way to had a simple rectangular shape and its windows completely darkened, with no electronic lights on to illuminate the inside of the station. Aside from the windows, the station was painted entirely white. Scorch marks covered the station's exterior, and chunks of its metallic structure were drifting away from it, as if some great, destructive forces had tried to rip this station from the foundation which was rooting it in the moon below, without being able to completely destroy the facility itself.

"Seems like it was attacked." Lieutenant Anukis pondered to the captain.

"Hmm." The Captain mumbled in response as he nodded his head, his hand firmly on his chin.

"Is this station even online?" Ren'e wondered on the deck.

"Life support systems are fully operational." Onyx stated.

"I wonder if anyone's there." The captain muttered quietly.

"The stations' communication systems and cameras are offline." Onyx said to the Captain.

"So there'd be no way to see if there's anyone actually over there without actually physically going onto the station." The captain replied to Onyx, as he looked to the android's face.

"That is correct." Onyx affirmed. Hernandez nodded once more, and he started thinking to himself.

"I say we send a team in to investigate." Ren'e suggested. The captain looked upwards to think to himself about her proposal.

"Agreed." he replied.

"I volunteer." Ren'e declared.

"That's probably a good idea." Captain Hernandez answered in agreement. "If there are people aboard, they could need medical assistance, so bring Tika. And if the systems are offline, Javal's the only one among us who can bring it back."

"Agreed, Captain." Ren'e stated simply in compliance.

Moments later, Ren'e, Javal and Tika were on a shuttle to the station. Ren'e and Javal piloted the ship as Tika was sitting in the back. Tika was waiting patiently for them to arrive, while tapping her Affix.

"What might you be doing?" Javal asked Tika curiously.

"Checking the station's systems." Tika answered. "Seems like the facility had an emergency shut down of all systems but life support to conserve power."

"For what reason?" Javal wondered.

"One of their generators were destroyed. Probably from some kind of firefight." Tika replied.

"That's strange." Ren'e quietly uttered. Tika said nothing in response, she only tapped her Affix. Suddenly, Bryna's voice came over the intercom.

"This station seems to have a very simple automated intelligence system responsible for maintaining control over the power systems. I've hacked into the station's A.I and having it activate the lighting and power to other non-critical systems." Bryna explained. "You won't have to find out what happened here in the dark."

"Very good." Ren'e responded in a grateful tone.

Morenko walked about the bottom of the Enforcer ship, staring occasionally at the few men guarding the ship's power core. Several other Enforcer staff drifted about the ship, but the core was mostly guarded by Morenko, the Torrie woman he saw in the night club, and the human with brown hair that she was dancing with. Morenko glanced to the tag on her Constable uniform, recognizing the name "Jai." Something that sounded familiar. Something his mother or father used to remark to about the Torrie.

Morenko took the flask strapped to his belt, and started sipping his drink. The burn of the cheap alcohol calmed his nervousness, and slowed his reflexes just a bit, not too much for him to notice, but enough to make a small difference in how he walked. The headset on Morenko's purple face was tuned into the Enforcer's public communications.

Morenko pulled the left sleeve of his Constable uniform up slightly, just enough to see the scar on his arm, left by the cigar burn from the Amras woman he'd met. Jai walked up to him, slowly, behind his back. Morenko felt suspicious of her presence, but didn't want to give away his ensuing betrayal. So he attempted to remain calm, slow his breathing, act as though everything was normal. Morenko reached his hand to pull up his sleeve when Jai gently stopped him, placing her fingertips on his wrist. Jai's warm breath was gently being felt on Morenko's neck, making him slightly more uncomfortable.

"Yours matches mine." Jai whispered, pulling back the sleeve on her Constable uniform, revealing the same cigar burn left on Morenko. Morenko looked to her eyes slowly.

"You too?" He asked. Jai nodded, smirking while she did it. "Anyone else?" Morenko wondered.

"Fiyush, and the other three humans, except Alexander." Jai answered.

"Is that your human play thing?" Jai nodded. "Why not him?" Jai shrugged, over exaggerating a frowning face, trying to be playful, but the intensity of her eyes couldn't help but tell the tale of her insanity and viciousness toward everyone she knew. Morenko looked off at Alexander, noticing that he was staring at the two of them. "You don't mind getting rid of him?" Morenko wondered.

"He was fun." Jai responded, starting to feel Morenko's chest. "But I haven't had someone purple in my bed in a little too long." Jai stated, starting to feel the top of Morenko's head. "I'd love to see what you'd look like embracing war."

"Crew!" Captain Hernandez shouted, via intercom. "We're getting a distress call, I'm putting it on public comm."

A frantic sounding young woman's voice came through Morenko and Jai's headsets. "We need assistance. Our crew is scattered, our people are dissipated, and they're inside, and we can't get away!" She screamed. Morenko recognized the secret phrase.

"Well." Jai started. "It seems like it's time." Jai pulled away from Morenko slowly, and started walking toward Alexander. Alexander saw a grin growing on her face as she paced closer and closer to him. Alexander smiled, hoping for affection.

"I was getting a bit jealous." Alexander said. "Haven't forgotten about me?"

"Not at all." Jai replied, playfully. She started reaching for her pistol strapped to her belt as she walked behind him. Jai raised her gun, aiming it at Alexander's head, and pulled the trigger. A bullet ripped through the back of Alexander's head, brain matter flying through the air, blood splattering onto the deck. Alexander's head was mostly left only with his nose, jaw, and mouth, his tongue loosely dangling as his body hit the floor. More blood and red matter spilled onto the floor from the hole left in Alexander's head.

"He's dead." Morenko muttered. Jai laughed in response. "We have to destroy the Slipstream Drive." Jai nodded.

"Mhm." She mumbled, nodding her head, and still staring blankly at the dead body.

After docking the shuttle, and walking into the station, the lights flickered on to reveal something atrocious to each of them:

Eviscerated organs, massive amount of blood, massacred bodies that were hardly even counting as people anymore.

"What the hell did this to them?" Ren'e screamed in alarmed outrage. Tika examined the bodies covering the marble floors, the nearly unbreakable glass looking out into space, and the moon nearby. Tika's pupils danced around in her sockets as she mumbled to herself and paced in the mixed blood that was soaking into her boots.

"No. No, no, no." Tika muttered. "Too big, too big. Karsh native to Amras since the invasion. Unlikely. Crime scene shows signs of humanoids. Can't be. Can't be. Unless androids. But no, too messy for androids. Not logical to make them like this. Someone fed. Signs of fecal matter left behind. Signs of insanity and rage." Tika kept whispering to herself.

"Any news on opening the locked rooms on this station?" Javal inquired as he tried to keep his eyes aware from the gory sight and his nose distracted from the disgusting, corpse ridden scent all around him.

"I don't think so." Bryna answered over the intercom. "The A.I. has some kind of protocol I can't override. Whoever designed this is smarter than I am, sad to say."

"So you can't do anything to find the things that did this is what you're saying." Ren'e said, aggression in her voice. Clearly, the dead Constable scientists were getting to her. Bryna shrugged.

"Not from here, no. We'd need to get to the source of the programming. I'm guessing this facility has the A.I. unit in one of the rooms. I maybe slightly distracted here on the ship we had a distress call come in from a nearby vessel. I'll give you more details in a few minutes." Bryna responded.

"Oh, Architect." Tika whispered in a frightened revelation, her hands pulling her hair slightly in disbelief.

"What?" Ren'e inquired.

"This… this is Red Rage." Tika muttered.

"What?" Ren'e asked, bewildered by Tika's statement. Tika pointed all throughout the room, where some small bright red smudges were about the glass that looked out to the eternal vacuum of space, on the bodies, and the entirety of the facility. It looked like speckled bits of red powder, and was difficult to notice for the untrained eye. This powder is what was making Tika become nervous, afraid.

"Someone gassed this facility with Red Rage. And these people, I think they were scientists." Tika's bright purple eyes widened, her mouth trembling and her hand cramping in a frightened tick. "Someone gassed this place with a vaporized form of Red Rage. They tore themselves apart. They went insane and just eviscerated each other. Until every last one of them were dead."

Captain Hernandez started tapping on his chair, nervously. "Suggestions?" Hernandez asked.

"The distress call is of Constable origin, Captain." Onyx stated. "If they need assistance, surely, we should oblige."

"Sure." The Captain agreed. "But, it--"

"Slipstream drive inactive!" The A.I. screamed at the crew.

"Architect!" Shouted a crew member.

"Danger! Cloak inactive!" The A.I. blared once again. The ship's lights flickered on and off.

"What is going on?!" The Captain screamed.

"Please don't do it. Please." A woman pleaded on her knees. Morenko's rifle was aimed at her head. Dead bodies piled the hallways. For every moment that the ship's screams and its beeping blared, the only thing that could be heard was gunshots and Jai's laughter.

Morenko started to feel pity for the human before him and started to lower his gun. Just as the woman started to smile relief, Jai jammed her blade into the woman's pale throat. Blood dripped over Jai's fingertips as she held one of the woman's arms back, and started flailing the woman's body about. Blood started spitting on the deck and on Morenko's boots.

"What's worse?" Jai whispered into the human's ear. "That no one can save you, or that you'll know you're never going to matter? Not your life, not your death, not anything you've ever done, you're just--"

"Shut up, Jai." Morenko interrupted. Jai looked away from the woman she was massacring to meet Morenko's eyes. "I'm tired of hearing you talk. We're supposed to do a job, let's do it. Drop her and let's go." Jai shrugged and let the now lifeless corpse flop to the floor, blood slowly spilling from the dead woman's neck.

On the engineering deck, the crew members started screaming, trying to get each other to find a solution, to get their cloak back up, to get their systems working.

Spontaneously, as if to destroy all hope or grasp of safety, three warships arrived, carrying artillery that could obliterate the crew of the U.S.S. Enforcer. With the Enforcer's cloaking systems down, its shields offline, and with no chance of escape, missiles ripped through space to hit the Enforcer's armor again and again. The crew inside the ship felt the hit each and every time, and it nearly knocked them from their seats every time. They were now wearing their seatbelts to strap them in.

"Armor integrity compromised!" A crewman cried out, his face full of shock, disarray, and utter panic. He had no choice but to look to the man he was forced to call "Captain" for direction. Miguel Hernandez was confused and broken. His face showed it. His lips trembled, his eyes were wide in bewilderment, and his body shook in terror.

Tika, Javal, and Ren'e Anukis watched the repeated attack on the U.S.S. Enforcer, as missile after missile barraged the ship they'd know to call home.

"What… what do we do?" Javal trembled as he said the words, hoping to find answers from any of his allies for an answer to get him in action, to help his friends, his crewmates. He needed purpose. And his Lieutenant could not answer. Ren'e was speechless.

"Architect's forsaken hell." Ren'e whispered to herself.

"Come on. We need to keep looking through this facility."
Tika demanded. Javal looked to Tika in fumbling confusion.

"Keep looking?!" Javal screamed in confusion. "Our friends
are getting attacked!"

"I can't pilot that shuttle into battle. It doesn't even have long
range travel or adequate weapons systems to go up against those
warships." Ren'e bluntly uttered. "I don't think we'll be able to
save them. All we can do is try to discover what happened here.
What experiments were going on inside this damn facility. Find
out who killed these people and why. And upload a recording of it
to the Flow Council, or to anywhere. That way, if we die, our
deaths mean something."

Tika nodded. "Bryna was probably right about the A.I.
having a physical location. We should find it." Ren'e and Tika
starting wandering through the base of the station.

Javal had no other purpose, and no other direction. He
followed Tika and Ren'e to discover what had happened to this
facility.

Onyx rose from his seat and rushed through the bridge.
Captain Hernandez's fear turned to rage. Death was never Miguel
Hernandez's phobia. So he knew only one thing to do; get angry.
Gain his will.

"Fuck this!" Captain Hernandez shouted in outraged refusal.
For the Captain, it was time to stop being afraid and fly his damn
ship. The Captain took the helm from the ships automated systems,
and he started masterfully dodging attacks from the missile
barrages.

Each and every missile he dodged was another victory over
whoever was attacking him. No longer would he feel this
unfamiliar fear for himself and his crew. He'd do only what he was
meant to do, what he was born to do: fly.

Onyx rushed off the bridge so quickly, that the Captain didn't
even notice him rise from his seat. Onyx started running through
the hallway that connected to the ship's level lifters. Only one

thing was on the android's automated system: "Get in a mining torpedo."

Tika, Javal and Ren'e wandered to a room to find holographic interfaces. Each were designed to look like a person and would look at the nearest person to pass it. As the three Constables walked through this shined steel room full of vials, research notes, and studious details of equations and formulas all over the walls, Javal felt unnerved by the automated people made of light staring at him. Tika felt no such fear.

Tika stared at each and every one of them, noticing their subtle differences. One looked muscular and like that of a soldier, one a female with features of a thin face and light hair. Tika noticed that each and every one of these people looked familiar, and that each of them were dressed in the same exact attire of a Constable uniform.

Tika put her hand to one of the holographic interfaces, in curiosity. It was of a woman, a Daporan, like Javal. Her blue skin and fins on her neck showed a differing contrast to the rest of the alien ambassadors, but her eyes looked dead, lifeless, just like the rest of them.

"I do not act without opportunity." The Interface started muttering, in its high pitched female voice, with just a tad of echo due to it being a hologram. "I pretend, I put on a play for you, my friend. I do not make mistakes, I wait for your own." The female interface stated. "What am I?" She asked the three Constables. Ren'e squinted and looked up to the ceiling, confused by the question and the statements. Javal thought to himself for a moment, realizing that this was a riddle.

"Oh!" He exclaimed. "You're a--"

"—traitor." Tika interrupted.

"Acceptable enough answer, Tika Shamari, medical expert. Your record redacted at the request of Constable Director Tollus. Your existence was debated as legal or illegal." The interface replied, as it smiled at the two Constables.

"Who did you betray, exactly?" Javal wondered, rubbing the back of his neck in confusion to the point of this program.

"A forgotten people." Every single interface declared in unison. "A forgotten world. A forgotten series of worlds."

"What worlds? What forgotten worlds?" Tika twitched in place for a slight moment as the words left her mouth. Immediately, each of the holographic figures morphed and changed into new people, some altogether disappearing. Their outfits looked ever so slightly different. Only one did not change. One that Tika recognized. The android Ambassador of the Flow Council named D.A.X.

"In the 193rd year of the Flow Council's formation--" The interfaces began stating. "—the Flow Council forced restrictive laws and rules upon its civilians, forcing them to live elsewhere. To find a Mystic Sea of protection and salvation, free from the restrictions the Flow Council put upon them."

"What does that have to do with these worlds? What does this have to do with anything?" Ren'e wondered.

"This event caused the Flow Council to cut off much needed resources--" The interfaces continued, seeming to not care whatsoever as to the lieutenant's question. "--attempting to force them to return to the Flow Council's systems, hoping not lose power or influence over their people." Tika nodded, as her eyes darted around the room, as she remembered the events the artificial minds were describing to her.

"Right, right." Javal stated in acknowledgement as his head nodded ever so slightly. "Then the Mystic Seas organization attacked the Flow Council, stealing food, water, and whatever other resources they needed to survive."

"Correct." The interfaces responded in unison.

"Then a war happened." Tika interjected. "A war that the Flow Council won. The Mystic Seas rebellion lost most of its citizens and what was left of it became a mercenary and terrorist force."

"The Mystic Seas." Ren'e muttered in understanding. "But what does that have to do with anything?" Ren'e investigated in confusion.

Onyx was finally loaded into one of the mining torpedoes after removing its explosive components. He knew that Captain Hernandez was always the best pilot in the Flow Council, so he knew that if there was any chance to do what he planned, it was best in his Captain's hands.

"Captain." Onyx stated, attempting to gain his leader's attention through his affix.

"What, Onyx?" Captain Hernandez responded in irritation. "I'm trying to keep us alive!" The Captain screamed.

"As am I." Onyx declared, with the slightest bit of emotional inflection in his voice. "I'm in one of Aiden Dakar's mining torpedoes. I need you to fire me at one of the rival ships, Captain. The torpedo will bore into a rival ship, and I will be released, enabling me to eliminate some of our enemies."

"Fine!" The Captain yelled, then cut off communication, obviously to focus his attention on retaining control over the ship. As Onyx closed the hatch of the torpedo he was ready as the automated loading sequence began to place the torpedo into the firing tube.

"I've got a clear shot of Constable Dekar as he's trying to repair the damaged systems." Jai whispered with a slight sadistic giggle, as she aimed her pistol at the engineer's head.

"Don't kill him. I actually like the guy. Leave him be" Morenko stated. "It's smarter to just get to the escape pods and get out of here. Then beg to the Architect for them not to find us."

"But what's the fun in that?" Jai wondered, her tongue licking her lips as her finger tugged on the trigger slowly, but still not pulling it all the way.

"No." Morenko commanded. Jai made eye contact with him, seeing his will and determination for a smarter action, and shrugged.

"Fine." Jai agreed, lowering her firearm. "If you're so damn sentimental, then perhaps you're too weak for whoever our client is."

"I'm not weak, Jai." Morenko denied. "We need to go and cause chaos another day. For now, let's just stay alive." Jai giggled.

"Fine. But I'll need some other kind of fun later." Jai replied, clacking her teeth together silently, as she tugged at Morenko's inner thigh with her off-hand. Morenko shook his head at the savage woman he was forced to call an ally. But giving this maniac the violence she craved was worth it, if he could be granted his freedom.

Inside the hull of one of the enemy ships, a group of a mixture of Mystic Seas mercenaries, Amras men and women, and Constables fired missile after missile into the Enforcer's armor plating, and tried their best to chase down the ship as it began evading them. Miguel Hernandez's piloting skills had started to infuriate the red-skinned Amras pilot.

He kept muttering to himself curses over and over as he grunted in frustration, being unable to put the U.S.S. Enforcer into submission. The pilot's brash arrogance had blinded him to a compartment of the Enforcer that opened, and the firing of the mining torpedo with a drill at its nose into the bridge that he sat in.

The torpedo slammed into one of the Enforcer's would be enemies, and a powerful drill erected and grinded through the powerful glass that was supposed to protect this crew from the outside vacuum of space. Within seconds, the terrified and screaming crew started abandoning their posts, without any success.

The unforgiving drill grinded into the glass, breaking it and ripping crew members out into the vacuum of space. Their screams couldn't be heard in the void as they started dying slowly, their bodies being covered in ice, their eyes being frozen, and terrified in asphyxiation. The crew members that did manage to hold on for their lives were crushed quickly by the torpedo, now nothing but red and purple paste spread across the walls, monitors, and control consoles of this ship.

As the metal emergency hatches closed the ship's bridge, the paste that was previously being ripped into space hit the floor of the deck. The drill to the mining torpedo stopped, and Onyx opened his hatch, and was ready to find the secondary piloting room, and help the men and women he called crewmates. Onyx grabbed the shotgun on his back and cocked it, ready to kill anyone he needed to.

Onyx walked through the bridge, past the desecrated corpses, destroyed machinery, and started wandering the ship going through hall after hall. The entire ship now had red lights flashing, and a loud high-pitched beeping blaring in emergency to alarm its crew, letting it know it was in danger.

The nanites that covered his body hardened, forming a crystalline shell. The horrified crew members tried firing their assault rifles at Onyx, with no success as the bullets merely bounced off him. Onyx shot once into the neatly organized crew members and saw flesh being ripped apart after the powerful high speed fragments roared through his gun's barrel. Their bodies hit the floor. Onyx knew this would be easy.

Tika, Ren'e and Javal saw the holograms of these people all fade, each and every one, until one remained. One they recognized. The red skinned Amras ambassador named Vaskis Sinzo. Unlike the other holograms of the former ambassadors, Vaskis was very much full of life.

"You want to know why, Javal?" Vaskis asked. The three Constables realized that this was no hologram or an A.I. This was truly, the one and only Vaskis Sinzo. Whether it was a hologram, showing what Vaskis truly looked like from some other location, or if it was a recording of him saying something, they weren't sure. But they knew that it was truly him, not a fake imitation. "Because the Flow Council, with its laws, with its regulations, with its idiocy and interpersonal bureaucracy, they let my planet burn. They let my people get raped and murdered and put into slavery. And it still happens. To dozens upon dozens of worlds. Mercenaries, slavers, pirates, and the like… they are a disease on this galaxy. I will force them to be purged."

"How?" Tika wondered. Vaskis smiled.

"The only way that they could be destroyed, Miss Shamari. By destroying themselves." Vas'Kis began. "You walked through this facility. You know what this new Red Rage can do."

"It's been you?!" Ren'e yelled in outrage. "Doing all of this?!" Vas'Kis nodded.

"Yes. I hoped to destroy Scar with the Solar Sword, but you and Santos' child--" Vas'Kis said, referring to Captain Hernandez "--made sure I couldn't. So I continued my plan, to simply destroy all the mercenary worlds with Red Rage."

"So, at the Treasure Planet Casino, where we had to rescue Jaffar… what was that?" Javal wondered.

"Some scientists wanted to see how the Red Rage would affect random people." Vas'Kis started. "So we sent agents to poison people's drinks with an ingested form of Red Rage. Unfortunately, we poisoned the wrong boy, and Director Tollus had your crew get involved. Which made things messy."

"I was stabbed because of you." Javal stated, almost in anger, the closest thing to anger his people could be capable of feeling.

"Yes." Vas'Kis agreed.

"And the Mystic Seas?" Ren'e wondered. "You paid them to ship your crates? I thought you hate mercenaries." Vas'Kis shook his head.

"They aren't mercenaries, because they don't attack anyone but the Flow Council and their forces." Vas'Kis responded. "They believe I'm going to obliterate the Flow Council." Each of the Constables' brows raised in alarm. Vas'Kis shook his head. "I'm not." Vas'Kis stated in response to their shock. "They're fools, but they gave me the power to do what is necessary."

"So, what will you do, exactly?" Javal inquired.

"I will infect every single planet's civilized areas with a vaporized form of Red Rage, and every citizen and mercenary will become berserk and out of control." Vas'Kis detailed. "At which point--"

"They'll rip themselves apart." Ren'e muttered in understanding. Vas'Kis nodded. "Why? There are innocents on those worlds! People who were like me when I was a child!" Ren'e screamed.

"Yes." Vas'Kis agreed, his demeanor changing ever so slightly, to almost sound like regret. "But they'll do what needs to be done. The slaves will kill their masters, and the parasites of the worlds will rip themselves apart."

"But why?" Tika asked. "Why like this? You could have killed them so many other ways. So many more efficient ways." Vas'Kis nodded in agreement.

"Yes. I could have." Vas'Kis affirmed. "But this death. Watching them claw and tear at each other until they die slowly and brutally, this is the death they deserve." Vas'Kis closed his eyes. "And on this day, my ancestor's will smile, as I destroy their worlds. As I destroy them."

"You can't do this!" Javal roared in revolting cry. "Those are people! Innocent people! You have no right!" Vas'Kis chuckled once more.

"I have every right in the world." Vas'Kis replied in disagreement. "And it isn't something I plan on doing. It's something I've already done."

The U.S.S. Enforcer couldn't take much more damage. It's exterior armor was reduced to nothing, and the ship's internal systems made it near to impossible to actually pilot the ship. Morenko stepped into his escape pod, ready to be rid of this forsaken ship that held him prisoner. Jai practically skipped in disregarded arrogance and glee, as a bullet grazed the neck of the treacherous Constable from behind her. Jai inhaled deep in shock and started firing blindly in the direction from which the bullet came.

"I knew it!" A scream from Bryna Stoli echoed throughout the hall of the escape pods. "I knew the damn Torrie mercenary was nothing but scum!" Jai looked down the hall to see that Bryna had taken cover to avoid Jai's gunfire. Jai saw her opportunity. She continued her array of bullets with her pistol in one hand and signaled for Morenko to follow her.

"Let's kill us a big bitch!" Jai howled, insulting Bryna's affluent height. Morenko knew that he might be able to follow the psychopath he was forced to call an ally and help her kill Bryna Stoli. Maybe, just maybe he could. But in this moment, he knew he had a better chance of escaping. And he also knew that Bryna Stoli was famous for escaping near death situations. So he shrugged his shoulders. He turned on his escape pod. And the door closed, as he left Jai alone to deal with Bryna.

Jai knew her ammo was running low and her intensity turned to fear, as she heard Morenko's escape pod door close and it jetted off, leaving her by herself. Jai felt the familiar click of depleted ammo for her pistol, and simply turned to where Morenko once was and screamed.

"No!" She cried. "No!" She stomped, her back toward Bryna. Bryna stared at the back of Jai's head, pulled out her combat knife and hurled it, watching as the blade flipped though the air, until it dug its way into the back of Jai's head. Jai let out a gasp of air from her lungs, as she was rendered unable to move, and hit the floor quickly. Blood dripped from her hair to the steel floor as her lifeless body would now call a place to rest.

"Architect's forsaken hell." Aiden's oh so familiar voice muttered, as he walked into the hallway, seeing the gory sight.

On the two remaining enemy ships, the crews were frantic, hoping to fire weapons back at their attackers as plasma lasers were used to weaken their shields, but they were unable to pin down a single shot, thanks to Miguel's masterful and using sporadic flying technique. None of them were Onyx or Ren'e Anukis, they hadn't the skill to keep up with the only pilot that could save the lives aboard the U.S.S. Enforcer.

But even Miguel Hernandez couldn't overcome the ship's limit. He knew it. The crew knew it. And the woman who spoke through the intercom knew it. She smiled at Miguel as sweat dripped down his face, and he used every maneuver in his arsenal to keep himself and his crew safe.

"Give it up, Miguel." The woman stated. "We don't want you dead, and the other six of your main crew are about as valuable to us as you are."

"Fuck you!" Miguel denied in fury. The woman giggled.

"Your ship is malfunctioning." The woman repoted. Soon, your most basic systems will go offline. You know as much as I know that this is in vein. Don't be a fool. Don't fight us. To be frank, we aren't your enemy anyway."

"Not my enemy?!" the captain shouted. "You attack my ship, threaten my life, my crews' lives, and you say you aren't my enemy?"

"We never wanted this, but you kept getting in our way. We can't keep wasting our time with you. Surrender or die." The woman stared straight at Captain Hernandez, even through a hologram, he could see her resolve. Her will. The captain knew that, even if he could somehow dodge every missile, every assault, every danger, eventually, the ship would stop working. It had taken damage from the traitors within its walls, and wounds from the missiles that had already ripped apart most of the exterior integrity of the ship.

Miguel let his eye wander to the crew around him. He saw criminals, outlaws, and people that the universe had not wanted. People who, like himself, saw no other purpose but to rebel. Miguel might not have known why each of his crew had chosen a life of crime, but he did know that they all shared one common link; that they had no one but each other.

"If I stop, if I don't fight back, you'll let the crew live?" Miguel inquired. The woman on the intercom's black eyebrows raised in slight surprise. She then took in the statement and nodded.

"By my honor as one of the Amras, by my honor as a Constable, and by my honor of my friend's cause, I will not be the cause of your death, Captain Hernandez." The woman responded. Miguel looked to the men and women whose lives were in his hands. Even if they were a group of miscreant criminals, they were his crew. He knew the value of his command. He knew the honor in his own command. He knew he couldn't sacrifice them.

"I've been stubborn all my life." Miguel began. "I've fought back against everyone and everything I knew, because I could." Miguel looked off to the confused faces around him. "I risked my life because I could risk it. Because it was a thrill to risk it. But these people won't die because I'm too stubborn to lose. I surrender."

PHOE-NIX NEBULA

Star Enforcers: Chapter 20

Captain Hernandez watched as the enemy ships surrounded the U.S.S. Enforcer, and like a virus, the unrelenting and unison sound of boots stomping on metal paraded throughout the entire ship. The captain was ashamed that all he could do was watch. He observed this large group of men, most of them having the red skin and black hair of the people from Amras as they aimed their guns at his crew, even at him. The Enforcer's bridge crew was escorted out of the command center leaving Hernandez along, and (Sinzo's 2nd) walked before him, staring him in the eye with the intensity of a person who'd seen so much violence, so much bloodshed, and had ascertained just the right amount of knowledge of atrocities, so that she may enact them on the captain if he disobeyed anything she said.

Miguel raised his hands in obedience. Not only for the sake of his crew, but in the faith that Bryna, René, Onyx, and the rest of the Constables could save him, and save the rest of the ship's personell.

"Welcome to the U.S.S. Enforcer," the Captain stated in sarcastic compliance. (Sinzo's 2nd) recognized this right away and smirked from Miguel's obvious wish for rebellion.

"I'm wondering, Captain Hernandez, if you'll be privy to what we have to offer if you are blatantly told what it is we are doing," (Sinzo's 2nd) stated.

"What are you talking about?" The captain obliviously wondered.

"I'm talking about joining us, Miguel Hernandez. The squadron of the Enforcer, the other highly trained and powerful Constables have escaped, but we'll find them. You see, we're doing something beautiful. We're cleaning out the part of the galaxy that the Flow Council and the Constables would love to ignore. My commander has elected not to ignore them. And neither should you."

The Captain tilted his head in interest and slight fear towards what the woman before him was uttering.

"Do you remember what you saw on Scar? On Royale? Those places, those planets filled with people with no power and no will to change their situation. People that are broken, beaten, completely and totally destroyed beings ruled by the cowardly, the disgusting, the mercenaries and slavers and the other despicable creatures of this galaxy? Do you remember that? Do you remember all of it?" (Sinzo's 2nd) wondered, trying to invoke something from Miguel, some kind of answer that could form a middle ground.

"I do," Miguel replied.

(Sinzo's 2nd) cracked a small smile in response to Miguel's reply, as she hoped that she could coerce him.

"Then you'll understand what we're doing, what my commander is doing."

"What is he doing? What are you doing?" Miguel honestly wondered. "To me, it just seems to be random chaos, followed by greed to distribute Red Rage."

(Sinzo's 2nd) laughed. "There is no such thing as random. Not with this universe, and not with us. We let it spread intentionally. We let this happen to evil people intentionally. The only error we made was that boy. The son of the Ambassador. The one who killed the hooker. We didn't anticipate that. The hooker we paid did not know who he was. And the owner of the casino saw too grand of an opportunity to pass up. It wasn't something we could stop, and we are so glad you could."

Miguel balled up hands into fists.

"For what? Why are you doing this?!" Miguel screamed.

"Testing this product. To see if we can use it. As the weapon it is intended for. On the people who deserve so much death, so much destruction, so much suffering. On Scar and all places like it."

Hernandez squinted his eyes in confusion.

"You--you think I'd approve?!" Miguel cried in outrage. "You think I'd join you?! That I'd want this? I'd never want this! Fuck you! Fuck your drug! Fuck your sick and twisted idealogy! Fuck you!" Hernandez yelled in emotional distress.

(Sinzo's 2nd) shrugged.

"Ah, well. I tried," she replied, as she reached for her pistol, and shot Miguel several times.

Enough times to hurt him. Enough times to make him lose just enough blood to lose consciousness within a couple of minutes, but not die.

Captain Hernandez screamed in atrocious agony. An undeniable pain claimed that which was his insides. A spot between two of his ribs felt nothing but searing, hot, piercing pain, that forced him into consciousness. As his eyes drifted about the room he was in, a room that was steel, filled with tables that had torture devices. Torture devices like knives, screwdrivers, torches, broken glass, things that are medieval and primal.

Hernandez's eyes raised to look into the depths of the eyeballs of a true monster. A man whose eyes were powerful, bold, green, and lusting for nothing but domination and power. The eyes looked familiar, yet distant. He'd seen them before. But before they were filled with rage and vengeance, not disgusting desire. He'd seen those eyes in Bryna's head before. And Miguel knew who this man was. Forlka Skine. Bryna's father. Bryna's torturer. Bryna's passion and desire for vengeance for her entire life.

"You refused us," Skine muttered in assured confidence and cruel simplicity. "You refused us and you will know the consequences."

Miguel looked down to his ribs to see the device that was causing him such undeniable pain, a sharpened metallic spike, that was made red hot, presumably by putting it to one of the lit torches that cascaded the room in a dark red.

"Fuck you," Hernandez replied in confident defiance. "Aaaaahhhhhh!"

Miguel screamed as the spike drove deeper into his flesh. The bold Captain could smell and hear the intensity of his flesh burning, smelling of a thick and disgusting roasted meat. "Where--where's Bryna? Where's Aiden?" Miguel asked Skine.

"In another room," he replied. "My daughter spent so much time away from me. I think she believes herself to be a person. I'll have to strip her down and remind her she's a thing. Just like you. Just like the blonde boy.

"You're a strong man," Skine began. "I break strong men. And strong women. Then I make them something else."

Skine drove the spike deeper.

"Grraaaaaagh!!" Hernandez screamed louder as he bit his lip.

"The question will not be when you will break, but what I can make you into afterwords. What potential you'll have after you learn to stop defying. The question is, Miguel Hernandez, who will you become?"

Captain Hernandez could not stop feeling the intimidation

that was Skine's enormous stature. Over seven feet tall, with nothing but meat and muscle, covered in black and red sleek, shiny armor that protected his vital organs, but left his arms free. Skine's hair was dark and gray, and receded, giving him a sharp and deep widow's peak. Skine's scars about his body were intense, but only a further sign of how unstoppable this monster was, and how far he was from a man.

The constables drifted to the nearest solar system, as each of them gathered to the stolen enemy ship's pilot area. They'd been hoping to get some form of agreement as to what to do in reaction to this betrayal. Onyx had docked onto the research facility as per captain's orders, and retrieved Tika, Ren'e and Javal as he narrowly escaped the captivity of (Sinzo's 2nd) Now Javal sat in the conficated ship's pilot's seat, staring into his console, wondering what to do. René leaned her back against a wall, rubbing her temples due to stress.

"They have the captain," Tika stated. "We need to get him back."

René shook her head.

"Wherever he is, he's surrounded, he's their prisoner. We don't have the capacity to get to him, and we don't know who to trust, so we can't call for backup," René responded sternly.

"If it was us, he'd do anything," Tika declared. "He deserves salvation from this... this group of people."

"We don't even know who they are," Javal interjected, with a nervous tick in his voice. "Why would they do this?"

In the Flow Council meeting room, Santos Hernandez stood before his fellow men and women who intervene on the Galaxy's most pertinent and resilient threats. Santos looked behind him, to see his friend, Vas'Kis Sinzo standing, awaiting his introduction.

"--and with that point, I introduce Councilor Sinzo. As you may remember, he single handedly freed his planet by invoking a conscriptive deal of trust between his planet and the Flow Council. Please, give this man's thoughts respect, as he might have a solution to this Red Rage problem, one that the rest of us just cannot see," Santos declared to the entirety of his people proudly and efficiently in order to ascertain their attention.

Vas'Kis lightly, but sternly approached the stand in order to plead his case. His face forced a quick tick, a slight muscle jolt in his cheek before he started to speak.

"Councilors. You must know the truth. All of it," Vas'Kis looked about the room and saw men and women that were loyal to him.

Guards. Fellow Council members. Respected Elumeni. People of considerable power, each and every one of them.

"Those of you who are loyal to me, those who I knew could respect my dream, my vision, I thank you. Your predecessors or friends or fellow Councilors who did not who were dealt with... I thank you for your understanding regarding the actions I took against them."

Santos' eyes widened as he looked across the room, noticing the shocked faces that were all around him, which was disturbing. But what was more disturbing yet was the faces that were not surprised, that some of them were even smiling, like they'd been waiting for this moment and now it had finally come to show them salvation.

A deafening boom roared throughout the meeting room, as an Elemuni forced a large amount of air to lift those guards who were not loyal to Vas'Kis into the air. They reached for their rifles or sidearms. They screamed as they felt themselves dropping and crashing to the ground. The sound of bones snapping and chairs breaking forced the room into a moment of silence.

The guards seemingly loyal to Vas'Kis pointed their guns at all of the Councilors, all except for Santos and the portion of Councilors who were loyal to Vas'Kis.

"Most of you weren't in your positions when I came here. When my planet burned. When mercenaries and savages and despicable creatures from beyond our solar system invaded us. When our people were raped and sold into slavery and beaten and murdered," Vas'Kis began, as his fist beat against the podium. "But now! Now you let other worlds burn! You let the innocent die and the guilty go unpunished. Scar, the mercenary world is unburned because of people like you! I hoped for the Solar Sword to crush the planet and the entire system around it, but you forced my hand! You forced my decisive brutality!"

Santos looked about the room, as he noticed that not a single guard had a gun pointed at him. And so, he reached for his pistol that was strapped to his side, and rushed to Vas'Kis, pointing the gun in his face.

"Stand the hell down!" Santos screamed to everyone in the room. "Stand down or I'll shoot him! I swear to whatever Gods you hold dear, whatever philosophy you follow, to whatever fucking planet you call home!"

"You won't kill me, Santos," Vas'Kis merely laughed in response.

Santos simply glared at Vas'Kis, ever determined.

"And why is that?" Santos wondered.

"We all know many things about you. You're so obvious about who you are and what you want. Which makes you respectable. Honorable. But it makes you weak. Susceptable," Vas'Kis stared into Santos' eyes, giving him the impression that he has the upper hand.

"What makes me weak, Vas'Kis? The gun? The bullets in it?" Santos sarcastically asked with a grin on his face.

Vas'Kis shook his head with a blank stare, and then started tapping his Affix.

"No," Vas'Kis sincerely remarked. "Your children."

Vas'Kis put a display of Miguel being tortured by Forlka Skine. Santos' jaw dropped, his eyes widened and his fingers trembled at the sight of his son being horribly eviscerated. Miguel's screams over the intercom echoed throughout the Council meeting room.

"Drop the gun, Ambassador Hernandez."

Santos' pistol clacked against the floor.

"If you kill my boy, Vas'Kis, nothing will stop me from killing you," Santos threatened.

Vas'Kis smiled and nodded.

"Your boy and his crew were a remarkable experiment. Disregarding several failures, they've been a complete and total surprise. Because you had faith in him. Because you saw potential in him. Because, above all else, past his previous failures and misgivings and criminal mistakes, you wanted him to succeed in being a point of pride for you," Vas'Kis ranted on. "He discovered and tried preventing the Red Rage. If you'd like to know, to truly know, what's been happening with this new creation of the drug, I'll gladly tell you. It's my doing. It's always been my doing."

Santos squinted his eyes in disbelief.

Bryna raised her eyes to see the face of (Vas'Kis 2nd) gazing upon her. (Vas'Kis 2nd)'s scarred face and piercing black eyes would intimidate most people, but not Bryna. The constable looked down to see that she was still in her armor, but her arms were chained to a wall that she was leaning against. Her knees rested on the metallic ground below her, and she looked to her right to see Aiden, still unconscious. He was in the same position, but his chest armor was stripped off, and a white tank-top was covering him.

"You know—" (Vas'Kis' 2nd) began, "--we were actually going to recruit you first."

Bryna lowered her head slightly, in reaction to (Vas'Kis' 2nd)'s statement.

"It's true." (Vas'Kis' 2nd) replied in response to Bryna's vaguely confused expression, as she raised her eyebrows.

"Recruit me for what?" Bryna wondered.

(Vas'Kis' 2nd) raised her arms, pointing to the room.

"This. This glorious cause."

Bryna raised a single eyebrow in feigned curiosity, trying to keep (Vas'Kis' 2nd) talking.

"Which is?" Bryan asked.

"To destroy everything you hate, and to give you the opportunity to change." (Vas'Kis' 2nd) answered.

"Change?" Bryna inquired.

"Yes, Ms. Stoli," (Vas'Kis' 2nd) nodded. "You see, we've had this plan, Vas'Kis and I and so many of his followers. This plan to wipe out the scum of the universe. The people that descended on our planet. The people that killed our families and friends and loved ones and brethren. The people that raped our women and children, and enslaved our people like they were livestock."

"By people, you mean mercenaries?" Bryna wondered.

Again, (Vas'Kis' 2nd) nodded.

"Well, not mercenaries," (Vas'Kis' 2nd) rephrased, and then proceeded to pause,

Clicking her tongue to the roof of her mouth and looking to the ceiling, she gave the impression she was thinking.

"More like scum. That's the only word, really. Scum."

Bryna smiled.

"Scum, huh?"

(Vas'Kis' 2nd) nodded.

"See, we were going to recruit you, but Director Tollus interrupted our plans, discovered you were arrested because of that Elumeni, Harmony. When she was discharged from the Elumeni, it made a big stink amongst the Constables, they found out about you, and Tollus wanted you on the Enforcer. Bad."

Bryna smiled and chuckled ever so slightly in response.

"So how? How were you going to wipe out the scum?" Bryna asked.

She then looked to her right, as she noticed Aiden was finally grunting and shaking himself to consciousness.

"Hmm. I'll show you, sweet Bryna. Angry Bryna. Vengeful Bryna," (Vas'Kis' 2nd) responded, with a very large, a very disconcerting smile.

Then, suddenly, (Vas'Kis' 2nd) injected Bryna with a needle containing a light blue liquid, and Bryna started to fall asleep. She knew this anesthetic. Bryna couldn't keep her eyes open.

All she could say was "Lover's Lie", the name of the poison, as she drifted, again, into unconsciousness.

Tika paced back and forth on the enemy ship, with her hand on her mouth, and her eyes darting around as she mumbled to herself.

"No, no. Constable design. Constables attacking us. No word from Flow Council. Who. Who, who, who," Tika kept repeating to herself as Javal, Onyx, and René each looked for their own solutions to the problem before them.

"I just don't get what is even going on," Javal bluntly stated. "Is that just me? Am I the only one who has absolutely no idea what's going on?!"

Javal slammed his fist against a panel, making a small dent, and vaguely alarming René from flying the ship.

"We need to find Captain Hernandez," Tika declared. "We need to find our captain, we need to find Bryna, and we need to find Aiden."

"What we need is reinforcements. Whoever these people are, they've outmatched us," René interjected.

"Reinforcements are unreliable." Onyx vocalized in disapproval to René's statement. "Medical Expert Shamari was correct. They were of Constable origin, had Constable training. This ship itself is an exact replica of the 38-77 class Constable fighter ship. Meaning that our enemies could be anyone, could be anywhere. The only ones who can be trusted are those on the Enforcer who did not betray us, and those of us in this very fighter ship."

"That actually makes sense," René agreed. "The Enforcer has a tracking signal. Reaching out to it will more than likely alert attention."

"I don't think we have a choice," Javal spoke with a soft,

and nervous tone.

Tika looked down as the ship's messaging system started beeping. The ship put something on the display that was being projected from the holograms within the ship. Something horrifying and shocking.

"By the Architect...," Javal gasped, putting a hand on his mouth.

In the council meeting room, Vas'Kis stared at the majority of the Ambassadors, the majority that was not on his side.

"I want to show you, to show all of you that it's possible to wipe out Planet Scar. To wipe out that casino, Treasure Planet. To destroy the dozens of worlds that filth inhabit that are a virus on our systems, our worlds, our people. Without decisive destruction, we will be obliterated, and the innocent will be persecuted," Vas'Kis ranted.

"Where will it end, Vas'Kis?" Santos demanded, forcing Vas'Kis to turn his head to his former friend. "You justify wiping these people out, and when will you stop? What is your justification for those who are caught in the crosshairs of your vision? For Gollic, one of our own Ambassador's sons," Santos pointed to the display of Miguel being slowly tortured. "What is your justification for my son?"

"A necessity in acquiring a soldier," Vas'Kis responded.

Santos laughed as he tried to hold back tears in response to seeing his son being tortured as his flesh and blood was being forced to scream, wriggle and squirm from immense pain.

"How convenient," Santos responded. "How convenient that your sick and twisted dream comes at the price of my son. Of me. Of all of us."

Vas'Kis remained silent and turned his head away from Santos. Santos' lip trembled in uncontrollable anger. "We gave you a seat on this Council! We gave your people a voice, your voice! We gave you everything that is possible to achieve for a man of honor, and you twisted it! You defiled it! You--!"

"QUIET!!!!" Vas'Kis roared in undeniable rage.

The roar that made glasses on the tables shake.

"You weren't there! You let my people burn!" Vas'Kis screamed, as he waved his arm at the room. "All of you! All of you let my people be raped and murdered and sold into slavery! And you thought for a second--FOR A SECOND--!" Vas'Kis roared again, "--that I would not let the people that did this to me go unpunished?! That I would tolerate your indifference?! That I would let another world, any world go through what I went through?!"

Vas'Kis slowly approached Santos and stared into his eyes.

"Not every world has a Vas'Kis Sinzo! Not every world has a person who can lead his people to salvation! So I need to give it to them! That rage! That fire in their heart! That ability to rip their enemies apart, and for their enemies to rip themselves apart!"

Santos stepped back in nervousness, in shock.

"What have you done, Vas'Kis?" Santos asked in fear.

"What is necessary," Vas'Kis replied, before tapping his Affix and showing the room what the finality of his plans were.

The display in the Council meeting room showed Scar. The planet of mercenaries and savages. The planets of slaves and beggars. The planet of chaos, where ash rains down on little children's heads like rain. It showed the entirety of the civilized parts of the planet being covered in a red dust. And its people tearing each other apart. Men, women, and children ripped into each other with anything they could find; guns, knives, big rocks, their bare hands. Eyeballs were gouged, innards were spilled, people's necks were eviscerated. Each and every horrorific atrocity upon the people was more monstrous than the last. Blood spilled all about the wasteland, and the Council room witnessed, in terror, the consequence of allowing Vas'Kis Sinzo a seat on The Council.

"I didn't want to do this!" Vas'Kis screamed, "But you forced my hand!"

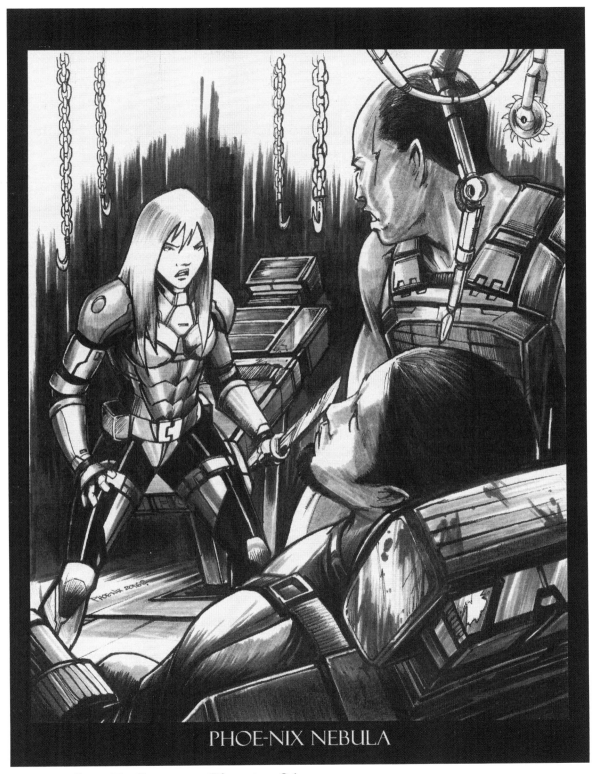

PHOE-NIX NEBULA

Star Enforcers: Chapter 21

Bryna rose, once gain, from unconciousness. She felt herself hanging from the chains. A disturbingly painful feeling to most, but it was somehow pleasantly familiar to her. She looked over to her left, and saw more chains dangling, and noticed the room she was in was of some solid metal, perhaps steel. It looked like a torture room, with a big bright light bearing down on her, blinding her if she were to look upwards. She looked to her right, and saw Aiden Dakar dangling as well, unconscious, and in pain.

"Aiden!" she screamed, jolting Aiden into consciousness.

"Wha--?" he uttered as he awoke.

Aiden twisted and grunted in pain.

"My wrists," he whispered, just loud enough for Bryna to hear, as he looked up to his wrists to see how he was chained.

The chain connecting the shackles around his wrists was looped over a beam a few feet above his head.

"For the sake of the Architect, that just seems so unecessary."

Bryna looked around, and noticed the layout. Knives, screws, hot pokers. This was definitely the torture room of her father. So primal, so vicious, and so much bloodshed. And best of all, he could do it with his bare hands.

"Aiden, I need you to break your left thumb."

Aiden looked over to her, making eye contact.

"Now, I get that you're trying to get me involved in something sexually vile, but breaking just seems so... so...," Aiden couldn't finish his sentence as his eyes started to flutter around.

Bryna looked close at his temple and noticed it was bruised. He had a concussion. He was delirious.

"Aiden, I need you to focus." Bryna grunted at him.

Aiden looked over at her before his eyes shut again.

Aiden smiled. "Mummy, I'm hungry. Does Aiden get supper?"

Bryna squinted in displeasure.

"Yes, Aiden. Aiden gets supper. But first, Aiden has to get free. Aiden has to break his left thumb."

Aiden smiled and laughed.

"But that's Aiden's favorite thumb," Aiden replied in defiance.

"Then the other one," Bryna commanded.

Aiden nodded.

"Aiden don't like that one as much."

Aiden started to clench his thumb in his fingers and push. Hard. Then harder. Then harder. Aiden gritted his together in pain.

"Don't scream," Bryna said to him, trying not to gain attention from whoever had been holding them where they were.

Aiden bit his lip in compliance. Then, suddenly, Bryna heard a snapping sound come from Aiden's right thumb, as Aiden's eyes widened in extreme pain. He did not scream though. Even while delirious, Aiden was as loyal as ever. Aiden pulled his wrist down through his confinement, and got his right hand free. Aiden, now without a counterweight of his right hand, fell a foot down to the ground and boots thumped the floor. His left hand pulled the chains across the beam and they pooled around his feet as they clanked to the floor.

Aiden walked over to Bryna and started to loosen her chains, and get her free. As Bryna's wrists were freed, her chains hit the floor, and she too hit the ground. Bryna noticed her coat wasn't on top of her, and so it was just her body armor. Aiden was still wearing just his white tank top. Her arms were free, and she was wearing no gloves. Bryna looked around her to find something to use, and she grabbed a short knife and picked it up. She smiled, knowing she'd soon feel her father's blood drip to her bare hands.

The rest of the crew, Javal, Tika Shamari, Lieutenant René Anukis, and Onyx were all nearly powerless to do anything as they watched through the stolen ship's intercom of Vas'Kis Sinzo's mad rant. They listened to the horrid screams and gurgles of death and agony.

"We have to do something," Tika said to the group.

"We have to do something," she repeated.

Javal nodded.

"But what can we do? We're in a stolen ship nearly half the galaxy away," Javal noted.

"The Slipstream Dive is still operational on this ship to get us to the Flow Council," René stated.

"But what about our captain?" Javal inquired.

René shook her head.

"Our first responsibility is to the Flow Council. Even if we are all criminals, we're Constables, dammit," René grunted with pride.

Onyx nodded in agreement. The very slight sound of metal on metal shifting in his head made a small echo within the small ship's alternate bridge.

"Lieutenant Anukis is correct. Captain Hernandez, Bryna Stoli, and Aiden Dakar must all find their own way to defeating this enemy. We have our own," Onyx iterated.

Javal looked around the ship, shifting his eyes to try to find anything useful about it.

"If we get to the Flow Council, what can we even do?" Javal wondered. "We have to assume that Vas'Kis Sinzo has taken control of Integra's force field, so we can't get to the Flow Council in time, and neither can any other Constable," Javal stated to the group.

"If we had Bryna, we might be able to hack into it. But it's possible even she couldn't do that," Tika muttered to the group.

René looked to Onyx.

"Could you do it?" Lieutenant Anukis asked.

Onyx looked at her and took a moment to think.

"It's possible," Onyx replied. "What we truly need is the full force of the Cybernetics."

René raised an eyebrow.

"What good will that do?" she wondered.

"Through the Neural Network, they can collectively bring down the force field, and we can invade Integra and subdue Vas'Kis Sinzo and his followers with force," Onyx replied.

"So the rest of the world hasn't found out about Vas'Kis' plan? Just us. Otherwise the Cybernetic Peoples would have probably done it already," Javal stated.

René nodded.

"Is the world in our hands?" Tika wondered.

"Well, one world most definitely is. One planet," René replied.

"So some criminals on a stolen ship are going to save the most important representatives of the most important peoples," Javal said aloud.

"Yes," Onyx replied.

"Very good. Just wanted to make sure that's what was happening," Javal smiled, as Onyx tapped his Affix, and prepared the message to the Cybernetics.

Captain Hernandez kept grunting as the hot iron stake was being shoved into his thigh. The smell of his flesh burning like a piece of meat was the thing that was the most horrible. The pain itself started to feel dull and like it didn't mean a whole lot. Like the sensation of his body saying "Something is wrong. Something is wrong." meant less and less with each and every stab, poke, and prod. Really, it was the smell that was becoming torture. And the loneliness. There was just Skine. Only Skine. Until Miguel looked up. Looked up into the opened door that led into the hallway and saw Bryna and Aiden standing there.

Bryna had a smile on her face, a knife clenched in her hand. Aiden's eyes were widened and horrified. Miguel knew what he had to do. He had to give in to what Skine wanted. He hung his head down after Skine pulled out the stake from his body. Miguel kept panting like a dog. And Skine merely watched him. Watched as Miguel seemed to be giving up on resistence.

"Now, you are no longer Miguel Hernandez. That is another man. A dead man. A man I killed. Because I could. Because I am stronger than he was and he was stronger than you."

Miguel pulled his head up and nodded. As the man who used to call himself Miguel Hernandez looked into the eyes of Forlka Skine, with an expression of helplessness and fear, he started to open his mouth. Skine raised an eyebrow and turned his ear to listen.

"Yes?" Skine grunted to the former captain.

"Master...," Miguel muttered in a weak voice.

Skine leaned forward to look into Miguel's eyes and Skine smiled and chuckled.

"That's right, boy," Skine replied. "That's--"

Before Skine could reiterate his sentence, Captain

Hernandez cocked his head back, and rammed his forehead into the bridge of Skine's nose as hard as he possibly could.

The loud "CRACK" and the vibration that went into Miguel's forehead from the breaking of Skine's nose was one of the most satisfying things he'd felt in his entire life. Skine reeled back slightly, and looked downwards to see Captain Hernandez, proud and confident. Smiling. Skine grabbed the back of his head, and took a blade into his hand.

"You'll lose an eye, boy! Just for that, you'll lose an—"

"FORLKA SKINE!" Bryna roared at him.

Skine turned to see his daughter walking towards him along with Aiden.

"Girl," Skine replied to Bryna.

Bryna shook her head.

"Bryna Stoli," Bryna stated with confidence and defiance.

Skine laughed.

"Stoli? Bryna?" Skine asked her, as he released Miguel's head, and walked towards his daughter.

The two were closer and closer, getting to be spitting distance within each other.

"Just two names you took from a dead man and a coward retired bounty hunter," Skine shook his head. "Names are something parents give you. And when I took your mother, when I raped her, when you popped out, you never got a name. You never will. Even with the protection your mother gave you, she never gave you a name. She was still disgusted with you."

Forlka Skine smiled.

"How does it feel? To know that your own blood hated you? To know that your mother couldn't even bother to give you a name, and I knew you for what you were? A thing. A tool."

Bryna said nothing. Just stood defiant. She did not answer his question.

"You raped my mother. You killed the first man to ever defend me. You tortured me. You...," Bryna hesitated as she couldn't quite find the words.

But then she did. Then she knew what she had to say. What truth she could not tell the Captain.

"You stuck yourself inside me,"

The Captain looked up in disgust and shock.

"You will die by my hand."

Skine laughed and then he charged at her, with a knife clenched in his hand. Bryna ducked his first few swipes. He might have been faster than he looked for a man his size. But he was wild and crazy with his swings. Bryna had discipline. Bryna ducked and dodged and moved herself to Skine's left, and took a stab at him. She cut into his side a bit, the part of his torso that wasn't covered by his armor.

Skine grunted and punched Bryna across the face. A smaller person would've hit the floor and felt an intense pain from Skine's blow. They probably would've fell unconscious or maybe even died. But not Bryna. Her stature and mental resilience forced her to simply take the hit, and spit out the blood filling in her mouth. Skine took the back of Bryna's head and stabbed into her. She held the blade into her side and grunted.

Aiden ran at Skine, trying to save her. Skine pulled his blade out of Bryna, and kicked Aiden in the groin. As Aiden reeled from the strong and extremely painful blow, Skine picked up Aiden's body with one hand, and slammed him to the ground. Aiden's torso cracked as his body hit the ground. Skine had broken a rib. Then, Skine held his boot on top of Aiden's head and started to push. He pushed and pushed and pushed, trying to crush Aiden's head.

Before he could, Bryna lept onto his back, and tried stabbing into Skine's neck. Skine had grabbed her body, and threw her off of him. She landed to the ground and rose to her feet to face him again.

Bryna switched her blade to a reverse grip, keeping the blade sticking out from her pinky rather than her index finger and thumb. Skine kept his stance. And just tried to intimidate her with his enourmous, hulking stature. Bryna waited for the next attack.

"You will die by my hand," Bryna said again.

Skine walked a couple steps towards her and started to make stabbing motions at her mid section, head, and throat. But she dodged them all. With each and every duck, dodge, and step backwards, she was backing herself into a corner. She was getting closer and closer to the wall behind her.

It was then that Skine made his lunge to stab her. As he lept towards her, Bryna twisted and turned to get out of his way just narrowely enough to slice his achilles' tendon. He grunted in pain as he dropped to the ground, and held his ankle in pain. Skine looked up to see that, in the distraction of battle, Aiden Dakar had somehow managed to rise to his feet and free his captain. Miguel was now leaning on his blonde comrade in order to stay standing.

As Skine scanned the room to find Bryna, her knife plunged into him. Right into his eye.

"How does that feel, fucker?!" Bryna screamed with intense

ferocity. "How does that feel, you piece of shit rapist mother fucker?!"

As she twisted the blade into his eye. He grunted and squeeled in agony as the knife twisted and turned in his eyeball. Blood seeped into Bryna's hands and dripped to Skine's chest and to the floor.

In the Flow Council meeting room, Vas'Kis Sinzo kept pacing back and forth between his fellow Ambassadors and Santos Hernandez. Santos just watched him. They watched him as he kept in his own mind, in his own rage. Then, a sudden disorienting beeping sound blared throughout the entirety of Integra.

"FORCE FIELDS DEACTIVATED. FORCE FIELDS DEACTIVATED. HOSTILES DETECTED. HOSTILES DETECTED."

The female voice was loud and annoying, and on most days, people would just feel mild irritation at the sound of her automated voice. But not today. Not for Vas'Kis Sinzo.

"No!" Vas'Kis screamed. "No, no, no!"

Ambassador D.A.X. looked up to Vas'Kis and opened his robotic mouth.

"My people have torn down the Force Field, Ambassador Sinzo. Constable ships are arriving here and now. Your only option is to surrender peacefully, or there will be consequences." Vas'Kis nodded.

He paced and he nodded.

"Peacefully. Peacefully." Vas'Kis repeated to himself.

Then, Vas'Kis shook his head.

"PEACE? PEACE?!" Raising his arm, Vas'Kis shot D.A.X. with his blaster. He shot the mechanical ambassador multiple times. The guards who were on Vas'Kis' side started to approach him so that they could defend him against the aggression of the room. But it was too late. Though some of these men and women might have been peaceful politicians, many of them were accomplished warriors. And when a comrade dies, you fight.

The sounds of gunfire, stabbing of pens, punching and choking filled the great hall, as it devolved into chaos, as the Ambassadors started to kill Sinzo's men.

"NO!" Vas'Kis screamed. "This wasn't how this was supposed to happen!"

Ambassador Santos Hernandez walked before Vas'Kis and looked him in the eye.

"You killed D.A.X," Santos stated to Vas'Kis. "Drop the gun."

Vas'Kis did as Santos demanded. Then, Vas'Kis collapsed onto the floor.

"I heard he was the first person who recommended that we keep you on this Council. That we give you and your people a place here," Santos started to iterate.

Vas'Kis nodded.

"He gave you a chance and you killed him."

Vas'Kis looked up at Santos, to make eye contact with him.

"Call off your men, Vas'Kis. Tell them to surrender. No more bloodshed. Not here."

"Stand Down," Vas'Kis commanded.

The sound of death stopped filling the room, and while a few Ambassadors were dead, the majority still lived. Vas'Kis' guards dropped their rifles, and all knelt to the floor at Vas'Kis' word. The Torrie Ambassador kept beating one guard in the face with her fist over and over again. She laughed as she did it.

Perhaps she knew the fighting stopped. Perhaps she didn't and needed some violence in her life, and this was the way to get it. This was a Torrie, after all. And in society and in blood, violence is their nature.

With the surrender, everyone in the room knew that a swarm of Constable soldiers had to secure the meeting room, and arrest Vas'Kis. Vas'Kis knew he'd lost his freedom. But he'd accomplished his mission. And with that thought, he smiled.

In the artificial atmosphere of Integra's city, an armada force of Constable ships rushed Integra, and destroyed Vas'Kis Sinzo's remaining opposing ships. Leading the fleet was the stolen ship piloted by René Anukis and Onyx. They may not have been as skilled or fluid as Captain Hernandez, but what they lacked in agility, they made up for in brutal efficiency and speed.

The ship docked and the four Constables rushed into the Flow Council's Arua Great Hall. Lieutenant René Anukis, Onyx, Javal, and Tika Shamari ran at the front of a large group of men and women, Constables of all the Council races. They ran in unision alongside one another, their simultaneous footsteps making a daunting sound.

As soon as they arrived into the Flow Council meeting room, Lieutenant René Anukis walked to Ambassador Vas'Kis Sinzo and raised her rifle to his head. She did not even focus on the other Ambassadors, the surrendered Constable traitors who were loyal to Vas'Kis, or the Constable that the Torrie Ambassador was still beating to a pulp. She could only focus on Vas'Kis. The man behind every pain, every struggle, every death that had haunted the Enforcer for the past month.

"Vas'Kis Sinzo," René began. "Ambassador to the Amras

peoples. You are under arrest for conspiracy to commit mass murder, treason . . ."

René was interrupted by Santos Hernandez, who raised his hand.

"No, he isn't," Santos interrupted.

René looked upwards and recognized Santos Hernandez from the previous Flow Council meeting she'd attended, Recognized him as her Captain's father.

"Sir?" Javal inquired.

Santos merely gave Javal an expression of irritation and straight forward aggression. Javal stood down from his confusion, and kept silent.

"If any of you have learned anything from serving amongst my son, it should be this, what the public knows, and what actually happened, are not always the same thing," Santos stated.

A few Ambassadors threw in "Yes." "Agreed." "Yes."

"We must keep the peace," Santos continued. "There are enough people that love this man, that look up to this man, who will be inspired to go against us, and angered at our decision to punish him. We can not punish him. At least, not publicly."

"Then what?" Vas'Kis asked Santos. "What will you do to punish me if you don't do it publicly?"

Santos looked over to his former friend and co-Ambassador.

"You can't kill me. Too many questions. Can't put me in prison. I end up talking."

The Daporan Ambassador walked before Vas'Kis, a woman of blue skin and sharp fins, with eyes that were as red as a dying sun.

"You take a leave of absence," the Daporan woman began.

"The stress of what you had to do to save your people and what you've done to serve them, it was too much for you."

Santos nodded, understanding the lie that the Daporan woman started to weave for the public.

"You need time to yourself. And in your absence, one of your own people will be annointed as Ambassador," Santos continued with her.

"It will be put to a vote amongst your people," another Ambassador chimed in, one of Green skin, with horns that were grown from her brow.

The Torrie Ambassador rose from the pummeled body she'd made, and wiped the blood from her knuckles on his shirt.

"And during that time, we'll lock you in a room. A room where you'll be able to use that brilliant mind for something," the Torrie woman added to the conversation.

"You won't kill him?!" Tika screamed. "After what he did? People will find out what happened! To the men, women, and children who were massacred!"

Vas'Kis Sinzo shook his head.

"No, they won't," Vas'Kis looked up to Santos. "Will they, Santos?"

Santos Hernandez shook his head at his old friend. Santos walked before his fellow Ambassadors, and he knew what he had to do. But first, he had to warn his son. Before it was too late.

The scream of Forlka Skine kept echoing throughout the torture room. And each time a guard ran in to try to help him, either Captain Hernandez or Aiden Dakar gunned them down with a sidearm that they'd found in the room. When Bryna finally pulled out her blade, Forlka Skine panted, and then he started to laugh.

Captain Hernandez looked over to the body armor and Affix that was torn off of him, and he walked over to it. As he picked up the beeping Affix, he listened to a message from his father.

"Miguel! This is your father. We're sending out the Solar Sword. It's going to destroy all of it. It's going to destroy the solar system you're in, so that there's no evidence of what Vas'Kis Sinzo had done. I need you to leave, son. Now."

"Shit," Aiden responded to Santos' message.

He kept grabbing his head, coming out of his delusional state slowly.

"We... we need to go..."

Aiden kept stumbling, and then raised the pistol in his hand to fire a round through a man's head who was trying to rush into the room like a wild dog.

"Yeah," Miguel agreed.

Bryna smiled at her two comrades, then turned back to her father.

"Goodbye, Father,"." She said and raised her blade.

"Wait!" her father cried out. "Don't you want to know your mother's name? Hmm? Don't you want to know your mama's name so you can find out where you come from?"

Bryna shook her head.

"I am the best hunter in the galaxy. I found out who she was over a decade ago."

Skine's smile turned to a frown, as Bryna stabbed him in the groin, shredding through his clothes, and squirting blood all over her fingertips.

"AAAAAAGH!" Skine screamed in agony.

Bryna laughed. Then, she brought the blade to his neck and cut at it, while holding the back of his head. Every so often, Skine would hit her in the face, trying to get her to stop, but even with the amount of brusies and blood and broken ribs or her face, Bryna did not stop. She just kept cutting into his throat until Skine bled onto her arm, and then she cut deep enough and fast enough to cut off his head. She pulled the severed head of her father off his neck, and tossed it to the ground, forcing his blood to spill all onto the ground.

Bryna looked up to Hernandez, and she saw his body. She saw the blood, the cuts, the burns, and pain he'd gone through. She saw that he endured through it. She saw that he might truly be worthy of his command. And now, with Bryna having no more Forlka Skines to kill, she smiled and nodded to him.

"Shall we leave--?" Bryna started, "--Captain?"

Miguel smiled, noting that this was the first time she had ever called him Captain. He nodded to her.

"Right now. Right now, Architect save us," Miguel replied.

Bryna walked to Captain Hernandez.

"The Architect won't save us. You will."

The three left the torture room, and noticed that all the men were trying to escape the complex, and so they gunned a few down on their way out, and made a path to a ship.

They made their way onto the fighter vessel, started the drive, and shot the ship into space. As they left the docking are, the Solar Sword zoomed past them, and it started to head towards the sun.

The decently large space vessel that was nearly the size of an aircraft carrier with similar features and a dark grey skin hull had a huge blade at the front of the ship. It also used an unknow form of faster than light type of drive which was faster than current Slipstream Drive technology. The Solar Sword also had a highly efective cloaking device of its own. Once the large blade was activated it gathered surrounding energy from space debris and particles from space which merged into to blade itself forming a purple hue of color. Then suddenly the particles became super charged, the purple hue around the huge blade became blue and shot a beam straight into the center of the sun. Once that occurred the sun's fussion began to change from yellow to red, and within twenty seconds the sun exploded from inside out. The energy shockwave was immense killing every single planet in the targeted solar system. Then, it jumped to multiple solar systems till its task was completed.

The other solar systems that were targeted were the planets that Vas'Kis Sinzo had destroyed. Scar, Royale, the mercenary world of Scar, and other worlds he'd unleashed the Red Rage upon. Without any form of objection or resistence, billions were killed. Just like Vas'Kis had wanted in the first place. The devastation would forever be questioned by the public. And the Flow Council would never give an answer.

Captain Hernandez, Bryna, and Aiden all escaped, barely with their lives before the shock wave over took the ship they confiscated.

Star Enforcers Epilogue

Captian Hernandez limped his way over to his father in the hallway of this strange building. It was all white, the walls, ceiling, and floor all were made of a strange smooth material that Miguel did not know. It was hard as stone, but as smooth as silk. There was no hint of wax giving it the smooth composition; it was some strange material he'd never encountered before. And somehow, everything was vibrant. With no hint of light source, the entire area was bright and everything was easy to see. The hallway had no doors to it; it was just a simple corridor that was 10 yards wide and 10 yards tall. Odd thing was, the building itself was enormous. The outside look was of simple faded grey stone. This place, on this planet he'd never been to, was eerily strange.

"What is this place, Dad?" Miguel asked Santos.

Santos looked over to see his son.

"It was an Elumeni training area, my son. It was designed by the Minostas. They made this area so that Elumeni could train and use their abilities without harming themselves or each other," Santos explained.

"So, this place was made so that an Elemental could walk into this hallway and practice their abilities?" Miguel wondered.

Santos shook his head.

"This place is so much more than a hallway."

Santos looked to the wall in front of him, and placed his hand in front.

"Santos Hernandez. Open," Santos uttered his words like a command.

And at this command, the walls shifted and turned, they turned into a strange material that receded, and they saw Vas'Kis

Sinzo, sitting alone in his room. He had books, paintings, a large comfortable bed, and large amounts of food and water, along with a tiolet and sink.

"You," Miguel said to Vas'Kis.

Vas'Kis looked over to the young Captain and nodded.

"Yes, me. Your father didn't tell you why he brought you here?"

Tika Shamari sat in a room, alone. Director Tollus had told her to wait, but she did not know why. She simply sat, nervous, anxious. It was Director Tollus' office. A hint of boring with the usual desk, holographic projections, and papers laid all about. And a hint of brutal, with the skull of some exotic and dangerous creature casually laid on one of his shelves, its head was nearly the size of Tika's torso. It had fangs erupting out of its face seemed to call to Tika every time she looked at it, but she had to break the stare with this deceased creature when someone walked into the office, finally.

It was not Director Tollus. No. It was someone else. Someone who she had never recognized. Someone with a different hairstyle than Director Tollus. Someone who was still a Torrie, but a woman. One who had an expression that was rooted in decisiveness, almost brutality.

"Thank you for waiting, Medical Officer Shamari."

Tika nodded in response, and gave a slight nervous smile. The woman walked over and sat down in Director Tollus' seat.

"Do you know who I am?"

Tika shook her head

"I am an Agent of Chan."

"What is Chan?" Tika wondered.

The Agent looked upwards at the ceiling for a moment, then back down to Tika.

"Chan is a Goddess in Torrie culture," the agent explained. "She demands that her children protect their world and cherish the land they walk on. It is my duty, my sacred oath, to protect the planet that the Torrie call home."

Tika nodded, in understanding.

"I see," Tika responded.

"Have you ever been to the Torrie homeworld, Miss Shamari?"

Tika's eyes widened a bit.

"Um--," Tika shook her head, once again, as she mumbled a few incoherent words. "No," she finally spoke.

"A desolant wasteland. Where people only favor their firearms or their spaceships. My people have not cared about protecting or salvaging our gracious homeworld in hundreds of years. Not since before the creation of the Flow Council."

Tika shrugged her shoulders for a second.

"And what can I do about that?" Tika wondered. The agent smiled.

"A lot, I'm hoping. I've heard you've made good progress in your research of Red Rage," Tika nodded.

"I have," Tika replied.

The agent continued smirking.

"Have you tested in on a Torrie subject?"

Tika shook her head.

"No humanoid subjects. Only rodents, small animals and the like. What effect does it have on the Torrie?"

The woman laughed for a moment.

"Oh, Ms. Shamari. You'll find out soon enough. I have a

task for you."

Bryna sat on her office chair, researching with her Affix. A holographic interface display was before her eyes, and she was looking at different records. Articles, birth certificates, identifications of address and occupation were all laid out before her. Aiden sat on the floor behind her.

"So, I was delirious, eh?" Aiden inquired.

Bryna chuckled and nodded. "You kept calling me 'Mummy'."

Aiden started to laugh, coughing a bit at the end of it.

"That's hilarious. And I was all chained up?"

"All three of us. You, me, and Captain Hernandez."

"Captain?" Aiden remarked. "You're calling him Captain now?"

"Well, I respect him now," Bryna responded. "I always thought he was just some Ambassador's brat who could never hold his own against someone like my father. Turns out, my father couldn't break him. And for that, I respect him."

Aiden nodded.

"Must feel good, huh?" Aiden stated, "Knowing he's dead."

Aiden was prodding to get a reaction out of Bryna, but all she did was stop her tapping, look down to her desk, and then continue to do her work.

After a few seconds of awkward silence, Aiden decided to change the subject.

"So, what're you looking for there?"

"Records of my mother," Bryna sharply responded.

"Oh?" Aiden stated. "Find anything interesting?"

"Apparently she was married."

"Huh. So you've got a step-daddy out there somewhere?"

"No. Seems Skine killed him when he took my mother."

Aiden looked down to the floor.

"I'm sorry."

"Why?" Bryna genuinely wondered.

Aiden just rolled his eyes in response, irritated at being unable to connect with her. Aiden always had a subconscious demand to connect with everyone on the ship. But Bryna was still the hardest. Everyone else seemed to like, or at least be somewhat more relaxed in his presence. Even Onyx responded with some form of comradery. But not Bryna.

"Well, at least you--."

Suddenly, Bryna took a deep breath. A gasp so loud that it cut off Aiden's sentence.

"What?" Aiden wondered.

Bryna pushed herself away from her desk, tears rolling down her cheeks. For the first time in decades. Vomit roared from her mouth and splashed on the ground. Bryna coughed and held her gut and cried, as little spittles of greyish yellow vomit dribbled to the steel floor.

"What?" Aiden wondered. "What is it?"

"He--he..."

"What?!" Aiden demanded to know.

"She had a son! A son named Jamie Joreau! I had a brother! I half brother! And--and..."

Aiden started shaking his head, confused, as he knelt down before Bryna putting his hand on her shoulder.

"What? Did something happen to him?"

"I happened to him!" Bryna cried in horrid pain. "I killed him! I killed my big brother!"

Bryna sobbed. Aiden just held her, her face nuzzled into his shoulder. Then Aiden started to cry.

"It's okay," Aiden responded. "I know what it's like. I killed someone I loved too."

THE END

STAR ENFORCERS GLOSSERY VOL. 1

LOCATIONS

A

Amras: Planet of the Amrasians, red skin humanoids with black hair, limited technology and weaponry. Amras was taken over by space mercenaries who raped the planet and made slaves out of the inhabitants.

Aquis IV: A water world planet and home to the family of Ambassador Santos Hernandez, and Captain Miguel Hernandez

The Great Hall **Aura**: Fifty story building where the Flow Council meets. The outer structure looks like a bronze metal flame. The base of the building was mirror coated white and black marble flooring. Thirty one pillar assembly on the interior of the hall sits the ambassadors of the Flow Council. At the top of each pillar is seating for four people.

B

Black Jack Pub: A bar saloon in the Chalice space dock on the promenade level.

Briefing Room on U.S.S. Enforcer: On Deck 2, semi circle room, one table with three chairs for head officers. Chairs are in the semi circle with computer terminals on the armrests. Large plasma monitor behind the tables.

C

Chalice: Space port made out of an asteroid that orbits planet Primus. Its five miles in diameter. It's a port for merchants and constable space cruisers. This port is also the training facility for Space Constables. The U.S.S. Enforcer and its sister ships are docked here. It took three years to construct. It has a mixture of military, constable, and civilian inhabitances.

Constable Head Quarters: 55 Story building Pyramid shaped with black mirror windows. The building also has the Flow Councils alternate location. The opening to the chamber is a huge gold door with the imprint of all the ambassadors' insignias.

Cronar System: The area of space where the planet Scar is located. It was renamed the Penal Solar System. Five planets orbit the sun. Scar is the only planet with life.

D

Dapora: Water planet that Constable Javal is from. The inhabitance is technologically advanced.

G

Garka: A slum planet which was once controlled by the Torrie and affected by the Eliminator-Elumeni War. The planet was bought by the Mystic Seas mercenary group which forced the Torrie off the planet.

I

Integra is a moon. It is the base of the Flow Council and all of their operations. The moon is about the size of Pluto, so its gravity is about the same. However, there is a huge city about the size of a small country that the Flow Council uses, known as Overdrive. The mega-city is constantly given energy and artificial gravity by a nuclear fission reactor, which Aiden Dakar's father had invented. Integra is the sixth out of the twelve moons that orbit Primus.

L

Lictora: A planet on the outer rim of the galaxy. Mercs fought for control of the planet.
Lylax: Forest Planet, and home world of Ambassador Larrott.

M

Martin VI: Planet owned by the Mystic Seas and has a base of operations.
Melva IV: wine and beer vineyard planet. The planet is known for the best liquors produced.

R

Research Base EVA 9: Is a facility located on a moon where the Red Rage Drug was released on the inhabitance. (Experimental, Viral, Area)
Roul'e: A gaming moon that is under the control of Voltory Bolare who owns the main gambling establishment Treasure Planet Casino.
Royal III: Home world of Lt. Ren'e Anukis

S

Scar: A volcanic world that has two moons and is located in the Cronar System. The planet at one time was a mining colony then it was converted into a hard labor penal colony. Years later it became a home planet for mercenaries and criminals. The volcanic atmosphere constantly has ash that falls to the surface like light snow. The planet is a breeding ground for mercs, bounty hunter groups, and underground terrorist organizations.

T

Talon: A moon orbiting Primus and has life, and is a training area for the Elumeni.
Tango Quadrant: A sector of the Andromeda Galaxy
Treasure Planet Hotel & Casino: Located on the Roul'e Gaming Moon. Owned by Voltory Bolore. 40 stories tall establishment, has a protective shield dome, and armaments for defense. Guards wear red and black armor.

V

Voodoon: A province on the planet Scar.

W

Wicked Titties: A bar and saloon on the planet Scar within the Voodoon province.

CHARACTERS, SPECIES, & ORGANIZATIONS

A

Acidpod: Giant centipede that squirts corrosive acid. They are territorial, hostile, and native to the planet Scar.

AIDEN DAKAR- (Male Human) White American Male in appearance. He is a Constable Officer aboard the U.S.S. Enforcer. He is a Core Engineer and Explosives Expert. Once a brilliant scientist and prodigy of technology since he was 12 years old. He had tried at his best to avoid all confrontation of battle and at all possible, the enlistment of being apart of the Flow Council. But because of an explosion that he had caused, he had been forced to live with the guilt of killing an entire building of men, women and children. He has memorized all of their names and home planets. The Flow Council is now offering him amnesty for his mistake if he works for the crew. The question of whether he will forgive himself is still and may always be at play in his mind. He has blonde hair, a semi-muscular form, and a five O'clock shadow.   Aiden stands at about 5'8, and even with his guilt and depression, tends to have a mocking smile on his face and is always quick to a joke. He carries his guilt quietly and privately.

Alexander: U.S.S. Enforcer crew member.

Al'ra Stoli: (Male Humanoid) leader of the bounty hunter group Martai. His wife and family were killed by the Rycuda.

Commandant **Amadus**: (Male Human) A legendary Space Constable who was assaulted by Lt. René Anukis for attempting to rape her. Athletic build, olive green skin, and grey eyes.

Arako: (Male Humanoid) Spearhead Terrorist and messenger for Brillen Cardac, the leader of the organization. He is a humanoid with orange skin, and blue hair. The hair on his head is half burnt off.

Elumeni **Aratar**: (Male Torrie) He has a shaved head, and a cybernetics right eye. There is a burn mark from his forehead to his chin that he received from training on Talon.

Assaulter: War Machine robot that is eight feet tall and a deadly arsenal. It walks on two legs and has an armored football player appearance.

Az`Ramo: (Male Amrsian) General of a squad of Mystic Seas Mercs.

B

Brillen Cardac: (Male Humanoid) He lives on the planet Scar in the province called Voodoon. He is the head of the Spearheads Terrorist organization. He has grey skin which is rough and pitted, and blue eyes. He has a large scar on his left cheek, and a second scar that runs down his right brow and extends to his upper cheek. The tattoo of the Spearhead organization is on his forehead.

BRYNA STOLI- (Female Human) is White European in appearance. Constable Officer aboard the U.S.S. Enforcer. She is a Bounty Hunter/Computer Specialist. Her father Falka Skine was a warlord of a warrior society. His means of murder and thievery were known throughout the universe. She was physically abused by him, brutally. He mother died in child birth. Bryna had thought of ways to kill him on multiple occasions. Bryna was later kidnapped and was being held for ransom. Her father refused to pay because he thought his daughter was worthless. However, the leader of the rival mercenary group trained her to become a bounty hunter herself and an expert on computers in order to hunt and kill whoever the group needed killed. Her mentor/father figure was killed by her father. She had then wandered across the galaxy, taking jobs from mercenary groups until the Flow Council arrested her. Now, they have given her a choice, work off the debt of murders and illegal means and possibly get the chance to kill her father, or rot in a prison cell. She had chosen to be apart of the U.S.S. Enforcer crew.

She wears blue armor, and blue boots. She carries a high tech sharp shooter rifle.

D

Declan Dekar: (Male Human) He is the builder and the designer of the Great Hall Aura. He is also Constable Aiden Dakar's father.

Ambassador **D.A.X.**: (Unknown sex identification) Cybernetic thin build Eliminator that sits on the Flow Council.

Daporans: A species with blue skin, amphibious in nature and appearance. They have highly adaptable bodies to fire, water, acids, frost, and toxic atmospheres. Vulnerable to a vacuum atmosphere. Constable Javal is of this species.

F

Fiyush: U.S.S. Enforcer crew member

Forlka Skine: (Male Human) He is the leader of the Rycuda Mercenary group. He has a muscular build and a scar that runs from his forehead to the left side of his cheek. He is also Constable Bryna Stoli's father.

G

Elumeni **Golic**: (Male Human)Earth Elemental that has Pilipino features and a short hair cut with a pony tail that reaches his 4th lower back vertebrae. He has honey brown eyes, wears a bronze robe and armor. He also carries a battle staff.

Gonz: (Female Idol) The Goddess of War to the Torrie race.

Guard 7-8-20: Assaulter robot in Brillen Cardac's tunnel that is under his fortress on planet Scar.

Gul Nar: (Male Human) He is a bounty hunter, Native Indian in appearance with tan skin, well built and unshaven face. He loves to carry around his main weapon that is a portable Gatling Gun.

H

Elumeni **Harmony**: (Female, unknown alien species at this time) Air Elumeni with jade skin and black hair. She has slightly thin horns that come from the side of her head and curves downward towards the chin.

Hornwing: Winged beast that is similar in appearance to dragons and as large as a horse with horns, tail, and short dark, grey fur. It has large talons on its feet with extreme crushing power.

J

Jaffar Krytis: (Male Humanoid) Caught in an altercation on the Gaming Moon Roule, and in a drugged out state murdered a prostitute. Skin paper white with black dots.

Jai: U.S.S. Enforcer crew member.

Ensign **James Felipe**: (Human Male) Bridge officer aboard the U.S.S. Enforcer.

JAVAL (Male, Last name unpronounceable by the human tongue) is the Chief Engineer of the U.S.S. Enforcer. He is a 45 year old blue skinned humanoid who was born on the water planet Dapora. He is amphibious with gills that are located on his upper back for breathing in water, and has a set of fins on the top of his head. His body is highly adaptable to harsh environments such as extreme heat and cold and toxic atmospheres. His only weakness is the vacuum of space. His blood purple blood also glows. Later in the series he has a small addiction to coffee.

He wears a full body black spandex uniform but it doesn't cover his hands, feet, or head. He carries a repulsor rifle and pistol.

K

Kaisa: (Male Daproian) Younger brother to Constable Javal. He is a brilliant hacker.

Kaisin: (Female Humanoid Amrasian) She's an elder with a burn mark on her left eye which was rendered useless. She is also a religious figure to her people as she taught forgiveness and peace. She is also knowledgeable about Amrasian history and their language. But later she became more vengeful like Vas'Kis Sinzo.

Elumeni **Kalama**: (Female Depora) Water elemental.

Kenkias Loro: (Male Humanoid Amrasian) A Mercenary who works at the Treasure Planet Casino. Also has an addiction to the Red Rage drug. He was a Constable and discharged for taking bribes from criminals that he previously arrested.

Kill Hounds: Canines the size of tigers. Large snouts with shark teeth. Droolers, large claws on all four paws, and wolf like ears.

 Ki'Sha: (Female humanoid Amerasian)She was taught at a young age by an artificial intelligence to pilot and navigate an Oppressor's starship.

Kora Nagotu: (Female Human) Japanese in appearance and a professional assassin. She wears navy blue body armor with red trim. She's in her young 30's.

L

Ambassador **Larrott Krytis**: (Male Humanoid) Sits on the Flow Council and father to Jaffar. Skin is paper white with black dots.

M

Martai: Bounty Hunter group, they wear blue armor with gold impressions.

Martos Royal Family: High class rich individuals who live on Integra.

Mia Diaz: (Female Human)Capt. Miguel Hernandez's girlfriend before he became a Space Constable. She was a Space Pirate, and killed by Commandant Mintog.

CAPTAIN **MIGUEL HERNANDEZ** who is Latino in appearance was born and raised on the planet Aquis IV, a water planet. He is the Captain of the U.S.S. Enforcer, and lead Constable of his crew. He has four brothers and two sisters, him being the youngest. His mother is a very nurturing person and his father Ambassador Santos sits on the Flow Counsel. Their father has a high expectation of his children. All his children excelled at math and science, but except one; Miguel was intelligent but he always seemed to get into trouble with the law. During his teenage years he had a string of misdemeanors and public disturbances due to his association with the wrong type of crowds. He refused to be like his siblings. He wanted action and adventure, not stuck in a lab all day or teaching as a renowned professor at a university; it was just not his calling.

Later in time Miguel became a space pirate and was arrested by Space Constables while on the luxury space cruiser Utopia. Once Miguel was apprehended in the neighboring star system he was brought up on extreme charges. The Flow Council sentenced Miguel to serve out his eight years in the Space Constable Academy. Once he completed his two years at the Academy he graduated at the top of his class and became a first officer of the USS Grand Torino. Since Miguel was more familiar with gangs and illegal operations he decided to become an undercover constable and was given command of the U.S.S. Enforcer.

He carries two silver pistols, Chaos and Mayhem. He carries special clips in his arsenal for these guns. He loves to wear black denim jackets.

Commandant **Mintog**: (Male Torrie) Capt. Miguel Hernandez's personal trainer during his time in the Constable Academy. Highly respected among the Constables.

Monitor: The person assigned to reside over the Flow Council to keep things in order. The person wears a grey robe and carries a pewter *gavel.*

Morenko: (Male Torrie) A Mystic Seas security guard. Purple skin, shaved head, blue eyes.

Mystic Seas: Mercenary Organization, which is a rebel movement to break away from the laws and guidelines of the Flow Council. These people want true freedom, and they despise the Flow Council. Their logo is a white crescent moon.

O

ONYX: Cybernetic being, classified as an Eliminator. Onyx is the Chief Tactical officer of the U.S.S. Enforcer. He has grey metal skin and can shape shift the appearance of his outer shell, and has an endoskeleton. He carries a high tech shot gun, and a glock pistol.

R

(Lieutenant) **REN'E ANUKIS** (Female Human) is the second in command constable aboard the U.S.S. Enforcer. She is a Black female who was born and raised on the casino planet Royale III. Her upbringing had some rough roads. Her father and mother loved her dearly but they had become addicted to narcotics a few years after she was born. Later René was placed into foster care for her own safety by the authorities due to her home environment. While in foster care she learned that her parents were killed by an Acer after her mother and father owed money for their addiction to one of the major drug lords in their galaxy. René vowed to bring whoever was responsible for her parents' death to justice, so she pursued a career as a space constable.

She carries a high caliber compact assault rifle, and wears black and gold trim armor.

Rik'Tal Shivasti: (Male Amras) He is a Martai Bounty Hunter that raised Constable Bryna Stoli when she was 8 years old.

Rycuda: A mercenary group which holds a special interest to find Constable Bryna Stoli. They were black armor with a red painted wolf's head in the chest plate.

S

Santos Hernandez: (Male Human)Ambassador on the Flow Council. Male Human with slightly tanned cocoa skin, short cut hair, and clean shaven face. On his Flow Council Garb there is a water drop symbol. He is an even tempered man and father to Captain Miguel Hernandez of the U.S.S. Enforcer. He is the ambassador of Acquis and multiple planets in that sector.

Shalah Vallair: (Female Human) Assassin that Constable Tika Shamara takes the appearance of during some of her missions.

Sinzo: (Female Idol) A goddess idol to the Amrasian race and a warrior that slaughtered the guilty and protected the innocent.

Solara: (Female Human) Fire Elemental, Acer. She works as the head of security at the Treasure Planet Casino. Carmel skin complexion, black hair, red lips and red eyes. Wears skin tight top with belly showing. Tight black pants, and black boots. She carries knives and a sword.

Spearheads: Terrorist organization that has the spearhead tattooed on their foreheads.

T

TIKA SHAMARI (Female Human) is a 15 year old chief medical officer. She is an Indian in appearance human who was born on the planet Tazmal which is very much like Earth. She had an illness that caused brain seizure. Her parents violated the law by using an experimental drug to treat Tika's illness. Her brain repaired itself and she became a child genius. She received her university degree at the age of 11 years old. Her passion is in medical science, she is a fabulous cook and an expert on herbal plants. Tika had the ability to use 20% of her brain which enables her to retain a wide range of information. She sees the galaxy as a child would, but has an old soul of maturity. Later a drug test was done on Tika which indicated that she had been injected with the experimental drug, and she was forced to serve aboard the U.S.S. Enforcer and become the youngest space constable in history, and she enjoys a challenge.

She carries a repulsor pistol and a dart gun. Her hair is black and extends down to her lower back.

Director **Tollus**: (Male Torrie)Head of the Constable Task Force. Purple Skin, black hair, blue eyes, and short bull horns to the side of his head. He has a muscular build and a Mohawk. His species is know as Torrie, a warrior race.

Torrie: Purple skinned humans with unique muscular builds and Mohawk hair, both males and females. They also have blue eyes. They are a race of warriors and they had taken a number of planets for themselves until the Flow Council was established. Later the Torrie relinquished control of planets to the original inhabitants and negotiated peaceful trades for goods and services.

Tuk Nar: (Male Human) He is a professional jewelry thief, Native American in appearance with tan skin. He is the brother of the bounty hunter Gul Nar. And word has it that he was killed by the Bounty Hunter Kora Nagotu.

V

Valya: (Female Huanoid) Pale Skin with a shaved head. She is second in command of the Martai Bounty hunter group. She has tech implants giving her the ability to merge with technology and blue glowing cybernetic eyes.

Ambassador **Vas'Kis Sinzo**: (Male Humanoid Amrasian) His parents were killed in front of him when he was a child. His people were drafted as slaves of the mercenaries as they used their planet for food, land, water, and other resources. He has a tattoo constable symbol on his neck

Voltory Bolore: (Male Human)Casino Owner of Treasure Planet. Athletic build human, trim mustache, he likes cigars, and he likes Korona Suits. He is sophisticated and adventurous.

Y

Yannis: (Male Human) Mercenary Captain that tried to assault the Constables at the Treasure Planet Casino.

TECHNOLOGY, STARSHIPS, WEAPONRY & EXT.

A

Affix: A metal device for communication, and universal translator, which is mainly worn on the wrist.

Artington: Powerful six shell shot gun. A heavy weapon to carry with powerful stopping power. This weapon is mainly carried by Constable Onyx.

C

Constable Insignia: Gold horizontal infinity sign with one gold star in the oval areas of the symbol, and four gold stars that run vertically in the middle of the infinity symbol.

E

Eliminator – Elumeni War: The machines and the Elumeni fought or 60 years, and the Cybernetics waged war to defend their sentient rights to exist.

U.S.S. **Enforcer**: United Star Systems, Stealth Destroyer Starship. Used by the Space Constables. The ship is 120 meters long with 4 decks. Exterior is blue and black. Armaments- torpedoes, laser torrents, rocket launchers, counter measures, and cloaking device. Engines- Slip Stream Drives: faster than light speed, and sub-light engines. Crew of 35 non militants and the rest are Constables.

F

Flow Council Garments: Dark blue colored robes with the constable symbol on the shoulders. Each ambassador has the insignia of their world on the front of the garments.

G

U.S.S. **Grande Torino**: Battle Cruiser that Capt. Hernandez served on as first officer before he was reassigned to the U.S.S. Enforcer as captain.

Gravis Gun: Repulsor field gun. Non-lethal, able to propel targets backward.

H

Hammer-Head Class Warship: Older space cruiser warship used during the Eliminator-Elumeni War.

L

Level lifter: Elevator system

M

Matrix Collective: Mechanics that are registered and forced to obey the collective A.I. network.

Mystic Seas Symbol: White cresset moon.

N

Neural Network Law: Any robot or cybernetic is to be linked to the Matrix Collective. If not they must be destroyed. Excluded from this law is Constable Onyx for his uniqueness.

P

Parises Dice Table: Casino Game similar to Craps but played with 3 dice.

R

Red Rage: Is an inject-able, air pathogen, or oral drug which causes a person to increase in strength. Some mercs and military forces use the drug for combat. The drug causes an increase in testosterone levels within higher evolved organics. It increases feelings of anger, violence, and sexual aggression. The drug also has a mysterious red glow.

S

Slip Stream Drive: Faster than light speed system that is powered by the centrifuge of liquid isotopes.

Solar Sword is a starship that is the size of a large aircraft carrier. The A.I. on the ship is a robotic pilot; it informed the explorers that the ship is called the Solar Sword. The reason for the ship's name is because the vessel has the ability to destroy a star and cause the planets in the solar system to be eradicated by the devastating shockwave. The Flow Council, once informed took immediate hold over the entire planet and the moon inhabiting it. The Solar Sword was used only once, to destroy an uncontrollable and deadly disease spreading in the Darwin System. The Solar Sword has since been used as a looming threat towards whole planets. It is never stated that the Flow Council would use the weapon, but the few populated planets that are not aligned with the Flow Council do fear the possibility of the Solar Sword being used. However, the only planets not aligned with the Flow Council are mostly planets that have inhabitants that have not discovered space travel yet or planets ruled by mercenary gangs.

T

Train tube: Transportation system used on the Chalice Space dock.

U

U.S.S.: United Systems of Space

Pleasure ship **Utopia**: A large space cruise liner.

W

U.S.S. **Warlock**: Sister ship to the U.S.S. Enforcer.

STAR ENFORCERS: *Sketches and Preliminaries*

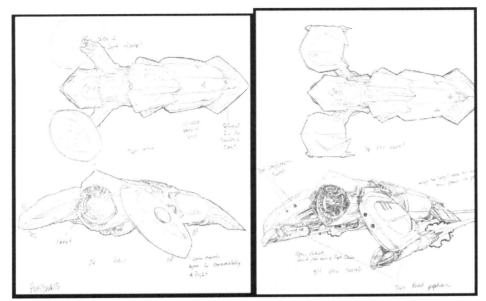

U.S.S. ENFORCER by Donovan Petersen

Captain Miguel Hernandez by Phoe-Nix Nebula

Lieutenant René Anukis by Phoe-Nix Nebula

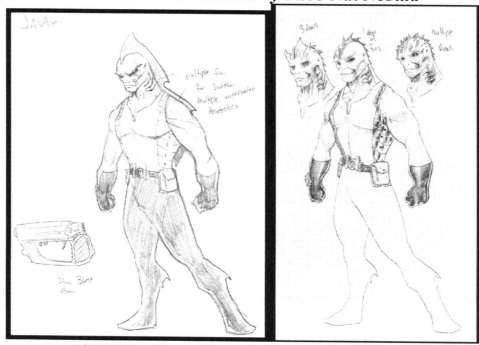

Chief Engineer Javal by Donovan Petersen

Chief Medical Officer Tika Shamara

Original Bryna Stoli by Donovan Petersen/Revision by Jonathan Piccini

Chief Tactical Officer Onyx by Donovan Petersen

Bounty Hunter Kora Nagotu by Phoe-Nix Nebula

Director Tollus by Phoe-Nix Nebula

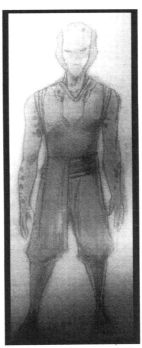

Jaffar Krytis by Phoe-Nix Nebula

Voltory Bolore by Phoe-Nix Nebula

Voltory Bolore / Young Bryna Stoli & Al'ra Stoli
By Donovan Petersen

Solar Sword by Phoe-Nix Nebula

Main Cover by Phoe-Nix Nebula

95452048R00182

Made in the USA
Lexington, KY
08 August 2018